Maine

Maine

COUPLES TORN APART ARE REUNITED
IN THREE HISTORICAL NOVELS

Carol MASON PARKER

BARBOUR
PUBLISHING

Published by Barbour Publishing, Inc., P.O. Box 719, Uhrichsville, Ohio 44683, www.barbourbooks.com

Our mission is to publish and distribute inspirational products offering exceptional value and biblical encouragement to the masses.

Member of the
Evangelical Christian
Publishers Association

Printed in the United States of America.
5 4 3 2 1

CAROL MASON PARKER writes inspirational romance because she wants to present romantic relationships that have Christian values and ideals. After many years in northern Michigan, she now makes her home in South Carolina and enjoys keeping up with her four grown children and their children.

Dear Readers,
Although this is a novel of fiction, some of the characters are real people and some of the facts are true. This story was written in memory of my great-grandfather, Captain Frederic T. Mason (1844–1909). Captain Fred served with the Union Army in the Civil War, and this book is dedicated to all his descendants.

Carol Mason Parker

Waterville

Within Her gates doth Wisdom sit enthroned,
The sceptre governs with its gentle sway;
And Plenty smiles through all Her woodland aisles,
Blest is the coming of the perfect day.
We may not pledge thee in the sparkling wine,
Since Bacchus doth no place of honor fill;
But here's a health in nectar old as Time,
Whose name is linked with thine. . .sweet Water(ville).
—Anonymous

(Taken from the *Old Waterville* picture book and used by permission of the Waterville Historical Society, Waterville, Maine)

A Haven of Peace

To my husband, Herb,
for all his love, patience, and encouragement.
With special thanks to our daughter, Kimberly Parker Christmas,
for transferring my completed manuscript onto computer disks.

Chapter 1

A peaceful hush flooded the countryside. It was early July 1865, and three short months since the bitter war between the North and South. Frederic Mason shifted the haversack on his shoulder as he limped along the dusty gravel road leading to his family's farm in Waterville, Maine.

His right leg, the one with the ball still in the thigh, started to drag, and he needed to rest. A huge elm tree by the side of the road beckoned and provided welcome shade as he lowered his weary body into the tall grass. Leaning against the elm's rough bark, he rubbed his hand up and down, massaging the wounded leg. He untied the bandanna from his neck and wiped huge beads of sweat from his face and brow.

He had been wounded April 9, the last day of the war. His company, the 11th Maine, under General Edward Ord, had pushed toward the Confederate line and seen the roofs of the hamlet of Appomattox Court House in the distance. The gallant Lieutenant Colonel Jonathon A. Hill, his regiment's immediate commander, was told to close and hold the pike.

"Charge that battery!" Colonel Hill had shouted, pointing to the Confederate forces on the ridge across the field. Frederic's regiment had sprung from the woods into an open field, meeting a barrage of grapeshot and bullets.

Remembering brought tears to Frederic's eyes. His close friend, hit with a bullet in the chest, had screamed and fallen to the ground. Frederic had knelt beside him, cradling his head in his arms. Helplessly he had watched his friend die. "Good-bye, ole buddy," he whispered, then jumped to his feet, his stomach tied in knots and his eyes brimming with tears.

Midway across the field, grapeshot and shrapnel had hit his right thigh, knocking him unconscious. He learned later that Lieutenant Colonel Hill had been injured in the same battle.

Frederic remembered being transferred to a hospital in Chesapeake, Virginia, his thigh full of shrapnel that had shattered the bone and caused the right leg to shorten. One ball they were unable to remove. It would remain with him, a constant reminder of a nation torn apart, each side dedicated to its own cause.

The war was finally over, though, and he was back home again. Now he could pick up his life. Get back on the farm and work with his pa and grandpa. Marry Becky Sue, just like he'd promised all those years ago before he'd left for the war. Thinking of Becky Sue, he smiled; soon, very soon, he would see her again. He hadn't heard from her, not since he was wounded, he remembered, and his smile flickered, but no doubt her letters had been held up.

As if in answer to his thoughts, a lone rider approached on horseback, startling Frederic out of his daydreams.

"Hullo there!" A large-framed, middle-aged man peered down at Frederic from his horse. "Well, if it ain't young Fred Mason jest back from the war! Almost didn't recognize ya with the mustache ya growed. Does yer pappy know yer comin'?"

Frederic stood to his feet and smiled. "Nice to see you, Mr. Collins." He took a deep breath and extended his hand to Becky Sue's father. "No, the folks don't know I'm coming. I wanted to surprise everyone. The hospital released me quicker than expected. I just got into town on the noon train and felt like walking home."

"Yep." Hiram Collins eyed Frederic's bad leg. " 'Peers ya were able ta keep the leg after all. Back in April, talk was that ya'd lose it shore enough."

"The Lord's been good, Mr. Collins. The leg's still with me. . .just dragging a little."

"Reckon yer pap will be mighty glad ta have ya home in time fer harvest." Hiram Collins squinted a little in the bright sun as he peered down his long nose at Frederic. "Bet yer shore glad to get out of the army."

Frederic pulled his twenty-one-year-old body up to its full six feet. His dark hair, damp with perspiration, curled around his face like a child's, but his blue eyes were a man's. "My papers state, 'Captain Fred Mason honorably discharged on account of wounds at Appomattox Court House,' sir. But I'm thankful the war is over and our great nation is one again. Being away for three years made me mighty anxious to get home." He hesitated a moment. "Sir, how's Becky Sue? She never wrote me in the hospital."

"Yep, yer letters came ta the house." Hiram Collins frowned as he spoke. "Becky Sue run off and married Zack Turner right after she heered about yer leg. Broke her ma's heart, too. She was plannin' on a nice church weddin', her bein' our oldest daughter and all."

Frederic's face turned ashen, and tears brimmed in his eyes. Clumsily he wiped a hand across his face. When he finally spoke, his voice was halted and broken. "But, sir, we were promised. Becky Sue promised to wait for me until after the war."

"I know, boy," Hiram Collins admitted, "and I'm right sorry about it. Thought yer folks had writ ya, but maybe they thought otherwise, ya bein' in the hospital and all."

Frederic's frame slumped as he sat down on the edge of the road, his head in his hands. Sobs racked his body as he fought for control.

"Anythin' I can do fer ya?" Mr. Collins asked kindly as he got down from his horse. "Let me take yer sack there and other belongin's to yer place."

"I'll be okay, sir," Fred said hoarsely as he waved him aside. "Thanks for offering your help. Guess I'll just get along now. It's not much farther, and I'm sure anxious to get home."

A HAVEN OF PEACE

Hiram Collins mounted his mare, touched his hand to his hat, and rode off. He knew Frederic needed to be alone with his thoughts.

The Collinses' property butted up to the Mason spread on one side. Often the men had helped one another during harvest season, while the women sewed, canned, and quilted. Fred and his sisters, Cassie and Emily, had walked to the little red schoolhouse with the Collins children, Becky Sue, Billy Bob, and later on little golden-haired Sarah Jane.

Becky Sue's face flashed before him, and in his mind he saw her dark flowing hair and sparkling green eyes. They had both been eighteen when he had joined up, proud to serve his country. "The Union must be preserved at any cost," he'd told her. "But I'll be back, Becky Sue. Mr. Lincoln will have this war over in no time." Frederic had drawn her close and whispered against her silky dark hair, "I love you. I've always loved you, even when we were kids. Will you be my wife, Becky Sue? Will you marry me when I get back?"

Frederic could almost hear her soft voice and feel her clinging arms. "Oh, yes, yes, yes, Frederic! We'll be married as soon as you get home. I'll be waiting for you, if it takes forever!"

"How long is forever?" Frederic mumbled to himself now. Her "forever" hadn't even lasted three years. He felt tired and empty inside, but he ignored his bad leg and quickened his step a little. He wanted to be home now, wanted to be with his own people and see the love in their eyes. They could not take away the wound that Becky Sue had dealt him, he knew, but they were the only thing left to him now.

Still, the pain in his heart eased just a little as he looked across the green hills toward his family's land. How he loved this countryside with its woods and graceful trees. Tall spruce and pine, along with birch, maple, oak, and elm, lined the narrow country road. A wave of feeling washed over him. "This is my kind of country," he mused. "This is where I belong."

Just around the next bend, Frederic saw the large white farmhouse his grandpa had built for his bride on the rolling hundred acres. The house sat back from the road a good piece, on a hill overlooking the surrounding area. Farming had always been a way of life for the Mason family, and now Frederic saw the cattle and horses grazing on the hillside with the tall outbuildings just beyond.

Frederic knew every inch of this land. He knew it by heart and loved every part of it. Many times he had visualized these scenes during the past three years, wondering if he would ever see home and family again. "Terrible waste, this war!" he muttered. "Many didn't make it. Young men blown apart, others like myself crippled for life. Boys turned into men overnight. Some of us became hard and bitter, others callous and indifferent."

Frederic remembered those who had found the horrors of war so dreadful they were unable to cope. When the going had gotten too tough, they'd deserted their posts and filtered away into the woods, weakening the ranks. Frederic shook his head. "Yep, war brings out the best and worst in men. Much as I hated the killing, I'm thankful it didn't make me bitter. It's only by God's grace I'm alive today."

He squinted in the sun as he looked toward the homestead. "The war is over, and I'm home at last. But, God," he said, his whisper filled with pain, "what do I have to live for now? Becky Sue is married to someone else. Help me, God. Help me be able to bear it."

Chapter 2

With a deep breath, Frederic shifted his haversack and started up the long gravel drive to his family home. Large trees dotted the front yard that sloped toward the house. "I reckon it looks just the same," Fred murmured as he paused a moment to let his eyes drink in the scene.

The clapboard house, with its green shutters and huge chimneys, was etched clearly against the azure sky. Small-paned windows, gingerbread trim, and steep gables and dormers made the house look as though it were trimmed with diamonds and points of lace. A summer porch ran across the front of the house and wrapped itself around the side. Everything was just as he remembered; even the wooden swing his grandpa had made was still in place.

Laddie, the collie, began barking furiously as Fred continued up the long drive. Suddenly, Laddie stopped barking and met Fred halfway, his tail wagging. The dog jumped in delight at having his old friend home.

Fred knelt down and gathered the dog to him. "Lad, old boy. It's good to see you," he murmured into the dog's soft, furry coat. He patted the noble head and stroked the soft ears. Laddie rolled over so he could rub his belly. "You're getting fat, old fellow." The dog danced and ran in circles as the two of them headed for the house.

"Fred, is thet you?" Grandpa Caleb sat on the porch in his old wicker rocker, sipping a glass of cool apple cider. He pulled himself slowly up to greet his only grandson, and Fred noticed how much older and grayer he seemed. He knew his grandma had died of pneumonia two years back while he was away at the war.

"Gramps!" he cried as he flung his arms around the old man. "Gramps, how I've missed you. I'm so sorry about Grandma."

After a quiet moment, Caleb spoke, "The Lord wanted her real bad, Fred. She's with Him now. There's an empty place here, thet's fer sure." The elder Mason touched his heart. Then his face brightened. "But we'll see her agin one day."

Fred's eyes filled with tears, not only for his dear little grandma Mason, but also for Becky Sue, who was lost to him forever.

"Yer ma's inside, Fred. She'll be fit ta be tied. Yer pa's out on the back property fixin' fences. Always so much ta do and I'm no help taday with this confounded lumbago actin' up. My joints ache and pain most of the time. But listen ta me, would ya? Yer the one thet's hurtin'. How's that leg doin'? Ya shouldn't a-walked from town, boy. We coulda brung the wagon fer ya."

"No, I wanted to see everything slowly, Gramps, and drink it all in. I was so thirsty for this land, every tree, every trail, the rolling hills. There were times I thought I'd never see any of this again."

"Land-a-Goshen, Frederic!" Mary Jane Mason came bustling out the kitchen door onto the porch. A small, stout woman with hazel eyes, she pulled her brown hair straight back into a bun at the nape of her neck. Her round face beamed, and her pink cheeks flushed with excitement. "My boy! My boy! Yer home safe!"

Fred had to stoop as she gathered him to her bosom, her whole body convulsed with sobs. "But oh, Frederic, yer poor leg. We've worried so about ya."

"Ma, don't cry. My leg's fine. I'm all right, honest. I'm tired from my trip, but I'm home now. That's what counts."

Mrs. Mason released him and wiped her eyes on her checkered apron. "Let me look at ya, son. Ya sure are a sight fer these eyes. We're all so proud of ya. We prayed every day, and thank the Lord yer safe. Now ya jest rest some in the swing while I get ya somethin' ta eat."

"Thanks, Ma," Fred said as he slumped his body onto the swing.

Mrs. Mason reappeared shortly with a pitcher of apple cider and a plate of sandwiches. "This will hold ya till supper. Yer pa will be back from the fields about six. Some of the cattle were gettin' out of the pasture, and he found the spot. Grandpa helped him yesterday. Taday he's jest finishin' up."

"Where's Cassie and Emily? Are they away?"

"It's a wonder ya didn't pass 'em on the road," Grandpa said. "They went ta town in the buggy hours ago."

"They needed ribbon and dress material," Ma offered, "and I needed some staples. They like an excuse ta go fer me, but they should be back soon."

"I guess they are young ladies by now," Fred exclaimed between mouthfuls. "When I left, they were just my 'little sisters.'"

"Yep, not so little anymore," Grandpa agreed. "Leastwise they think they're growed up, bein' seventeen and eighteen. Can't keep 'em young forever."

"And I suppose they've been courted by some of the local fellas, too?" Fred asked.

Before his grandfather could answer, the family buggy, pulled by old Nell, flew up the drive. Two girls dressed in calico, giggling and laden with packages, stepped out. Fred left the swing and hurried, limping, to meet them.

"It's Fred!" they screamed simultaneously. Packages flew everywhere as they hugged Fred and fired questions at the same time.

"Cassie! Emily! You sure grew up on me." Fred held them admiringly at arm's length. "How come you grew up so fast?"

"You've been away a long time, big brother," Cassie said teasingly.

"We just growed!" Emily laughed. "It was easy!"

Grandpa Caleb cared for old Nell while the girls chattered constantly, filling Frederic in on all the local news. He listened to some sad information about friends killed in the war, and his heart ached as mentally he relived the horrors of his own experiences at Petersburg and Appomattox.

"There's been lots of weddings since the war ended," Emily was saying. Suddenly she faltered as Cassie shook her head and gave her a meaningful look. Fred's face became drawn and tight.

"It's all right, little sisters," he said gravely. "I already heard about Becky Sue. Mr. Collins met me on the road, down a piece. I could see that it bothered him to tell me."

"It's terrible of her!" Emily exploded. "Downright mean! She's just so fickle and two-faced, I declare!"

"Now, Emily, be kind," Mrs. Mason warned. "It's done and over, and we can't change it a whit. This kinda talk won't help Fred none. Son, we wanted ta spare ya the news as long as we could." Seeing his downcast expression, she added, "I'm sure ya want ta wash up and rest a bit before supper. We can all talk some more then."

"I would, Ma, thanks," Frederic replied and headed inside. The pain in his injured leg was surpassed only by the throb in his heart. His entire body screamed out in pain over the loss of Becky Sue to another.

"Why, God? First my leg and now this. Becky Sue couldn't stand the idea of being married to a cripple!" He spat out the words, and they choked in his throat. "Ma knows how hard it hurts," he sighed as he settled himself back in his old room.

The room was just as he'd left it, the same single bed with the patch quilt his grandma made him when he was a boy. Lovingly he fingered the quilt, so full of memories. Across the room stood a pine dresser and commode, with bowl, pitcher, and kerosene lamp. Grandpa had crafted the furniture from huge pine trees on the family property. Most of the furniture in the house had been made by his pa and grandpa. They were craftsmen, both of them.

Fred had the same inner desire to work with wood. He remembered his grandpa helping him make a pine cutting board, shaped like a pig, when he was ten years old. It was to be a gift for his mother's birthday, but he made a wrong cut and messed up the shape of the pig so that it was lopsided. Then he refused to give it to her.

"It's ruined, Grandpa; it's ruined!" Fred moaned as he hid the board behind some scraps of lumber.

"Now, Freddy, yer ma'll love it jest the same because ya made it, boy," Grandpa insisted. "Don't ya go a-hidin' it on her."

Later his mother found it, loved it, and didn't care a whit that it was crooked. She only cared that it was from her boy.

Frederic took off his dusty clothes, washed up, and threw back the quilt. As he stretched out on the neat pine bed, he whispered, "Ma knew how bad I felt then, and she knows now. Ma always knows when I'm hurting."

Chapter 3

S on, wake up!" Frederic's father shook him gently. "Fred boy. . .ya've come home ta us."

Fred opened his eyes to see his pa's face smiling down at him. Chase Mason was an older copy of Fred: the same dark hair, though now touched with gray, the same deep blue eyes that squinted when he smiled, the same tall, lean frame that knew hard work from farming. "Pa!" Fred's voice broke as the elder Mason embraced his son.

"Come on, boy, Ma's got supper on the table. Let's get it while it's hot."

Supper was a joyous occasion. Ma prepared two of their choice hens, along with dumplings, Boston baked beans, johnnycake, and apple pie. "Fit fer a king!" Grandpa exclaimed, patting his belly.

"Ma," Fred said, "I dreamed of your cooking for three long years while away at the war. I have to say it, your cooking just gets better and better."

"Pshaw, Fred," Mary Jane Mason said. "It's jest plain cookin'. It does do my heart good ta see ya eat so well, son."

After the meal, Chase took the worn family Bible and read a portion of scripture. Their family custom included meditating on God's Word each evening and having a time of prayer. Grandpa Caleb prayed this time, waxing eloquent in thanking God for His bountiful blessings. "And thank ya, Lord, fer bringin' our Fred boy home ta us. In Jesus' name, amen."

Now the family besieged Fred with questions. They were eager to hear about his experiences in the war. He talked for some time but kept the horrors of war brief and omitted much of the pain and sorrow.

"But yer leg, son. Is it terribly painful to ya?" his mother asked.

"I'm just thankful I could keep it, Ma. At first the doc said I'd lose it for sure. There's no pain now, unless I get overtired, but even that will go away, the doctor said. It's just a nuisance to me, that's all."

While Mrs. Mason and the girls cleared the table, the men continued their discussion in the parlor.

"Pa, what a tragedy about Mr. Lincoln being shot. It made me angry when I heard about the killing while in the hospital. It makes no sense. . .no sense at all."

"Abe Lincoln was a good man," Chase agreed. "A warm and understandin' president, even brilliant the way he held this nation tagether. But there are still strong and bitter feelings against him, especially in the South."

"It's right hard to understand why he was killed," Grandpa interjected. "But

God, in His plan, knows all about it. He's the One who's in control."

"Some people say we're in a depression. Is that right, Pa?"

"Well, son, we never had prosperity," Chase answered. "So how can we have a depression?"

While Mrs. Mason put away the food, Cassie and Emily quickly did up the dishes. "When can I tell Fred about Bill and me?" Cassie asked her ma. "Bill's coming around tonight, courting."

"It will hurt him, Cassie," her mother warned.

"Ma, the wedding's in September, so I have to tell him." Cassie's hazel eyes clouded as she shook her chestnut curls. She had tied yellow ribbons in her hair to match her dress of calico and muslin.

"Fred must be told." Mrs. Mason sighed. "I jest hope it don't hurt him too badly. He's been hurt so much already."

"Bill's coming!" Emily shouted as Laddie started barking and a lone rider appeared galloping up the long drive.

Cassie patted her hair, pinched her cheeks, and fairly flew off the porch to meet him. How grand and tall he looked, she thought as he swung his lean body down and tied his gray gelding to the hitching post. Bill Collins had a thatch of reddish gold hair, bright blue eyes, and a smile that lit up his whole face. Cassie greeted him warmly, and they walked together hand in hand toward the porch swing.

"You're pretty as can be in that yellow dress, Cassie. I'm glad you're my girl."

Cassie's cheeks burned under his steady gaze. "You are a flatterer, Bill."

"It's true, Cassie. . .it's the honest truth."

"Oh, Bill." She went into his arms and lifted her face to his.

After a moment, she drew away and led him onto the porch. "Frederic's inside," she said. "You'll have to talk to him before you leave. It's so good to have him home safe at last."

"How is he?"

"He seems okay. He limps. And he's quieter than before. But he's still the same Frederic."

"Pa said he took the news about Becky Sue hard."

Cassie nodded. "He hasn't said much. But you can see he's hurting bad."

Bill shook his head. "I know she's my own sister, but I can't understand what got into her. I know she was scared when she heard Fred was going to lose his leg. But why did she have to up and marry Zack so fast? You'd think she didn't have a brain in her head. What a thing to do to a guy just back from fighting for our country. Fred deserved better, and that's the truth."

"I know, Bill, I know."

They sat close together in the porch swing, silent, thinking of Frederic. After a few moments, though, they turned toward each other once again, and soon they had entered their own small world. They talked softly, oblivious to anyone in the house.

"Pa and I have the cabin almost done, Cassie," Bill said. "You haven't seen it since it was roughed in. I wish you'd come see it tomorrow. You need to tell us how you want some of the finishing done. That's your department. Let Emily come with you if she wants to."

"I will, Bill," Cassie replied eagerly. "I've been meaning to come for quite a spell but just been so busy with my sewing. My wedding dress is done. I have two more dresses to make, and then I'll start on curtains. It's such fun planning our own place." Cassie squeezed his hand and laid her head on his shoulder. "Look at that moon coming up, Bill, just for us."

The couple sat in silence for several minutes, their hearts full of love and bursting with plans for their future. The swing creaked and groaned as they rocked back and forth, back and forth. Laddie was curled up in one corner of the porch fast asleep, while fireflies darted here and there, dancing in the twilight.

The men finished their lengthy discussion in the parlor. Grandpa yawned and excused himself. "This old man needs his sleep," he muttered and headed upstairs. Chase and Fred stepped out on the porch for a breath of fresh air.

"Mr. Mason, sir." Bill jumped to his feet. "Fred! Heard you were back. Good to see you." He held out his hand.

"Billy Bob!" Fred squinted in the twilight. "Say, are you courting my sister Cassie?"

"Yep, I been courting her nigh on a year now. We're both eighteen, and your pa gave his permission. We plan to be married come September."

"Pa, is that true? Cassie. . .you never told me. Your letters said nothing about it."

Cassie slid off the swing and put her arms around her brother. "I. . .I wouldn't let them tell, Fred. It was to be a surprise. Bill and I wanted to have a double wedding with you and Becky Sue." Her last words faded as she moved away. "I'm sorry, Fred, so sorry."

"Don't worry about that none, Cassie," Frederic mumbled quickly. "I'm happy for you and Bill." He shook Bill's hand and slapped him on the back. "Congratulations, Billy Bob. You have yourself a special girl there. Take care of her."

"You bet I will," Bill Collins said heartily as he drew Cassie close.

"It's gettin' late, Cassie," Mr. Mason warned. "We best be gettin' inside."

"I'll be leaving, sir. Good night." Bill Collins moved toward the steps.

"Pa, I'll be coming in just a few minutes," Cassie said.

A full moon cast its lengthening shadows on the young couple as they walked hand in hand toward Bill's gelding. Trees silhouetted against the soft sky seemed to whisper their good nights.

"I feel badly for Frederic," Cassie said. "We're so happy, and he's hurting so."

Bill cupped her small oval face in his large, rough hands and looked into her hazel eyes. The moonlight lit her face with a silver glow.

"I know, Cassie, and I feel bad, too. But we can't change what's happened. Life goes on, and we make the best of it. Frederic is strong. He'll make out fine. We just have to trust God."

Chapter 4

Fred awoke early the next morning before any in the household were up. The light from the full moon penetrated his room, and he dressed quickly. Silently he crept from the house, nudged Laddie where he slept on the porch, and headed for the back pasture. Laddie trotted beside him, delighted at this early morning walk. Down the trail they went, the young man and his dog, with the towering trees rising around them in the fading darkness. The trail led around a bend, then through the smooth clay fields before coming to the creek.

"This is my favorite spot, quiet and secluded," he said aloud. "I like the peacefulness of the countryside where I can mull things over."

He lowered himself to the ground with his back against a giant maple. The ground had a fresh, sweet smell and was moist and spongy from a heavy dew. The solitude was broken only by birdsong and the low sounds of the cattle grazing in the field.

"Kinda wet, eh, Laddie?" He nuzzled the dog's head and scratched his ears. Laddie laid his head on Fred's lap as if to say, "All's right with the world." The creek bubbled and gurgled on its way downstream. It was shallow and narrow at this point but broadened out and got deeper farther back.

"This is nice," Frederic said. "Far away from the bloody battlefields and smell of the dying. I wish I could get it out of my mind."

Presently the sun started to rise on the horizon. "Look at that ball of fire, Laddie. What a sight for these eyes. There's nothing prettier, nowhere!"

A twig snapped, and Laddie jumped to his feet.

"So here you are, Fred! I knew I'd find you here." Emily sat down by her brother in the damp grass, pulling her skirts around her. "This has always been our special place."

"Look at that sunrise, Emily! God splashes His flaming color against the bluest of skies. It's to remind us of Himself and His goodness to all His creatures."

"What goodness?" Emily snapped, her blue eyes flashing. "Is it good that you have a crippled leg? Is it good about Becky Sue breaking her promise, running off and marrying someone else? I declare. . .God doesn't seem very good sometimes at all. Why does He let these terrible things happen?"

"I can't answer that, Emily. God is God. He is perfect. I love Becky Sue, and I'm fighting bitter feelings. I've asked God why it happened. He let me keep my leg and my life. I'm not bitter about the war, but I feel bitter toward Becky Sue. She betrayed my trust."

Suddenly Emily, tomboy that she was, took off her shoes and stockings, gathered her cotton skirts to her knees, and started across the creek, jumping from one rock to another. "Come on, Fred," she called. "Get a move on!"

Fred quickly took off his shoes and stockings, rolled up his pant legs, and followed her cautiously, favoring his injured leg. He lost his balance more easily now, but he made it safely to the other side. Laddie splashed his way through the creek and proceeded to shake himself, spraying Fred and Emily with the cold, clear water.

"Hey, Laddie!" Fred and Emily sat down on the mossy bank amid the clover and wild daisies, laughing.

"I'm glad you are home, Fred. Will you stay and help Pa and Gramps with the farm? It's getting harder all the time for Grandpa to keep up." Emily's blue eyes searched his.

"Yep," he drawled. "Farming's inborn in me. I've been waiting three years to get back to this." Fred gestured toward the surrounding landscape. "There's something about working with the soil, just feeling it in your hands, planting crops, and seeing them grow. And the animals. . .well, they're like friends. What about you, little sister? Do you have a beau, too, like Cassie? Will you be getting married on me one day?"

"Nobody around here catches my fancy!" Emily declared emphatically. "I don't want to be a farmer's wife like Ma, and like Cassie will be. I'm tired of farm life. . .I want to live in town. I want to do something with my life. I'll marry a rich fella maybe, if I ever decide to marry. Ma says I can take a teachers' course at Colby College while staying with Aunt Maudie in town. Aunt Maude's so lonely now that Uncle George passed on, and no kids of their own."

"Can Aunt Maude put up with that hot temper of yours?" Fred teased.

Emily pushed Fred affectionately. "It's better now than it was. I'm more grown up."

"Well, I remember those times when you were so mad you'd hold your breath until you fainted."

"Yep, and I remember what you and Cassie did to me."

Fred laughed. "You were about nine, I guess, the last time you held your breath like that. You were madder than ever just because you couldn't have your own way. Cassie and I picked you up and dumped you headfirst in the rain barrel."

"Ma was real mad at you, too. She said I might have drowned."

"Naw. We just dunked you up and down a few times, fast-like. We didn't hold you down. It cured you, too, didn't it? You never held your breath after that."

"I got over it. . .but who wouldn't after such horrid treatment?"

Fred was thoughtful a few minutes. "Billy Bob seems like a fine young man. He grew up while I was away. I guess he and Cassie will be mighty happy."

"Bill is nice," Emily agreed. "He and his pa are building a cabin for Bill and Cassie on a piece of the Collinses' property. Cassie is so excited. She wants me to ride over with her this afternoon to see it. It's going to be different with Cassie gone. That's another reason I want to go away. I'll miss her."

"She'll only be a short ways off. You could see her anytime. It won't change that much."

"Yep, it will. . .it will change. It will be mighty different with her being married. She won't be my playmate anymore. We've always been so close, being just eleven months apart. Like twins sorta, Ma always said. Now she'll have Bill. He doesn't like being called Billy Bob anymore. Anyway, I'd just be in the way."

Their thoughts were broken by the tolling of the old dinner bell. Ma used it whenever they were to come, for a meal or whatever. This time it meant breakfast, so they hurried across the creek, put on their shoes and stockings, and started up the trail. An aroma of fried bacon reached their nostrils as they rounded the last bend.

Fred sniffed deeply. The sweet morning air, punctuated with the smell of coffee and crisp bacon, saturated his being. "If God's heaven was on earth, Emily, this would sure be it!"

Chapter 5

Breakfast was a sturdy meal at the Mason farm. Oatmeal with fresh cream, molasses doughnuts, and Ma's homemade blackberry preserves started it off. Then bacon and eggs followed with huge mugs of strong coffee. Fully satisfied, the men left for chores while the womenfolk set to theirs.

Fred eagerly fed the pigs and chickens, watered them from the spring, and checked on the horses and cattle in the pasture. Then he worked the garden, down the rows of beans and into the corn. He loved the smell of the earth as he turned it over again and again. The carrots and onions were half grown, and little green tomatoes hung from the vines in abundance. "It will be a good harvest," he muttered.

After the noon meal, the elder male Masons took Fred out to their workplace in an old log shed. On one side sat the huge bellows and tools used to shoe the horses. The other half of the shed contained lumber and woodworking tools. They had been working on a four-poster bed for Cassie and Bill's wedding gift.

"It's beautiful!" Fred exclaimed, running his hand over the smooth pine posts. "Has Cassie seen it?"

"Not yet. We've warned her ta stay away till it's done. Jest a little more sandin' and then the finishin' stain. Grandpa does all the finish work," Chase explained. "He's the real craftsman."

"You've made this shed into a dandy workshop," Fred stated as he glanced around. There were wooden swings, tables, chests, and baby cradles partly assembled. "What do you do with all these?"

"We sell them ta neighbors and townsfolk who hear about our work. In late September we'll take 'em into Waterville ta the fair. Ma sells her preserves and pickles, and Grandpa and I sell our wood pieces. The ladies also sell a few patch quilts and some fancywork. Gives us some extra money fer the long winter."

"I want to do this," Fred said seriously. "Do you think I could learn this trade?" He caressed the fine pieces and inhaled deeply, letting the odor of the new wood linger in his nostrils. "Working with wood is the next best thing to working with the soil."

"Sure ya could, Fred, and ya'd be good at it, too. Maybe ya could make us some breadboards fer the fair, shaped like pigs," Grandpa suggested with a sly smile.

Fred and his pa laughed heartily.

"I'll do it," Fred agreed. "Pigs are my favorite for breadboards, if I can just make them so they aren't lopsided."

"It's good ta see ya laugh, son," Chase said. "Grandpa and me hoped ya'd have a hankerin' ta work with wood. We got kinda a trade goin' here that ya might like ta carry on. There's enough timber still ta be cut on the property, more than we need fer the woodstove and fireplaces. We figger there's ample ta spare fer woodworkin'."

"Can't think of anything I'd rather do. I'm anxious to start."

"Are ya sure ya want ta work the farm, Fred, and jest stay here?" Chase asked seriously. "Yer ma wondered if ya might want to go to Colby and get some more book learnin'. Emily's got that idea in her head, says she wants ta get away and get some schoolin'."

"I'll leave that for Emily, Pa. My heart is here on the farm, working the soil, tending the cattle, and learning the woodcrafting. This is the only place I want to be."

"We sure do need ya, boy." Grandpa placed gnarled hands on his grandson's shoulders. "Ya don't know how bad yer needed, or how long we've wished it."

"It's settled then," Fred said. "You need me, and I need you. We'll work side by side on this great land that God has given us. We'll plant, and He'll give us the increase, teaching us a few lessons besides."

The two elder Masons showed relief at Fred's decision. Being native downeasters, they were a tough and independent lot. They would never have pressed Frederic to stay on the farm, but they were glad that for Frederic, like for themselves, the greatest joy came from wrestling with the land.

In the early afternoon Cassie and Emily took the buggy and old Nell over the land that led to the back of the Collinses' property where Bill and his father were building the cabin. Timber had been cleared, and the cabin sat on a little knoll with a view of the countryside. Bill and Mr. Collins heard them coming and hurried out to greet them.

"It's beautiful, Bill!" Cassie exclaimed. "Oh, Mr. Collins, thank you. I love it; I really do."

"I'm glad you like it, Cassie," Bill said as he placed an arm around her tiny waist. "It's ready now for the woman's touch."

He walked her through the rooms: a large kitchen, living room, and two bedrooms. "We can add on as our family grows," he said shyly. "We'll have a bigger place later on." They were lost in their own little world.

"How do ya like it, Emily?" Mr. Collins asked as she lingered behind.

"It's nice, Mr. Collins. You and Bill have worked very hard; I can tell. It's the perfect house for Cassie."

"But do you like it?" he persisted.

"I like it for her, but not for me. I want to be in town. I want to be with people," Emily said honestly.

"So that's it." Mr. Collins smiled. "The country girl wants ta leave the country, spread her wings a little, is that it?"

MAINE

"I plan to attend Colby, the liberal arts college in Waterville, and live with my aunt Maude. That will suit me a whole lot better than staying here."

Cassie, captivated by the smooth logs of the cabin's walls, didn't let her sister's remarks dampen her spirits. She looked out the front window at a view of wild apple trees, clumps of birches, and fields of blowing daisies. Deftly she set about measuring the windows for curtains.

"I'll make them quicker than you can shake a stick," she exclaimed. "I have yellow calico for the kitchen and blue for the living room. And one bedroom will have blue and the other yellow. They're my favorite colors."

Cassie and Bill planned where they would put their furniture. They had very little, but each set of parents gave them extra pieces from their attics. The poster bed was to be a wedding gift, and they could count on a cradle later on when needed. The womenfolk made scores of dish towels, rag rugs, and bed quilts.

Bill and Cassie walked out onto the porch. "This house doesn't need a thing," Cassie insisted as she turned to Bill and their eyes met.

"I can think of something important," Bill said softly.

"What does it need?" Cassie smiled saucily up at him.

"Only you, my darling," he whispered in her ear. "It won't be complete until you are here."

Chapter 6

The weary days of harvest were at hand. As quickly as the men harvested the crops, the womenfolk canned them. Nothing could compare with their sweet corn. The thick blanket of snow in winter was part of the reason for the sweetness of Maine's corn crop. Wild berries that grew in abundance on the hillside were carefully picked and made into jellies and preserves. They stacked the field corn in corncribs and pitched hay into huge mounds by the barn. They would have enough to feed the animals through the long, hard winter ahead.

Everyone was involved. The hard work helped Frederic heal, saturating his being like a tonic. He liked being busy and drove himself constantly. He wanted no time to think about Becky Sue.

He had seen her at a distance at church a few times, but he avoided meeting her face-to-face. When she headed toward him, he bolted for the door. Seeing her in the flesh and knowing she belonged to another was just too painful, and his bitterness cut into his heart like a knife. He suppressed the urge to let his eyes linger on the soft white countenance, full lips, and mass of ebony hair, forcing himself to escape after services were over as quickly as possible. As a result, some at church decided Frederic was unfriendly, probably because of the war and his crippled leg. But his family understood. If he left after church in a hurry and started walking, they picked him up along the road on the way home and said nothing.

Plans for Cassie's wedding progressed swiftly and kept the household in a high fever of excitement. Cassie had finished her sewing. Her dresses and underclothing were done and the calico curtains up. She and Bill moved their used pieces of furniture and handmade items into the cabin. The beautiful four-poster had been lovingly finished and placed in the larger bedroom. Ladies at church held a bridal shower, and shelves stood stocked with canned goods, preserves, towels, quilts, bedding, dishes, and cooking pots. The completed cabin stood ready and waiting for the bride and groom.

Frederic avoided visiting the cabin. Each time Cassie asked him to see it, he made an excuse, and his heart tightened up inside. Seeing the little house only reminded him that he, too, might have had a cabin like it, the one he had planned to build for Becky Sue.

"Please, Fred, just come and see what we've done," Cassie begged one afternoon. "Tell me if you like it or not. . .that's all I ask."

Frederic finally gave in. "I'll come."

The ride was a quiet one as he, Cassie, and Emily took the buggy over to the cabin. Frederic walked through the rooms in silence, his mouth set in a firm line.

"Don't you like it, Fred?" Cassie asked. "Tell me what you're thinking."

"It's a fine cabin, Cassie. It's exactly what I planned to build myself. Bill and his pa did a good job on it. And your curtains. . .well, they're prettier than fair to middlin'."

Cassie hugged her brother. "I'm so glad you like it. I knew you would. Emily doesn't like it a bit."

"I do so, Cassie," Emily sputtered defensively. "I like it a lot, for you and Bill. It's just not what I'd want, that's all."

At that moment a horseman flew up the trail, raising a cloud of dust, and stopped abruptly at the porch. Frederic noted that the rider was a girl, but she was an odd-looking character in faded coveralls a mile too big. Her red gold hair was formed into a braid that reached to her waist.

"Hello!" a feminine voice shouted as the girl jumped from her sorrel mare.

"Who is that?" Frederic whispered.

"You know her—that's Bill's sister Sarah Jane," Cassie replied softly. "Sarah," she called. "Come on in."

"Been out riding and saw your buggy," Sarah said. "Thought maybe Emily and Frederic might be along. Hello there, Frederic." Sarah's smile lit up her small oval face. "I've seen you at church, but you always rush off so fast. I'm glad your leg is okay and that you're home safe."

"Thanks, Sarah, my leg's fine. Well, I wouldn't have recognized you. You've grown taller since I left. You were just a little freckle-faced kid."

"I'm almost fifteen," Sarah declared indignantly. "And I'm the best rider in these parts. I can outride anyone. . .even you, Frederic."

"Well, that's quite a boast. We'll have to see about that." Frederic laughed.

"When, Frederic?" Sarah asked quickly. "When will you ride with me?"

Frederic studied this slip of a girl in her baggy coveralls. She certainly was straightforward and outspoken. Loose wisps of red gold hair framed her pale, delicate face. She gazed at him expectantly with her dark violet blue eyes, waiting for his answer.

Emily broke the silence. "Sarah's a tomboy, like me. You'd have to ride some to beat her, Fred."

"When can we ride?" Sarah asked again.

Frederic smiled at her persistence. "We'll give it a try one of these days and see who outrides whom. I haven't done much riding in the past three years, but I reckon I can outride a little whippersnapper like you."

"Ho. . .just you try!" Sarah declared confidently.

Cassie took Sarah on a tour of the cabin. The younger girl hadn't seen it since it was finished and all the furniture in place.

"It's beautiful, Cassie," Sarah exclaimed. "I knew it would be. Your curtains make it real home-like."

They talked some about the wedding, and everyone avoided talking about Becky Sue. Eventually Cassie, Emily, and Frederic climbed into the buggy and headed home.

"Don't forget, Frederic," Sarah called as she hopped on her mare. "We'll race together; you promised. Shall we have a prize for the winner?"

"Yep, and you decide the prize, Sarah. How about cookies? Remember, I'll be the one winning it."

"Don't count your chickens!" Sarah shouted as she rode off, her long red gold braid trailing in the breeze.

Chapter 7

Cassie's wedding day, early in September, dawned beautiful and sunny. The hot, humid days were past, and the breeze was fresh and invigorating. Trees had started to change color, and a definite promise of autumn filled the air.

Excitement reigned at the Mason household. Ma pressed Pa's and Grandpa's best suits. Frederic purchased a new suit in town, his old prewar one not being suitable for his sister's wedding. Ma dressed in palest pink, her favorite color that brought out the roses in her cheeks. Emily also wore pink, though a deeper color, with matching bows in her dark brown hair. Cassie and Bill were having only Bill's friend, Peter Jordan, and Emily stand up for them, since they wanted a small wedding. Frederic hoped to stay in the background. He wouldn't miss his sister's wedding for anything, but he wondered how he would avoid Becky Sue.

"I'll just have to grin and bear it," he decided. "Guess I'm not the first man to be thrown over for another by a fickle woman."

Nervously he dressed and prepared to leave with his parents and grandfather in the larger buggy. Cassie and Emily went ahead in the small buggy with old Nell.

The little church was full of people. Friends and neighbors came in their buggies from miles around. A wedding gave an occasion and excuse to get everyone together for a social gathering. No one wanted to miss it.

Cassie looked beautiful and radiant. Her chestnut hair, pulled back from her face, cascaded into curls around her shoulders. The dress of purest white fit snugly around her tiny waist, then billowed out into layers of ruffles and lace. She had sewn pearl-like beads on the bodice neckline and on the crown of the veil.

Bill stood at the front of the church, nervous but handsome in his dark suit and tie. His hair was plastered down, and his blue eyes sparkled. The little lines in his face twitched occasionally as Chase Mason walked his daughter down the aisle to give her away.

Aunt Maude McClough, Pa's widowed sister, sat with the family in the front pew. Medium in height, her slightly rounded figure was draped in lavender and lace. Her dark, snappy eyes commanded attention, and her thick dark hair, streaked heavily with gray, nestled under a perky straw bonnet complete with elegant feathers.

Being ten years older than her brother, Chase, she tended to be doting and somewhat bossy. Upon hearing about Cassie's upcoming wedding, she spoke out against it. "Fiddlesticks, Chase," she protested loudly. "Cassie is too young. Mark my words, it will never work. Why, they are both babes."

Despite her repeated warnings, the young couple continued with their plans. Maude sat, lips pinched together, and fidgeted impatiently with her gloves. Although the wedding did not have her approval, she had presented the couple with a generous gift of money so they could travel to Boston for their honeymoon.

Maude lived comfortably in a large brick home in Waterville near the common. Her late husband, a doctor for many years, had left her well off financially. Having no children of her own, her brother's three children held special places in her heart. She had been allowed the pleasure of showering them with gifts on special occasions through the years.

The pastor of the little church, Rev. Clyde Davis, was a short man in his early seventies. He had thin gray hair, a waxed handlebar mustache, and wore thick horn-rimmed spectacles. He spoke the marriage ceremony in a deep, resonant voice and quoted scripture verses from memory. After the young couple repeated their vows, he admonished them to love one another "till death do you part."

When the marriage ceremony ended, Mrs. Mason was sobbing quietly. Frederic, seated on one side of her, placed a comforting arm around her shoulders. She leaned against him and dabbed at her swollen eyes.

"Now, Ma, don't take on so," her husband whispered from the other side. "Don't let Cassie see ya cryin'. Ya don't want ta spoil it fer her."

"Land-a-Goshen." Ma sighed. "Jest look at me, would ya? I'm happy my little girl is married to sech a fine boy. These are jest tears of joy, Pa."

As everyone moved outside, the people gathered around the newlyweds with affectionate hugs and well wishes. Quickly, trestle tables, made of wooden sawhorses and planks, were set up on the grounds and laden with food. Neighbors brought picnic baskets filled with goodies to share in the feast.

Frederic wandered to the back of the property away from the crowd. He sat with his back to the group, surrounded by a small clump of trees. He hoped to be alone and unnoticed in all the excitement. This was Cassie's big day, and he wouldn't brood over it. He just wanted to be by himself.

Lost in his own thoughts of self-pity, he was startled by a voice behind him. "Frederic, you've avoided me all these weeks since you came home."

The voice was soft and familiar. Fire rushed to his face as he jumped up and turned to face Becky Sue. Even if he hadn't seen her, he would have recognized her by the delicate sweet scent that met his nostrils.

"Frederic, I've missed you," she continued, moving closer. "Remember how it was with us before you went away?"

"Becky Sue!" Frederic's voice sounded strange in his ears, and he caught his breath. "Where's Zack. . .your husband? Isn't he here?"

Becky Sue reached up and touched Frederic's face with her soft hand. "Your mustache makes you look some older, Frederic, but I like it. I like it a lot."

Frederic backed away as though stung. "Where's Zack?" he asked again hoarsely.

"Don't bother about him none, Frederic. He's working all day at the mill. I made a terrible mistake marrying Zack. I know now that I want us to be like we were before." Becky Sue moved closer and gazed steadily at Frederic. Her sea green eyes held his with a sad and wistful appeal.

Frederic felt himself becoming lightheaded. He shook his head and took a deep breath. "Becky Sue, you are married to Zack," he said firmly. "Things can't be like they were before. We can't go back. God knows I loved you. I planned for three years to come back and marry you. I counted on you waiting for me. You broke your promise as if it meant nothing. You're a married woman; you belong to Zack now. Didn't you hear what the preacher just said? Marriage is 'until death do us part.' That's the way it has to be." He spit out the words and looked away. "Don't you see—it's too late now!"

Frederic turned abruptly and headed back to the festivities. He could hear Becky Sue crying softly, but he didn't turn around. "Don't you see," he muttered to himself bitterly, "it's too late for us now!"

Chapter 8

Over here, Frederic," Emily called from a group of people gathered to one side. "Come join us."

Frederic wanted to be swallowed up in the crowd so he wouldn't have to face Becky Sue again. Quickly he joined them and greeted many of his old friends, some who were now married. Peter Jordan had a cousin with him, Collette, visiting from Portland, Maine. She was small with lots of dark hair and striking black eyes. Her stylish pale yellow dress highlighted the depth of her olive complexion. When introduced, she smiled demurely and held out her hand.

"Nice to meet you," Frederic said.

Time passed quickly as Frederic spent it in lengthy conversation with this interesting and well-educated young lady. Collette spoke French fluently.

"My mother is French," she explained, "and we've been to France many times. I grew up learning the language."

Fascinated by her perfect diction, Frederic found this well-traveled miss very enjoyable company, and the distraction welcome. Collette's father was a successful Portland businessman. His shipyard boasted a number of ships involved in the trade market. He had established his headquarters in New Orleans, married her mother there, and until the war, spent winters in New Orleans and summers in Portland. The war had caused heartache and hardship for her family.

"Southerners were naturally suspicious of us," Collette said in her light Southern drawl. "This resulted in our moving permanently to our home in Portland for the duration of the war. Mama and I are so homesick for New Orleans."

"Will your family move back now that the war is over?" Frederic asked.

"Not right away. It may take years to gain confidence with the South, although we have many ties and relatives there. I do so want to go back. My heart has always been in the South."

"How sad that they are suspicious of you. Your family was as much a victim of this war as we soldiers. I have an idea that it will take a little time for all of us."

Frederic learned that Collette would be visiting the Jordans for a few weeks and requested permission to call on her.

"Bond's Cornet Band from Boston will be in town next week at the meetinghouse. They are well-known for their music. Would you go with me?"

"Why, Frederic, it would be a pleasure."

They said their good-byes, and Frederic hurried to help his family clear away food and place wedding gifts in the large buggy. Cassie and Bill had slipped away earlier and caught the train for Boston. They would be gone a week.

Frederic carried an armload of gifts to the Collinses' wagon, as they were also transporting gifts to Cassie and Bill's cabin. He was deep in thought about Collette. *Did she notice my crippled leg? She never asked any questions. Probably too polite. I wonder if it matters to her.* As he turned around, he bumped into someone standing directly behind him.

"Sorry, Sarah," he exclaimed. "Where'd you come from?"

"Been right here, Frederic," she said, laughing.

Frederic hadn't noticed her all afternoon, but all of a sudden here she was. The slender slip of a girl with reddish golden hair looked older somehow. Her hair wasn't in a braid today; instead, it was tucked and curled around her shoulders for the wedding. Could she really be only fourteen? He noted that her soft, misty green muslin dress complimented her fair coloring. What an improvement over the ridiculous baggy coveralls.

"Don't be draggin' your feet about riding with me," Sarah Jane reminded.

"Mercy, Sarah, you can't be the same girl I saw at the cabin in baggy britches, can you?" Frederic teased. "I reckon you look a mite older today in that fancy dress."

"I like baggy britches!" Sarah exploded. "Can't ride fast in a dress. When are we taking our ride? You promised, remember?"

Frederic grinned at her impatience. "Things have been busy, Sarah, with the wedding and harvest."

"But will you ride with me sometime?"

"I promised, and I will. . .sometime. I can't say when just now."

Frederic thought about the day's events as he and Emily rode home together in the small buggy. Emily chattered constantly about the wedding, the people, and the visitor from Portland.

"Peter's cousin is a real lady, don't you think, Frederic? She's older, twenty-five, someone said, and does have some fancy ways. Guess she's bored to death around here."

"Oh, I don't know about that," Fred said thoughtfully.

"What do you think of her? You were talking to her a lot. Is she to your liking?"

"She's very nice. As a matter of fact, we're going to the band concert at the meetinghouse on Thursday. We both enjoy good music, and she agreed to go."

"Do you think she's pretty?" Emily pressed. "She sure has a lot of dark hair."

Frederic was quiet for a moment. "She's a fine-looking woman, even pretty, I guess." He looked away, avoiding Emily's gaze. "She's not as pretty as some," he added softly.

Emily suspected Frederic was thinking about Becky Sue, and she changed the subject quickly. "Aunt Maudie is anxious to have me live with her while I attend Colby. She gets so lonely in that big house."

"I'll miss you at home. You'll come back weekends, won't you?"

"I won't go until after Christmas when they start the winter term. So I'll be around for a while yet. Don't know about coming home weekends. . .I might have too much studying to do."

"You'll be meeting new fellas and be busier than can be with your social life," Fred teased.

"I know there will be lots going on at the college. I'll like getting involved."

Just then a small buggy came from behind and pulled up beside them on the road. It was Sarah Jane traveling alone and recklessly at a high speed. "Want to race?" she shouted.

"No, Sarah, no!" Frederic yelled. "Slow down! Don't drive so fast! You'll overturn!"

Sarah waved and pulled on ahead. Her red gold curls had fallen loose and blew carelessly around her shoulders. Frederic and Emily heard her laughing as she left them behind.

"That child needs a good spanking," Frederic said as he pulled old Nell to a slow trot. "She could have caused an accident."

"You know, Fred, she's really not a child anymore. She'll turn fifteen soon."

"Well, what do you think has gotten into her. . .riding up on us like that?"

"I wonder," Emily mused. "I wonder."

Chapter 9

The day of the Waterville fair arrived. Pa and Grandpa filled the wagon with wood furniture that had been lovingly handcrafted especially for this event. Frederic had helped them finish the pieces and now carefully arranged them in the wagon so they would not get broken on the way into town.

Ma and Emily took their quilts, rag rugs, jellies, preserves, and pickles in the buggy. Since the fair lasted all day, the picnic hamper had been filled with food and drink. Cool weather, darkish and damp, threatened, but the sky brightened some as they packed the wagon. Hopes were high.

Grandpa Caleb, though, planned to stay home and nurse his lumbago. The all-day affair was hard on the older man.

Still visiting at the Jordans, Collette had told Frederic she would be at the fair. He had enjoyed the band concert with her at the meetinghouse, and he'd called on her a few times since. Today they would be together again.

"Seems like you and Collette are getting chummy," Emily teased. "Didn't you say she wants you to visit her in Portland?"

"Yep. I'll probably do it. She's a very persuasive person."

"I noticed." Emily laughed. "She seems to have you in a whirl."

"It might be good for me to get away for a while," Frederic said soberly. "I need to mull things over."

Waterville's fairgrounds bustled with activity. The family quickly set up in an area designated for those with food and craft items to sell. Judges were on hand to judge the best pickles, pies, and other desserts. Ma had entered her blueberry pie and some of her sweet and sour pickles.

At the far end of the area, a lean-to shelter was provided for the animals that would be judged. In previous years, before the war, Frederic had entered a calf, steer, or pig. This year the family decided against it. The wood products and canned items would keep them busy enough.

About midday, Collette appeared, dressed in fine blue muslin with a picnic basket on her arm. "Can you leave for a while?" she asked. "I fixed a picnic lunch, and we could take it down by the river."

When Frederic hesitated, the family insisted that he go and enjoy himself for a spell. Cassie and Bill had arrived and planned to help for the remainder of the day.

"Go ahead," Ma insisted. "This is your first fair in three years, son. Look

34

around and don't hurry back."

Frederic and Collette found a quiet spot to picnic away from the mingling crowd. Frederic spread a blanket on the deep grass, and they relaxed while they ate. Collette had brought fried chicken, rolls and cheese, and some little cakes. They laughed and talked about little things, then strolled around the grounds visiting the various booths.

"Do you like fairs?" Frederic asked. "We have one every year. I've come here since a little boy, as far back as I can remember. Pa used to carry me on his shoulders."

"I like fairs," Collette assured him. "Especially this one. There are so many quaint, homemade items. . .a great variety to choose from."

They approached the contest area and watched as the judges tasted one pie after another. Then they started on the other desserts.

"How can they decide?" Collette asked. "It must be a very difficult decision."

"I'm sure it is," Frederic agreed. "It would be interesting to be one of the judges. I wouldn't mind tasting all those delicious pies."

Collette tilted her dark head and laughed, a sound like tinkling little bells. "You might get sick," she warned, "or fat."

They walked toward the game booths and stopped at the shooting gallery.

"Would you like a doll, Collette? I'll try my hand at shooting those ducks." Frederic took the gun and started shooting. He hit enough ducks to select a prize for Collette.

"I'd like the stuffed bear, the big brown one," she said. "Fred, you are an excellent marksman. Have you always shot so well?"

"Pa taught me as a boy. It came in handy during the war."

"Tell me about the war."

Frederic turned away. "No, Collette. It was a terrible war. I want to forget about shooting and dying."

"I understand," Collette said quickly, hugging her bear. "Let's go see the animals instead. They should be interesting."

"Right!" Frederic agreed. "Just wish I had one to show today. There'll be a riding contest, too."

Frederic steered Collette toward the back lot where the livestock were kept. Judges graded an assortment of ducks, geese, chickens, pigs, cows, lambs, goats, and horses. Collette stopped suddenly short of the shelter, keeping her distance from the animals. Frederic coaxed her to take a closer look.

"You go on ahead, Frederic." She smiled sweetly. "I'm not used to the smell of animals. Most of them, especially the pigs, are so dirty." She wrinkled her nose in disgust. "Take your time. I'll just wait here." She patted her hair and fluffed out her gown, then she pulled her wrap tightly around her shoulders to keep out the chill, dabbing her handkerchief at her nostrils.

Frederic hurried eagerly forward. The animals were like friends to him, and he even relished the smell. "Yep," he grinned, taking a deep breath, "it just goes with the territory."

He wandered along the stalls until he came to the far end of the shelter where there was a fenced area and several people on horseback. "This has to be the horseback riding contest," he muttered. Just then he noticed a slip of a girl in baggy coveralls astride a sorrel-colored mare. "Can that be Sarah Jane?" he said aloud. "It must be her, with that red hair and baggy britches."

Sarah spied him and rode over. "Frederic! Will you watch while I put Star through her paces? You'll have to come around to the other side."

Frederic nodded and hurried as fast as his bad leg would permit. Standing by the rail, he watched Sarah trot Star out to the center of the ring. Forgetting the time, he watched her entire performance as she trotted, cantered, jumped, and galloped her mare in the competition before the judges.

When finished, Sarah rushed up to him. "How did I do, Frederic? Did I do okay?"

"Better than okay, little one. I'd say you will probably win yourself a ribbon, if I'm any judge."

"Last year I got a third-place ribbon. This year I worked harder and I'm older. I'm hoping to get a first place."

Frederic gazed steadily at this youngster in her baggy britches. "Do I look older to you, Frederic?" Sarah searched his face intently with her deep violet blue eyes. He found it difficult to look away and stood gazing back at her for some time.

"Someone's calling for you, Frederic," Sarah said finally. "It's that fancy French lady from Portland."

Frederic spun around to see Collette walking toward him. She had a look of determination on her otherwise pretty countenance. Frederic had forgotten her completely. Hurriedly he said good-bye to Sarah Jane and apologized to Collette.

"I'm sorry, Collette. I got so interested in watching the horseback-riding contest."

"Who is that odd child you were talking to?" she asked.

"She's a neighbor," Frederic answered. Then he added thoughtfully, "But she's really not a child."

Chapter 10

Autumn's glorious colors blazed across the land. Towering trees with their leaves of gold, yellow, red, and orange painted the countryside. Warm days prevailed, and completion of the harvest was at hand. Nights were cold and crisp, with clear, starry skies overhead.

The men cleaned, repaired, and readied the barn for the animals that spent the long winter inside its walls. Cassie joined the womenfolk as they did up squash and pumpkins. They made applesauce, apple butter, and jugs of apple cider from an abundance of apples grown in the orchard. The cider filled the air with a delicious aroma that was both tantalizing and inviting. As they completed their canning, they stored the jars on shelves in the pantry or in the cellar under the house.

Cassie took a share of canned products with her to her cabin. Divinely happy in her new role as housewife, her conversation centered around her new husband and their little home. Emily, unable to share in her sister's enthusiasm, grew more and more impatient to start college.

Aunt Maude had generously offered to put up the funds for all of her brother's children so they could receive a college education. She was disappointed that Emily was the only one to take advantage of her offer.

While visiting the farm for dinner one crisp fall Sunday, Maude pressed upon Frederic the importance of higher education. "Frederic," she said in her commanding tone. "You need to get more schooling and make something out of yourself. Farming is all right for your pa and grandpa. They didn't have the opportunity given them for advanced learning. But you, boy, you need something more challenging. Have you no goals? Have you no ambition?" Aunt Maude was known to speak her mind and never very tactfully.

"I do have goals, Aunt Maude. I plan to wrestle the land. As far as more schooling is concerned, no. I'm happy here on the farm. I feel close to my Maker when I'm out in the fields. God speaks to me, and we commune together in the beauty of His creation. Yep, everything I want is right here."

"Talk some sense into him, Chase. Do you want to be a farmer all your life, Frederic? Surely you can't be satisfied. . ."

Chase interrupted, "Now, Maude, let the boy alone. He's been away ta the war and seen a lot of terrible things. He's old enough ta know what he wants ta do. Farmin' is a good way ta live. . . . Grandpa and I can tell ya. Anyway, it's his life; let the boy decide."

Maude sat tight-lipped for a moment. She didn't take defeat easily. Being outnumbered, however, she resigned herself and added, "If you change your mind, Frederic, just say the word. The funds are there for you." As an afterthought she said, "Are you still seeing the young lady from Portland?"

"I haven't seen her for a few weeks. She's gone back to her family in Portland."

"She invited Fred to visit her," Emily said with a grin.

"Is that so, Frederic?" Aunt Maude asked. "You should go and meet her family. I understand they are important people and quite wealthy."

"I'm thinking on it," Fred answered. "Maybe now is a good time to go with the harvest about done. What do you think, Pa?"

"You've been workin' hard, son, and it'd do ya good ta get away fer a while. Grandpa and I can carry on here. There's not much ta do right now. We got all the hard stuff done."

"Watch out fer the fancy lady," Grandpa added slyly. "I think she had her eye on our Fred boy."

Frederic shook his head. "She's a nice friend, Grandpa, that's all. I've enjoyed her company. It kept me from thinking about other things. It'll be just a friendly visit. . .no strings attached. It would be nice to visit Portland."

"That's right, son," Ma agreed. "Jest go, meet her people, and have yerself a good time. Portland is a nice place fer visitin', and ya can stay with Cousin Amos and Sophie. They'd be so pleased."

"Now, Frederic," Aunt Maude snapped, "it wouldn't do any harm to think about the possibility of marrying into such a fine, well-to-do family. This young woman might be just the one for you."

"She'll press you, Fred," Emily teased. "Collette has marriage on her mind."

A shadow crossed Frederic's brow as he answered. "I'm not ready for a serious relationship. Not now. Maybe never. I'm still not over Becky Sue."

After an awkward silence, Emily said quietly, "Becky Sue has left Zack and is living back home. She wants out of her marriage. . .says it was a mistake."

Frederic muttered an excuse and quickly left the table. He couldn't trust his feelings. Emily's words pounded in his brain: *"Becky Sue has left Zack. It was a mistake."* First a glad feeling of hope flooded his being. Then despair washed over him.

He clenched his fists and pounded his injured leg. "It's no good this way," he confessed bitterly, alone in his room. "Please help me, Lord, to win over these feelings I have. I know they're wrong. I need to put Becky Sue out of my mind forever. How can I love someone and hate her at the same time?"

❧

After a fitful night with very little sleep, Frederic arose early and hitched up old Nell to the wagon. He'd wrestled with his painful emotions and made a decision. "Come on, Nell, old girl," he said. "Let's head for town and see if we can get this straightened out. I need to talk to Zack."

A HAVEN OF PEACE

The movement of the wagon along the rutted, bumpy gravel road lulled Frederic into a state of sleepy depression. Fleeting glimpses of Becky Sue in all her loveliness flashed before him, taunting him, teasing him. He could almost hear her speaking.

"I made a mistake marrying Zack, Frederic. I want us to be like we were before." Her soft, inviting words pulled at his heart, and he shook his head wildly to rid himself of her face. . .her voice. Memories tortured him. . .of her hand in his as they walked together, of her touch as he encircled her waist and drew her close. When they kissed, it was tender and gentle. . .soft as a summer breeze. Becky Sue would laugh and pull away, then look up at him with an impish grin.

"I've got to block out these memories!" Frederic fairly shouted the words. "Becky Sue is married to Zack, and she will never be my wife! I must accept it and try to forget."

Frederic forced himself to repress thoughts of Becky Sue for the remainder of his ride into town. With an anxious heart, he approached the mill shortly before opening time. *Will Zack talk to me? He's probably angry and blames me for Becky Sue's return to her parents. I've got to convince him it's not my idea and hope he believes me.*

Mr. Turner, Zack's father, was startled to see Frederic so early in the morning. "What can we do fer ya, Fred? Yer pa need some more lumber?"

"Not today, sir. Is Zack around? I'd like to speak to him, if I may."

"He's inside the office catching up on some paperwork. Go right on in, Fred."

As Frederic entered the small office, he cleared his throat and fumbled for the right words. "Morning, Zack. How are you?"

Zack Turner pushed back a shock of sandy hair as he looked up from his desk of papers. He seemed haggard and sunken-eyed, while his body, always wiry, appeared thinner than usual. "Fred, what can I do for you?" he mumbled. "Do you need more wood?"

"I need to talk to you, Zack. Could you spare me a few minutes?"

"Sure," Zack replied, leaning back in his chair. "Sit down. Is it about Becky Sue? You want her back, don't you?"

Frederic hesitated, then said hurriedly, "No, Zack. . .she's your wife. She belongs with you. I didn't know she'd left you until last evening."

"She's not in love with me. . .never was," Zack muttered bitterly. "She's left me because she's still in love with you."

"Becky Sue might think she's in love with me. She's not. . .or she would never have married you."

"Aren't you glad about this, Fred? Now's your chance to get her back. She only married me because she thought you'd lost your leg. I just happened to be around when she needed someone."

"I'm not happy about this situation one bit," Fred said emphatically. "I loved Becky Sue. . .thought about her every day for three years. But she didn't wait for me. She married you, and that's it. Don't you love her, Zack?"

The sandy-haired young man stood up. He looked stricken, tears brimming in his eyes. "I love her more than life itself. . .and always will."

"Then go to her," Frederic said firmly, "and ask her to return. Don't wait another day."

Zack brushed the tears away and grasped Frederic's hand. "Thanks, Fred. I'll do just that."

As Frederic headed old Nell back to the farm, he struggled with his inner feelings. "I know it's right that Zack and Becky Sue get back together. That's the way it has to be. But, God, why does it have to hurt so much?"

Chapter 11

The train followed the scenic Kennebec River lined with its magnificent birch trees. Frederic stared thoughtfully out the window, watching the river as it hurried toward the sea. He needed this time to get away for a while. His pa's cousin Amos, a seaman, and his wife, Sophie, lived in Portland, Maine. Frederic would stay with them for a spell. He'd packed a few belongings, planning to return within the week.

He slumped in his seat, more absorbed in his thoughts than in the scenery. The monotonous *clickety-clack, clickety-clack, clickety-clack* of the train wheels seemed to laugh at him and say, "Becky Sue, Becky Sue, Becky Sue." He struggled unsuccessfully to put her out of his mind.

As the train neared Portland, he glimpsed the harbor town bathed in shimmering sunshine, displaying the magnificent granite bulwarks of the coast. The town stood like a sedate lady, surrounded by her jewels, the islands of Casco Bay, bidding a hearty welcome to crafts from many ports. The coast was granite ledges and twisted pines, while roads rambled, dipped, and curved, following this mysterious wonder. Lobstermen and fishermen dotted the harbor in their small dories as they set their twine or baited their trawls.

A short walk from the train station, his cousin's stately old house lay near the harbor. Frederic had visited there many times as a boy, and he loved the salt spray of the air and gray granite coast with its pounding surf. He watched sea-birds spread their wings and fly gracefully on their way out to sea.

Sophie and Amos Mason, a warm and homey couple, greeted Frederic heartily. They welcomed his visit and listened to all the family news from Waterville. Sophie, a small, chubby woman with a round face, seemed always to be smiling. Amos, the "old salt," had a tanned, leathery face and large gnarled hands. He owned a fishing boat and made his livelihood from the sea. The raw winds from the sea stiffened his joints, and he hobbled slightly as he showed Frederic to his room, a simple alcove with a bed and chest of drawers.

Sophie served a delicious supper of hearty fish chowder, fish cakes, baked beans, and suet pudding. At their request, Frederic related some of his war experiences. Their only son, Samuel, had been killed early in the war at Bull Run. Sadness and pride shone in their eyes as they listened to Fred's stories. He purposely made them brief and minimized the horrors and killing.

With a little encouragement, Amos then related colorful tales of the sea. His stories were endless. With good humor, he spun yarn after yarn late into the night while they sat around the fireplace.

The next afternoon Frederic called on Collette. The Jordan home turned out to be a beautiful Victorian mansion. A servant opened the door and ushered him into a large library filled with shelves of various books. The furniture looked imported and was covered with expensive brocade tapestry. Fine pieces of porcelain from around the world sat on beautiful carved tables.

When Collette appeared, Frederic was studying the books on the shelves. "Father does have a great collection," she said, holding out her hands to him. "Frederic, I'm so glad you've come."

The fall day was glorious, and the couple spent the afternoon on a tour of Portland. Frederic felt a strange sense of importance as they rode in the fancy carriage with its beautiful thoroughbred horses. The driver handled the horses well along the rambling, curving roads that followed the sea. They stopped briefly at his cousins' so Frederic could tell them he would be having dinner with the Jordans.

Sophie and Amos made a fuss over Collette and offered her some tea and cakes.

"Oh, no thank you," she said curtly. "We must be getting home."

As they headed toward the Jordan home in the carriage, Collette commented on the simpleness of his cousins' home. "Your father's cousins are so quaint. Is fishing all he does for a living?"

"They're rare down-home folk," Frederic said defensively. "The best. I've always loved visiting Pa's cousins by the sea. If I wasn't a farmer, I would probably turn to the sea."

Dinner at the Jordans' was a lavish and delicious meal served in the formal dining room. Frederic felt ill at ease, but his host and hostess received him warmly. Mrs. Jordan was another Collette, only older and heavier. Mr. Jordan, tall with a lean, angular jaw, had a firm mouth and keen, observant eyes. He talked at great length about his shipbuilding business, the cargo trade from port to port, and his desire for a young man to learn the business. His talk centered only upon his work, and Frederic suspected that it consumed his entire life. Frederic listened politely and after a length of time realized that, for some strange reason, Mr. Jordan was hinting that Frederic might be the "young man" he was looking for.

❧

In the days that followed, Frederic and Collette walked or rode around the scenic spots of Portland. Mr. Jordan insisted on showing Frederic his buildings and offices located near the harbor. He seemed determined Frederic would consider a position with him.

"Mr. Jordan, I appreciate your confidence in me. But I'm a farmer. I know nothing about the trade business."

"I'll teach you," Mr. Jordan said forcefully. "You can learn it just as I did."

The pressure made Frederic uncomfortable, and he welcomed an escape with Collette to walk along the sea. They watched the fog roll in and enshroud them like a heavy mantle. They laughed when the deep blue of the pounding surf caused the salt spray to sting their faces. They saw the large boats come in and listened to the tolling of the bell buoys, and then slowly they walked back toward town.

Later that night, Frederic shared with Sophie and Amos his hurt and bitterness over Becky Sue and also Mr. Jordan's offer of a position. In their kind way they offered words of wisdom.

"God will mend yer heart," Sophie said. "Ya jest have ta give it over ta Him completely. Time heals. God allows these things ta happen fer a purpose."

Amos gave him words of warning about the position with Mr. Jordan. "Don't be acceptin' it jest because it means a lot of money. If yer heart's not in the work, don't do it. Money isn't that important. God gives us a choice as ta how we're ta make our livin'. Me, I chose fishin' and the sea. Freddy, yer a farmer. Ya say ya love workin' the soil. Then do it. Don't let anyone change yer mind."

Frederic felt better after their talk. They had given simple and direct counsel that spoke to his heart.

The week, so enjoyable at times, passed quickly. His last evening with the Jordans, he told them his good-byes.

"There is a fine opportunity waiting for you, young man, in my shipping business. I need someone like you, enthusiastic, enterprising, with a fine head on his shoulders." Mr. Jordan extended his hand as he spoke. "I'll pay you well. It's an offer of a lifetime, so give it serious thought."

"Yes, sir, I will think about it. It's a very tempting offer, although I don't think I'm suited to an office job."

"Good-bye then," Mr. Jordan said curtly. "Let me know your decision as soon as possible."

Collette walked Frederic to the door. "You must accept his offer, Frederic. It would give me so much pleasure. We could be together all the time."

Frederic looked into her dark, pleading eyes. Were there strings attached to the job?

"I'll think about it, Collette," he said. "But I can't promise anything."

Chapter 12

Frederic walked swiftly in the brisk night air to his cousins' home by the sea. He was grateful to find Amos still up, reading quietly by the fire.

"Ah, lad. . .so soon ya have ta leave us, eh?" the older man said. "We'll miss ya when ya go."

"And I'll miss you and Sophie, Cousin Amos. You've been so gracious, I feel right at home here. And I've appreciated your advice about Mr. Jordan's offer."

Amos stared into the fire for some time before answering. "Ah, Jordan is a keen and shrewd businessman, that he is. He's amassed a fortune in a way that, according to rumor, was not allus on the fair and square. I jest say. . .don't be hasty, lad. We Mason menfolk have allus been men o' the sea or men o' the soil. I'm not sayin', mind ya, thet ya can't break out o' the mold. I'm jest sayin' ta ponder it slow-like and search this Book fer yer answer." Amos handed Frederic his worn Bible and bade him good night.

Frederic read Amos's Bible late into the night. This was something he'd neglected for a long time. He remembered Isaiah 26:3 from memory. "Thou wilt keep him in perfect peace, whose mind is stayed on thee: because he trusteth in thee."

"I haven't been trusting," he muttered. "That's why I haven't had any peace. Forgive me, Lord."

As he read and meditated on God's Word, Psalm 61 spoke to his heart. "Hear my cry, O God; attend unto my prayer. From the end of the earth will I cry unto thee, when my heart is overwhelmed: lead me to the rock that is higher than I."

Then and there he turned his broken heart over to God and left it with Him. A feeling of peace settled over Frederic. His bitterness toward Becky Sue vanished. . .and he realized he didn't love her anymore, nor did he hate her. "Thank You, God," he whispered.

Frederic enjoyed the train ride home. He had gone to Portland depressed and with a heavy heart; he came away contented and at peace with God. The prospect of a new job with a bright future entered his thoughts.

Could I refuse such an offer? Mr. Jordan made it clear that he wanted me for the position. Why would he want me? I'm just a farm boy. Of course it's Collette. She probably begged her pa to give me a job. She almost insisted that I take it. Amos is right. . . I need to give it a great deal of thought.

&

Back home the family listened eagerly as he told about his visit with Sophie and Amos. Frederic recited his good times with the cousins and how he and

Collette enjoyed touring Portland each day. His family was impressed when he went into great detail describing the Jordan mansion, the fine furniture, expensive brocade tapestries, and exquisite china. He mentioned Mr. Jordan's offer of a good position in his shipbuilding business. "He pressed me about taking it at every opportunity."

"Yep, the wheel thet squeaks the loudest gets the grease," Pa reasoned. "What did ya tell him, son?"

"I told him I'd think on it. Collette most likely put her pa up to it."

"What's he got in mind?" Grandpa asked. "A husband fer his daughter, maybe?"

"I wondered about that, Grandpa. Nothing was said, of course."

"But that's on Collette's mind, you can bet," Emily said, wrinkling her nose. "She's after you, Frederic."

"Son, ya might be leavin' us fer a job in Portland?" Ma's voice showed her disappointment. "Why, we jest got ya back home again."

"I'm to think on it, Ma, that's all. There's no decision yet."

"Be sure ya pray about it, son," Pa said. "None of us want ya ta go, unless it's God's will."

❧

The next week Frederic called on Becky Sue. She was still with her parents, separated from Zack. Fred knew he could handle seeing her now that God had changed his heart. He still cared for her as a friend and was concerned about her future. He'd hoped his talk with Zack would bring the couple back together.

"Evidently Becky Sue is being stubborn," he murmured. "Guess she needs to hear it from me. If I talk to her, maybe I can convince her to return to her husband. Zack still loves her and wants her. She must know that. God made them one, and they belong together."

Fred knocked on the old wooden door, cleared his throat, and heard footsteps approaching. He swallowed hard, ready to face Becky Sue.

Mrs. Collins, wiping her hands on her checked apron, seemed surprised to see him. "Frederic!" she exclaimed. "How nice of you to call."

"Hello, Mrs. Collins. Is Becky Sue at home? I'd like to talk to her if it's a convenient time."

"Of course, Frederic. Come on into the parlor, and I'll get Becky Sue. She mopes around the house a lot these days. It will do her good to see you. I'm sure it will lift her spirits."

Frederic paced back and forth as he waited for Becky Sue. *Lord, help me say the right words. Help me get these two back together. They need one another. I know that's what You want, too.*

Becky Sue burst into the room and ran toward him. "Frederic! I knew you'd come. I just knew it!" Her face glowed with color, and her eyes sparkled like shining green jewels.

"I came to talk to you, Becky Sue, as a friend," Frederic explained. "Can we talk a spell?"

Becky Sue took his arm and pulled him toward the sofa. "Let's sit down, Fred; it's so much cozier. And yes, we have lots to talk about, don't we?"

Fred disentangled her arms and settled himself some distance from her. He noticed her delicate ivory coloring, the slight lift of her chin, and her full, wistful lips. *She's as beautiful as ever*, he thought. *But she's acting like a spoiled child.*

"Becky Sue, I talked to Zack awhile back."

"I know about your conversation, Fred. What about it?"

"He wants you to come back. He's your husband, and that's where you belong."

"Why?" Becky Sue pouted. "I love you, and you love me. That's all that matters."

"No, it isn't, Becky Sue. I did love you, yes. But not anymore."

Becky Sue moved closer on the sofa and touched Fred's face with her soft hand. Her eyes searched his. "You do love me, Fred. You promised you always would. I remember your promise."

Frederic cleared his throat. "I did promise you that three years ago. I loved you, and you promised to wait for me until after the war. You broke your promise, Becky Sue, and that nullifies mine."

Becky Sue smiled up at him with her sweetest smile. "But that can be changed, Fred. I made a mistake marrying Zack. It was a terrible mistake, I know. Don't you understand? I can get out of this marriage, and we can be sweethearts again. You must know I don't love Zack. . .I only love you."

"No, you only think you love me. It was a long time ago, and we were young and in love. When I first came home, I thought I'd never get over loving you. Yes, I loved you, Becky Sue, but I almost hated you for what you'd done. God showed me how wrong I was to have such bitter feelings. He rescued me from the pit of bitterness, and now we can be friends. I'd like that."

"I don't want to be just friends," Becky Sue sputtered. "Don't you remember all the good times we had. . .the quiet walks. . .the picnics. . . . How can I forget everything we meant to each other?"

"God wants to help you, just as He did me. He'll help you love Zack. He takes our mistakes and works things for our good. He does it all the time. Go back to Zack and be a good wife to him. He loves you very much. I know God will help you learn to love him. Please, Becky Sue. Will you at least try?"

Becky Sue was crying softly. "I'll try, Frederic, if that's what you want."

"It's what God wants. That's what's important. We need to do His will. He can't bless us when we disobey His Word." Fred patted her arm and stood up. "I'll be praying for you," he whispered. "Everything will turn out fine, you'll see."

Frederic slipped out the kitchen door and heaved a sigh of relief. He felt like a heavy load had just been lifted from his shoulders. Becky Sue had agreed to go back to Zack and be his wife. "It will work out for them," he muttered, "if they both let God rule their hearts and their home."

Fred almost bumped into Sarah as she came in from the barn. She was dressed in her usual baggy britches, and her red gold hair was tousled and wind blown.

"Frederic!" she exclaimed in delight. "Did you come to ride? It's a fine day for it."

"Not today, Sarah. I've been visiting Becky Sue. We had some things to talk over."

Sarah's face clouded. "She's still married to Zack, you know. They're only separated."

"Yep, I know. That's what we talked about. I told her to go back to him. That's where she belongs. . .with her husband. Zack still loves her and wants her to return. They can work their problems out and put their marriage back together."

"Do you mean it? But she keeps talking about you two getting back together, like you are still in love. Are you?"

"It's over, Sarah. I've told her, and she knows it now. We are just friends, and that's the way it should be. God can help her love Zack. She thinks she doesn't love him, but God will help her if she'll let Him."

"You don't love Becky Sue!" Sarah said the words aloud as if to convince herself. "Do you love the fancy lady from Portland then?"

"Collette? She's a nice lady, but she's just a good friend. I'm not in love with anyone right now. I don't expect I will be for a long while." Frederic turned, waved good-bye, and left abruptly.

Questions haunted him as he set out for home. Could anyone ever replace Becky Sue in his life? Would he ever love again? The idea seemed impossible, and he shut it out of his mind.

But Sarah entered the house smiling, with a spring in her step and a song in her heart.

Chapter 13

The first two weeks of November were unusually warm and hazy, an Indian summer to finish the harvest and prepare for the long, black evenings of winter. Winters could be raw and cold with nor'easters blowing in storms and eventually mounds of beautiful white snow.

When Frederic learned Becky Sue had returned to her husband, he was grateful. He wanted things to go well for the young couple and for the marriage to survive. His talk with Becky Sue had proved easier than he had expected. "She knew she belonged with Zack," he muttered. "I only helped her make up her mind."

Collette wrote letters pressuring Frederic to accept her father's business proposition. Dwelling on the beauty of Portland, she reminded him how much they enjoyed being together during his visit. "Wouldn't it be wonderful to have these good times continue? Certainly farming doesn't compare with becoming a city gentleman? Life in Portland could be so exciting if only you were here at my side."

Mr. Jordan sent one terse note outlining the job and suggesting a generous salary. He intimated his offer to be something only a fool would pass up. The letter concluded saying he needed his answer by the first of the year.

Frederic, in a quandary, carried out his chores in a daze. He weighed the reasons for going against the reasons for staying on the farm. His family left him to piece out his own thoughts. Much as his pa wanted him to stay and eventually take over the farm, he knew what a tremendous opportunity his son faced. "Ya must make yer own decision, son," he counseled. "Ya are not beholden ta anyone. Let God be yer Guide."

Frederic reasoned he would make a large amount of money at Mr. Jordan's shipyard. He could give generously toward the needs of the farm. *But would I be happy? Money. . .is that what it's all about? I'd be giving up the farm, the land that I love, the animals, the fresh, pure air in God's great outdoors. For what? An office job, to sit at a desk every day surrounded by four walls.*

The thought stifled him. "How could I stand being cooped up day after day inside? But still, there's good things in favor of the job besides the money. It would be easier on my crippled leg. Much easier. I would sit instead of plow, hoe, cut wood, and do all the other duties involved with farming. But I'd be a traitor, wouldn't I?" he whispered alone in the open field. "I'd be a traitor to all I believe in."

The pure, crisp air caressed his cheeks as he dug his hands deeply into the dirt and let it trickle through his fingers. "This soil, this ground, is my life's work, same as Pa's and Grandpa's. God, I feel Your presence here."

⁓

Frederic remembered his promise to Sarah Jane to ride with her. He had postponed the ride many times, but since a promise must be kept, he arranged to meet her and ride before the snow fell.

One bright mid-November afternoon, they met on a ridge high on a knoll between the family properties. Riding was awkward for Frederic, since one stirrup had to be shorter than the other to accommodate his shorter leg. "I feel like a beginner, Sarah Jane." He laughed. "You'll probably leave me far behind in your dust."

"Where's your fightin' spirit?" she chided. "You sounded mighty cocky and sure of yourself earlier."

"Well, I'll give it my best shot and then some. Let's race to my place, and may the best man win!"

Frederic nudged Torch, his favorite buckskin, and started off ahead galloping across the field. He breathed deeply, letting the cold, crisp air fill his lungs, feeling exhilarated. He and Torch seemed glued as one unit. . .moving together smoothly and with perfect ease.

Sarah Jane was right beside him on Star, her long braid trailing in the wind. She rode fast, sure of herself. They were neck and neck all the way. A trail through the woods led them to the creek and finally into the back pasture heading toward the house.

"A tie!" Sarah shouted breathlessly as she jumped from her mare.

Frederic took longer to dismount. "A tie," he agreed. "But next time, I'll win."

Sarah heard the words "next time," and happiness washed over her. They tied the horses to the hitching post and went inside for cider and molasses doughnuts.

As the two riders entered the house, they found Mrs. Mason bustling about the kitchen preparing for the evening meal. "My, the two of ya look like ya could use some warmin' up. Yer cheeks are as rosy as can be. Did ya have a good ride?"

"Oh yes," Sarah exclaimed. "Fred almost beat me."

"Ma, she can really handle a horse," Fred added. "She sure gave me a hard run, but I managed to keep up with her. . .and like she said, almost beat her, too. Torch never let me down."

"Just set ya down at the table, and I'll get the cider and doughnuts. Ya must be hungry after sech a hard ride. The air is sharp taday."

Fred and Sarah pulled off their warm jackets and settled themselves at the kitchen table. Mrs. Mason heated the cider and served it with a plate of her homemade doughnuts.

"This will warm ya up," she said, placing the mugs before them. "Now eat and enjoy."

"Thanks, Mrs. Mason," Sarah replied. "That air did have a chill to it."

"Thanks, Ma," Fred said. "You always know just what a body needs."

Sarah chattered about school. "It's my last year, and I can't wait to graduate in the spring. That's enough schooling for me. The boys are all so childish and full of mischief. Last month they tipped over the outhouse. Miss Ragsdale was so mad!" She laughed.

Her laugh was infectious, and Frederic laughed with her, feeling more relaxed than he had in a long time.

"I'm glad you kept your promise about riding with me, Fred. Didn't it seem good to ride again? I'm sure you've been missing it."

"I'd forgotten how good it was, Sarah," he said soberly. "I always loved to ride. I guess I thought this ole leg of mine would limit my riding."

"It didn't hurt you none at all, Fred. You fairly flew along on Torch."

"Well, I feel honored that a nice young girl like you wanted to ride with me."

"And why wouldn't I want to ride with you?"

"I'm just an old crippled soldier from the war, that's why. Sometimes it matters to people."

"You're not old. . .and you're not crippled!" Sarah said emphatically. "And it doesn't matter. . .it doesn't matter at all."

"What do you call this then?" Fred asked, thumping his lame leg. "It's not the same as it used to be."

"Now, Freddy, ya hush," Mrs. Mason interjected. "Yer leg was hurt in the war, but don't call yerself a cripple jest 'cause ya limp a little. If ya refer ta yerself thataway, ya'll allus feel sorry fer yerself. Ya don't want that."

"No, I don't, Ma. You're right."

"Fred," Sarah said, "you'll carry that limp the rest of your life, as a reminder. Everyone knows our nation went through a terrible war. . .and you were part of it. You fought bravely, were willing to die even, to keep our country united as one and assure freedom from slavery. Remember what President Lincoln said when they dedicated the battlefield at Gettysburg? He said our nation was 'conceived in liberty and dedicated to the proposition that all men are created equal.' Not one soldier was injured or died in vain. Your injury is really a symbol of honor. I think you should be proud of your limp and how you received it. I am." Sarah sat back, out of breath.

"Sarah Jane, you amaze me. For a youngster of fourteen, you seem to have a good head on your shoulders. Do you know Mr. Lincoln's entire Gettysburg Address?"

"Yes, I do. Miss Ragsdale made us learn it and recite it in class as part of our grade. And, Frederic, I'm fifteen now. . .not fourteen. Just turned last week."

"Well, happy birthday, Sarah Jane," Mrs. Mason said. "Seems like only yesterday ya were jest a little tot. Yer growin' up so fast."

"When I turned twenty-two in September, I felt a lot older," Fred added.

A HAVEN OF PEACE

"Guess it was because of the war. Those were kind words you said, Sarah, and I appreciate them. I was proud to serve my country, and I'm thankful I could. The memories haunt me sometimes, but it's getting easier all the time. It was a war that had to be fought. There was no other way."

Emily came into the kitchen. "Hi, Sarah. You and Fred been riding?" She held out an armful of dress material. "Ma, I have some questions about this dress I'm making. Do you have the time?"

"Jest as soon as I put this apple pie in the oven, I'll come up and give ya a hand," Mrs. Mason answered.

"Hello, Emily," Sarah said. "Fred and I had a good ride, and he didn't beat me."

"It was a tie all the way," Frederic said. "But she's a fast rider, and it would be hard to beat her."

"Sarah, come with me upstairs and see the dresses I've sewed for college. I'm so excited about starting in January."

"She's anxious to get away from us." Fred chuckled. "With all her higher schooling, soon she won't want to associate with us peasants."

"Fred, you tease!" Emily gave him a clout on the back. "You know that's not true. Come, Sarah, let's leave this badgerer to himself."

Emily had several dresses, all completed, laid out on her bed. "That's a heap of fancy dresses," Sarah said, impressed. "When will you ever wear that many?"

"We have classes every day, and there are social activities. I'll need many different outfits. Aunt Maude is particular. She wants me to dress well. And I enjoy sewing."

"Fancy dresses are such a bother. I'd rather wear these old riding britches anytime. Can't ride horses in those kinds of getups."

"I enjoy riding just as you do. But sometimes it's nice to be a lady, Sarah. A fancy dress and hairdo might catch the eye of a certain fella. That is," Emily whispered mysteriously, "if you're interested."

Sarah Jane's face turned brick red from her hairline down to her throat. With a quick excuse, she ran downstairs and hurried outside.

Frederic called to her as she unhitched Star. "Wait, Sarah Jane, I'll ride home with you. Now that I've ridden Torch once, I see what I've been missing. Let's take our time and mosey on slow-like. I like to take it all in."

Sarah smiled her agreement and climbed on Star. She hoped her face wasn't still flushed. The afternoon had been so perfect, and she didn't want it to end. She glanced sideways at Frederic and felt her heart beating wildly.

Emily watched them from the upstairs window as they trotted side by side toward the back pasture. "Sarah's in love with him all right. It's as plain as the nose on her face."

51

Chapter 14

The latter part of November brought the snow, sifting down into the quiet, silent woods. It fell softly on the stone walls and fences, covering the evergreens until they bowed down with large puffs of fluffy white.

The Reverend Davis, in his seventies, decided to retire. He and his wife, Lucy, planned to stay until the new preacher arrived around Thanksgiving. Folks had grown so accustomed to the Davises that they dreaded to make a change. After all, the Davises had been with them for many years.

The church held a farewell "pounding" for them. The members brought staples of all kinds of canned meats and vegetables for the couple. The pastor's salary had been meager, though sufficient, and augmented through the years with "poundings" on a regular basis.

The new pastor, Robert Harris, was a twenty-two-year-old coming to them fresh out of seminary. The members of the church had mixed feelings about his capabilities. Many resented the fact that this would be his first pastorate. Would he be able to fill Pastor Davis's shoes? The young pastor had no wife to play the piano, head up the Ladies' Mission Group, and care for the parsonage.

The members decided since the new pastor was single, he would board with Deacon and Mrs. Meade. They lived near the church on Silver Street, and Mrs. Meade could take the young pastor under her wing. The parsonage would be closed temporarily until the young pastor married.

Robert Harris, a tall, slender young man with sandy-colored hair and green eyes, arrived a few days ahead of schedule. Not wanting to inconvenience anyone, he went directly to the Elmwood Hotel on College Street. He planned to stay there until the time expected by the congregation. This would give him time to get familiar with the town and feel at home. He felt excited, yet nervous, about his new pastorate.

He had no family except the grandmother who had raised him, and she had recently passed away. While attending seminary, he had worked to support her, and he missed enlisting in the war because she needed him.

Waterville would be his town now, he reasoned. Now that his grandmother was gone, these people would be his people, the church congregation his family.

After unpacking his few belongings, he left the hotel and walked briskly south along Main Street from the common to Ticonic Row. He crossed over the Kennebec River through the covered bridge and passed Lockwood Sawmill located below the Ticonic Falls. Circling back, he headed north on Main Street and wandered down several other streets: Elm, Pleasant, Water, and Silver. He noticed the home of Mr. and Mrs. Meade on Silver Street and decided, on an impulse, to greet them and let them know he had arrived earlier than planned.

The middle-aged couple greeted him warmly and urged him to move out of the Elmwood Hotel and in with them immediately. He declined until the morrow but agreed to have supper with them. His brisk walk all over town had left him with a ravenous appetite.

During the supper meal, the Meades told him of news about the church and its people. They were pleased to see the young preacher with such a good appetite and urged him to refill his plate.

"This is fine cooking, Mrs. Meade. I haven't eaten this well since my grandmother died three months ago. She was very dear to me." He told how his grandmother had raised him after his parents died in an accident when he was three. As far as he knew, he had no other relatives.

"You poor boy!" Mrs. Meade exclaimed. "No family. . .no one at all!"

"Well." Robert smiled. "I hope to make Waterville my home and the church folks here my family."

"We do tend to be like one big family at church, don't we, dear?" Mrs. Meade looked at her husband.

"Most of the time," Deacon Meade agreed. "But it will take some time for everyone to accept such a young and handsome preacher. Give us time, Robert. Many are hard-nosed and set in their ways, even though changes can be good."

"I plan to try very hard. It's important to me that this work out."

"Don't try too hard, son," Mr. Meade cautioned. "Just be yourself and preach the Word. That's all we ask."

"I will, sir. I'm anxious to get started. Will Pastor Davis still be here on Sunday?"

"Yes, for the morning service. He and his wife plan to leave in the afternoon. Pastor Davis will give you any help he can. Why don't you call on them before Sunday and get some counsel firsthand?"

"I'll do that tomorrow as soon as I've settled in here."

Robert thanked the Meades and left soon after supper. He needed a quiet time back in his room for study before bedtime.

As he walked slowly back to the hotel, the streets had a soft glow, lighted by kerosene lamps. All was quiet except the occasional *clip-clop* of a passing horse and carriage. Snow fell in large flakes that sparkled under the glow of the lamps. Soon his coat and hat were covered with the glittering flakes. The air was cold, but he had a warm feeling inside his heart.

"This town has charmed me already," he whispered. "Waterville, I'm home!"

Chapter 15

Ma and Emily gave the house "a lick and a promise," aired quilts and bedding, and started their baking for Thanksgiving. The menfolk cut timber in the woods and hauled it to the house to be cut in lengths for the fireplaces and woodstove.

The day before Thanksgiving the men loaded the wagon for a trip to the sawmill. Emily decided to go along and do some shopping. She dressed warmly to protect herself against the cold November chill.

Once in town, the men left her at the common while they went on to the mill. She planned to shop and then go to Aunt Maude's to be picked up later on their way home. The day was bright and sunny, with just enough snow on the ground to make it slippery in spots.

Emily purchased a warm hat, some needed staples, knitting supplies, and another length of yard goods. Overloaded with packages, she didn't notice a patch of ice as she came out of Miller's store and started down the street. In an instant, her feet flew from under her, tossing packages into the air. Feeling clumsy and embarrassed, she found herself sprawled awkwardly on the ground. A young man came quickly to her assistance.

"Let me help you, miss," Robert Harris said, smiling. Without waiting for an answer, two strong arms pulled her to her feet. The young man's eyes met hers and held for a long moment.

Emily looked away, shook herself free, and began brushing snow from her coat. "Thank you," she said stiffly, high spots of color rising on her cheeks.

Robert chuckled and began gathering her packages, which had slid every which way. Emily grabbed them from him. "Don't trouble yourself," she said coldly. "I can manage perfectly well."

"It's no trouble, miss," Robert insisted. "Let me carry your packages home for you. You have quite a bundle there."

He reached to take them, but Emily drew back. "No!" she said firmly. "I don't need your help."

He was still smiling at her, a wide, crooked grin that brightened his entire face.

Is he laughing at me? I must have looked foolish and ridiculous sprawled on the ground in such an unladylike fashion.

"It would be my pleasure to carry them," he said.

"I'm only going around the corner to my aunt's house!" she said haughtily. "I

54

don't need any help." She lifted her head, turned, and walked quickly away.

As she rounded the corner, she glanced back. He stood watching her with that silly grin on his face. "Let him laugh," Emily muttered. "I hope I never see him again."

Later, on the way home, Frederic noticed that Emily, usually so talkative, was quiet and deep in thought.

How shameful to fall in public and be helped by a handsome young man, she was thinking. *He is handsome, even with that crooked smile glued to his face. Well, I won't give him a chance to laugh at me again!*

"I talked with Zack today," Frederic said, trying to draw her out of her silence. He leaned back against the pile of pine boards stacked in the wagon bed. "He works at the mill, you know."

"Umm. . .yes." Emily's voice was absentminded.

"Well, he and Becky Sue are getting on fine. I told him it made me happy they are together again. He seemed glad I said that. We've always been good friends, so I guess everything is all right between us."

Emily snuggled closer to her brother to keep out of the cold. "I'm glad things worked out so well. . .for all of you."

They were quiet the rest of the way home, lost in their own thoughts. In the front of the wagon, Pa and Grandpa kept up a steady stream of chatter that blended with the rhythmical *clip-clop* of the team on the hard-packed road leading home.

❧

Thanksgiving arrived, the special day set aside by President Lincoln for giving thanks to God for His bountiful blessings. Ma prepared a large turkey complete with stuffing. The squash and mince pies and suet pudding stood in a row on the sideboard, waiting to be devoured. Emily set the table, then played the piano while waiting for Cassie and Bill. The young couple had offered to pick up Aunt Maude in town and bring her out for the feast.

Upon arriving, Aunt Maude bustled into the farmhouse as quickly as her stout legs could carry her. She bubbled with excitement as she greeted each of the family. Quickly she undid her wool wrap and warm hat and handed them to Emily.

"Frederic!" she exploded. "Frederic, do you know that Miss Jordan is coming to town? Well, of course you do. I heard from my friend Bessie that she'll be here in two weeks and stay through the Christmas holidays." Aunt Maude sat down heavily, flushed and out of breath.

"Yep, Aunt Maude. She wrote she was coming."

"Well, I must say you don't sound a bit excited. What is the matter with you, boy? I'd expect you'd be proud to have a fine lady like Miss Jordan wanting to see you. And she's wealthy, too. Bessie says it's common knowledge you and Miss Jordan are practically engaged and you are taking a position in her father's company."

"Whoa, Aunt Maudie!" Frederic exclaimed hastily. "There is no engagement. As for the job, I'm still thinking on it."

"What's to think about?" Aunt Maude insisted. "You can't turn down the offer of a lifetime! Think how important you'd be! Think of the money!"

Aunt Maude's outburst unsettled everyone. A hush fell over the room, and every eye turned toward Frederic. He faced his aunt and said softly, "Life doesn't consist in the abundance of things. . .or even money, Aunt Maudie. I'm praying about the job. But when I make my decision, it will be based on how God directs."

Chapter 16

Emily walked into the church the following Sunday and went straight to the piano. When Rev. and Mrs. Davis left, Emily would take Mrs. Davis's place as the church pianist. Emily flipped through the hymnal, pausing at one of her favorite songs as she began to play softly while she waited for Mrs. Davis to arrive.

"Mighty nice playing," a half-familiar voice spoke in back of her. "Are you the regular pianist—I hope?"

Emily whirled around to face Robert Harris, the same young man who had helped her up after her disgraceful fall. Color once again flamed in her cheeks as he stared at her with the same crooked grin.

"Yes," she stammered. "Or rather, I will be after the Davises leave. Mrs. Davis will play today. And you are. . . ?"

"I'm sorry. I'm Robert Harris, the new pastor."

Emily looked aghast and said nothing.

"Is it that bad?" he questioned, still with a grin on his face.

"No. . .I mean. . .I didn't think. . .I mean. . . ," she faltered.

"I see. You didn't think I could be a preacher, is that it?" he teased. "And may I know to whom I have the pleasure of speaking?"

Emily felt like a trapped animal. The church was beginning to fill with people, though, and she could not escape. Strange feelings filled her as her eyes met the steady green eyes of Robert Harris.

"I'm Miss Mason," she answered coolly, rising from the piano. She turned abruptly and walked away.

The church service that morning touched hearts. Rev. Davis reminisced about his many years with the congregation. "We've had times of joy and times of sorrow. You are a good people. Lucy and I have been blessed as we labored here—but it's time for us to move on and turn the reins over to a younger man. We hope you will support Robert Harris as he leads the flock from today on. Come up here, Robert, and tell the folks a little about yourself."

Robert Harris talked about his background and his plans for the future. "I look forward to serving as your pastor," he said. "Please feel free to come to me with any problems or suggestions. I welcome your help. I pray we can work together in a unity of the Spirit."

The congregation formed a line, bidding farewell to the Davises and welcoming Robert Harris at the same time. The Mason family, complete with

Grandpa and Aunt Maude, took their places in the line.

Emily could not avoid shaking hands with Robert Harris. He had a firm but gentle handshake and said warmly, "I'm so pleased to make your acquaintance, Miss Mason. I look forward to hearing you play the piano each Sunday."

Emily nodded and moved away. *There is something about those eyes. And that grin. . .crooked and teasing. Is he laughing at me underneath that polished exterior? Is he remembering my unladylike sprawl on the icy ground? Can I never get away from the silly grin?*

The family talked of nothing but the new preacher over dinner. Everyone liked the young man.

"We haven't heard him preach yet, but I think he'll be a good un," Grandpa said. "He sounds like he aims to please."

"We know he believes as we do. . . . It was all in his statement of faith," Pa agreed. "His schoolin' background is good. It'll take us some time, though, ta get used ta such a young fella."

Ma, Frederic, Bill, Cassie, and even Aunt Maude had only good things to say about the young Reverend Harris.

"He looks like a young man with backbone," Aunt Maude said. "I look forward to his preaching."

"Rev. Davis is a wise man," Pa said. "He knew when it was time fer him ta move on. At his age he needs a rest from all the responsibilities of a church. He's been our pastor fer a long time."

"I'll really miss Lucy," Ma added. "She's been sech a blessin' ta the ladies. She was sech a gracious person and did so many kind things. Young Rev. Harris will need a good wife ta share in his ministry. 'Course he's young and probably in no hurry. But I hope he gets one ta match Lucy Davis, when he does take a wife."

"Now don't ya go tryin' ta get him married off, Ma," Pa cautioned. "He needs ta get settled in first and get ta know the church folk. It might take awhile fer some of our people ta accept the new preacher."

Grandpa reached for seconds on the mashed potatoes. "Who knows, this young feller might have a special lady. . .back where he came from. Did ya ever think of that?"

"Well, he never mentioned it in his get-acquainted talk today," Maude said. "He told us he doesn't have any family. . .none at all. If he had a special lady friend, it seems he would have commented on it. He's probably been so busy with his schooling he hasn't had time for courting."

"I think it will be good for the young people to have a young pastor-leader as a role model. . .someone to look up to," Frederic reasoned. "They haven't had that in Rev. Davis, although he was interested in them and a dear man of God. The young people will relate better and share problems easier with a younger man."

"He's really taken you all in, hasn't he?" Emily asked. "Well, not me!"

"Don't you like him?" Cassie asked. "I saw you talking to him by the piano before church. Did he make a bad impression?"

"Did he say anythin' out o' the way ta ya, Emily?" Pa asked quickly. "I want ta know if he's not been a gentleman."

"Oh no, he's the perfect gentleman," Emily answered sarcastically. "It's just those searching green eyes of his and that silly, crooked grin."

"Aha!" Frederic laughed. "So that's it. You've noticed his eyes and his smile. I suspect you like him a whole lot better than you think."

Emily felt the color rush into her cheeks. "Oh, fiddle!" she exclaimed, jumping up from the table. "I wish I never had to see him again!"

Chapter 17

With the holidays fast approaching, Emily saw more and more of Robert Harris. He decided to have a Christmas program and needed Emily to accompany the children on the piano. The children would portray the Christmas story, sing, and recite verses. This would be the first Christmas since the end of the war and his first as pastor of a church. He longed to celebrate the Savior's birth in a spirit of love and peace. The congregation supported his plan with enthusiasm.

At each practice Robert Harris attempted to befriend Emily and call her by her given name. She corrected him each time, saying, "It's Miss Mason."

Emily held herself as aloof as possible, but during the practices she caught herself watching the young man as he worked with the children. He had an unusual way with them, and she saw they were trying hard to please him. He smiled a great deal, and she noticed the patience and gentleness he displayed.

The program would be fairly simple since they would have such a short time to prepare for it, but she had to admit the production itself would be a meaningful one. The children learned their parts, and the parents offered to help with the stage and costumes. Robert Harris worked hard, knew what he was doing, and carried the program out according to plan.

The day of the final practice, Emily arrived early. She planned to go over the music before the children appeared. As she was playing, Robert Harris came out of his study and approached the piano. "I wish you'd let me call you by your given name. Miss Mason sounds so formal after all these weeks."

"Only my close friends call me by my given name," she answered coolly.

"Can't we be friends, Emily? I'd like that."

"It's Miss Mason, and we hardly know each other."

"We could get to know one another if you'd talk to me. May I call on you at your home some afternoon?"

Emily ignored his question and continued to play softly. "Excuse me, Rev. Harris. I need to practice so I'll be ready for the children when they come."

~

Meanwhile, Frederic, who had brought Emily into town that day, was trying hard to make Collette understand his feelings.

Collette was visiting her aunt and uncle's place for the holidays, and Frederic had visited her several times since her arrival. The week before, he had taken her to the farm to join his family for dinner. He wanted her to see the place so dear to his heart. His own enthusiasm for the farm did not persuade her, however. Collette ignored the farm and conversed about Portland and her father's business. She explained the trade opportunities to other parts of the world and described the massive sailing vessels. The whole family noticed her indifference to their way of life.

Today Frederic would face Collette with his decision. Many nights he had slept little as he had wrestled with the problem of whether to accept her father's offer of a job, and he had sought earnestly for God's leading. Today, after leaving Emily at the church, he had headed Nell toward the Jordan home.

I'm ready to give my answer, and it will be a definite no. I must be true to God's calling for my life and true to myself. The job in Portland is not what I'm cut out for. I'll stick with farming.

As he tried to explain his decision to Collette that afternoon, she frowned. "My father offered you a chance to be a gentleman, with a gentleman's position, and you are turning it down?" she asked bitterly. "I can't believe you would choose farming. It's loathsome to me, and I could never, never consider being a farmer's wife!"

"That settles it then," Frederic said quietly. "I could never do anything else."

Collette's voice rose angrily. "You prefer farming to me? How could you?"

"I didn't say that. I only know farming is my life. I can't change. Collette, you don't understand. Farming is in my blood. I like the smell of the animals, planting crops and seeing them spring to life from tiny seeds, the feel of the soil as it sifts through my hands. Nothing compares with it. I wouldn't be happy sitting at a desk in a stuffy office. It just isn't me."

"Then it's good-bye, Frederic. I hope you'll enjoy groveling around in the dirt." Collette burst into tears and ran from the room.

A quiet and thoughtful Frederic was shown to the door by Collette's aunt. The older woman surmised something was amiss but said nothing.

The strain Frederic had been under left him physically drained. He headed Nell toward the little church to pick up Emily for the ride home. Little flakes of snow cascaded from the heavens. The flakes, like little balls of cotton, clung to the trees, but on the ground in front of him, they sparkled like diamonds. A cool, brisk air fanned his cheeks, reviving him. He felt a huge load lifting from his shoulders.

Evidently the job opportunity included an understanding Collette and I would marry. Certainly I never broached the subject. Did she read something into my words or actions? I thought we had a strictly friendly relationship. I never should have visited her in Portland. The opportunity came at a time when I needed to get away, but she obviously misunderstood. My intentions were for friendship and nothing else. But Collette is angry. She made it pretty clear that she wants nothing to do with me. . .no friendship, no nothing. What did she say? Farming is loathsome to her? She can't understand my feel for the soil. . .planting the seeds, nurturing them, and seeing them spring into a bountiful harvest.

Frederic knew that no matter how hard the work, the end results of farming were rewarding. God had called him to be a farmer, that he knew. His pa and grandpa already knew how hard the life of a farmer could be, but the challenge of the land excited him. He glanced at the little church as he reined Nell to a halt. "God," he whispered, "with Your help I'll be the sturdiest and best farmer I know how to be."

Chapter 18

The Christmas program was enthusiastically received. It set the mood for the spirit of Christmas, and parents proudly watched their youngsters as they performed. Most agreed the young Mr. Harris did a fine job and just possibly could be exactly what the little flock needed.

The holidays at the Mason farm were a relaxing time spent with the family. The menfolk chose and cut a large pine from the back property. Tree decorations, handmade and kept from year to year, nestled on the pine boughs. Each year the womenfolk added a few new ones, fashioned out of bits of cloth, lace, and ribbon. Fragrant boughs decorated the mantel, while candles burned brightly in several windows, giving a cheery welcome.

Cassie and Bill joined the family for Christmas dinner. Once again they picked up Aunt Maude, who would stay with her brother's family for a spell. She spoke out after dinner, ridiculing Frederic for refusing Mr. Jordan's fine offer.

"Why do you turn your back on a position that means wealth and prestige, Frederic? I understand Miss Jordan returned suddenly to her family in Portland. Was that your doing?"

Frederic pondered her question before answering. "Collette left of her own accord. I told her I was a farmer and would always be a farmer. That didn't set well with her. She's against farming as a way of life. In fact, she loathes it. Anyway, Aunt Maudie, everything worked together for good."

To avoid further discussion of the subject, Emily sat down at the piano and played Christmas carols. The family crowded around and sang, one of their favorite pastimes. Even Aunt Maude reluctantly joined in and soon got into the spirit. Their voices blended in harmony as the familiar carols filled the air.

Some time later they ended their singing when they heard Laddie barking on the porch. Loud knocking sounded at the door, and Frederic hurried to open it. Sarah Jane, bundled warmly against the chill, entered quickly with cheeks bright pink from the frosty air.

"Merry Christmas!" she called gaily. "Ma sent some currant jelly and Christmas cakes."

Frederic took her wraps and hurried her in by the warm fire to thaw. The family greeted Sarah warmly, and she expressed her delight at the lovely tree and decorations.

"Don't stop your singing," she pleaded. "It sounded so beautiful."

"You must be frozen," Emily cried. "Did you walk all that way alone?"

"Yes," Sarah replied. "Ma said I could come if Bill and Cassie would bring me back on their way home."

"Of course we will," Bill agreed. "We planned to visit the folks later anyway."

At Sarah's insistence they returned to the piano, and she joined in with her lilting soprano voice. Finally tiring, one by one their voices gave out, and they relaxed around the fire.

"Sarah, how about a game of checkers?" Emily asked. "We can go into the kitchen and play."

"Sounds like fun," Sarah agreed, and the two headed for the kitchen table. "Let's say the winner starts the second game."

Grandpa and Pa decided on a game of chess at a small table in the corner, while the others lingered lazily by the fireside. They could hear overtones of Emily and Sarah laughing and talking. Their sudden squeals of triumph echoed as they made an exceptional play.

"Sarah Jane is a pretty child," Aunt Maude said. "How old is she now?"

"She's fifteen, Aunt Maudie. Isn't that right, Bill?" Fred asked.

"Yep, fifteen going on twenty-one." Bill laughed. "She wants people to think she's older than she is."

"No need to grow up so fast," Aunt Maude said. "Time gets away from us, and we're old before we know it. I wouldn't mind going back a few years. Don't know why she'd want to hasten the aging process. She's at a splendid age. It does do me good to hear the young people laugh and enjoy themselves."

After a few stimulating games, Emily and Sarah rejoined the others. Sarah sat on a low stool off to one side and gazed into the fire. Frederic noticed the red gold glints in her hair highlighted by the dancing flames. Her small oval face and creamy complexion reminded him of a delicate cameo his grandmother used to wear.

"Who won the games, Sarah?" Fred asked.

Sarah turned and looked up at Frederic with her violet blue eyes. "Emily won two out of three," she said thoughtfully. "I'll have to catch her another time."

"Emily is hard to beat. I know. I grew up with her," Fred said, smiling. "How's school going for you? I know you're a good student."

"Miss Ragsdale wants me to go on for more schooling after I graduate. I never was interested, but she says I need to look to the future."

"How do you feel about it?" Frederic asked. "Would you like to be a teacher like Miss Ragsdale?"

"Never!" Sarah said emphatically. "Oh, Miss Ragsdale is nice. . .young even. . . and a good teacher. But I wouldn't want to teach like she does, to a bunch of students. Miss Ragsdale handles them well, but I wouldn't have the patience."

"Maybe some other field then?" Frederic asked.

"If I did go on for more schooling, I'd be a nurse. I always like taking care of our animals when they need fixin' up. It's a good feeling to ease their pain.

Guess it would be even more rewarding to take care of people. . .and know you could do something to help them. More and more women are doing that now, you know."

"That would be a mighty fine calling, Sarah. And I know you'd be good at it, caring the way you do. I think you'll succeed at whatever you take up."

Ma decided it was time for a supper snack for everyone, and she pulled out the leftovers. Cassie and Emily helped put out sliced turkey, homemade bread, canned pickles, Ma's special fruitcake, the currant jelly and cakes, and various pies. As the group gathered around the table, Ma brought a pitcher of frothy, hot mulled cider, spiced with cinnamon. Mugs were passed down the checkered tablecloth until each person had one. The frothy brew was sweet to the taste and warming to the body.

"How do yer folks like the new preacher, Sarah?" Pa asked as he passed her the plate of turkey.

"They think he's a fine preacher, Mr. Mason," Sarah answered. "Pa usually goes over his message each Sunday during dinner. Says he can't find a thing wrong with his preaching."

"We think he's a good un," Grandpa said. "Leastwise, most of us do."

"I thought he did sech a fine job on the Christmas program," Ma added. "Ya could see he put a lot o' time into it."

"And you had a big part in it yourself, Emily," Sarah said. "Your piano accompaniment was lovely."

"Thanks, but it was the children who made the program so beautiful. They worked very hard," Emily said.

Emily observed that Sarah, sitting by Frederic, seemed quite grown up. In fact, she was fast becoming a very pretty young lady. Her freckles were fading, and her red gold hair hung loosely curled around her shoulders. Forgoing her usual garb, she wore an attractive soft blue wool dress that highlighted her violet blue eyes. It seemed Sarah Jane had taken Emily's advice about dressing in a more feminine style. Emily knew, without a doubt, that Sarah felt a great attraction for Frederic. None of the others suspected, she was sure, and least of all Frederic. He joked and talked with Sarah completely unaware of her growing affection for him.

"Sarah, where are you putting all that food?" Frederic teased. "I thought sure a little thing like you would eat like a bird."

"Ho, look at your own plate, would you!" Sarah said quickly. "Do you plan to stuff yourself like Mr. Turkey?"

"Fred, ya hush!" Ma said. "Quit teasin' Sarah Jane. She's not eatin' much at all. And we have plenty."

"Just gettin' her goat up, Ma." Fred laughed.

Frederic felt an easiness talking to Sarah. He had not spoken to her, except briefly at church, since that day back in November when they went horseback riding, but now they talked at some length, discovering they had several things in common. Both appreciated good music, good books, the outdoors, and, of course, horses.

Later, when Cassie, Bill, and Sarah left, the family relaxed around the fireplace again. The logs snapped and crackled as the flames shot upward, dancing and glowing brilliantly.

The family discussed this month's convening of the United States Congress. With twenty-seven states having approved it, the Thirteenth Amendment to the Constitution, abolishing slavery, was formally put into effect.

"President Lincoln signed the Emancipation Proclamation back in January 1863," Frederic noted. "But that meant only the slaves in the rebel states were free, didn't it?"

"That's right," Grandpa declared. "But now they've finally passed this here amendment and all blacks are free. Abe Lincoln, if he were alive, would be mighty pleased."

"They say that the war wasn't about slavery," Frederic ventured, "but I daresay it was the underlying cause."

"War is in man's nature," Pa added thoughtfully. "He'll find a reason. It's allus been that way. There will be wars and rumors o' wars, accordin' to the Bible. I pray to God that there will never be another as bloody and terrible as this one."

One by one the older generation left for bed, leaving Emily and Frederic alone. They watched the fire curl upward for some moments before Emily spoke. "Big brother, are you aware of your ardent admirer?"

"Admirer? What are you talking about?"

"Sarah Jane. She adores you, and you can't see it, can you?"

"You always were a tease, Emily. Sarah Jane doesn't give beans about me. She's a youngster. There must be a dozen young men to catch her eye. I'm an old man. . .a crippled one at that. She did tell me once it didn't matter. But hey, she's just fascinated because I've been to war."

"I knew you didn't recognize her feelings. She's not a child anymore. She's grown up quickly over this past year, and she converses in a mature manner. You must have noticed that."

"Well, I do enjoy talking to her, and we found we have a lot in common. She has a level head on her shoulders—she's not giddy and light-headed like some young women."

"I daresay she understands her emotions, and they are very strong ones."

"Well, if that doesn't beat all." Frederic was stunned. "If you are right, I'd best be on my guard. I must take care not to encourage her."

"Why not? Sarah is a lovely young lady."

"It takes time to heal, Emily. I can't think about anyone seriously right now."

"You still care for Becky Sue, don't you?"

Frederic gazed into the fire for several moments, searching for the right words. "Becky Sue is only a memory that lingers in my mind sometimes. She was my childhood sweetheart. I thought we were in love. We planned a life together for after the war. But time changes things, and life goes on. I'm grateful she and Zack are back together again. I hope they will always be happy." He shook his head. "No, I don't care for Becky Sue anymore, not like I did. But Sarah—I couldn't—" He shook his head again, feeling both bewildered and strangely pleased.

Chapter 19

Through the long, hard Maine winter, the women baked bread; mended, sewed, darned, and knitted clothing; quilted bedcovers; and hooked rugs. The menfolk donned heavy woolen caps and shirts and wore snow packs on their feet as they spent much time in the woods. The harsh winter had unpredictable thaws that sent the maple sap flowing and the farmers scrambling to gather it. They drilled holes, caught it in tin buckets, and carried it out of the woods by horse-drawn sleds. The men also hunted, fished, and trapped. Cutting and hauling wood to take to the sawmill took up much of the daylight hours. Firewood had to be cut and split continually to keep the cookstove and fireplaces supplied.

Frederic took Aunt Maude home on a cold and crisp winter afternoon. Emily, trunks piled high with her belongings, rode along. She was moving to Aunt Maude's in town where she would begin her college studies at Colby.

Soft, pure white snow touched the evergreens, graced the maples, and covered stone fences. Frederic hitched up the sleigh as the roads were packed and icy from the abundant snowfalls. Nell snorted in the brisk air. Her thick winter coat glistened in the sun as she pulled her passengers safely to their destination.

Frederic unloaded Emily's trunks and many packages. "Looks like you've got everything you own," he teased. He carried them into one of the bedrooms upstairs in the magnificent brick home.

Maude had a cook/housekeeper, Martha, and a neighboring handyman, Zeke, to help keep her home running smoothly. She had become accustomed to such amenities when her husband had been alive and could continue them now that he was dead because he had left her comfortably well-off.

Emily, excited about starting college, bubbled with enthusiasm. Her friend Louisa Bradford would start Colby at the same time, and they hoped to share several classes. Louisa lived in Waterville, near the common, and they expected to spend much leisure time together. "Louisa and I can hardly wait to get started. It'll be such fun."

"It's what you've always wanted, Emily," Frederic said. "I'm glad it's all worked out. I need to say good-bye, though, and get back to the farm. Pa and Gramps will be working in the woods. They need me."

"Go along, Frederic. Thanks for all your help."

"Try and be good, and don't get in Aunt Maudie's hair," he teased, giving her a hug.

"I declare, Fred. . .I'm always good. We get along just fine, don't we, Aunt Maude?"

"We do indeed, child, and I'll be appreciating the company. So get along with you, Frederic."

Emily spent the rest of the afternoon settling in. She had brought enough of her personal things to feel right at home. Of course she had spent many other times with Aunt Maude, but that was different. Those were just visits and always ended too soon. This seemed pretty final. Her stay would last until she finished school.

She relaxed herself on the large four-poster with its soft quilts and coverlet and let her eyes take in the loveliness of the room. Twin hurricane oil lamps stood on the polished cherry chest and table. French wallpaper in soft pink roses with matching curtains, an ornate gold-framed mirror, and an exquisite English bowl and pitcher on the walnut commode completed the beauty of the room.

When her aunt called her for dinner, she was surprised at how quickly the time had passed. "What fun to be waited on," she murmured. "Dinner is all prepared and ready to be served. I like this kind of life. I think I was born for this."

After dinner Aunt Maude had an unexpected caller. When Emily realized it was Robert Harris, she made an excuse to leave the room, using the pretense of helping Martha with the dishes. Her aunt would have none of it.

"Emily, sit down. Rev. Harris has come to call, and I'm sure he would enjoy talking to both of us."

Rev. Harris was indeed pleased to see Emily, for he had not expected to find her there. He made social calls on members of his congregation during the week. The fact that Emily happened to be there was a pleasant and welcome surprise.

After inquiring about Aunt Maude's health, he looked directly at Emily. "Did you have a pleasant Christmas with your family, Miss Mason?"

"Fine, thank you, Rev. Harris," she replied and looked quickly away. When she turned back, she saw him watching her intently. When she had no further conversation, he turned to her aunt.

"Mrs. McClough, how are things with you? Is there any way I can help you? As your pastor, I want to be of service if you need anything."

Maude expressed her thanks for his concern and assured the young pastor that everything was fine. "Did you know that my niece will be staying with me while she attends Colby College? She's the only one of Chase's children with enough wit about her to go on with higher schooling. I wanted Cassie and Frederic to attend, but they refused. At least Emily has her priorities in the right place."

Robert Harris smiled. "I'm sure you will be an excellent student," he said, glancing at Emily. "What courses do you plan to study, Miss Mason?"

"Fiddlesticks!" Aunt Maude exploded. "Don't be so formal, young man. You must call her Emily. That's her given name."

"Thank you, Mrs. McClough. I would like to very much."

"I plan to be a teacher, Rev. Harris," Emily stated coolly. "I'm not sure what my classes will be as yet. Whatever is necessary for a degree in teaching little children."

"I'm sure you will be a fine teacher one day, Emily. Emily." Softly he said her name again and then hesitated. "It's a nice name."

Their eyes met and held briefly before she glanced away.

Chapter 20

Emily threw herself enthusiastically into her studies. She and Louisa shared most of their classes, and they often stayed on at the college to study and do research. She was busy and rarely got home to the farm.

Aunt Maude enjoyed having her niece with her and appreciated their visits late in the evening before bed. Emily related happenings at school, and Maude, gratified that at least one of her brother's children was taking advantage of higher education, shared her excitement. Although Maude tended to be bossy and Emily high-spirited, they formed a truce early on, hoping to avoid any clash of a serious nature.

Robert Harris called frequently on the widow McClough, hoping each time for glimpses of Emily. Often he would be there when she arrived home from Colby. She would come bouncing into the room, bubbling over with witty bits of Shakespeare from her literature class, and Robert was eager to discuss them with her.

Emily stubbornly held him at a distance, though, responding coolly but courteously. Still, he persisted, and eventually, in spite of herself, she found herself warming toward this kind and humorous young man. She began anticipating his visits and felt disappointed when he missed several days in succession. He told amusing stories, catching her off guard, and she laughed in spite of herself. She found herself looking at him quickly from time to time, catching him looking at her with a soft, wistful expression that warmed her blood.

After one of his visits, he bade her farewell and took her small hand in his larger one, holding it briefly. Emily felt a tremor of excitement at the warmth of his touch, and color rushed into her cheeks.

"I can see who the reverend is really interested in seeing," Aunt Maude said bluntly after Robert left.

"Oh, Aunt Maudie, of course he comes to see you. I just happen to be here, too."

"That young man has a serious look about him, Emily. I don't doubt he has marriage on his mind." Aunt Maude always came straight to the point. "The life of a preacher's wife is a hard one, and you don't want that. Mind my words, child. You finish your schooling and become a teacher. Don't get sidetracked!"

"Fiddlesticks, Aunt Maudie. Marriage is the farthest thing from my mind."

Warm thoughts of Robert Harris flashed through Emily's mind, however, more often than she cared to admit. His serious deep green eyes and crooked grin had caught her fancy. His entire face lit up when he smiled, which was often. But marriage—well, of course that was out of the question.

Toward the end of February, Aunt Maude came down with a chill. She'd gotten her feet wet, refusing to wear her boots, and now had the croup. She took to her bed and wouldn't eat, coughing laboriously late into the night. The doctor feared it would turn into pneumonia, and he limited her visitors to the family and the preacher. Frederic and the family came but, under doctor's orders, stayed only a few minutes.

The "grippe," as Maude called it, hung on into March, and then she seemed to rally and do better. Emily constantly tried to get soup and liquids into her. Maude, feeling stronger, determined to get up and go downstairs, against the doctor's orders.

"I'm better. I'm better," she insisted. "Let me be!"

Emily could not deter her. Aunt Maude would do as she pleased. But as the doctor feared, she took a turn for the worst. Pneumonia took over and gripped her body with a vengeance. Her once stout, robust figure quickly became frail and emaciated, until she became a whisper of the woman they'd known.

Emily neglected school to nurse her beloved aunt, ministering medicine and encouraging liquids whenever possible. By the end of March, Maude had wasted away and breathed laboriously amid constant coughing and spitting.

One morning after a difficult night, she took Emily's hand and whispered faintly, "Emily, dear child, I want you to have my home and all my fine furniture. I know you will care for the house and all my nice things."

"Hush, Aunt Maudie, hush!" Emily cried, bending close to her aunt. "Don't say such things! You're going to be fine. You're going to get well. . .I know you are!"

After a fit of coughing, Maude continued with difficulty. "No, child. I'm ready to go. I'll see my Maker and my beloved George. He's been waiting for me."

"No, Aunt Maudie, no! Don't say such things. I can't bear to hear you talk like that. You'll be better tomorrow. . .much better."

The faint trembly voice continued amid spasms of coughing. "There's money set aside for your schooling. The rest will be divided between Cassandra and Frederic. The house is for you. Cassie has her home with Bill, and Frederic won't leave the farm. You will take care of my house."

Emily burst into tears and threw her arms around Maude's frail, wasted body.

"Don't cry, child," Maude whispered sternly. "I've already talked to your father about my desires, and he'll have it taken care of with my lawyer. Now I'm tired, dear child." She waved Emily away weakly. "I'm so tired."

Emily stumbled blindly from the room, her eyes brimming with tears, and bumped into Robert Harris in the hallway.

"I'm so sorry," she faltered. "I wasn't watching where I was going."

Robert Harris put his strong hands on her shoulders to steady her. "Emily, what's wrong? Has Maude taken a turn for the worst?"

"Yes, she's very bad." Emily was sobbing openly now, the tears streaming down her cheeks.

Robert released her and pulled out a clean handkerchief. "Let me wipe away your tears," he said. Gently he stroked her face, but the tears kept falling. "Is the doctor here?" he asked. "There may be something else he can do."

"He'll be here later today, but Aunt Maude needs him now," she cried. "She's very tired. She sent me away so she can get some rest."

"I'll go in and pray with her," Robert said. "If she is already asleep, I'll still pray for her. God loves Maude, and He cares about her. Will you be all right?"

"Yes," Emily answered, wiping away more tears. "I'm going to check with Martha and make sure we have plenty of chicken soup. When Aunt Maude wakes up, she'll need some broth and tea."

Twenty minutes later Robert Harris descended the stairs and entered the kitchen. Emily and Martha were preparing chickens to make a broth so that it would be ready when Maude wakened. Emily looked up from her task. "How's Aunt Maudie? Is she awake?"

"She's sleeping quite peacefully at the moment," Robert said. "I'm sure the rest will be good for her."

"Did you pray? Did you pray and ask God to heal her?"

"Yes, I prayed. I asked God for healing of Maude's body. Then I committed Maude to His keeping and prayed His will be done."

"But it *is* His will for Maude to be healed. Why didn't you demand God heal her?"

"Emily, we don't demand God to do anything. He is God. . . . He is in control. The Bible tells us to pray 'according to His will.' He knows the end from the beginning and what is best for all His children."

"I don't care. . . . I want Aunt Maudie to live!"

"We all do, if it's His will. The church people are praying. I'll be back tomorrow, Emily, or sooner if you need me."

Emily closed the door as Robert left, then she turned back to the kitchen. "Don't You let her die, God," she cried fiercely. "Don't You dare let her die!"

Chapter 21

Maude McClough lingered until mid-April and then passed away in her sleep. The frail body could hold up no longer, and she was tired of fighting for life. She was reconciled to her Maker and ready and willing to go.

Emily became quiet and withdrawn. She believed God had failed her. He had not answered her prayers for healing, and she could not accept Maude's death. She went through long periods of crying, praying, and asking God, "Why?"

The service held in the little church was Robert Harris's first funeral. Emily refused to attend, and so she did not hear the message of comfort and hope.

"We will all miss Maude McClough," Robert Harris told them. "She was a fine Christian woman. When something like this happens, it's hard to understand God's ways. We would rather have our sister here with us still. It's hard to understand how a loving God could take her away from us now, when we had expected to have many more years together." He shook his head. "I can't deny that death hurts. Even Jesus wept when his friend Lazarus died. But we know from God's Word that our sister Maude has gone to a far better place. . .where there is no pain, no sickness, no sorrow. She is at peace, living in heaven with her Lord. And though we are sad now, this story will have a happy ending, for one day we will see her again."

Rev. Harris went on to quote many portions of scripture and closed with Psalm 116:15: "Precious in the sight of the Lord is the death of his saints."

They buried Maude in the little cemetery behind the church. She was placed next to her husband, George, and near her mother and a sister who had died as a child.

Emily would not be consoled. She dropped her college classes and buried herself in her grief. Bitterness toward God gnawed away at her insides, making her miserable. The family tried comforting her but without success; her attitude did not change.

"I can't help how I feel," she said sadly. "Where is God, anyway, when we need Him?"

Chase insisted she return home for a spell, but she resisted. The others persuaded him to let her stay in town to work things out alone. She wouldn't be completely alone as Martha, the housekeeper, lived at the house and would remain as long as Emily needed her. Emily's friend Louisa lived close by and tried her best to get Emily back to her normal self again.

"Come back to school," she begged. "It will be good for you. Things aren't the same without you. I miss you terribly."

"I can't go back, Louisa. I have to work things out first. I have to understand why God did this, and I don't want any pat answers."

Robert Harris called several times, but Emily refused to see him. She knew he would criticize her behavior, and she couldn't handle that. She needed answers instead.

≈

Spring came, and balmy breezes penetrated the air. They reached down and kissed the earth with their soft touch. The birds, perched high in the treetops, sang their sweet melodies.

Martha hauled mattresses outdoors to sun them and put rugs on the line to beat. She was giving the house "a good turning out," as she called it. This meant an old-fashioned spring-cleaning from top to bottom. Emily, pale and wan, offered to help, but Martha insisted she rest instead. "Go into the backyard and relax, child. You look so peaked. Do some reading; enjoy the sunshine and the fresh, pure air. It will do wonders for you."

Halfheartedly, Emily obliged. She took her Shakespeare along, hoping to find solace in its pages. She read aloud, "This above all, to thine own self be true, and it must follow as the night the day, thou canst not then be false to any man."

Beautiful words. But they don't fulfill the need of my heart. From just a little girl I was taught to turn to the Bible for comfort and strength. How can I now, when I am at odds with the Author? He's failed me. Will I ever have faith again? Will I ever have faith to believe He can help in times of need?

Emily glanced around her. Everything was coming alive, and the apple trees and lilacs had burst forth in full bloom. Maude's flower gardens were a veritable showplace, for she had taken pride in spending endless hours planting, weeding, transplanting, and nurturing. Some of her favorites included the twin flowers, purple lilacs, daffodils, violets transplanted from the woods, ground phlox, and yellow Scotch roses.

Emily eyed the plants, some already blooming and others that would soon be transformed into beautiful flowers. She spoke to the plants in a sad voice, "Your mistress, who loved you, is gone. She won't be coming back to enjoy your beauty." Emily felt tears trickling down her cheeks.

"Emily, may I speak with you?"

Emily glanced up to see Robert Harris standing just outside the gate.

"I thought I heard you back here in the garden," he continued. "I've been trying to see you for weeks."

"I didn't want to talk to you," she mumbled, dabbing her eyes with her handkerchief.

"I'm sorry. Do you want me to go?"

She sighed. "You may stay if you promise not to preach to me."

"I'd never do that, Emily. But can we talk?"

Emily agreed they could talk, and Robert tried to keep the conversation as light and cheerful as possible as he told of current happenings with the congregation.

"I've missed you, Emily. Everyone at church misses you."

"Can't anyone else play the piano?" she asked absently.

"Mrs. Meade is filling in for now. But that's not what I meant. Emily, when are you coming back to church?"

"Why doesn't God answer prayer?" she countered. "Can you answer that?"

"I'll try if you won't think I'm preaching."

"Then try."

The young pastor was quiet for a few moments, collecting his thoughts. Then he said soberly, "God is not accountable to us for what He does or does not do, Emily. He doesn't have to reveal 'why.' He owes us no explanations."

"God isn't fair. Why would He take Aunt Maude?"

"When we think God is not fair, what are we measuring His fairness against? Who invented fairness? Wasn't it God Himself?"

"You sound just like Frederic!" Emily exclaimed. "He never blames God for anything!" Emily pressed her lips together, and then she burst out, "I don't care if you think I'm awful; I don't care if I'm committing some awful sin. I just don't understand why God could fail me like this."

Robert's lips curved. "I don't think you're awful, Emily. I don't think I ever could. And you're not committing a sin by questioning God. Why, even Christ on the cross felt forsaken and cried out to God." He touched her face gently, then withdrew his hand. "We can't understand everything about God. We never will. If we did, He wouldn't be God. Sometimes it's hard to trust blindly—but we know He has promised that nothing will ever separate us from His love. When we really believe that, then all our hurt and anger don't really matter anymore, because then we know that everything that comes our way, both good and bad, can never stop God's love from reaching us."

Emily bit her lip. "I don't know," she said at last. "I feel so angry at Him. If I could really believe that Aunt Maude was still alive in heaven, I wouldn't feel so bad. I want to believe it; I want to believe it more than I ever have in my life. And yet I'm filled with so many doubts."

"Your doubts can't change what's real." He took both her hands and pulled her to her feet. "Walk with me through Maude's garden. God touches each of these blossoms and causes them to spring to life. Our lives are like that, too. God touched Maude's life, and she sprang into everlasting life with Him." Robert stooped down and plucked a violet that had unfolded into a delicate purple blossom. He held it out to Emily. "It's new life," he said softly, "the resurrection. Once it was dead, and now it's alive."

Emily stood deep in thought, gazing at the flower for a long time while she held it cupped gently in both her hands.

Chapter 22

Sarah Jane Collins was very perceptive for a young lady going on sixteen. She knew Frederic avoided her whenever possible. Brief encounters at church or in town were all she could hope for, and they were not very satisfying.

She had cared for Frederic since before the war between the North and South. She was eleven and he eighteen when he courted her sister, Becky Sue. While he served on the battlefield, her childish fascination grew into a deeper, lasting affection. Becky Sue shared Frederic's war letters with her younger sister, not realizing Sarah's feelings for him. Sarah hung on every word, pretending the letters were meant for her. . .even memorizing portions of them. The family knew nothing about her attachment.

Sarah was distressed when she heard Frederic was wounded severely in battle at Appomattox Court House. Would he die? When Becky Sue eloped with Zack, she felt a door being opened to her. Would Frederic notice her now? She was fourteen by this time and experiencing grown-up emotions. Could her dreams become a reality?

She didn't mind that Frederic returned home wounded and crippled. The limp wasn't important when he could have lost the leg. Even that wouldn't have mattered, though. The person remained. . .the same boy. . .the young man she cared about. Her feelings never wavered, only became stronger and surer since Frederic returned home.

Frederic showed, on numerous occasions, that his feelings for Becky Sue were over. She and Zack had worked out their marriage problems and appeared to be happy, especially now that a child was on the way.

Sarah assumed no one else held Frederic's attention. *Frederic is twenty-two, and I'm yet fifteen. The war aged him. . . . He feels older than he is. He thinks I'm just a child. I'm not a child! How can I get him to see I'm a woman, with a woman's heart?*

She approached him after church at the end of May, detaining him in the churchyard. A bright, sunny day boasted the sweet scent of purple lilacs and apple blossoms.

"Frederic," she asked, "will you come to my graduation? My mother is having a get-together afterwards at our house. Your whole family is invited, but I especially want you to come."

"Are you old enough to graduate, Sarah Jane?" Frederic teased. "How did you manage that? Aren't you a little young?"

"I skipped a grade some years back," Sarah declared testily. "But I'm old enough! At least my teacher thinks so."

"When is it?" Frederic asked, changing to a more serious tone. "The graduation?"

"It's next Friday afternoon, two o'clock at the school. I would be pleased if you'd attend. It's important to me."

Something in her tone of voice caught at Frederic. She spoke with a pleading quality, and her eyes held his without wavering. He found he could not look away from her deep violet blue eyes.

Suddenly he grinned, reached out, and patted her on the head. "I'll come, little one. I wouldn't miss it for the world."

She smiled, and her eyes whispered her thanks. *He still considers me a child, patting me on the head. But at least he's coming! I'll find some way to prove I'm a grown-up and not the little freckle-faced kid he remembered when he left for the war. Mama was married at sixteen, and I'll be sixteen in the fall. That's a good age.*

～

Frederic rode his horse and arrived at the school for the graduation exercises the following Friday as promised. His family, the Collinses, and other spectators were already there. The students thronged together in the school yard, waiting until time to march in. Each grade would march in procession, with the graduates last.

Frederic's own graduation seemed so long ago to him, and yet like yesterday in some ways. Since then, though, had come the war years, the battles, his disability, and the time in the hospital. Suddenly he felt very old and questioned why he had come. His eyes searched the group for Sarah Jane, and he discovered her standing under a tree, surrounded by several male students.

As soon as she spied him, she called out and waved. "Frederic! Frederic! I'm so glad you came." She wore a lovely sea green dress with a large lace collar, clasped at the throat with a cameo brooch. Her red gold hair seemed redder than usual. It was tied with green ribbons and fell in a mass of curls around her shoulders. Her youthful, creamy complexion glowed with a tint of color on her cheeks.

Frederic viewed this lovely creature hurrying toward him and caught his breath. Sarah took his large hand in hers and pulled him, limping, toward the others.

"Are those young men all your beaux, Sarah Jane? I'm not surprised you have so many."

"Of course not, silly," she replied, laughing. "They're just youngsters. . .kids in school."

"Youngsters?" Frederic quipped. "Youngsters like you?"

Sarah faced him squarely, her violet blue eyes intent upon his. "I'm not a youngster, Frederic. Not anymore. Can't you see that I've grown up? Can't you see that I'm a woman?"

Frederic gazed steadily at this grown-up vision of loveliness. He agreed in his heart that she was, indeed, a woman.

Chapter 23

Frederic thought about Sarah Jane as he rode over to the Collinses' farm for her graduation party. She was a lovely creature, and he struggled with his rising emotions. The deep and special feelings he once had for Becky Sue were gone. Only memories remained, and they no longer pulled at his heart. He was a prisoner set free, no longer shackled by a lost love. Now that his heart was free, he was ready and able to love again.

"But Sarah is too young for me," he muttered. "I shouldn't be thinking about her like this. She needs someone her own age, one of those young men I saw at the school. There were several who seemed smitten with her."

Frederic tied Torch to a post and joined the group of family and friends gathered in the backyard. He spied Sarah Jane over by the punch bowl, talking to one of the young men he had seen earlier. Sarah smiled and waved. As he turned away, he almost bumped into Becky Sue and Zack.

"Hello, Frederic," Becky Sue said, smiling, as she clung to Zack's arm. "I guess you heard about our expected little one."

"That's great news," Fred said. "I'm very happy for you."

"We'll be a real family now," Zack said. "It's made a big difference in our lives."

"Frederic." Becky Sue paused. "I want to thank you for what you did. You helped bring Zack and me back together again. We'll be forever grateful." She reached out and lightly took Frederic's hand in an expression of friendship.

"Yes," Zack added as he shook Fred's hand wholeheartedly. "We appreciated your wise counsel. We took it, and we couldn't be happier."

"It was nothing," Fred insisted. "I'm just glad for the way things worked out."

"Here you are, Frederic!" Sarah Jane said, taking his arm. "Come with me. . . . I want you to meet my teacher, Miss Ragsdale. Will you excuse us, Becky Sue?"

"Of course, Sarah. You two run along."

Sarah half pulled him toward the punch table where an attractive brunette was talking to Mr. Collins.

"Whoa, Sarah, not so fast," Fred cautioned. "Remember this bad leg of mine."

"Oh, fiddle," Sarah said, laughing. "It's as fit as can be!"

Somewhat out of breath, she cornered Miss Ragsdale. "Miss Ragsdale, I'd like you to meet Frederic Mason. You met the rest of his family earlier."

"Yes, I remember. How do you do, Mr. Mason?" Hannah Ragsdale looked at him keenly with dark, wide-set eyes. "It's a pleasure to meet you."

"The pleasure is mine, Miss Ragsdale," Frederic said, taking the hand she extended.

"Why don't you two get acquainted?" Sarah suggested. "Ma told me I had to mingle with the guests. There are plenty of chairs over there by the oak tree."

"Good idea," Frederic said. "Miss Ragsdale, would you care for some cake and punch?"

"Thank you, I would. Please call me Hannah. And may I call you Frederic?" she asked demurely.

"I wish you would. Frederic. . .or Fred, either one, Miss, er, Hannah."

Hannah laughed as she settled herself into one of the wooden chairs under the large oak tree. Frederic noticed her fair complexion and delicate hands, which she folded in her lap. When she smiled, her eyes sparkled, and her otherwise plain features transformed magically into something pretty.

"Hannah, I've heard what a good teacher you are," Frederic said. "Do you enjoy teaching?"

"I do very much. As to my being a good teacher, I'm afraid Sarah Jane is prejudiced. She's a very bright girl. I hope she'll go on and get some more education. She has the mind for it."

Frederic wasn't certain how long he and Hannah Ragsdale talked together. When he saw the crowd thinning out, he felt it was time to make his departure. On an impulse, he invited Hannah Ragsdale to the band concert the following week in Waterville.

"How delightful!" she exclaimed. "I would love it!"

After getting her address and setting the time, Frederic bade her farewell. He searched for Sarah to say good-bye and found her talking to an older couple from the church. She saw him coming and hurried to meet him. "Fred, you're not leaving, are you? We haven't had time to talk to one another."

"I need to get home, Sarah, and help Pa with evening chores. A lot of people have left already."

"I hoped you'd stay on. Did you and Miss Ragsdale get acquainted? She's such a nice person."

"We found we had a lot to talk about," Fred answered. "And you're right; she's a very pleasant person."

Sarah fell into step with Frederic as he headed toward his horse.

"Before I leave," he said, "I have a small gift for you. . .for your graduation. It's in my saddlebag."

"Fred," she cried, "you bought me a present? Really?"

"Really," he said, smiling at her excitement. *She's such a child*, he told himself. *A sweet child, and so pretty, but just a child, and. . .* He could feel her close presence as he fumbled in his saddlebag for her gift. She brushed against him, and he breathed in the sweet, delicate scent of lilacs. *She's just a child*, he reminded himself sternly, but his pulse was pounding.

"Congratulations, Sarah," he said huskily as he handed her a neatly wrapped package.

"Thank you, Fred." She tore open the wrapping and held up a small volume of poetry.

"It seemed right for you, Sarah. I hope you like it." He had spent a long time deliberating over what to give her. He watched her face, hoping he hadn't made the wrong choice.

She opened the book to the flyleaf page and read aloud: "To Sarah from Frederic, June 1866." Then she clasped the book to her and looked up at him. Her eyes were moist and wistful. "I love poetry," she said softly. "It's something I've always wanted. I'll cherish this book, Fred."

Frederic gazed at her sweet, upturned face and felt a sudden desire to take her in his arms and hold her close. Instead, he took a deep breath and said, "I'm glad you care about it, Sarah. I like poetry, too."

For a long moment, their gazes locked, as though time had frozen around them. *She's just a child, just a child, just a child*, Fred was repeating over and over inside his head, but the words were meaningless. He wanted to touch her so badly that his muscles ached from holding them still.

He swallowed hard and swung himself into the saddle. "I'll be seeing you, Sarah," he managed to say, and then he trotted Torch down the drive. When he looked back, she waved. She was still standing in the same spot. . .watching him go.

"Why did I ask Hannah Ragsdale to the band concert?" he mumbled. "She's a sweet and interesting person, and we'll have a good time. But I'm afraid Sarah Jane will be on my mind most of the time. There's something unique about her. She's special. I can't pinpoint it actually, but I get sort of light-headed when she's around. Just thinking about her makes me feel happy inside. Only then I remember I shouldn't be feeling that way. Not when I'm so much older than she is."

He nudged Torch into a gallop and felt the early summer breeze caress his face. "Yep, Torch, that young lady has my heartstrings all entangled. I just wish she wasn't so young!"

Chapter 24

Robert Harris visited Emily several times after their talk in the garden. She was more receptive with each call as he pointed out God's love and promises from the scriptures. Emily asked if she had been a disobedient Christian. . .angry with God and asking why Aunt Maudie had died.

Robert smiled and shook his head. "Everyone has doubts sometimes. Even the authors of some of the Old Testament books asked God why sometimes. I think maybe our faith grows the most during those times when we're filled with doubts. We'll never know all the answers," Robert told her. "We just need to trust God and claim His promises from His Word. You will see your aunt Maude again someday."

Robert's words were a soothing balm to her heart. After his visit, Emily fell on her knees and poured out her heart to God. "Forgive me for not trusting You in every situation. I have been so miserable because I've been out of fellowship with You and other Christians. Please, God, fill me with the mind of Christ."

Emily felt God's presence wash over her. His peace and comfort drew her close. She no longer felt at odds with her Maker. "I'll go back to the farm," she cried. "The folks have put up with my bitter attitude and pouting long enough! Oh, it will be so good to be with the family again! I'll spend the summer at home!"

Immediately she made preparations to return and left Martha in full charge of the house in town.

The family greeted her with open arms. Emily felt like a prodigal returning after a life away from God and the comforts of family. They had been waiting for her to come out of her depression and return home.

"I'm still sad over Aunt Maudie's death, the same as all of you," she told them. "But I'm not asking God why anymore. I don't need to know why things happen. I accept with faith what He sends. . .what He gives and what He takes."

Chase and Mary Jane rejoiced at the change in their daughter. She had accepted Maude's death and matured from the experience. Cassie and Bill joined the family for supper that evening, looking as happy and as much in love as ever.

"We have some wonderful news, Emily," Cassie confided, smiling. "I'm going to have a baby."

Emily shrieked with delight and hugged her sister. "How wonderful! I'm so happy for you both. When?"

"Around Christmas or thereabouts," Cassie replied.

"He will be our special Christmas gift," Bill said proudly. "This will be the best Christmas ever!"

"Bill," Cassie said sweetly, "it might be a girl."

"Either one—it will still be our special Christmas gift," he said, kissing her lightly on the cheek.

That evening the talk centered around the new baby. The family had known about it earlier, but they shared in the excitement of the moment.

"So everyone knew but me? Why didn't I hear this good news earlier?" Emily demanded.

"Cassie thought it best ta wait," Ma offered. "We all agreed ya had enough on yer mind."

"We wanted you to work through your unhappiness first," Cassie murmured. "We knew you would, in time."

"I'm afraid I wasted a lot of time feeling sorry for myself," Emily said. "I learned a lesson through this. God is always there waiting for us to come to Him."

"Just think, I'll be an uncle," Frederic said lightheartedly. "Uncle Fred, the farmer. It sounds good."

"Do you have any names picked out?" Emily asked. "I suppose it will be Bill Jr. if it's a boy."

"No Juniors," Bill said emphatically. "I like Ethan or Jeremiah, but we've not settled on anything."

"I think we'll name a little girl Rebeccah," Cassie said softly, "after Grandma."

Grandpa smiled broadly. "Thet would be a fine name, Cassie. Yer grandma woulda been proud."

"Grandpa made the cradle, and Ma and I are working on the layette," Cassie said. "Why don't you come over tomorrow and see the nursery, Emily? You can help me with some sewing."

"Oh, I'd like that," Emily agreed.

"We need Emily in the field, don't we, Pa? With it being seed-planting time and all. You plan to help us at five tomorrow morning, don't you, Emily?" Frederic teased.

Emily smiled. "Yep, Frederic. After I show you, Pa, and Gramps what to do in the fields, I'll hustle over to Cassie's and sew!"

"Now, dear, yer brother was jest foolin'," her mother said soberly. "The menfolk do the farmin'. We got woman's work ta do."

"Just teasin', little sister," Fred agreed. "By the way, Robert Harris asked about you at church."

"Is that young man interested in ya, Emily?" Grandpa asked.

All eyes turned toward Emily, and she felt color rising in her cheeks. "We are good friends, Grandpa. Robert Harris called on me last week, and we talked. He helped me get my thoughts straightened out and work through my bitterness. He was very kind."

"Does he have marriage on his mind?" Grandpa persisted. "Seems like he's up in the clouds lately."

"He's not discussed anything like that," Emily said, embarrassed. *Why do I blush so easily?* "I'm sure marriage is not on his mind."

The following day Emily spent with her sister at the cabin. They talked, sewed, and laughed like old times, and their good time had a therapeutic effect on Emily. "You are so blessed, Cassie. A fine husband and now a baby coming. I'm very happy for you."

"You'll find happiness someday, Emily, when you marry a fine young man. . . like Robert Harris, for instance. I know you are attracted to him."

"He wouldn't want to marry me, Cassie. I wouldn't make a good preacher's wife."

"And why not?" Cassie demanded.

"Look at all the doubts I had about God when Aunt Maudie died. I was bitter. . .only thinking about myself and my loss. A problem comes along, and I waver. I'm such a weak Christian. Robert needs someone stronger in her faith."

"Someone like Louisa?"

"Is Robert. . . Is he seeing Louisa?"

"They've been together some. But I think his mind is really on you. He's cared for you from the first."

"I've been such a ninny, the way I've treated him. But I want an education. I don't want to get married."

"Are you sure, Emily? Make sure you sort out your feelings. Don't let something you really want pass you by."

"If he cares for Louisa, it's too late anyhow," Emily said sadly. "She's my best friend. I wouldn't want to hurt her."

"What would hurt most? Losing Robert? Ask yourself."

Cassie had touched on a tender subject, and Emily couldn't sew any longer. Tears brimmed in her eyes and overflowed, till she could no longer see the stitches. She stuck herself with the needle twice. Thoughts raced wildly through her mind.

Does Robert love me? Does he want to marry me? What about school? I've given him no encouragement at all. His eyes spoke to mine many times, and his crooked, endearing smile seemed for me alone. I've probably ruined any feelings he might have had for me by my selfish and bitter attitude toward God. "Cassie," she cried, "why have I been so stupid? I'm in love with Robert Harris!"

Cassie gathered her weeping sister into her arms. The proud Emily had taken the first step. She'd admitted her feelings for Robert, and now a healing process could take place.

Chapter 25

Later that week, Emily rode into town with Frederic and planned to visit Louisa while he took some pine boards to the mill. He dropped her at the common, and she walked first to Maude's brick home to check briefly with Martha and make certain things were running smoothly. From there she went directly to the Meade home, secretly hoping to see Robert. Mrs. Meade welcomed her graciously and seemed genuinely pleased to see her.

"We've all missed you at church these weeks, dear," Mrs. Meade said kindly.

"Thank you, Mrs. Meade. I'm doing well now."

"Does this mean you'll be back playing the piano on Sunday?"

"Yes, I'm ready to take over again if you want me to."

"Oh, I certainly do," Mrs. Meade said quickly. "I'm not the player I used to be. I'll welcome you taking it on."

Emily glanced around the room. "Is Pastor Harris here or at the church?"

"Neither, dear. I'm sorry. He's away for the day. Shall I tell him you called?"

"No, thank you," Emily hastened to say. "I just wondered whether he was here. Nothing important."

Emily tried her best to sound nonchalant but knew Mrs. Meade had seen her disappointment. She made an excuse, said good-bye, and headed toward her friend Louisa's home on Water Street. Lost in her thoughts, Emily walked swiftly along the path, oblivious to the beauty of the day around her. She reprimanded herself for asking about Robert. *What will Mrs. Meade think of me? But then it was a simple question. I was merely curious. Oh, I do hope she understands.*

Emily reached the Bradford home and knocked lightly, and Mrs. Bradford answered the door. "Emily, it's been awhile since we've seen you. How nice of you to call. Louisa will be so pleased."

She ushered Emily into the parlor, where Louisa was conversing with Robert Harris. Startled at seeing them together, Emily's face turned crimson, and she mumbled, "Oh, I'm so sorry to interrupt. I really can't stay."

Louisa jumped up from the divan and grabbed Emily's hand. "You silly goose. . .you aren't interrupting anything. I'm so happy to see you. Come and sit down."

"Yes, Emily," Robert said, smiling at her with his crooked grin. "Please stay and visit with us. Louisa and I have been having an interesting conversation."

"Perhaps it's of a private nature," Emily suggested stiffly as she sat across from them.

Louisa and Robert exchanged mysterious glances. "We are done with that conversation anyway," Louisa said, changing the subject. "Is it nice being home on the farm for a while? Martha said you plan to spend the summer with your family. That will be good for you, Emily. Will you start classes again in the fall? Frankly, I'm glad they are over."

"I'm not sure," Emily faltered. "I've not decided what I'll do as yet."

"Martha says your aunt Maude left you her house. How generous of her. I suppose you plan to keep it. It's such a lovely old home and furnished so beautifully," Louisa added.

Robert seems unusually quiet and even a little aloof, Emily thought. He said nothing but watched her carefully.

"I do love Aunt Maudie's home," Emily said. "The furniture, the garden. . . everything is so beautiful. She was a dear to leave it to me. She knew I loved it and would take care of it."

Robert's lips were set in a firm, unsmiling line. Emily cast quick glances at his face, wondering what his expression meant. She had never seen him look so serious before. Was he resenting her presence there? Had she interrupted an intimate moment between him and Louisa? Emily shifted uncomfortably in her chair. An awkward silence had fallen over all three of them, and Emily was searching for an excuse to take her leave.

Before she could say anything, though, Robert finally spoke, "Will you be coming back to church Sunday, Emily?" His eyes were strangely intent on her face.

"Oh yes. I've told Mrs. Meade that I'll play the piano again. Thank you, Robert, for helping me get my thoughts together recently. I've overcome my bitterness toward God, I'm happy to say. I was being very childish."

"Not at all," Robert said sincerely, and for a moment his face softened. "You suffered a great loss. Those things take time." He pulled his eyes away from her face and appeared to be intent upon studying the book titles on the shelf beside him.

Mrs. Bradford came bustling into the room with tea, cookies, and small cakes. As they ate, the conversation turned to lighter things, and they all seemed to relax a little. Still, Emily sensed that Robert was avoiding looking at her, as though something about her displeased him. Had she done something to offend him? He had been so kind about her doubts and anger after Aunt Maude died, but perhaps he disapproved of her now. Perhaps he imagined she would be a bad influence on Louisa.

Emily studied her friend's face, trying to read her expression. She thought Louisa looked unusually pleased with herself, as though she knew some happy secret. Emily's heart sank a little lower. What else could Louisa have been discussing with Robert to make her look like that except love? *Louisa and Robert must be in love with each other, and Robert must have just confessed his feelings to her.* No wonder Louisa looked so pleased; no wonder Robert was so resentful of Emily interrupting them.

Emily was eager to leave. When Frederic finally arrived for her, she heaved a sigh of relief. She smiled her good-byes, but underneath she was hurting.

"I'll see you soon," Louisa promised. "We have so much we need to talk about." She smiled, her face secretive again, and glanced quickly at Robert.

Emily returned her smile, but she knew her lips were stiff. She could not force herself to look at Robert. Instead, she mumbled, "I'll see you in church Sunday," while looking down at the gloves she was pulling on her fingers.

"It will be a pleasure to have you once more at the piano, Emily," he answered, but his voice was cold and distant.

Emily hurried out the door before they could see the tears that had risen in her eyes at the ice in Robert's voice. She averted her eyes so that she could avoid looking at either of them and mumbled her good-byes over her shoulder.

My best friend and Robert! They certainly are well suited to each other. Louisa, with her golden hair and pale coloring, is very attractive. How could Robert help but notice how delicate and feminine she is? I must seem drab in comparison. Why didn't I see this coming? Cassie prepared me somewhat, but that doesn't make it any easier. I guess they were talking of very private, intimate things when I arrived. . .perhaps even marriage. My timing couldn't have been worse. Well, at least now I know the truth. I won't be wasting any more time thinking about Robert.

Emily greeted Frederic soberly, then climbed into the wagon with a heavy heart.

Chapter 26

The ride home seemed unusually long. Frederic was very quiet, and Emily appreciated the silence. When she finally took a good look at him, she noticed his clothes were disarrayed, his hair was rumpled, and he had a small cut on the side of his right cheek.

"What happened to you, Fred?" she cried, reaching out to gently touch his face.

"I had a run-in with someone down at the mill. There I was, minding my own business, but he seemed to want to pick a fight. It was really nothing."

"Why, Frederic? Who was it? Anyone you know?"

"Actually, it's a coincidence, because I have met him before. Briefly, while I was at Petersburg during the war. He was assigned to my company for a short time. I remember he was a hothead. He didn't like me and tried every way he could to show it. . .called me bad names because I said I hated slavery. I pointed out that God created us all equal and no human being should be in bondage to another. He didn't care beans about the black man's plight. He fought simply because there was a war. He seemed to enjoy fighting. The fact that I didn't gamble, curse, or drink with the men bothered him. He called me a sissy and other names I won't mention. Since I was a captain and he an enlisted man, there were times he had to be disciplined. That galled him and made matters worse."

"Did you try to befriend him back then?"

"I did, Emily. . .even went out of my way. But he would have none of it. He hated me, and we had several confrontations because of it."

"I wonder what he's doing in Waterville," Emily mused.

"Well, that's it," Frederic said. "I recognized him right away and tried to be friendly. . .forget the past. So I greeted him and asked him why he was in town. He swore and said it was none of my business. Then he shoved me against the boards on the wagon. I shoved back, and it turned into quite a scuffle. Zack Turner and his dad pulled us apart, and he left. They don't know anything about the man. . .said he was just hanging around the mill today killing time."

"We don't need his kind around here," Emily said emphatically. "I hope he's just passing through."

❧

They arrived home in time for supper, and their mother had a hot meal waiting. Cassie and Bill were there also. Frederic explained his disheveled appearance and the cut on his cheek, giving them a brief description of what happened.

After supper and a short devotional time, their father said seriously, "I have an important letter to read to you, one that will affect each of you children. That's one reason we asked Cassie and Bill to be here. It's from Maude's lawyer, Josiah Williams, who was a close friend of Uncle George.

"Dated June 1866. 'Dear Mr. Mason,'" read their father, "'This letter is in regard to the estate of your sister, Maude McClough. I must inform you that George McClough had a son to his first wife, and since Maude's death, he is the legal heir. His whereabouts were difficult to obtain and unknown to me until recently. I have finally located him, and he is in town at the present time.'"

"Uncle George was married before he married Aunt Maude?" Frederic asked. "We never knew that."

"Your mother, Grandpa, and I all knew it, and of course Maude. We knew that George had made a mistake when he was younger, married a girl who left him and ran off with another man. She divorced him, didn't want anything more to do with George. But there was never anything said about a son."

"Maybe he's an imposter," Emily suggested. "Maybe he's someone claiming to be a son so he can get the money and the house."

"Let me finish the letter," Chase said gravely. "'My friend George McClough supported this son, through me, for the first eighteen years of his life. His mother was one of low morals but received the money eagerly for the boy's care. However, she refused to let George see or write his son during all those years. The mother passed away two years ago, shortly before George's death. George left instructions that upon his death, everything go to Maude. But upon Maude's death he directed that everything go to his son and heir, Peter McClough, of Boston. I shall call upon you, along with Peter, on Friday next at 2:00 p.m. Sincerely, Josiah Williams, Attorney.'"

"That's tomorrow!" Frederic exclaimed. "What a jolt!"

"It's a shock all right," his father agreed, "a real surprise. This means there is no money for you, Frederic or Cassie, no home for Emily, and no money for schooling."

Emily started to cry softly.

"Don't cry, little sister. It's not important, not really," Frederic soothed, placing a comforting arm around her shoulders.

"It's not the house or the money," Emily said, sobbing. "I never expected them anyway. It's just that an intruder, someone we don't even know, will have the house and all Aunt Maudie's lovely things."

"Well, I hope he's a decent sort of fellow," Frederic said. "If he's anything like Uncle George, he will be."

Cassie agreed the money didn't matter. She and Bill were too happy to let anything spoil their joy.

"Remember, children," their father cautioned, "Peter McClough has been brought up without a father and by a woman of questionable morals. We don't know what kind of a person he will be. We'll see fer ourselves tomorrow."

"For his sake we must try to be gracious about it," their mother added. "He hasn't been blessed with a lovin' family as ya children have. Cassie, you and Bill best join us tamorra and meet Peter McClough."

"Let's see," Gramps said, "Maude an' George were married twenty years afore George died two years ago. This young feller must be 'round twenty-five years old. George McClough came here from Boston twenty-four years ago, in April, and set up his medical practice in Waterville. He won yer Aunt Maudie's heart in a hurry. Yep, George was a fine man. We all liked him, and especially yer grandma. George's son, Peter, has no family now." He paused thoughtfully and added, "Maybe, jest maybe, we can be his family."

Chapter 27

Josiah Williams arrived with his companion promptly at 2:00 p.m. the following day, and Mr. Mason ushered them into the parlor where the family had gathered. Mr. Williams was a short, portly man, and his vest stretched tightly across his midsection. His head was bald except for two patches of gray fringe along both sides. Deep-set dark eyes peered from behind spectacles perched carefully on his rather prominent nose. He made a stark contrast to the tall, muscular young man beside him.

Frederic was startled to see that Mr. Williams's companion was Peter Graham, the young man he had found troublesome in the army and again yesterday at the mill. *How could Peter Graham be Peter McClough?* he wondered.

Mr. Williams shook hands with Frederic and his grandfather, then bowed politely to the ladies. "This is Peter McClough, George's son," he stated in introduction. Peter McClough merely grunted, shifting from one foot to the other and eyeing them suspiciously. Peter was well dressed, just under six feet tall, with a muscular build and dark hair and eyes. He would be considered handsome except for a hardness around his eyes and his firmly set mouth. Peter looked closely at Frederic and said gruffly, "Eh, Mason. . .it's you!"

"Do you know one another?" Josiah Williams asked. "How can that be?"

"Yes, sir," Frederic answered. "We served together for a short time in the war."

"Then you knew him as Peter Graham," Mr. Williams continued matter-of-factly. "Peter carried his mother's maiden name all those years, and I had a difficult time locating him after Maude's death. He's George's son and officially Peter McClough now." Mr. Williams continued to explain George McClough's wishes that were to be carried out upon the event of Maude's death. "He directed everything go to Peter, his son and heir."

"We understand," Chase said. "I've read yer letter ta the family."

"Just want you to get it straight," Peter interrupted hoarsely. "The house. . .the money. . .it's all mine. I'll not share it with any of you."

Josiah Williams spoke up quickly. "Mr. Mason, I have a paper for you to sign. It relinquishes any claims you might have against your sister's estate. I'll need each of the family members' signatures to validate it."

"Of course," Chase agreed. "We have no problem with it. Our daughter Emily had been livin' there with Maude. Maude wanted her ta have the house. Emily will need time ta move her things back home."

"That should be handled as quickly as possible," Josiah Williams suggested.

"Peter plans to move into the house as soon as it's vacant and make Waterville his home. He has no family or ties in Boston anymore."

After signing the agreement, Mrs. Mason hurried to the kitchen and returned with molasses doughnuts and glasses of cool cider from the springhouse.

"Won't ya share in some refreshments?" she asked.

The two visitors eagerly agreed to partake before they started the journey back to town. "This is very kind of you, Mrs. Mason," Josiah Williams murmured. "Very kind indeed, under the circumstances."

"Well, we appreciate meetin' George's son," Grandpa said. The others nodded their agreement. "We thought a lot o' George. He was a kind and thoughtful man, one o' the best. But we never knew he had a son."

Josiah Williams stood up, consulted the gold watch he pulled from his vest pocket, and prepared to leave. "Folks, thank you for your kindness and cooperation in this legal matter. I have another commitment this afternoon, so Peter and I best be on our way."

"Peter, why don't ya stay ta supper with us tonight?" Mrs. Mason asked. "Frederic can take ya ta town afterwards. Where are ya stayin'?"

"I'm at the Elmwood Hotel temporarily, until I move into the house. But I'll pass on the meal," he muttered gruffly.

"Ya'd be welcome," Mr. Mason added. "We'd all like a chance ta get ta know ya."

"Why?" Peter asked quickly. "Why? I won't change my mind, if that's what you think. The money and the house are mine, and I intend to have it all."

Mr. Mason put an arm lightly around Peter's shoulders. "We are only interested in you, Peter, not yer house or yer money. We'd all like ya ta stay, but the decision is up to you."

Peter shuffled his feet awkwardly, hesitating. *What is with these people anyway? I'm out for all I can get, and never mind about them. Why would they want to be nice to me? I'm a stranger to them all except Frederic. And I always hated Frederic and his goody-goody ways. Strange, Frederic hasn't said one word against me.* Peter touched the bruise over his left eye, put there yesterday at the mill by Frederic. He glanced at Frederic's cut cheek. The cut was scabbed over but there nonetheless. *And Frederic is smiling at me. They all are.*

"I have to leave, McClough. Make up your mind whether you are coming with me," Josiah Williams said.

"Please stay," Mrs. Mason said warmly. "George's son will allus be welcome in our home."

Peter's mouth relaxed from its hard, firm line. He looked at first one and then the other. No one had spoken so kindly to him before. He was a rough character and had been treated as one. This was all new to him. He had to find out if these people were genuine. "I'll stay," he said and managed a slight grin. "It will be a treat to have some home cookin'."

A HAVEN OF PEACE

Grandpa and Chase took Peter on a tour of the farm while Frederic tended to the chores. Cassie and Bill headed home, and Emily helped her mother prepare the meal, a delicious boiled ham dinner. Peter ate with a vigorous appetite. Gradually, he began talking about his childhood. "I shifted for myself growing up. Ma wasn't home most of the time. I never did know where she went. She didn't tell me anything about my pa. Just that he was no good. Guess he left her when I was a baby. When I asked about him, she told me he was dead.

"I got out. . .went into the army as soon as they'd take me. It gave me a paycheck. I sent most of it to my ma until she died."

"Yer pa was a fine man. . .a doctor," Chase said. "Ya know, accordin' ta Mr. Williams, he sent money ta yer ma fer yer upbringin'. George was like that. . .took care o' his obligations."

"My ma must have drank up all the money. . .she and her men friends. Oh, she had plenty of them. She never had money left for things we needed, like food and clothes," Peter said bitterly. "I'm afraid I don't have any good memories. I was in Ma's way when I was a kid. I cramped her style. I couldn't wait to get away."

Peter chewed his food thoughtfully as he reached for another chunk of Mrs. Mason's thick-cut, homemade bread. Methodically he spread butter and blackberry preserves over its surface. "You say my pa was a good man. . .a doctor in Waterville?"

"His life was dedicated ta the medical profession," Chase replied. "Many a night he didn't get a scrap o' sleep, out carin' fer his patients."

"Yep," Grandpa agreed. "Healin' people and bringin' comfort from pain came first ta George McClough. He was the kind o' man ya can be proud of, Peter."

Peter glanced at the Mason family seated around the dinner table. Their faces expressed an invitation to warmth and friendship. "My old man doesn't sound anything like what my ma described. She couldn't say enough bad things about him. I always figured he was a good-for-nothing slob." He looked down at his plate and added pensively, "I wish I could have known him. I wish I could have known my pa."

Chapter 28

A thoughtful Frederic hitched up the buggy to take Peter back to town. He was grateful Emily decided to ride along. Now he wouldn't have to worry about a lack of conversation. She could handle that, and Peter would be more apt to mind his manners with a lady along.

As they started down the drive, Emily began telling Peter about her aunt's house. "Martha is an excellent housekeeper and cook, if you decide to retain her," she offered. "She's been with Aunt Maude and Uncle George for years. You couldn't find a better one."

"She won't want to stay on with me," Peter said gruffly. "I'm a complete stranger to her. I don't want her living in my house anyway. I can manage alone. I always have."

"You probably won't need Zeke either," Emily continued. "He's a neighbor who has helped Aunt Maude since Uncle George's death. . .keeping up the place. She paid him, of course. I planned to retain them both when I owned the house. But then. . .things are different now."

"I guess you wish I didn't exist," Peter said cynically. "Now you don't have the house or the money. But they are rightfully mine. . .you know that!"

"Of course," Emily agreed, smiling. "The house is lovely, you'll see, and the furniture mostly imported. I do love the place, but mainly because I loved the people who lived there. . .Aunt Maudie and Uncle George." Tears welled up in her eyes. "But, Peter, I never expected to have the house, not in my wildest dreams, so it's no loss to me. I just hope. . ." She hesitated, then added softly, "I just hope you will care for it and appreciate it. Aunt Maude and Uncle George would want you to."

Peter looked away and didn't respond. They rode for some time in silence, with only the sounds of the horses' hooves clip-clopping on the hard clay roadway.

Frederic finally spoke. "Will you be looking for work in Waterville, Peter?"

"I might," he replied. "I'd like to work at the mill. I've always liked the smell of cut wood. Do you know if they need anyone?"

"No, I don't," Frederic answered. "But my friend Zack Turner works there. His pa runs the mill, and I'll put in a good word for you."

"You'd do that. . .after the way I've treated you?" Peter asked in amazement.

"Why not?" Frederic asked. "You look like a hard worker, and I know how strong you are." Frederic touched the scab on his right cheek and grinned. "I know firsthand."

A HAVEN OF PEACE

Peter McClough sat quietly for some time, as if trying to decide what to say. Finally he spoke, and his voice had lost some of its gruffness. "I'm sorry about how rough I've been, cursing and knocking you around. But hey, you carry a hefty punch yourself." They laughed together, and a barrier between them seemed to break.

Emily picked up the conversation once again and chattered about the points of interest in Waterville. In a short time, Frederic stopped the carriage in front of the Elmwood Hotel.

"I'll move my things tomorrow," Emily said as Peter climbed down. "Shall I tell Martha she is no longer needed? And Zeke also? Martha has a sister living nearby whom she can move in with."

"I'd appreciate it," Peter replied. "I'd like to go it alone, at least for a while."

"Would you join us for Sunday services?" Frederic asked. "We attend the little Community Church here in town. It's the church your pa attended."

"Naw. . .I'm not into church," Peter mumbled quickly. With a wave of his hand, he turned and walked briskly toward the hotel.

They watched as the lonely figure disappeared from sight. With a sigh, Frederic snapped the reins and headed Nell toward home. A soft summer breeze had come up, and Emily pushed back straying wisps of hair. "I know he's treated you shabbily, Frederic, but I can't help feeling sorry for Peter."

"Well, he has a fine home now and is financially stable. I'd say he's pretty well set."

"Peter has no family. . . . He's really quite alone in this world. It must be a dreadful feeling."

"He's got our family, Emily, if he wants us. We tried to make him welcome. I have no qualms about being his friend."

"When I spent those weeks in town after Aunt Maudie's death, it was unbearable. I was so lonesome. I missed the family, but my pride and anger kept me away. At least I knew I had a family. . .a family who loved me and cared about me."

"Yep, it has to be painful for Peter. He never knew his pa. I'm sure Uncle George loved him but was unable to see him and express his love. And it's hard to imagine someone like his ma. . .not caring a hoot about him. We have much to be thankful for, Emily. God has blessed us with a loving family."

"Fred, you've been courting Hannah Ragsdale some, haven't you? Do you enjoy her company?"

"Very much. She's a fine person, and I admire her. We get along well together."

"I've seen Sarah Jane accompanied by a young man in her graduating class a few times. He's very handsome and attentive. I wonder if she's interested in him romantically."

Frederic shrugged. "She should be seeing someone her own age. She's so. . .so young."

The following day, Frederic hitched up the wagon for the return trip to Waterville. He and Emily talked at length about their half cousin, Peter, and the turn of events during the past few days.

Frederic helped Emily load her trunks and other personal belongings on the wagon. Martha and Zeke were told about the new owner and the unusual circumstances of his birth. They were surprised at the news, but neither seemed disturbed.

Emily took Martha aside. "I'm so sorry you will be relieved of your position here. You've been with Aunt Maudie for so many years."

"Don't you fret none, child," Martha insisted. "That's just it, I've been working here for a long time. Why, I wouldn't leave Maude as long as she needed me. Then when she passed on, you needed me. Fact is, I'm ready for a change. My sister's been wanting me to live with her for a long time. She's alone, too, you know. So it will be good for both of us. I've put some money aside, and we can do some things together. Don't you fret one bit. Everything will be just fine."

Emily hugged Martha and said her farewells. She lingered a time in the garden, noting the brilliant blossoms that seemed to beckon her. *What will become of you?* She took a deep breath and let the delicious fragrance fill her nostrils. "Farewell, sweet blossoms," she whispered, then hurried to the front gate where Frederic was waiting in the wagon.

"Could we stop by Louisa's for a few minutes?" she asked, looking up at him. "I need to talk to her. . . . I want to tell her what's happened."

"Yep, I'll drop you off, Emily. I want to go by the mill and talk to Mr. Turner about giving Peter a job."

"I'll walk to Louisa's, Fred. It's such a lovely day. You can pick me up when you're finished."

Emily made her way through town to Louisa's home and was relieved to find her friend alone this time. "I thought I might be interrupting you and Robert Harris again," she said cautiously. "You two were having such a serious and private conversation the other day."

"Nonsense!" Louisa protested. "It was nothing serious."

"Are you quite sure, Louisa? Why were you so mysterious?"

"We didn't mean to be. . . . We were just having one of our quiet talks."

"Louisa, are you and Robert in love?" Emily demanded boldly. "I have to know. Is that why he was here?"

"Oh, you silly goose!" Louisa laughed. "You must know that Robert is in love with you. That's what we were talking about. . .you!"

"Me!" Emily's face turned crimson. "What about me?"

"Oh, just how he's been in love with you since the first day he saw you. . .when you fell on the ice and he helped you up!"

"That's ridiculous!" Emily exploded. "People don't fall in love that quickly."

"Not you, perhaps. But Robert claims he did, and I believe him."

"Why was he telling you all this? Why doesn't he tell me?"

"He confided in me since I'm your best friend. Robert is in love with you but says he can't ask you to marry him."

Emily's face paled. "Why not? Oh, I don't blame him really. I've had so many problems accepting Aunt Maudie's death. I neglected church. . .I became bitter. . .I even cried out against God." Emily burst into tears, and Louisa gathered her into her arms.

"Dear Emily, that's not the reason," Louisa soothed. "Robert knows you had a difficult time, but you have made your peace with God. He understands."

"Then why, Louisa? Why can't he ask me to marry him?"

"Do you love him, Emily? You must, dear friend. I can tell by your tears."

"I do, Louisa. I do! I think I've loved him for a long time but wouldn't admit it. I'm so headstrong. . . . I wouldn't listen to my heart."

"Robert says he can't ask you to marry him because he has nothing to offer you. You have your aunt's beautiful home, a large amount of money, and all that fine imported furniture. He feels as though he would be marrying you for your inheritance. He's too proud. . . . He couldn't bear that."

"Is that all?" Emily asked excitedly, smiling through her tears. She jumped up and whirled around the room. "Oh, he must know the truth, Louisa! It's all too wonderful what has happened. The house, the money—I don't have them after all!"

"What are you saying?" Louisa asked.

Emily sat down, caught her breath, and proceeded to tell her friend all that had transpired during the past few days. "I'm a pauper!" She laughed, jumping up again and whirling Louisa crazily about the room. "I can't go back to college. I don't have a house. . .or money. . .or fine furniture. But, Louisa, I don't even care!"

Chapter 29

Emily's words regarding Sarah Jane having a beau bothered Frederic. He had decided she was too young for him and had tried his best to keep her out of his mind. But the idea of her enjoying some young man's company filled his thoughts day and night.

"Yer mind isn't on yer work, Fred," Pa said one day while they sat at lunch. "Have ya got a problem? Want ta talk about it?"

"No problem, Pa," Fred said hastily. "Nothing I can't handle, anyway."

"Maybe he's in love," Emily said impishly. "He's been seeing the school teacher, Hannah Ragsdale, a lot during the past few weeks."

"Is thet it, son?" Ma asked. "She seems like a fine person. Mebbe we should ask her ta dinner."

"No, I'm not in love!" Fred said gruffly. "Hannah's very nice, but we're only friends. I think she enjoys the companionship. There aren't many men her age left. . .since the war."

"I'd guess she's about twenty-five or so," Emily stated. "But that's not old."

"No, it's not," Fred agreed. "She told me she was twenty-five. Her soldier friend was killed at Bull Run, early in the war. They had planned to be married."

"Thet's a shame," Ma said. "We lost so many of our fine young men in thet terrible war. It's only God's grace thet brought ya home ta us, Fred."

"God's been good ta us," Pa added as he rose from the table. "Well, Fred. . . ya ready ta get back ta work? We've got ta get thet fence patched down by the creek."

Frederic swallowed his milk and pushed back his chair. "Ready as I'll ever be, Pa. I'll try and keep my mind on the work at hand. Just crack me on the back if I get daydreamin'."

Emily picked up dirty dishes and carried them to the sink. "Sarah Jane's coming over this afternoon, Ma. She wants me to teach her to sew."

"Land sakes, thet's right. Her ma never did like ta sew. Can't understand it, neither. It's right pleasin' ta take a piece of material and fashion it into a dress. Don't know what I'd do iffen I didn't sew."

After cleaning up the dishes, Emily pulled out some scraps of material to get Sarah started. She had several leftover pieces that were suitable and would make good-sized aprons. Carefully she arranged them on the bed so Sarah could choose whatever color and pattern caught her eye.

Sarah chose a pale cotton calico with little pink rosebuds splashed on it.

"This is beautiful," she cried as she hugged it to her. "Is there enough in this piece for an apron?"

"We'll make it enough," Emily said, laughing. "We can always use a piece of plain fabric for the ties if we need to."

The two worked steadily, and Emily was impressed with how quickly Sarah learned the fundamentals. "You'll be sewing dresses in no time, Sarah. You seem to have a natural talent for it."

"Thanks, Emily. Ma sews, but she doesn't like to. . .doesn't have the patience for it. She said it would be a terrible chore to teach me, and if you were willing, I should grab at it. She's seen the lovely dresses you've made."

"Ma taught me everything I know," Emily confessed. "And I love sewing. . . . So does Cassie. It's hard to understand someone not liking it. We've been brought up by a ma and grandma who loved to sew and taught us at an early age."

The project was completed sooner than Sarah expected, and she eyed it with delight. "It'll be a gift for Ma's birthday next month. Won't she be surprised?"

"She'll be very pleased, especially since you made it yourself."

"You did a lot, Emily. I couldn't have done it alone."

"I only gave instructions. . . . You did the real work. I'm really proud of how quickly you learned. We can start a dress for you next week, if you'd like."

"Oh, would you, Emily?"

"Look over my patterns and pick out one you like. Buy the needed material and thread at the fabric shop in town. With my supervision, you are ready to tackle a dress."

Sarah left in high spirits, her apron neatly folded and wrapped securely. On an impulse, she headed Star toward the back pasture, hoping for a glimpse of Frederic. She waved at Mr. Mason, who was heading for the house from the direction of the creek.

"Maybe Fred's over there," she said aloud and pulled the reins to turn Star. "I'll just tell him about my sewing lesson."

She could see Frederic in the distance, bent over mending the fence that had been broken by a storm. Star snorted, and Fred looked up just as Sarah Jane slid to the ground beside him. She kneeled close to see what he was working on. Straying wisps of her red gold hair fell across his face, and he felt the familiar giddy sensation rising in his veins.

"Can I help, Fred?" she asked. "I've helped Pa mend fences before."

Frederic stood up and pushed back his dark hair, curly and damp from the summer heat. He pulled out a clean bandanna and wiped his face and brow. "Sarah, you do take a body by surprise. How did you know I was here?"

"Just a guess, Fred. Emily taught me to sew today. I made an apron for my ma's birthday, and Emily's planning to help me make a dress next week. Let me help you. Ma doesn't expect me home till supper time."

Frederic handed her a fence rail. "You hold, and I'll pound."

She smiled up at him and grabbed the rail firmly. For a moment her limpid blue eyes gazed steadily into his. He felt like a sailor lost in the depths of the sea. As he bent over his work, her hair brushed his face again, and he felt a sudden surge of excitement. Awkwardly, he reached for his tools, fumbled, and dropped them. "What a clumsy oaf! I'll never get this right. Pa will be back, and I won't be finished."

"Here, Fred. . .you hold the rail, and I'll pound." Sarah reached for the tools and felt his strong hands upon her shoulders. He turned her toward him and gently cupped her face in his hands.

"That's not a good idea, Sarah," he said huskily. He felt her trembling body close to his and once again suppressed a deep desire to take her in his arms. "You—you'd better go home now."

"Am I interfering with your work?" Sarah asked in a disappointed tone. "I only wanted to help."

"I know you did, and I appreciate it. But I can't do my work when I get distracted. Run along now."

Sarah climbed on Star and headed home. *Run along,* he said. *Like I was a child pestering him. That's all I am to him—a child. That's all I'll ever be, no matter how old I get.* She did not look back at him once. *I've learned my lesson. I won't pester him again.*

Frederic watched her ride away, then turned back to his task with a heavy heart. "What's a fella to do?" He sighed. "I can't fight these feelings much longer. Sarah Jane is so lovely. Whenever she's near me, all I can think about is pulling her into my arms. If only she weren't so young. . ."

Chapter 30

The lengthening days of summer brought busy activity to the Mason household: planting, weeding, nurturing the crops. Harnesses needed to be oiled and mended and the outbuildings cleaned and repaired. Frederic was happiest working in the fields or out in the pasture mending fences.

He had talked Mr. Turner into hiring Peter McClough on a trial basis at the mill, and all reports were good thus far. Peter proved a conscientious young man, willing to do an honest day's work. The Mason family invited him over for dinner often and could see evidence of changes in his life. As they showered him with friendship and concern, his attitude softened and he became less aloof. His gruff and raucous ways were gradually giving way to a more peaceful and gentler nature.

Although they exercised no pressure, the family felt it would not be long before Peter would willingly attend church with them. He had made his peace with man. . . . Now he needed to be at peace with God.

Peter felt overwhelmed because they referred to him as "family," giving him a feeling of belonging that met a need deep in his heart. He'd had no father's companionship, and his mother had cared little about him. . .had treated him as though he were in the way. The Mason family, on the other hand, made him feel welcome, even wanted, and he found himself anticipating each visit with greater pleasure than the one before. Although not accustomed to farmwork, he took pleasure in helping Frederic with chores on each of his visits.

❧

Emily wanted Robert Harris to know the facts about her impoverished state, as she called it. At a loss as how to tell him, she grew more impatient with each passing day. *Is Louisa right? Does Robert love me? If so, there is nothing to keep us apart.* The thought of marriage to Robert gave her a warm, peaceful feeling. *Oh, I've changed a great deal from the saucy young lady who wanted to be "somebody." God, You took me through some difficult times. . .but You showed me it doesn't take wealth and position to be "somebody." It's more important to be "somebody" for You.* "Robert's strong faith will have a strengthening effect on my own," she said aloud. "Together we will serve God. Yes, together." She emphasized the word, and it was a soothing balm to her anxious heart.

A few days later, Robert Harris appeared unexpectedly in the afternoon at the Mason farm. He explained he was making routine visits to members of his congregation and hoped he was not imposing.

The menfolk were out in the field, but Mrs. Mason was delighted with his presence and bustled about getting them some refreshments. Emily had been baking cookies and quickly pulled back wisps of hair and patted them into place. She took off her apron and felt her heart pounding as she entered the parlor where Robert sat looking at the old family Bible.

"Hello, Robert," she said somewhat breathlessly. "It's so nice of you to call."

Mrs. Mason reappeared with cool drinks and some of Emily's freshly baked cookies. The conversation was light and cheerful, with Robert and Mrs. Mason doing most of the talking. Emily sat quietly with her hands folded in her lap, saying very little but watching Robert carefully.

Finally, he stood up as if to leave. "Emily. . .would you walk with me for a spell? I'd like to see some of the farm."

Emily was sure her heart skipped a beat. She jumped up, then reprimanded herself for appearing too anxious. "Certainly, Robert," she said calmly. "Let's walk down the back lane to the creek. It's one of my favorite spots."

They walked in silence for a short distance, and Emily thought her heart would burst. *This is a good opportunity to tell him about losing the inheritance. Would I seem brazen and forward?* As she tried to find the right words, she could feel her heart pounding in her bosom.

Robert stopped abruptly in the path, reached for her hand, and faced Emily squarely. "Emily, I. . ." His husky voice took on a serious quality. Suddenly a broad smile spread across his face, turning into the familiar lopsided grin.

"What is it, Robert?" she demanded.

"My dearest Emily," he said, chuckling softly, "you are very beautiful—but you have smudges of flour on your nose." Robert pulled out his handkerchief and gently wiped the flour smudges from her face while looking directly into her eyes.

Emily wanted to run away from his teasing smile but felt glued to the spot. His words, "My dearest Emily," kept resounding in her heart.

Robert tucked his handkerchief back into his pocket. "My dearest Emily," he repeated, "I—" His voice faltered, but he continued to look into Emily's eyes steadily. He shook his head, and his grin flickered across his face for a moment. "Here I rehearsed what I came to say so many times—and now I've forgotten every word. You wouldn't think this would be harder than that first sermon I preached here in Waterville, would you? But it is, Emily."

He took a deep breath and tried again. "What I want to say—what I came here to say is—I care for you deeply, Emily. I know we haven't had a courtship as such—probably I'm putting the cart before the horse by saying all this before I've courted you properly. But ever since that first time I saw you, that time you fell on the ice, I've been sure of my feelings for you. I couldn't court you then, though. How could I when you would barely speak to me back then? Do you remember?" Once again Emily saw his lopsided grin, but his eyes still looked seriously into hers. "I couldn't very well court you when you wouldn't even let me call you by your first name, now could I?"

Emily blushed, but her eyes were glowing with happiness. Robert's eyes searched her face. "When your aunt died, you had so much to deal with, you were hurting so badly, that I didn't want to press myself on you then. I knew you needed time to heal, to straighten out things with God. But I wanted so badly to put my arms around you and comfort you. And then I found out your aunt had left you her house and money. I couldn't court you then. I was afraid you would think I was interested in you for the wrong reasons. And my pride got in the way. I could bring you nothing at all, while you already had so much. I pulled away then, tried to hide my feelings away inside myself."

He looked down at her, traced the oval of her face with one finger. "When Louisa told me you no longer have an inheritance, I was glad. That's an awful thing to say, isn't it? But it's true. For the first time, I felt as though nothing was standing between us." He drew in his breath. "I decided I'd better tell you how I felt right away, before something else came up to separate us. I love you, Emily. And you're just looking up at me, smiling, but you haven't said a word. Does that smile possibly mean you could care for me?"

Emily's smile grew wider. "Oh yes, Robert. I care for you a great deal."

He drew her close, and his lips brushed hers gently. Then he pulled back and grinned. "It's your turn now to talk. Tell me why you pushed me away when you first met me. Tell me what you thought. Tell me everything."

Emily looked away from his gaze, and her cheeks grew rosy. "I think I was attracted to you right from the first, too. But I was afraid I had looked like a fool that day when I fell on the ice. I was afraid you were laughing at me."

"I would never do that."

"Unless, of course, I had flour on my face."

Robert grinned. "Of course. But keep talking. I want to know everything."

"Well. . ." Emily looked through the trees to where the sunlight flickered on the creek. "I didn't like thinking someone might laugh at me. I was taking myself very seriously in those days, you see, and so I was angry with you. And I tried to regain my dignity by being very cool toward you. But I couldn't resist you for very long. During the Christmas program, you were so good with the children. And you were always dropping by Aunt Maude's and talking about my courses with me. I found myself thinking about you more and more. But when Aunt Maude died, I was so angry with God. I was hurting so bad I didn't want to let anyone close, not you, not even my own family."

She looked up at him, and her lips curved. "But it was your wisdom and gentleness that helped me heal, that helped me be able to come to God again. Only then I was sure you could never. . .care for someone who had been so full of doubts. After all, you're a preacher, and. . ." Her voice trailed away.

"You think preachers never have any doubts?"

"Do they?"

He nodded. "Everyone does sometimes. But no matter how many times we waver, God never does. And that's all that matters." Once again, he pulled her close.

After a few moments, they drew apart and walked together down the path arm in arm, feeling a contented closeness.

"I'm sorry you lost the money for your schooling," he said after a moment. "I know I told you I was glad you lost your inheritance—but I'm truly sorry about your having to leave school. I know how important it was to you."

"Don't be sorry for me, Robert," she said, hugging his arm. "I couldn't be happier than I am at this moment. I wouldn't want the inheritance—not if it meant losing you."

He stood still in the path and looked down at her. "After all these months of loving you from afar, I can hardly believe this is happening. I can hardly believe I'm hearing you say what you are." She saw him swallow and then take another deep breath. "I'm tempted to ask you what I really want to ask you right now. But I want us to have a courtship, Emily," he said. "It's important because I want you to be sure. My feelings for you will never change. But I realize the life of a pastor's wife can be a difficult one. It's something that needs a great deal of thought. I may be called to a pastorate far away from Waterville. I hope not. . . . I love it here. But if God calls me, I must go."

Emily had never considered the possibility that marriage to Robert might take her away from her beloved family. She set her shoulders squarely, though, knowing her place would always be at this man's side. "Do—do you think I would make a good pastor's wife?"

Robert looked down at her sweet, upturned face. . .radiant and full of love. Leaning over, he gently kissed her hair and held her close. "Yes, I do, my darling," he said huskily. "You'd be the very best."

Chapter 31

In July, Frederic, with his father's help, started clearing timber on a small wooded knoll overlooking the creek. This was the spot he'd selected before the war for his future cabin. It lay not too far back from the main house and outbuildings yet was somewhat secluded. They cleared only those trees needed for a sizable cabin, leaving the others untouched.

"It's the perfect spot for me, Pa, here in the woods. I like the quietness of it back here. Just the lowing of the cattle from the pasture, the songs of the birds, and the croaking of the bullfrogs. This will be my haven of peace."

"Yep, son, it shore be a pretty spot. Yer ma will miss havin' ya at the big house, though. She loves ta fuss over ya. While ya were away at the war, she fretted a lot about yer safety. She'd say, 'When our boy comes home, then things will be right in the world agin.' She shore enjoys cookin' all yer favorites."

Frederic laughed. "She sure does, Pa, and I love eating them. No one cooks like Ma does."

"Well, son, even if ya want this cabin of yer own, ya can still take yer meals with us. Yer ma wouldn't have it any other way. It's gonna be hard on her. Emily and Robert Harris are courtin' now. There might be a weddin' next summer. Cassie's weddin' was hard enough, even though we still had Emily and ya'd come back ta us from the war."

Frederic stacked the last log, wiped the sweat from his brow, and hobbled over to his pa, settling down on a grassy spot beside him. "Ma will do fine, Pa. You'll see. Remember, there's a new baby coming around Christmas. Can't you just picture Ma with her grandchild? Can't you just see her fussin' and spoilin' the little one?"

"Thet'll be somethin'," Pa agreed. "Fact is, we'll all be a-spoilin' him. . .or her, whichever the good Lord sends."

The dinner bell tolled in the distance, telling them the evening meal was ready.

"I knew it was time ta quit when I set down here," Pa said from his spot on the ground. "My belly reminded me thet it was supper time. Let's go git it, son."

They gathered their tools and headed down the trail toward the house, with Laddie at their heels.

"We accomplished a lot, Pa. Thanks for your help."

"Yep, we did. But it's slow goin', son. We did a full day's work taday, and thet's a good feelin'. There's no hurry, is there?" He gave his son a keen glance.

Fred shook his head. "Just so it's done by November, before winter sets in. I want to have it buttoned up by then."

"Any partickler reason ya've decided ya need yer own place, son? Wouldn't have anything to do with that pretty teacher friend of yers?"

Again Frederic shook his head. "No, Pa, like I've said before, Hannah and I are just friends."

Chase's eyes rested on his son's face. "Well, ya got something—or someone—on your mind, I can tell. I have a feelin' you're buildin' this cabin for someone special. But I won't press ya. Ya tell me when you're ready, son. And in the meantime, we'll be gettin' this cabin ready."

Frederic followed his father down the trail. He looked back once at the cabin, still visible through the tree trunks. He was building it for someone all right, or at least he hoped he was. But so far, he could only admit that to himself, and that was hard enough. He frowned, forcing himself to face the thought that he might be the only one who would live in the new cabin after all. Emily had said Sarah was in love with him—but now Emily said Sarah was seeing a boy her own age. *What if I've fallen in love with Sarah,* Frederic thought, *just when she's fallen out of love with me?* He shook his head, still uncomfortable with the thought that he might be in love with Sarah Jane, a girl so much younger than himself.

But before he and his father reached the house, Frederic looked back one more time in the direction of the cabin. He knew without a doubt his father was right: He was building the little house for someone, and that someone was on his mind every minute that he worked on the cabin. The cabin would be his haven of peace one day—but only if he could share it with someone special. And in spite of himself, his heart insisted that Sarah Jane Collins was that special someone.

❧

Mrs. Mason had supper waiting for them. Peter McClough had stopped by and been persuaded to join them. After washing up, Fred and his father met with the others at the table.

"Glad ya dropped by ta join us, Peter," Pa said, passing him a large platter of ham. "We hope ya allus feel welcome here."

"I do feel welcome, Mr. Mason, and I appreciate your generosity. You folks have been kind to a lonely orphan. . .much kinder than I deserved."

"How's the job at the mill, Peter?" Fred asked. "Is the work pretty hard?"

"It's hard enough. . .but it's good for me."

Fred buttered a chunk of homemade bread. "You don't have to work, do you? Couldn't you just live off your inheritance?"

"I could, Fred. I don't need the money. . . . I have more than enough. It's a strange feeling knowing I don't have to work. I guess I like the job better because I know I don't have to do it. The work keeps me occupied so I'm not lonely in that big house. Makes the time pass quickly."

"Peter, ya jest come visit us whenever ya feel lonely," Ma said. "We like havin' another young'un around."

"I'm planning to build my own cabin back by the creek," Fred mentioned. "The logs will come off our own property, but I'll be coming into town to the mill for some building supplies soon. I hope to have most of it completed before winter."

"Can I help?" Peter asked enthusiastically. "I could give you a hand and learn a lot in the process."

"I'll welcome all the help I can get, Peter. But aren't you busy most of the day? We don't work on Sundays."

"I could help after work, and I always have one weekday off. I'll squeeze in all the time I can. Sounds like a challenge."

"Ya can take yer meals with us when ya come," Ma said. "I can allus set an extra plate."

"Thanks, Mrs. Mason. Fred, why do you want a place of your own? You have the best right here." Peter glanced around the table at the family.

"Well, you have your own place, Peter. It will be a good feeling, at my age, to be on my own. . .but close enough for Ma's home cookin'." Fred winked and smiled fondly at his mother.

"At your age, Fred," Emily mimicked. "You sound like you are an old man!"

"I'm sure Peter would agree with me when I say the war aged us. I'm ready to move, just so it's on this property. . .back by the creek. I picked out the spot before I joined up with the Union troops. It's so quiet and peaceful back there."

"It always was your favorite spot," Emily agreed. "But won't you be lonely? Peter admits he is."

"Naw. I'll have all the wildlife around. Anyway, I'll be here at the big house most of the time, I reckon."

"Emily," Peter said, "I've hired Martha to come in once a week and clean for me. She's a very capable and thorough person. The day she comes, she fixes my supper and leaves it on the stove. That's the best food I ever get, except when I come here." Peter took a second helping of ham and potatoes. "Mrs. Mason, you are by far the best cook around!"

He chewed his food thoughtfully for a few moments. "Folks, I came out here tonight for a special reason. You've all been more than kind to me, and now I want to do something for all of you. Emily, there is money set aside for you to go on to school. Your aunt Maude wanted it that way, and I'm sure Uncle George, my pa, would have agreed. Fred, I can help you with physical labor whenever possible on your log home, but I also want to buy your needed building materials. For Bill and Cassie, I'd already planned to give them a substantial money gift for the coming baby. And for you, Mr. and Mrs. Mason and Grandpa—"

"Now jest wait a minute, young feller," Grandpa said. "We old folks don't need a thing."

The rest of the family sat spellbound. Emily recovered first. "That is a very kind offer, Peter, but I'm not sure if I want to go back to school."

"The money is there for you," Peter said seriously. "Isn't schooling what you always wanted?"

"Yes, it is. But there have been some changes in my life. I would have to pray about it and give it a great deal of thought."

"I couldn't take any money for building supplies," Fred murmured. "It's rightfully your money, Peter, and we don't expect a cent."

"I know you don't. But can't you accept it as a gift. . .a repayment for all the kindnesses shown me? I have more than I need and would like to share. It isn't a loan I'm talking about. It's a free gift."

Grandpa cleared his throat. "Thet free gift ya mentioned reminds us of God's love and His free gift ta us. . .the gift of eternal life through Jesus Christ, His Son. Have ya ever accepted God's gift, Peter?"

Peter looked down at his plate. He felt strange and uncomfortable. Something was going on inside him that he didn't understand. Usually any talk about God or religion angered him.

God never bothered about me. I grew up without a father. My loose-living mother never showed me any love. But I see love in this family. . .the way they care for one another. . .the way they care about me. I've been such a rotten character all my life. Could there really be a God somewhere who loves me?

Chapter 32

Peter's thoughts were troubled. He'd felt an uneasiness ever since his visit to the Masons and Grandpa's talk about God's free gift. The family had not pressed him or forced their beliefs on him, and for that he was grateful. He had none of the bitter feelings he'd often felt in the past when someone mentioned God; instead, he had a gnawing ache deep inside, as though something was missing in his life. Whenever it was convenient, he joined Frederic, his pa, and his grandpa to work on the cabin. Cassie's Bill and his pa, Mr. Collins, also lent a hand whenever possible.

By the end of September, the cabin was completed on the outside and able to stand against the elements of nature. The setting by the creek was impressive. Autumn had arrived with the Master Painter's brilliant splashes of color. Towering trees bedecked in red, orange, and gold stood gracefully among the green pines.

"Kinda takes your breath away," Peter said one Saturday, standing back to survey the picturesque setting. "I can see why you picked this particular spot, Fred. It's outstanding."

"I know. Words really can't describe it. Only God could create such beauty. . . and give it to us to enjoy. We don't deserve all the good things He pours out upon us every day."

Peter muttered something under his breath and turned away. He couldn't understand this family. They gave God the credit for every good thing that happened to them. And if there were difficulties, things they couldn't work out, they insisted God still cared about them and was in control.

I feel pulled in two directions. Maybe this God is on the level and does love everyone, good or bad, the same. Could this be what I'm missing in my life? Money hasn't been the answer. Oh, it's nice to have, but it doesn't satisfy my longing deep inside. Naw, it can't be as simple as that. Just accept God's free gift, through His Son, they say. If I could see God, really see Him in person, then I'd know He is real. Maybe. . .maybe then I'd be ready to accept His free gift.

"Peter," Fred's voice broke into his thoughts. "Let's join the others for lunch. Ma's probably waiting on us."

The two young men walked side by side down the trail toward the house.

"Zack Turner thinks highly of you, Fred," Peter said. "It's a fact."

"Well, I think highly of him also. We've been good friends for a long time."

"I heard about what happened. . .how he stole your girl while you were at the war."

"That was two-sided, Peter. Becky Sue heard the news about my wounded leg." Fred moved his hand up and down, massaging his bad leg. "She was sure I was going to lose it. I guess she couldn't handle that."

"Didn't you hate Zack and Becky Sue for what they did? He'd be my enemy. I'd have gone after him and beat him to a pulp."

"Would that have solved anything, Peter?"

"No. . .but it would have given me a heap of satisfaction."

"I don't think it would in the long run. The Bible tells us to love our enemies and forgive them. What's to be gained by a fight? I'd have lost Zack's friendship. Anyway, they were already married, and that can't be changed."

"Would you change it now if you could?"

"I'm not in love with Becky Sue anymore. Maybe it was just an infatuation. Sometimes God changes our plans. But I know He works things out for the best."

"Your mind is on the schoolteacher now, isn't it? I understand you've been courting her."

"I wouldn't call it courting, Peter. We've gone for walks in the park, attended some band concerts and a few picnics. Hannah is a fine person. She's easy to talk to, and I'm comfortable around her."

"Sounds rather dull," Peter said. "Aren't there any sparks there?"

Frederic laughed. "Not the kind you mean. We're good friends who enjoy each other's company. Hannah suggested we keep our relationship on a strictly friendly basis, and that suited me fine. What about you, Peter? Is there a fair maiden who has caught your eye?"

Peter shrugged. "I'm not sure any lady would look kindly on attention from me. I'm just a nobody."

Frederic put an arm lightly around Peter's shoulder. "You're somebody very special to God, Peter. He likes you just the way you are."

"Maybe so," Peter mumbled. "Maybe so."

"Peter, I didn't want you to buy all those building supplies. You sure work your way around a fella, bringing them out on your own. Thanks. You're a good friend."

Peter's face brightened. "I knew you wouldn't accept any money. It's one way I can help."

The two friends entered the kitchen where the others were gathered for the noon meal. After a hearty lunch, the men were eager to resume work on finishing the inside of the cabin.

"Ya men will need ta quit work early," Ma said, "ta be ready fer the potluck supper at church tonight. Why don't ya come with us, Peter?"

"Naw, I've never been inside a church. I wouldn't know how to act."

"Just be yerself," Ma insisted. "It's a git-acquainted time for meetin' new people. Ya'd be more'n welcome, and they'd all make ya feel right at home."

The others urged Peter to join them, and he finally agreed. "Hope God won't be too surprised to see me in church," he quipped.

"I'll introduce you to Hannah," Frederic said. "You'll enjoy talking to her."

The men finished work on the cabin early so they could clean up for the church potluck. Peter met them at the church, somewhat ill at ease. "Do I look proper?" he asked Fred as they entered the building.

"You look fine."

"What do I say to people?"

"Don't worry about what to say. The folks here are all friendly. They'll do most of the talking. As Ma said, just be yourself."

Frederic introduced Peter to several people, then seated him across from Hannah at one of the tables. "This is my cousin, Peter McClough."

Hannah took up the conversation, as Frederic knew she would, and kept Peter's attention during the meal. After dinner, chairs were moved into a semi-circle and the group joined in a time of singing. Hannah seated herself between Peter and Frederic. "Peter," she said, turning to him, "you aren't singing."

"Naw, I can't sing," Peter said awkwardly. "I hoped no one would notice."

"Of course you can," Hannah said, handing him a songbook. She smiled and turned to the correct page. Peter felt drawn to this cultured and self-assured young woman. She was pretty, and her inner beauty drew him like a magnet. He looked over at Frederic, but Fred seemed intent on watching someone across the semicircle.

Peter turned to follow Fred's gaze and saw the young Collins girl. He had noticed glances passing between Fred and her during the meal. When she smiled at Fred, Peter watched emotion rise in his friend's face. *Frederic is completely unaware that Hannah and I are even here. He has eyes only for Sarah Collins. Could he be in love with her? Does he know how much his face reveals?*

These thoughts haunted Peter and kept him awake into the long hours of the night. "It seems Fred and Hannah really are just friends," he mumbled. "I wonder. . .I wonder if she would consider allowing me to call. When she looked at me, I thought she looked like she might like me."

He rolled over and pressed his face against the pillow. *And if someone like Hannah could like me, then maybe it's true what Frederic said about God. Maybe He really does like me just the way I am. . . .*

❧

The next day when he finished work, Peter strolled past the house where Hannah boarded. He was trying hard to appear casual, but his shoulders were stiff with tension. As he drew closer to the house, he saw that Hannah was seated on the porch, and he was filled with both relief and nervousness.

"Why, hello there," he called, hoping his voice sounded calm and friendly.

Hannah stood up and came to lean on the porch railing. "Hello, Peter. How nice to see you again so soon. Would you like to come sit down and have a glass of lemonade?"

"Sure sounds good," Peter said, smiling.

He climbed the porch steps and seated himself in one of the wooden rocking chairs that sat on the porch. Hannah went to get the lemonade and soon returned with a tall, cool glass. Peter took a long swallow. "Mmm. Thank you. This surely hits the spot after a long day's work."

"How do you like your work at the mill?"

"I'm enjoying it. It helps fill my time. I enjoy working with the men."

"Do you get lonely living in that big house by yourself?"

Peter leaned back in the chair. "Yes, I do." He looked at Hannah's face and saw the genuine interest in her eyes. "I never thought I would. When I came here, I was so filled up with angry feelings, I didn't think I'd need anything except money and a nice place to live. I thought finally not having to worry about money would be all I'd need to make me happy. I found out I was wrong." He clenched and unclenched his hands, ashamed to admit these things to the gentle, cultured Hannah; somehow, though, being honest with her seemed important.

"I've learned a lot from the Masons," he said after a moment. "I never met anyone like them before. I never had a family of my own, not who cared anything about me. My ma didn't amount to much, and I never knew my pa." He shot a glance at Hannah's face again, waiting to see a look of shocked withdrawal, but he read only sympathetic concern in her eyes. "I expected the Masons to hate me—after all, I'd taken their aunt's money from them. And I'd known Frederic during the war—he and I didn't get along, and it was my own fault, I have to confess. Something about him always seemed to rile me—I guess the way he always seemed so at peace with himself and with God. So I came here ready to fight the Masons."

Peter drained the last of his lemonade and set the glass down on the small table that stood between his chair and Hannah's. He shook his head. "Instead, they've welcomed me like I was really one of the family. They actually seem to like me."

Hannah smiled. "I can see why they do."

Peter felt his face flush. "I've never been somebody who people liked."

Hannah looked away from his face for a moment. "I think," she said after a moment, "that we all need people to accept us just the way we are. And then we become likable even if we weren't before. Maybe you were so angry inside—and so unpleasant outside—because you'd never met people who just liked you as you were."

Peter leaned toward her. "Funny, Frederic was saying something like that to me the other day. Only he was talking about. . ." Peter cleared his throat nervously. "He was talking about God."

Hannah smiled. "God loves us just the way we are. Sometimes I find that hard to believe—"

"You do?" Peter asked, surprised that this lovely and composed woman would ever have feelings of doubt.

Hannah nodded. "But He really does love us." She reached across the space between them and quickly, gently touched his hand. "He really does love you."

Peter felt the warmth of her brief touch linger on his hand. *Maybe, just maybe, you don't have to see God to know He loves you,* he thought. *Maybe you can see His love through other people. People like the Masons. And like Hannah.*

Peter cleared his throat. "Uh, Hannah?"

"Yes?"

"Could I call on you again. . .sometime soon?"

"I'd like that, Peter. I'd like that very much."

Chapter 33

In early October, the Masons invited the Collins family, Robert Harris, and Peter McClough for a harvest dinner. Becky Sue and Zack were invited, too, but they were unable to attend because their young baby had a cold. Cassie had especially looked forward to holding the little one. "What a disappointment," she said. "I wanted to cuddle little Zack. He's such a sweet baby."

"You'll soon be cuddling your own, Cassie," Emily exclaimed. "Only a couple months to go."

"We can hardly wait," Bill commented. "It will change our lives having a little one in the house."

"I plan to spoil him," Emily said saucily.

"Or spoil her, don't you mean?" Robert asked.

"Whichever," Emily sighed in anticipation. "He or she will be spoiled by their aunt Emily, that's for certain."

While the others discussed the coming baby, Frederic watched Sarah's face. Was she avoiding him? he wondered; she seemed to be looking everywhere except at him. He hadn't talked to her in a long time now, not since that day when she had offered to help him with the fence post and he had longed so badly to take her in his arms. Had he frightened her away? Or was she busy with a beau, someone her own age?

For weeks now, Frederic had been unable to put Sarah out of his mind. She filled his thoughts day and night, and finally he had been forced to admit to himself that despite the difference in their ages, he had fallen in love with her. Lately, instead of lying awake tormenting himself with fears and hopeless longing, he had been praying about his feelings for Sarah. Now he had finally reached a feeling of peace. And he was pretty certain he knew what God wanted him to do.

He smiled to himself just as Sarah's eyes turned toward him. Their gazes caught and held, and he watched her cheeks flush. He leaned across the table toward her and said softly, "Let's go for a walk after dinner, Sarah. It's a nice day for one."

"Yes, it is, Frederic," she said breathlessly, the color rising still higher in her cheeks. "A walk would be fine." Excitement built within her until she picked at her food, barely able to swallow.

After dinner Frederic nodded to her, put his finger to his lips, and jerked his head toward the door.

"I'll go get my wrap," she said quietly, "and meet you outside."

Frederic was limping toward the back land when she caught up with him a few minutes later. The fall day was sunny with a cool nip in the air. The trees were brilliantly arrayed in their full panorama of color. Some of the leaves fluttered down, forming a carpet on the ground that crunched under their feet as they walked.

"What a glorious day, Frederic. I guess fall is my favorite time of the year."

"Mine, too," Frederic said thoughtfully, taking a long sideways glance at his companion. Her cheeks were flushed, and her curly red gold tresses bounced around her shoulders as she walked. Frederic could feel his heart thumping wildly within his chest.

"Pa's been telling me about your cabin," Sarah said. "Pa says it's big and mighty nice."

"I think so," Frederic agreed. "Would you like to see it? It's just over this hill and down by the creek."

Sarah clapped her hands in delight. "Oh yes, I would. . .very much."

They came to the clearing in a grove of pines where the cabin nestled. Sarah took a deep breath. "What a beautiful cabin, Frederic. There's something special about a log home. And I love the smell of new wood."

"The porch overlooks the back pasture and also the creek," Frederic said, excitement rising in his voice. "And the sunsets. . .well, they are magnificent."

Sarah stood on the porch, dreamily gazing at the landscape.

"Come inside, Sarah," Frederic called, "and see the layout of the rooms. Everything is finished except for the furnishings."

Sarah walked through the house quietly, taking it all in. Suddenly her voice became sad. "I guess this is the house you planned for Becky Sue. . . ." A little sob caught in her throat, and she looked away. "It's just too bad. . ." Her voice trailed off.

"Long ago I did plan on building this house for Becky Sue," Frederic said seriously. "But instead, I built this house with someone else in mind."

Sarah Jane turned to him with tears filling her eyes. "So you do plan to get married then? We've all been wondering about that—why you'd build a place of your own!" Her voice broke, and she struggled to go on. "The talk about you and Miss Ragsdale must be true. Everyone says you two are going to be married. I know you've been courting her these past months." She turned abruptly and ran out of the house and blindly down the path.

"Wait, Sarah Jane!" Frederic called as he limped after her. "Wait!"

Sarah kept running, choking back her tears, leaving Frederic far behind.

"It's for you, Sarah Jane," he called loudly, and his words echoed across the valley. "I built the cabin for you!"

Instantly she halted, then turned and ran back to him. She put her hands on her hips and stared at him, her red gold curls blowing in the wind. "What are you talking about, Frederic Mason?" Her voice trembled.

He took a step closer to her. "I'm talking about wanting to marry you, Sarah

Jane Collins." His voice was soft and husky. "I know maybe I waited too long to realize how I felt about you. And then I had to get up my courage to talk to you. By now you've probably found someone your own age, someone who's made you realize—"

Sarah reached out a small fist and thumped his chest. "Will you be quiet? You're the only one I want, the only one I've ever wanted. . . ." Her voice faltered, and she blinked tears out of her eyes, then grinned mischievously and added, "Even if you are old enough to be my grandfather. Or you'd think so from the way you talk."

He reached out, took her in his arms, and held her close against his chest. "I've wanted to do this for a long time," he whispered against her hair.

She pulled away and looked up at him. Her face, streaked with tears, wore a brilliant smile. "You really built the cabin for me?" she asked breathlessly. Her violet blue eyes searched his.

"For you, my darling," he said huskily, drawing her close once more. He gently kissed her tear-stained face. "I love you, Sarah Jane. I want you to marry me. Will you?"

He saw her answer in her eyes, and then his lips met hers. After a long moment, they turned back toward the cabin, and hand in hand, they walked through it once more.

Frederic took a deep breath, hardly daring to believe Sarah's hand was really in his. He remembered the long, hard days during the war, and then the pain, both physical and emotional, that had followed. The war was over, though; God had brought him safely through all the danger and pain.

And now at last, God had given him this home of his own to share with Sarah. Together they would build their own haven of peace.

A Time to Love

Chapter 1

1867

"Why, Robert? Why must you go? It isn't fair to ask you to leave." Emily Mason's clear blue eyes clouded. She pushed back straying wisps of dark, curly hair as she searched Robert's face. "Why is the church board sending you to start a mission church in some faraway place?"

Robert Harris, the young pastor at the Community Church in Waterville, Maine, had been courting Emily for some time. He stood tall and strong, with sandy hair. His serious green eyes took in Emily's beauty. Her creamy complexion against the dark ringlets, wide blue eyes, and full red lips always caused him to catch his breath. "Dearest Emily," he said huskily, "it will only be for one year. It's to a remote area in another state where there is no church now. They need someone to actually start a work from scratch and build it up by visiting people and inviting them to come for services. After one year, the work could be turned over to another pastor and I could return to my church in Waterville—if I desired to do so."

"If you desired?" Emily's full lips were pouting now. "Of course you would want to come back! Waterville is your home. You've said many times you love it here."

"I do love it here, and it would be my choice to return, darling. But I've been told that many times pastors want to stay on and nurture the flock they started. It's hard to leave a newborn church to someone else when you've seen it planted with seeds that spring forth into everlasting life."

Emily reached up and touched Robert's serious face. There was a special light in his eyes as he talked of building the mission church. Robert took her small hand in his and led her toward the sofa. "Don't you see what a tremendous opportunity this is for me, Emily?" His voice held an air of excitement, and he smiled his endearing lopsided grin. "I will be like a pilgrim, in a new area, reaching out to those who need God."

"Oh, Robert," Emily cried, laying her head on his shoulder. "I don't want you to go. I would miss you too much. Can't they send someone else? You are needed here in Waterville. I need you. The church people need you."

"There are people in remote areas who are spiritually hungry. They don't know our God as we do. And if they do know Him, they have no fellowship or opportunity to grow in the Christian faith. Because I'm single, I can devote all my time to such a project."

"What will we do for a pastor here in Waterville? Have you thought about that?" Tears gathered in the corners of her eyes and began to trickle down her cheeks.

Robert turned her face toward him and gently kissed away the tears. "Don't cry, dear Emily," he whispered against her dark hair. "I would never leave the people here without a pastor. Rev. Davis, your former pastor, has agreed to return for one year, while I go. If I decide to stay on after the one year, the board will find a permanent replacement for me at that time. The folks here all think highly of Pastor and Mrs. Davis and will welcome their return. They are looking forward to it. This arrangement will work out fine for everyone concerned."

Emily sat upright. She and Robert were sitting in the parlor of the Bradford home. Louisa Bradford was Emily's best friend, and she and Louisa were enrolled in the winter term at Colby College. Since the Mason farm was about four miles outside of town, Emily stayed with the Bradfords during the week. Her older brother, Frederic, picked her up on Fridays and took her home to the farm. Each Monday morning he brought her back to Colby College. The Bradfords were generous people and happy to share their large home with Emily. Louisa, an only child, was delighted with this arrangement, and Emily was happy here. Her face clouded now, though, as she realized how much of her happiness stemmed from Robert's companionship.

She sighed. "The Davises are wonderful folk, Robert, and everyone will love seeing them again. But you are our pastor now. The people have faith in you and appreciate your fine preaching of the Word. Don't you think you are letting them down?"

Robert's face had a special glow, and he spoke in a determined voice. "I can't let people interfere with my calling from God. If He wants me to go, I must be obedient. My commitment is to the Lord."

"What about me, Robert?" Emily pouted. "Don't you care how I feel? Don't you care that you are letting me down? You told me once our courtship needed time to grow. How can it grow if you are far away in another state?"

Robert drew her close. "I love you, Emily," he said with emotion. "You are all I want in a woman. But God must come first in my life and yours. This is most important. When I first came to Waterville, my first pastorate, I promised God I would be open to His leading. He is calling me now to this new ministry in another state somewhere. I will not break my promise. Please understand, my dearest."

"I don't understand," she sobbed. "I know God must come first in our lives. . . but why is He taking you away from me? Why must we be separated when we love each other? Why can't you stay here?"

"God isn't taking me away from you. You will be in my thoughts every day and every night. You will give me hope to go on—knowing we will have our time to love in the future. If I know you are here waiting for me, I can bear all things. There may be some hardships in the new work I am called to do. We can talk to one another through letters as we send our love and encouragement. I will write of my work, the people, and their problems. Hopefully God will bless my work, and I can tell you about lives being changed and folk growing in their Christian faith. You can write me about your courses at Colby, your family, the church folk, and all you are involved in here. I will want to know all you are doing so I can pretend I am with you. We can pray for one another and seek God's will. He will give peace to our hearts in the times of loneliness. The days will go fast for us, Emily."

"When will you know for sure, Robert? Have they given you a date yet? And what state will it be? Will it be far away?"

"I don't know all the details as yet. The arrangements are still being confirmed. There are many needy areas, and the board considers all the possibilities before making a decision. But if nothing interferes, I will probably leave in April."

Emily gasped. "It's January now! That's only three months away. Why so soon? But perhaps the arrangements will fall through, Robert. Maybe God will change His plans. Maybe you won't have to go after all."

"Your studies will keep you so busy," Robert teased, running his fingers through her dark tresses, "that I hope you find time to write. Remember last year when you first started college? You were so caught up in your classes—especially Shakespeare. You spent most of your extra time telling me about your courses and how wonderful it was to be getting higher education. It was gracious of your aunt Maude to pay for your schooling."

Emily sat quietly thinking about her aunt for a few minutes with her head resting on Robert's shoulder. "Aunt Maude didn't want me to drop out to nurse her when she got so sick, bless her heart," Emily murmured. "Remember how she scolded me for quitting my classes? It was my own choice, though, and I know it was the right one. I'd never have forgiven myself if I'd neglected caring for her when she was so ill. It was the least I could do."

"You were such a comfort to her, Emily. With her husband dead and no children of her own, your family was her whole life."

"When she died, I was bitter. God didn't answer my prayers for her recovery, so I turned my back on Him. I was a miserable creature, Robert, until you counseled me and helped me see the error of my ways. I'm a stronger Christian now because of the grievous time." She looked sideways at Robert, and the tears filled her eyes once again. "And now I'm to have another trial. . .another test of my faith," she whispered brokenly. "If God takes you away from me to some faraway place, I'll be devastated. I'm not sure I'm strong enough to bear a long separation." Emily clung to him in a last appeal as she buried her head against his chest.

Robert bit his lip as he held Emily close, and his face tightened. He loved this young woman. Her presence filled him with joy, and part of his heart longed to stay in Waterville so they could be married soon. But his heart also yearned to follow his God, and God was leading him to parts unknown to establish a work in His name. *God's will must come first in my life. He has promised in Romans 8:28 that "all things work together for good to them that love God, to them who are the called according to his purpose." I will never be truly happy unless I put God first.*

Robert sighed deeply as he stood up and pulled Emily up with him. She trembled and sobbed quietly against his chest as he held her close. Tears caught on her eyelashes and coursed down her cheeks. His strong arms closed around her. "Please don't cry, darling. Our love for one another will see us through separation. I hope to come back for short visits during the year. That will be something we have to look forward to."

"I hope you won't have to go," Emily murmured as she clung to him. "I'm going to pray that God will change His mind. I need you here, dear Robert. I need you close to me."

Robert finally said good-bye and left the Bradford home, bundled warmly against the January chill. Snow was falling lightly, dusting the roadways. He took deep breaths of the fresh, pure air and walked briskly toward the parsonage. *What a glorious night. The Creator is in this place and sprinkling His world with His beauty. Oh, dear God, help Emily to understand that I must follow wherever You lead me.*

The Bradford house was quiet as Emily climbed the stairs to her room. Louisa and her parents had already retired. Her throat ached as she flung herself, fully clothed, headlong on her bed. Louisa heard her sobbing quietly long into the night and wondered what ill wind had caused such heartache to her dear friend.

Chapter 2

The following day Emily confided her heartache to Louisa on the way to their college classes. "Robert doesn't seem to care about my feelings," she moaned. "We'll be apart for an entire year."

"I know you'll miss him dreadfully," Louisa said, trying to comfort her friend. "But if Robert is coming back a few times during the year, that should help. He does love you very much—I can tell. Has he said anything about marriage?"

"Not definitely. Robert is such a serious-minded young man. He wants to give our relationship more time. He feels I need more time to be certain of my love for him. But I do love him, Louisa."

"Of course you do," Louisa agreed as they climbed the steps to Colby College. The cold January wind had whipped blazing color into their cheeks. "Perhaps Robert believes true love will stand the test of separation."

"That is exactly what he believes," Emily said as she stamped the snow from her boots. "And he may not be convinced I would make a good minister's wife. Sometimes I wonder about that myself."

"How do you like your Introduction to Shakespeare class?" Louisa asked, changing the subject. "The new teacher, Dr. Matthews, is. . .interesting. . .don't you think? I have him for an advanced Shakespeare class in the afternoon. I must admit it's my favorite class."

Emily glanced sideways at her friend and noticed the sudden spark of interest on her face. "I didn't think you cared much for Shakespeare," Emily said teasingly. "Could it be the new teacher, Dr. Matthews, who has made the class so tolerable?"

Louisa's cheeks were pink from the cold, but underneath she could feel the color rising. "You are a tease, Emily," she said. "I have to hurry to my history class, or I'll never make it. Can we meet at noon for lunch?"

"I'll meet you at the cloakroom," Emily called as she waved and headed up the stairs toward her Shakespeare class. Taking her seat near the front, Emily looked keenly at Dr. Matthews, as if for the first time. *I can understand Louisa being attracted to him. He has a manly look about him and an interesting face. I wonder how old he is.*

As the classroom filled, Dr. Matthews stood up and leaned casually against his desk. He ran his fingers through his thick dark hair, then removed his glasses and slid them into his coat pocket. The class hour flew by as he lectured on his subject, holding his pupils' attention. As he dismissed the class, he added, "Miss Emily Mason,

123

please stop by my desk for a moment."

Emily's heart thudded as she shuffled her papers and gathered her books. As she approached Dr. Matthews's desk, she hesitated. When he did not look up, she cleared her throat. "You wanted to see me, Dr. Matthews? Is anything wrong?"

Dr. Matthews grinned, and Emily noticed that his dark brown eyes crinkled in the corners. "Not at all, Miss Mason. I just noticed you took this class last year with Mr. Lambert, who has taken another college position. Then you dropped it after a short time. Did you dislike the course?"

"Oh no, sir!" Emily said emphatically. "It was my favorite class, and I love Shakespeare. There were other problems." She proceeded to tell him briefly of her aunt's illness. "I needed to stay with my aunt and care for her. After she died, I went through a difficult time and had no heart to return. . .and no funds until now."

Dr. Matthews's dark eyes searched hers. "I'm sorry about your aunt," he said soberly. "And I am glad you decided to return."

Emily smiled, blushing slightly. "So am I. I do enjoy the class."

Emily and Louisa didn't have an opportunity to talk until later that evening. They had met only briefly for lunch before hurrying to their next classes. Now Emily noticed an air of excitement about her friend. "So what is happening, my friend? Tell me about it."

"This has to be confidential, Emily," Louisa said. "My parents would be upset if they knew I had eyes for one of the professors—someone they don't even know. You know how strict they are."

"I won't breathe a word—on my honor."

"Well, I know Betty who works in the registrar's office. She could tell I was interested in Dr. Matthews, although I tried to appear nonchalant. Betty showed me some papers as a favor. Emily. . .he's not married!" Louisa whirled around the room several times and fell breathlessly on the bed.

"How old is he?" Emily asked.

"He's thirty. But a young thirty, don't you think?"

"That's more than ten years your senior. What would your parents think?"

Louisa shrugged. "Listen to us go on. We're talking as though I was dating Dr. Matthews. His name is James, by the way. Dr. and Mrs. James Matthews. It has a nice sound to it, don't you agree?" Louisa stood up and curtsied. "Please say good evening to Dr. and Mrs. James Matthews." She laughed and fell backwards on the bed. Her mood was infectious, and soon the two girls were giggling uncontrollably.

When Emily could calm herself, she said, "Louisa, you don't know anything about Dr. Matthews's background or his beliefs."

"He's so kind, Emily, and good-looking. He inspires me to study hard and get good grades. I've never studied more in my life. I know my parents are happy to see me striving to achieve."

"Dr. Matthews has many fine points, Louisa. But you've neglected to consider the most important thing about his character. We don't know if he is a believer. He may not love our God as we do."

Louisa's face was downcast. "I know you're right, but I can't help being interested in him. Since the terrible war between the North and South, there aren't many available men left because so many were killed on the battlefields. Or if they did come back, they have wives or sweethearts. You have Robert, Emily. I would like to have a relationship like that."

"I know someone who is available," Emily suggested. "What about Peter McClough?"

"That raucous, uncouth individual!" Louisa cried. "I know he is your cousin, Emily, but he is very crude."

"Peter is a different person," Emily said. "That young man has done a complete turnaround. Some of Uncle George's fine traits have risen to the surface in the last few months."

"I remember him as self-centered, bitter, outspoken, and greedy when he came to town last year. I doubt he will ever really change."

Emily shook her head. "You know, Louisa, Peter never knew his father, Uncle George, who was married to my aunt Maude. But until his death, Uncle George supported Peter. Peter's mother was a very immoral woman. She neglected him and brought him up to believe his father was dead. His mother drank up the support money, had numerous men friends, and treated Peter as though he was in the way. As soon as Peter was old enough, he left home and entered the army, sending support to his mother until her death."

"He certainly had a miserable background," Louisa commented. "I know he has been generous to you, paying for your schooling."

"Uncle George left everything to Aunt Maude, with the stipulation all would go to his son, Peter, upon Maude's death. George's lawyer located Peter, and Peter got the house and all the money. Our family doesn't care about the money. We've been trying to show Peter love and concern, something he's never had."

"I'm sure that caused him to furnish the funds for your schooling, Emily, since your aunt Maude wanted you to complete your education."

"My parents didn't want me to take the money at first. They don't think women need further education. I had a time convincing them. It's something I've always wanted. They also knew Aunt Maude wanted me to have the opportunity. So when Peter insisted, they agreed."

"Well, maybe Peter does have one good quality," Louisa admitted. "But he can't compare with Dr. Matthews. Peter McClough is no gentleman!"

Chapter 3

Emily eagerly anticipated her return to the Mason farm each weekend. She loved the old homestead, built long before by her grandfather for his bride. The white clapboard, two-story home sat back a piece from the road, on a little hill overlooking the surrounding property. The Masons were farmers, and the hundred acres contained fertile soil for planting crops and expansive meadows for the cattle and horses to graze. At one side the land sloped down to a creek, and farther back the woods beckoned with its winding trails. Her grandma had died a few years earlier, while her brother, Frederic, had served with the Union forces during the Civil War.

Robert's news about leaving had been very unsettling, and most of the week Emily did not have her mind on her studies. She fretted and fumed, then scolded herself for doing so. When Frederic arrived on Friday to take her home, she climbed nimbly into the sleigh and pulled wool blankets snugly around her to ward off the chill. She welcomed the brisk breeze that fanned her cheeks and the lightly falling snow that covered the ground with a clean carpet of pure white. As they moved outside the town, the rolling wooded countryside closed around them.

"It's so beautiful, Fred." She sighed. "I miss the beauty of the outdoors when I'm in town all week at classes. Laddie, our collie, and all the farm animals—how I miss them!"

Frederic glanced at his sister as she snuggled against him to keep warm. He had the same dark, curly hair and bright blue eyes. During the war he had grown a mustache on his upper lip, which gave him a ruggedly handsome look. "It's Cassie's time," Frederic said soberly. "Ma said I should take you directly to Cassie's."

Emily jerked upright. Her sister, Cassie, wed to Bill Collins, lived near her family's farm in a little cabin on the Collinses' property. Their first child, expected around Christmas, was two weeks past due. "Is everything all right?" Emily asked. "Is the baby coming?"

"There are problems," Fred said grimly. "Cassie has been in labor since last night, and the baby is coming breech."

"Oh no," Emily cried. "Is the doctor there?"

"I picked him up this morning. The midwife came last night. Bill went after her at the first sign of labor. She left after Doc Sanborn arrived—nothing more she could do."

Frantically Emily prayed under her breath for her sister's life and the baby's. "Can't we go any faster, Fred?" she pleaded.

"Not safely on these snow-packed roads, Emily. There are too many hills and turns. The horses could lose their footing. Can't take the risk."

The soft falling snow added a glaze to the already slippery country lane. Emily knew her brother would do his utmost to get them safely to their destination. She had grown up relying on the wisdom of her older brother. He would not fail her now.

The cabin was well lit with kerosene lanterns when they arrived, and Emily hurried into the house while Fred unhitched the horses. Emily's mother, Mary Jane Mason, and Mrs. Collins were busy in the kitchen, boiling water and making other preparations for the birth. Mrs. Mason hurried to her daughter's side and gave her a warm hug. "Do what ya can ta help, dear. I need ta go back ta Cassie and be there iffen the doctor needs anythin'."

Emily could hear Cassie's soft moans in the back bedroom, and fear gripped her heart. Bill Collins sat, his clothing in disarray, his head in his hands. "Bill, are you all right?" Emily asked.

He looked up at her, his unshaven face haggard and gaunt, while tears streamed down his cheeks and splashed on his wool shirt. "It's Cassie," he choked. "I don't want to lose her. She's been suffering so long."

Emily wanted to scream, but she made herself affect calmness for Bill's sake. She sat beside him on the sofa and took his hand in hers. "Bill, she's going to be all right. Babies are born every day. Dr. Sanborn is with her and doing his best. I know you've all been praying. Let's you and I pray right now."

"I can't, Emily," he whispered hoarsely and covered his face again. "You pray for us both."

By that time Frederic had joined them, and the three of them slid to their knees on the hard pine floor. Amid Bill's choked and broken sobs, Emily, then Fred, prayed for Cassie's and the baby's lives to be spared, according to God's will.

The doctor came to the bedroom door, frowning and wiping his brow. "Bring more boiling water," he ordered. "I need to keep my instruments sterile and clean."

Emily ran to get a kettle boiling on the woodstove, while Bill rushed to the doctor's side. "Is Cassie all right, Doctor?" he muttered. "Is my wife going to live?"

Doctor Sanborn patted Bill's shoulder and spoke kindly. "Yes, son. Cassie is having a difficult time, but she'll make it." He hesitated, his brows knitted together deep in thought. "I'm—I'm not sure about the child. I'll do all I can."

Bill's face constricted in pain as Fred placed an arm around his shoulders and led him back to the sofa. "They are in God's hands, Bill," he whispered. "We must commit them to Him."

Bill's voice was broken and halted. "The baby—might—die, Fred. We won't—be able—to bear it. Cassie—has waited—so long for this day. It will—break her heart."

"Don't even think about it, Bill. It hasn't happened. And we know God is able to save the baby. Nothing is too hard for Him."

Frederic didn't want to think about death. He'd seen too much of it during his days as a captain of the Union forces during the Civil War. His best friend died pitifully in his arms. He himself was wounded in the right thigh at Appomattox Court House, on the last day of the war. One of the balls fired at him remained in his leg and had caused it to shorten. Although the pain was gone, he was left with a limp. It was a constant reminder of the death, bloodshed, and horror so prevalent during the war between the North and South. Absentmindedly, he massaged his right leg.

Mrs. Collins appeared from the kitchen with a tray of food. "Try and eat somethin'," she coaxed. "It's jest a light supper, and ya need ta keep up yer strength." They mumbled their thanks, but they had no heart for food and left most of it untouched. Bill paced the floor, wringing his hands and wiping his eyes. Each watched the bedroom door for any signs of activity. At last, late into the night, Emily dozed off, her head resting on Fred's shoulder.

Suddenly there was a commotion in the back room, and instantly all were alert. Cassie's moans grew in intensity, and her cries brought them to their feet. "Praise God, the baby must be finally comin'," Mrs. Collins whispered. There was a long period of silence while they looked fearfully at one another, not daring to speak. Bill's face was grief stricken. "Maybe the baby didn't make it," he choked.

Then they heard it, a loud slap and a faint cry, which grew into a strong wail. "The baby's alive!" Bill shouted. Tears flowed freely as they gratefully clasped one another.

After several minutes, Mrs. Mason came out with a tiny bundle, wrapped snugly in several blankets. "Thank God, ya have a healthy little girl, Bill. This little one had a mite of a struggle bein' born; thet's why the redness and marks on her little face. But thet'll be gone in jest a few days." She held the tiny bundle out to him. "Would ya like ta hold yer daughter? She wants to meet her daddy."

Hesitant at first, Bill reached awkwardly for his warmly wrapped little girl and held her close. "Cassie?" he asked. "How is Cassie?"

"She's plumb tired from the long labor, and she lost a lot of blood. She is somewhat groggy from the whole ordeal. Outside of thet, she is fine and anxious ta see ya. As soon as Dr. Sanborn comes out, ya can go ta her."

Bill pulled the blanket back so everyone could see the baby. The small head was covered with wisps of red gold hair. Her dark blue eyes were opened wide, and she had her tiny fist in her mouth, sucking.

"She has reddish hair like yours, Bill, and like your sister Sarah's," Emily said. "What a precious baby!"

"A miracle from God," Fred added as he smiled fondly at his little niece.

Bill Collins gazed at his newborn daughter with a look of awe. "She truly is a miracle, Fred. She's our miracle baby."

Before he left, Dr. Sanborn took Bill aside. "Cassie had a far more difficult time than expected. It would be unwise for her, in the future, to have another child. In fact, son, it would be detrimental to her health and possibly a matter of her life. She must be told, sometime in the future, because this is a very serious matter."

With the doctor's words weighing heavily upon his mind, Bill took his baby daughter into the bedroom and laid her in his wife's arms. Then he leaned over and kissed Cassie. "Thank you, darling, for our beautiful little girl. I love you both very much."

Cassie's eyes fluttered under a sudden rush of tears. She reached out to her husband and gently touched his cheek. "Are you disappointed, Bill? Are you sorry we didn't have a boy?"

"Not at all, Cassie. Our daughter is perfect. I'm so thankful both my girls are alive and well. As far as I'm concerned, our family is now complete."

Cassie glanced lovingly at the little bundle lying beside her. The baby wiggled, stretched her little arms, and yawned.

"I think my two girls need to sleep now," Bill said. "It's been very tiring for both of you."

Tenderly Cassie placed their daughter in the handmade pine cradle next to her bed. "Welcome to our family, Rebeccah Ann Collins," she said. "You are a precious gift from God. Maybe someday you will have a little brother to play with."

Bill kissed Cassie gently once again and quietly left the room. His heart was filled with thanksgiving for the graciousness of God. "How can I tell Cassie, Lord?" he muttered under his breath. "How can I tell her that she must never have another child?" He shrugged his shoulders and decided he would not rush to tell Cassie. Time enough for that in the future. Today was a day for joy and thanksgiving, not for sorrow.

Chapter 4

The Maine winters were usually hard and long, and this one was no exception. The snow sifted and swirled, completely covering the stone and rail fences. Winds from the northeast blasted across the hills and valleys, plugging the roadways. Frederic dug paths to the woodpile, barn, and outbuildings. The tunnel-like paths through the deep snow would invariably cave in and need to be shoveled out again and again. The animals in the barn were well fed, safe, and contented, but the birds and wildlife found it difficult to find food. Scraps and seeds were placed in various locations so they could endure the cold blasts of winter.

Time passed swiftly for Emily. The days seemed to hurry by, and each weekend, regardless of the weather, she was anxious to return to the farm. Robert called on Emily two evenings a week at the Bradford home and began picking her up on Fridays to take her back home. It gave them more time to be alone together and talk.

Robert had received his assignment from the board to raise up a mission church in Wampum, Pennsylvania. It was wilderness country, named after an Indian chief in the early pioneer days. The rolling countryside proved rich and fertile and was settled by farmers. In the 1860s, industry had found its way into the area. Coal mining, limestone quarries, sandstone quarries, and cement plants lured farmers from their fields to a more profitable involvement. Families lived far apart, some on hundreds of acres that included small rivers or springs.

Emily smiled cheerily as she climbed into Robert's sleigh one Friday afternoon. She felt warm and secure when they were together, although Robert's departure date was ever present in her mind. "Time is going by so fast, Robert, and in April you plan to leave," Emily cried. "Why must you go so soon?"

"The arrangements have all been made, Emily. The folk in Wampum are eager for me to come, and I look forward to the challenge God has for me."

"Where will you live? Is there a house for you in Pennsylvania?"

"I'll be living with Thomas Whan and his family. They live in a large log home one mile south of Wampum on three hundred acres of land. There is an abundance of wild game on the property, and I understand fish are plentiful in Big Beaver Run, just one mile away. Three other families besides the Whans are hungry for God's Word. They meet now in homes for times of Bible study. We've been given permission to use the schoolhouse for Sunday services until a church can be built in the future."

"You won't be there that long, Robert. It will take your entire year to build up a congregation. Then you'll be coming home. . .back to Waterville, and me."

"It probably will take the full year to bring the folk in, Emily. I'm trusting God will bless the work He has called me to do and show me His will for the future."

"For our future, Robert," she said, snuggling close to him. "And it's right here in Waterville, where we belong. I'll be so glad when your year in Pennsylvania is over."

Robert smiled and kissed her lightly on the cheek. Her face radiated a rosy glow from the cold, sharp air, and little snowflakes formed on her hair and eyelashes. "You are so beautiful, darling," he whispered against her dark hair. "I wish we could be married now so you could go with me."

Emily squealed in delight. "Why not, Robert? Why can't we be married now?"

Robert's voice took a serious tone. "You can't leave college in midsemester again, young lady. And anyway, I was given this opportunity because I was alone. They didn't want a married man. There is no place to live for a couple or a family. Although their house is large, the Whans have several children. It was determined a single person would be more dedicated to the work at hand, since he would have no distractions."

"Do I distract you, Robert?" Emily teased saucily, looking deep into his green eyes. She playfully tousled a lock of sandy hair.

"You know you do," he said huskily. "You caught me in your web long ago!"

"Robert!" she protested. "How can you say that?"

"It was inevitable." He laughed. "Actually, I was caught unbeknownst to you. And I'm not trying to get out of your web, Emily. It's the kind of entanglement I relish, as long as it's with you."

"Then how can you leave me for an entire year?" she demanded. "Maybe you'll meet someone else. . .some beautiful girl in Pennsylvania. Maybe you'll forget me."

"Not a chance," Robert said seriously. "It is going to be hard leaving you, but it's something I must do before we get married. We'll have our entire lives together, darling. Our own desires must be overruled. God wants me to go to Pennsylvania alone, of that I am certain. But a time for love lies ahead of us, when you and I become man and wife. Can you understand? My reason for going is to follow God's will for my life."

"I'm not happy about you going away, Robert," she said, pouting. "But I will try my best to be gracious about it. It's hard to understand what God is trying to do, but I won't ask Him why." She sighed. "I've learned that much at least."

The following day, a Saturday, Emily spent much of her time helping her sister with the baby. Cassie's strength was not back to normal, and she tired easily from the late-night feedings. Her face was pale and drawn as she greeted Emily. "You are a cheery sight, Emily. Come in by the fire and get warm."

"How is that precious little niece of mine?" Emily demanded. "Her aunt Emily wants to hold her."

"She's a good baby and sleeping more all the time." Cassie untied her apron and flung it over a chair. Pushing back locks of stray chestnut hair, she steered Emily toward the sofa.

"Cassie, you look so tired. You rest and let me do some chores for you. What needs to be done?"

"Everything's under control, and Rebeccah is asleep at the moment. Let's sit by the fire and have some tea. I had the kettle on for just such a treat. It will warm us up, and I'll feel better after relaxing a bit." Deftly Cassie poured tea from her blue china teapot into two china teacups. "This was Grandma's set, do you remember? Gramps gave it to me when Bill and I got married."

"It's lovely. . .and yes, I do remember it, Cassie. Grandma used to pour cups of weak tea for us when we were little girls, and we had tea parties with her. Those days were so much fun. It was sweet of you to name Rebeccah after Gram."

"I'm glad Bill was agreeable to the name. He's been such a help to me, Emily, since the baby came. He adores her. Everyone has helped so much. I'm getting spoiled. Ma and Mother Collins do laundry and bring in food. And Bill's sister Sarah comes over whenever she can and lends a hand. I'm afraid Rebeccah has many people to spoil her."

"Can't spoil new babies, Cassie. They need lots of loving and cuddling. It's when they get a little older that we'll have to be on guard. We don't want her to be ornery like I was."

Cassie laughed and hugged her younger sister affectionately. "So how is my sister the student doing these days? And tell me about Robert. Is he really going away for a year?"

Emily's face clouded. "Yes, for an entire year. He's going to some place in Pennsylvania to start a mission church. He will live with a family while he visits people and invites them to meet for services. The church will meet in the school-house for the time being, until funds can be raised for a separate building. The job opportunity is for a single man, Robert says, one who doesn't have a wife or family to distract him from his work."

"You sound a little cynical, Emily. Don't you want him to go, when the Lord is leading him to this place? He is a pastor, you know. Often they are called to different places."

"I know." Emily sighed. "It just isn't my choice to have Robert so far away in another state. But I'll keep busy with my studies—and seeing Rebeccah whenever I get a chance."

Just then they heard a familiar fussing coming from the handmade pine cradle. Emily jumped up and ran to get the baby, returning with her held snugly in her arms. "She must know her aunt Emily." She gazed fondly at the baby. "As soon as I picked her up, she stopped crying."

"Did you know Robert made a call on us awhile back? He knew I wasn't able to get out for services yet, and he wanted to see Rebeccah. It was sweet the way he held her. He didn't seem a bit nervous. I think he will make a fine father someday."

Emily blushed. "I think so, too." She looked away, and Cassie noticed a small tear slide out of the corner of her eye. "Robert hints at marriage, but he's never really asked me. I think he wants me to grow up a little."

"Tell me about your classes," Cassie said cheerily, changing the subject. "Do you like being back with your nose to the grindstone? Are you and Louisa studying hard?"

Emily talked for some time about her various classes and how much she enjoyed the course and her professors. "And Louisa is infatuated with the new Shakespeare teacher, Dr. Matthews. I have him for my Introduction to Shakespeare class, but she's in his advanced class. She talks about him constantly."

"Is he interested in her?"

"She says it's strictly teacher and student at the moment. But she loves the class, and I've never seen her work so hard at anything. Her parents don't know about her interest in Dr. Matthews, but they are pleased she is taking the course so seriously."

"Is he young. . .good-looking. . .single?"

"Yes, on all three. He's a very warm and friendly person. I can understand why she is attracted to him."

"You do make him sound interesting," Cassie said, reaching for Rebeccah, who was beginning to fuss and needed to nurse. "But what about Peter? He's changed so much. Does Louisa seem at all interested in him?"

"No. She has a real problem with his background. She still sees Peter as the rather crude person he was in the beginning. He's really cleaned up his life on the outside. . .but his heart is not changed. Peter McClough needs the Lord."

Chapter 5

Frederic labored tirelessly the entire winter making pine furniture for his log home, built on the Mason property. He had been given a chunk of land back in the woods on a little knoll overlooking the creek. It was his favorite spot, and he and his sisters had spent many hours there as children. This was the spot Fred had chosen to build a log home for his future bride, Sarah Jane Collins. His pa and grandpa, able craftsmen, lent their experience in building the cabin and making the furniture. The trio spent many hours cutting, planing, and staining the fine wood pieces.

Peter McClough, a frequent visitor to the Mason farm, offered his help on the wooden furniture pieces whenever the opportunity presented itself. "This isn't work, Fred. I enjoy doing this," Peter said one afternoon. "It amazes me how a chunk of wood can be transformed into such a beautiful piece of furniture. It'll look very nice in your log home. I think I like the homey pine pieces better than all the imported furniture in my place. Seems downright cozier somehow."

"You have a lot of expensive things, Peter, and they are beautiful. But Sarah and I will be pleased with these handmade pieces. They mean a lot because the trees are from our property and made by Pa, Gramps, and us. We'll always remember those who had a part in creating the furniture for our cabin." Fred gave his friend a gentle pat on the back.

Peter smiled. "Say, Fred, I was wondering. I understand you planned to build your cabin for one woman and ended up building it for Sarah. Can you tell me about it?"

"I chose this spot in the summer of 1862, Peter, when I was leaving to serve my country in the Union forces. My sweetheart, Becky Sue Collins, and I pledged our love and made a commitment to marry after the war. When I was wounded at Appomattox, word got back that I might lose my leg. When Becky Sue heard the news, she ran off and married another man. She couldn't cope with the situation—thinking she might have to marry a man with one leg."

"I'm sorry, Fred. That must have been a terrible blow."

"It was a shock, and I had a hard time getting over it. In fact, I grieved for quite a spell. But God worked it out for good. He always does. Becky's sister, Sarah Jane, is the only woman for me."

"Sarah is a lovely young woman. Why didn't you notice her before?"

Frederic chuckled. "Peter, she was only eleven, a redheaded, freckle-faced kid when I left for the war. How did I know she would grow up to be such a beautiful young woman? And anyway, I thought I was in love with Becky Sue."

"I've never been in love, Fred. But I've been thinking—do you think I might call on Louisa Bradford? I've been thinking about her a lot lately—can't seem to get her out of my thoughts."

"What happened with you and the teacher, Hannah Ragsdale? I thought you were courting her. The two of you seemed to hit it off good."

"Well, I thought so, too. I did see her several times, but. . ."

"What's the problem?"

"She's still grieving over her fiancé, the one killed in the war. I don't think she wants any kind of a serious relationship, and I'm hankerin' for one. I'm ready to settle down and get married."

"Well, that does beat all!" Fred laughed heartily. "I didn't know you had your eyes on Louisa. She's a very nice girl."

Peter laid down his saw and pushed back a shock of dark, unruly hair from his forehead. "And very beautiful. I know I'm not good enough for her. My background isn't the best. But I've tried hard to clean up my mouth and my life. I'm not interested in the kind of women I knew before. I've set my goals higher."

"You certainly have, Peter. Louisa is a fine Christian young lady and from a very strict family."

Peter looked down at his feet, and his face clouded. "You're saying it's hopeless, aren't you? I'll never be good enough for someone like Louisa Bradford."

"I didn't mean that. You've cleaned up your life, friend, but you've never gotten into a right relationship with God."

"So I have to go to church—is that it?"

"It's a start. But going to church doesn't get you into heaven. It will be important to Louisa and her family for you to be a believer."

"I believe in God, if that's what you're saying. Sure, there is a God up there somewhere. Guess maybe He looked after me all through the war years."

"That's just it, Peter—He isn't real to you. You think of Him as someone far away. God is a personal God. He cares about you. The Bible calls Him 'a friend that sticketh closer than a brother'."

"I've been such a rotten person all my life. God wouldn't want to be my friend."

"Yes, He would. When you come to Him through His Son, He blots out all your past sins and makes you a new person."

"I was pretty rotten to you, Fred, when we were stationed together for a time during the war. I knew you were a godly person, and it bothered me. Maybe I can clean up my life some more and then God will accept me."

"Anything you do on your own will still miss the mark. Jesus is the only way to God."

"I'll have to roll that around in my mind a bit. Might start going to church every week if you think it would help get Louisa's attention. I want her parents to think I'm a nice person."

Frederic eyed Peter soberly and shook his head. "You're a hardhead, my friend. But," he added, "you are not too hard for God."

❧

While Frederic had been busy making furniture, Sarah and her mother pieced quilts, braided rag rugs, and sewed curtains. With Emily's guidance, Sarah fashioned her wedding gown and veil. As she tried it on for her final fitting, Emily beamed and gave her a warm hug. "You'll be a beautiful bride, Sarah. The veil has a halo effect against your red gold hair. Frederic's eyes will pop out of his head when he sees you in this."

"Emily, I'm so grateful you taught me to sew last year. I couldn't have made this bridal dress without your help. Ma wanted me to have it in the worst way, but she couldn't handle it herself."

"I loved helping you, Sarah. But are you sure you want me to wear the pink gown I wore for Cassie's wedding? I could try and get something else made."

"I wanted a shade of rose for your gown anyway, Emily. It's such a lovely dress and so becoming on you. This gives you another opportunity to wear it."

"Yes." Emily sighed. "My bridesmaid dress. It seems I'm always a bridesmaid but never a bride."

Sarah hugged her gently. "You will be in another year. When Robert finishes his work in Pennsylvania, you'll have a beautiful wedding. It's something you can look forward to and plan on."

Emily's face looked pensive. "A year is such a long time, and he'll be so far away. I don't like waiting. I'm not a patient person."

"Waiting is hard when you're in love with someone. Did you know I've been in love with Fred since I was eleven? I know that is very young, and it may have been puppy love at first. My sister used to read Fred's letters from the war aloud, and I pretended they were for me. When she heard about his wounded leg and that he might lose it, she ran off and married Zack. I wondered then if there was any possible chance for me. I was only fourteen when Fred came home, and he still thought of me as a little kid." Sarah put an arm around Emily's shoulders. "God was in it, I know. All our prayers kept Frederic safe through the war years. He could have been killed on that battlefield instead of wounded. And God worked the time out for Fred to fall in love with me. He has the right timing for your marriage, too."

"Sarah, you are a wise one for your sixteen years. I wonder if Fred knows what a treasure he has in you. I guess he must, because he finally proposed."

"Poor Fred—he didn't have a choice. I just kept after him until he finally noticed me. It took a long time to get his attention!" Sarah laughed gaily, and Emily joined in. "Have you seen the lovely pieces of furniture in our log home? Fred and your pa and grandpa have worked long hours in order to have them done before the wedding. Even Peter lent a hand when he could. All the furniture was moved into the cabin last week, and, Emily, it looks beautiful."

"I've been so busy with my studies and visiting our sweet niece, Rebeccah, I've not visited the cabin recently. But I will soon, I promise."

"It's our dream house," Sarah said, taking off the bridal veil and laying it neatly on the bed. Her eyes misted and took on a faraway look. "Sometimes I think I must be dreaming! Will I wake up and discover none of this is true? Could it all be a little girl's make-believe?"

Emily smiled, reached out, and pinched her gently. "It's all true, Sarah. Anyone can see you and Fred were meant for each other. You grew up, young lady, just in time!"

Chapter 6

The president of Colby College scheduled a tea for students and faculty to allow them an opportunity to meet in an informal atmosphere. The primary purpose was to promote friendly discussions and answer students' questions or concerns as they mingled with their professors.

Louisa Bradford was excited as she dressed for the occasion. She went to great lengths styling her hair and preparing her wardrobe, hoping to make a favorable impression.

"Is that a new gown?" Emily asked, surveying her radiant friend. Louisa wore a slate blue wool dress complete with lace collar and cuffs. The dress highlighted and enhanced the gray of her eyes. Her golden blond hair, tied with matching slate blue ribbons, had been brushed until it shone and cascaded in ringlets around her shoulders. "It's lovely."

"Thanks. I needed something new, something eye-catching, for the tea. It's a rare occasion to meet our teachers on common ground and actually talk with them. We did this last year, and it proved very worthwhile."

"Are you dressing for one of your teachers in particular?" Emily teased. "Dr. Matthews, perhaps?"

Louisa's face reddened. "I'm trying to look my best for all the faculty," she protested. Then she smiled, and her face relaxed. "Oh, Emily, do you think Dr. Matthews will notice me? I've tried several times after class to get his attention, but he's all business. He doesn't seem to know I'm alive."

"He can't help but notice you today, Louisa. Your dress is striking. You will probably catch the eye of every professor and student there."

"I'm not interested in students. They are so juvenile. Dr. Matthews is the only person I'm interested in. In fact," she said, giggling, "he is the only single man on the faculty except for dear old Mr. Parsons. He's a widower and must be at least seventy."

Classes had been canceled for that day, and it was early afternoon when the girls entered the large banquet room at Colby College. Louisa, excited and nervous, held on to Emily's arm for stability. "Go with me to talk to Dr. Matthews," she implored. "I never know what to say. You are always so composed and in control."

"You're just shy, Louisa. But being shy is an asset, really. It makes you more mysterious and attractive. I'll go with you to get the conversation going and then bow out. Three is always a crowd."

"Speaking of crowds, Emily, we may not get near him. Did you ever see so many students? Where is Dr. Matthews anyway?"

"I see him over on the far side of the room, Louisa. But he is surrounded by students. Let's get some tea first and wait until the crowd thins out."

Emily and Louisa made their way to the long tables in the center of the room. White linen tablecloths and festive centerpieces added an air of elegance. The silver tea server was polished to a brilliant sheen, and silver trays held an assortment of cookies and small cakes. The girls each took a few of the choice sweets on a china plate and sat down at one of the small tables set for the occasion. A number of students greeted them as they passed by, engaging them in small talk.

"It looks hopeless," Louisa stated finally, taking another sip of her tea. Her eyes searched the room for Dr. Matthews. "There is still a crowd of students surrounding him. It just shows how popular he is. I don't see the other professors being mobbed that way. What shall we do? I must speak to him."

Emily finished her cookies and washed them down with the last of her tea. "Let's go over and wait. It's never going to get any better. We can't spend our entire afternoon eating cookies!"

Louisa laughed nervously and jumped to her feet. As they waited in line, she mentally rehearsed several questions she planned to ask Dr. Matthews. She planned to hold his attention as long as possible. After a lengthy time, they greeted Dr. Matthews, and he responded cordially, "Two of my favorite students." He smiled. "What can I do for you?"

Emily discussed some notes of interest from her Shakespeare class and expressed her pleasure in the course. "It has been enlightening and most enjoyable to study about Shakespeare the person. But I'm taking up too much of your time, Dr. Matthews." Emily smiled and held out her hand. "My friend hasn't had an opportunity to say a word."

Dr. Matthews smiled warmly, took her hand, and held it longer than necessary. Blushing, Emily pulled it away. "I need to discuss some matters with Mr. Gray, my history teacher," she mumbled. "I'm having a difficult time memorizing the dates of historical events." With cheeks still flushed, she turned quickly and walked away.

Emily spent the remainder of the afternoon meeting with Mr. Gray and her other professors. Keeping an eye on Louisa and Dr. Matthews, she noticed they talked alone together for a long time before Louisa moved on to talk to others.

Tired, Emily headed for the tea table and poured herself another steaming cup of tea. She found an empty table near the back and settled down for a relaxing moment, letting her gaze wander across the crowded banquet room.

"May I join you?" Dr. Matthews's familiar bass voice asked as he juggled a plate of cookies and a cup of tea. "I need a spot of tea to refresh myself."

"Of course," Emily stammered, caught off guard. "Please sit down."

"It's always nice to share tea time with a lovely young lady. Don't you agree?"

Flustered, Emily blushed and said nothing.

"Miss Bradford and I had quite a long talk," Dr. Matthews said.

"That's nice," Emily mumbled. "Where is she now?"

"Off with her other teachers, I believe. She seemed to have a lot of questions. She also told me you are involved in a serious relationship with a young preacher. Is that true?"

"You discussed me?" Emily asked testily. "Louisa had no right to talk to you about things that concern me! My personal life is my own affair and not to be talked about casually."

Dr. Matthews reached out and covered her small hand with his. "I'm interested in you, Emily. I'd like to know more about you."

Immediately Emily jerked her hand away and stood up.

"Sit down, please," Dr. Matthews said. "You haven't finished your tea."

"I need to leave now, sir," she said quietly but firmly. "Good-bye."

Emily lost no time finding Louisa and waited until she finished her discussion with one of her teachers. "Let's go home, Louisa," she said impatiently. "Are you ready to go?"

"I was going to have another cup of tea," Louisa protested. "Why are you in such a hurry?"

"We've been here all afternoon. It's time to go home now."

"You sound upset about something. What happened?"

"Louisa, you and Dr. Matthews discussed me. . .and my relationship with Robert. Why?"

"I only told him the truth. He asked about you. He wanted to know if there was any special man in your life."

"Why would he ask that? I thought you had many more interesting things to discuss with him. What about all those questions you planned to ask?"

"I tried to keep his attention." Louisa sighed. "But he seemed interested in talking about you. He kept probing. I thought if he knew you were practically engaged, he would lose interest in you."

"That's ridiculous! Dr. Matthews isn't interested in me personally. He just wanted to make conversation."

"He seems very interested in you, Emily. I could tell by the way his face lit up when we talked about you. And all the time I was hoping he would notice me. A lot of good this new dress did for me. He hardly knew I was there." Louisa glanced forlornly at her friend. "We might as well go home."

Emily could see that her friend was distressed. But she couldn't understand why Dr. Matthews would be interested in her. She'd never given him any reason to believe she thought about him except as her professor. The way he held her hand so long had been odd. He was an excellent teacher of Shakespeare; surely whatever he felt about her wouldn't pose a problem in the classroom. And especially she hoped it wouldn't pose a problem with Louisa. After all, Louisa was her dearest friend.

The two young ladies left quietly and said little on the way home. Later that evening, Emily tried vainly to find the right words of encouragement. "Everything will work out for the best, Louisa. Dr. Matthews will come to appreciate your beauty and sweet depth of character."

Though disappointed in the turn of events, Louisa found it difficult to harbor a grudge. She shook her head, tossing her golden curls carelessly around her shoulders. "I'll probably never get married!" she exclaimed dramatically, giving her friend a sad smile. "I'll end up an old spinster!"

"Ha! A spinster!" Emily teased. "You're only nineteen, young lady. You'll never make it to spinsterhood!"

"And why not? I don't see any eligible young men knocking at my door."

"I wish you would be open-minded about Peter, Louisa. You haven't been around him lately to notice how he's changed. I think you should be fair in your evaluation by giving him a chance."

"Pompous Peter?" Louisa exclaimed. "That young man has a brazen air about him toward women. I doubt he's changed in that respect. Anyway, I'll keep you up-to-date about Dr. Matthews. I haven't given up on that relationship!"

Chapter 7

The final days of March passed like a whirlwind. Emily felt on guard in her Shakespeare class with Dr. Matthews, trying to avoid any personal encounters. At times it was difficult to concentrate because she felt his eyes on her. She decided she couldn't let it bother her, though, as she loved the class and intended to finish the course.

Cool days with soft rains permeated the earth with a sweet smell and promise of spring. Trees stood tall, eager to burst forth and deck their lofty branches with new leaves. The time was fast approaching for Robert Harris to leave for Pennsylvania. As Emily faced the thought of their long separation, she became moody and withdrawn. She accepted Robert's decision to go, but she could not feign happiness.

The first Saturday in April, Fred and Sarah's wedding day, Emily pulled her rose pink gown over her head and surveyed her image in the mirror. Her dark, curly hair fell in a mass down her back, held back with pink bows that matched her dress. Emily forced herself to smile at her reflection. She was happy for her brother and his young bride. They were so in love and so right for each other. She would not allow any personal sadness to overshadow this special day. *Fred and Sarah,* she mused. *No one expected this to happen, not even Fred. But I saw it coming. I knew they were destined to be together.* Emily let out a little sigh and said sadly, "I just can't help wishing it was my wedding day."

The little church in Waterville was decorated for the afternoon occasion. Huge pots of flowers, artistically arranged, banked the front altar. Large pink satin bows on the ends of each row of pews added brightness and color. The Mason family and Collins family sat on opposite sides at the front, with close friends seated behind them. Bill and Cassie sat at the very back with little Rebeccah. The baby was wide-awake, and her deep blue eyes were alert to the people around her. Cassie was concerned that the service be quiet and meaningful for her brother and his bride. "If Rebeccah cries or gets fussy, I'll leave the sanctuary quickly and not disturb the ceremony," she had told them.

As Rev. Davis's wife played softly on the piano, Emily walked slowly down the aisle and took her place at the altar. Her heart skipped a beat as she looked at Robert, standing next to the elderly Rev. Davis. *How tall and handsome he looks in his fine suit. Robert, can you hear my heart crying out to you? I don't want you to go away. I want you to stay here so we can be together.* Robert glanced at Emily, and his eyes held such emotion she was certain he could read her thoughts.

Reverend Davis and Robert would share equally in parts of the wedding service. Frederic stood nervously with his attendant, Peter McClough, and watched a radiant and flushed Sarah walk down the aisle on the arm of her father. She created an angelic image in her white satin gown, overlaid with Irish lace. Her red gold hair, which cascaded about her shoulders, spilled out from beneath a filmy crownlike veil. When she approached the altar, Frederic took her hand firmly in his larger one and looked deeply into her eyes.

The message was an inspiring one of commitment, punctuated with verses of scripture. Fred and Sarah knelt for prayer, and when they arose to their feet, Rev. Davis pronounced them man and wife. Frederic's heart pounded wildly in his chest as he turned toward his bride. Lifting her veil, he took her into his arms and drew her close. "My darling wife," he whispered huskily against her red gold hair. "God made you mine." Sarah looked up at him, tears glistening in her violet blue eyes. His lips sought hers, and they kissed sweetly and tenderly as husband and wife.

The Collinses opened their large farmhouse for the reception for the couple, and it filled quickly with family and guests. Peter McClough looked striking in his new dark suit. His dark, wavy hair had been neatly trimmed and combed. He filled his plate from the long buffet table and searched the area for Louisa. When he located her in a far corner of the room, he made his way to her side. "Hello, Louisa. Fine wedding, wasn't it?" Peter smiled pleasantly as he sat down beside her.

Louisa only nodded absently and looked away. "A gentleman would ask a lady for permission before he sat down," she fumed under her breath. "This boor is no gentleman."

Peter tried vainly to draw the evasive Miss Bradford into conversation. "I plan to be in church tomorrow," he said eagerly, leaning toward her. "It's been on my mind for a long time. Seems like now would be a good time to start. I'm looking forward to the service."

"That's nice," Louisa said vaguely, turning away from him. Suddenly she motioned to one of her friends across the room with a bright smile and little wave of her hand. Quickly she stood up and walked away without looking at Peter. Dejected by her apparent disinterest, Peter sat alone with his thoughts while he finished his plate of food. Eventually he moved toward the parlor where Fred and Sarah were surrounded by a group of well-wishers.

Peter slapped Fred on the back and shook his hand vigorously. "Congratulations, friend. I thought you'd never ask her. What took you so long?" His dark eyes gleamed with a mischievous twinkle.

Fred laughed. "I had to wait until she grew up a bit." Then, with an admiring glance at Sarah, he added, "And she did just that!"

Sarah blushed, giving her oval face a soft, rosy glow. "It took some doing to get him to notice me as a woman. . .but I finally got his attention." She reached up and tousled his curly, dark hair in her fingers.

"You got his attention, all right," Peter said as he leaned over and kissed Sarah lightly on her flushed cheek. "All the happiness, young lady. Just be sure and keep this fellow in line. If he gives you any trouble, you can call on Uncle Pete."

Fred and Sarah ate a little supper, opened gifts, and expressed their appreciation. "Thanks to all of you," Fred stated. "We hope you'll feel free to visit us sometime in our new home. You are all welcome."

"Can you cook, Sarah?" someone shouted.

"Yes, I can, after a fashion. Come by, and I'll show you, even if it's only tea and cookies."

After an appropriate length of time, the couple slipped away to their little cabin in the woods. It was completely furnished and stocked with food. They had no desire to go anywhere but home.

Emily helped her mother and Mrs. Collins clean up the kitchen after the guests were gone. Since the Mason family shared in providing the food, Mrs. Collins insisted they take a good amount of leftovers home with them. Robert waited for Emily so he could take her home, while the rest of the family went on ahead. He lifted her easily into the wagon, and they rode in silence for several minutes, listening to the *clip-clop* of the horses' hooves on the hard-packed clay road. "Wasn't it a lovely wedding?" Emily said finally. "Sarah looked so beautiful and angelic."

"Brides always look beautiful," Robert answered seriously. "There seems to be an inner glow that radiates and lights up a bride's countenance. It's hard to describe. I just know all the brides I've ever seen have it. It's like an inner, magical, ethereal beauty."

"You sound like a philosopher," Emily whispered as she snuggled against Robert in the buggy. The horses trotted along the road with an even gait, lending an air of peace and tranquility to the countryside around them. "I don't like good-byes, Robert," she said suddenly. "I wish you weren't leaving so soon."

"My train leaves early Monday morning for Pennsylvania, Emily. This will be our last opportunity to talk alone. Will you write me often?"

"Oh, Robert, of course I will. And you must write me first and tell me about this new area you are going to. I want to know all about the people and what they are like. Tell me about your work—raising up a new church. Let me know about any problems or special joys so I can pray intelligently. And I'll keep the others informed of your progress."

Robert was quiet for a few moments. "Emily, I know we aren't actually engaged. It probably wouldn't be fair to ask you to wait for me," he faltered, glancing sideways at the slight figure so close to him. "But I wish you would."

"And I will, Robert," Emily said eagerly. "I want to wait for you. Could you see my eyes upon you all during the wedding service? You looked so fine and handsome. I was waiting for you to smile your special lopsided grin at me, but you looked so serious the entire time."

"I had to be serious, Emily, during the ceremony. But my heart was thumping in my chest when I looked at you. . .so beautiful." He cleared the huskiness from his throat.

Emily smiled up at him. "I'll be counting the days until you return, Robert. It isn't going to be pleasant with you so far away."

"I hope to return in September for a few days, but it will depend on how things are progressing whether I can leave at that time. If not September, then Christmas at the very latest."

"The months we are apart will seem like years, Robert. I know you have your work to do and it's important. It is where God wants you to be. God has plans for me also. I want to finish my year of college, just as I always dreamed. Maybe I'll even go on to be a teacher."

"Would you prefer being a teacher instead of a preacher's wife?" he asked, tracing the oval of her face with his hand.

"Of course not," she said quickly, grabbing his hand and holding it against her cheek. "I wish we could be married right now, before you leave."

"Dearest Emily," Robert whispered hoarsely as he released the reins and let the horses go at their own pace. He turned toward her, kissing her lightly, first on the cheek and then on the lips. "I do love you, Emily. And we shall be married, my darling. . .in God's time."

The horses had slowed to a walk, but Robert snapped the reins and turned them up the long drive to the Mason homestead. Emily's head rested contentedly against his shoulder. "In God's time," she echoed. "In God's time."

Chapter 8

The long, uneventful train ride to Pennsylvania seemed endless. Landscapes throughout New England were picturesque and breathtaking. Trees had leafed out in majestic splendor, and there were vast areas of farmland with small ponds and creeks. Large farms and outbuildings dotted the area, while cattle and horses roamed freely within the confines of fences surrounding their pastureland. Robert tried to make conversation with the various passengers. He was disappointed that none opened up to him except for brief discussions. Even those who seemed to have difficult problems became disenchanted when he turned the conversation toward a higher power. Stiff barriers rose as the travelers turned their attention elsewhere and became absorbed in their own plans. He noted complete disinterest and an apparent lack of concern.

What have I let myself in for, God? I expected people to be eager to hear about You—especially since the brutal war between the North and South caused so much heartache. Some of these passengers are obviously relics from the war, some without an arm, leg, or eye. They need to know the God who brought them through the horrible battles. Do these people forget so soon?

Robert glanced at the couple across the aisle from him. The man was obviously a disabled veteran, with only one leg. His crutches leaned against the seat beside him. The wife seemed interested when Robert approached them, but the veteran was brusque and spoke roughly. "We don't need no talk about God," he said and turned away.

After leaving Waterville, Robert had made a side trip to the war-torn battlefield in Gettysburg, Pennsylvania. Nearly four years earlier, on July 1, 2, and 3 of 1863, brave Americans fought the bloodiest single battle of the Civil War. Twenty-five square miles of countryside had been blown apart by shell and shrapnel. Tears brimmed in Robert's eyes as he toured the famous areas of combat: Seminary Ridge, Cemetery Hill, Big and Little Round Top, and others. Men from both North and South gave their lives on the blood-soaked battleground. Robert had seen pictures taken shortly after the battles occurred. They were unforgettable scenes of the appalling aftermath of war.

Here, he remembered, in November 1863, President Lincoln gave his heartrending Gettysburg Address at the dedication of the Gettysburg National Cemetery. "Our great nation has been preserved," Robert whispered with emotion. "We must never forget the price that was paid."

Robert's mood was thoughtful as he departed Gettysburg for his final destination. Now he must look ahead to the challenges God had for him in Wampum, Pennsylvania. He was eager to meet his host family and the others interested in building a work among the farmers and factory workers. *How will the people react to an outsider? Will they be on their guard around the new preacher? Thomas Whan believes many are hungry for the Word. I pray he is right. There are many needy people, and I have the message of hope. I'll soon see whether attitudes will be hostile or indifferent. No matter, God. I know You are with me.*

Thomas Whan, a husky farmer with dark hair and eyes, met Robert at the station. "Glad you're here, Preacher," he said with a warm smile and hearty handshake. "We've been waiting for this to happen for a long time." He took Robert's gear and loaded it onto his wagon. "It's a good two hours back to Wampum, but my wife will hold supper for us. Elizabeth and the kids are mighty anxious to meet the new preacher. I hope the kids don't overwhelm you. They are quite a handful."

"I'm looking forward to them, Thomas. You and Elizabeth have six youngsters, don't you?"

"Yep. Three boys and three girls. Turned out just right. The boys help me with the chores, and the girls help their ma. The baby is not yet two. He has the same name as you—Robert."

"I was an only child, Thomas, and I haven't been around children very much. Living with a family will be a treat for me."

The Whan homestead, a large log home, had been built by Thomas's father, John, one mile south of Wampum in Big Beaver Township. It was built on a knoll above a spring of running water. Another smaller building was built over the spring and was called a summerhouse. It kept butter and milk cool during the hot summer months. Caves had been dug into the sides of the hill to keep the vegetables and potatoes from freezing during the winter. In the yard, ovens made out of stone and mud had been built to bake the bread.

As Thomas drew the horses to a halt beside the large summer porch, several youngsters burst from the house. Robert climbed down from his seat on the wagon and found himself surrounded by babbling children, all talking at once. "Mind your manners!" Thomas shouted. "You can all meet the preacher, one at a time." Immediately the chattering ceased, and the children stood quietly, looking at Robert.

Such well-behaved children, Robert mused.

Thomas told them to step forward, one by one, and introduce themselves. The tallest, a sandy-haired lad, shook Robert's hand. "Welcome, Preacher. I'm Samuel, age thirteen. I'd like to help you call on people here. I know all the neighbors."

"Thank you, Samuel. I would appreciate your help. I don't know the people or the territory."

"I'm Mary Matilda, and I'm twelve," said a smiling miss with dark, curly hair, offering her hand and curtsying at the same time.

"How do you do, Mary Matilda," Robert said, taking the offered hand. "I'm very happy to make your acquaintance."

A shy, small voice greeted him next. "My name is Margaret." The little girl looked down at the ground. "I'm nine." The youngster's honey blond hair was pulled back into a long, neat braid.

"I'm so glad to meet you, Margaret," Robert said, lifting her chin to look into her clear blue eyes. Blushing profusely, she hurriedly stepped back into line with the others.

The next young man had a bold and vigorous handshake. "I'm William Thomas, seven years old. But I can plow and plant and help Pa do lots of things."

"I'm sure you can, William," Robert agreed. "You and Samuel must be great help to your pa with the farm chores."

"My name is 'Lizabeth, and I'm four years old," a winsome little lady said with a curtsy. Her golden curls peeked from beneath her pink-checked sunbonnet.

Without a word, Robert picked her up and held her high in the air while she giggled merrily. When he set her down, he glanced at each of the youngsters. "I hope we can become fast friends," he said. "But isn't there one more of you?"

Thomas chuckled. "Little Robert is with his ma. He's just a wee tike, and we can't trust him outside alone. He gets a lot of care and attention from the other young'uns. I dare say they do their best to spoil the lad."

Elizabeth Whan appeared in the doorway, holding a chunky, dark-haired toddler. He had chubby cheeks and was chewing on a piece of bread. Mrs. Whan's sandy hair was pulled back into a bun, and her blue eyes sparkled. "Thomas, bring our guest inside," she called. "It's getting late, and I have supper waiting. I'm sure everyone is mighty hungry."

The children bounded inside, eager to taste the hearty meal their mother had prepared. After washing up, Robert joined them at the long harvest table in the large dining room. "We're right proud to have you with us, Preacher," Elizabeth Whan said. "And we're hoping you'll feel right at home here."

"Thank you, ma'am. I feel very welcome already. The children greeted me and introduced themselves, and I feel right at home. You have a fine brood of youngsters here."

Robert was seated between the two oldest children, Samuel and Mary Matilda. Little Robert sat in his homemade wooden high chair opposite him, waving his chubby hands and demanding food. "We pray first," Thomas said firmly as he took one of baby Robert's hands. Elizabeth Whan took the baby's other hand, and each around the table joined hands for the blessing.

The home-cooked meal was delicious, and Robert ate heartily of the ham, potatoes, and vegetables. He slathered large chunks of homemade bread with freshly churned butter and raspberry preserves. It was a peaceful meal as the older children had been taught to be quiet at the dinner table unless spoken to by an adult. Little Robert was too young to understand and kept up a lively babble of baby talk, much to the delight of his brothers and sisters. The other children giggled at their baby brother's antics.

Later that evening, after the children were settled in their beds, Robert had an opportunity to discuss the work with Thomas and Elizabeth in the large living room before a roaring fire. "I understand there are two other families who meet with you for Bible studies, Thomas. I'll want to meet them first before I call on any new folk. And where is the school—the one we will be using for our church services?"

"It's just down the road a piece," Thomas said, pointing toward the south. "It's the Whan School, built on the Whan property. My grandpa came over from Belfast, Ireland, in 1792 when my pa was only a year old. When Pa became of school age, my grandpa and some neighbors built the school out of logs on the property. The one-room schoolhouse served my pa, myself, and now my children and many neighbor young'uns. They come from miles around. Some walk, and some come on horseback. It will do us fine for a church until we get a good work started and can afford to build something else."

"Sounds fine, Thomas. What about the two families already meeting for Bible studies? Are they close by?"

"James Davidson's farm meets our property at the line. He and his wife, Abbie, and their youngsters come, and the other family is the John Wilsons. They are about a mile in the other direction. These are all dedicated people, Preacher, and they desire to see a work grow. But we've needed a leader—someone who can call and visit, someone to preach and teach us from the Word of God."

"That will be my privilege," Robert said soberly. "I trust God will bless His work here and that many will come to know Him and become members of His family."

"Abbie Davidson, Lettie Wilson, and I get together and piece quilts and sew rag rugs one afternoon each month," Elizabeth said. "If there's a family in need, or one who's been burned out, we have them handy to take over to them. It's our way of saying we care."

"A fine outreach," Robert said. "Neighbors will respond to genuine love most of the time. Tell me about some of the other families in the area, some of the folk we hope to reach."

During the next hour Robert listened and took notes regarding some of the prospects in Wampum and the surrounding area. Finally, he bid them good night, took a kerosene lantern, and mounted the steps to his room on the second floor. It was amply furnished with a wooden poster bed, dresser, and washstand. One wall boasted a large desk and bookcase. "What a comfortable room," Robert murmured, placing the lamp on the desk's smooth surface. "This is an excellent place to study, and there is room for all my books."

Yawning, he placed his belongings in the dresser drawers and hung his dress clothes on pegs along the east wall. Pulling his quickly jotted notes from his pocket, he sat down at the desk to review them. He had written names and facts about each family to aid him when he visited them.

"Old man Larson is grumpy and ornery. Won't let the missus or youngsters come to any meetings," he read softly.

"Olivia Mayer lost her man in the Civil War and has been bitter ever since. She lives in a large farmhouse and has three young children to raise.

"Miss Johnson, the schoolteacher, is too intelligent, she thinks, to need any help from a higher power.

"The Morrison family is a likely prospect. They have a son who was badly injured at Bull Run during the Civil War. They have two younger children and a young man who came back from the war with their injured son living with them.

"The young man has amnesia due to a war injury and remembers nothing previous to being in the hospital. It was in the hospital that young Morrison befriended him and asked him to return with him to his home. He gladly accepted the offer, since he had no name tags on him and knew nothing of his family or their whereabouts. He goes by the name of John Smith and helps the Morrisons on their farm. Seems he's a kind of therapy for the injured son.

"Then there's the Stevens family, the Kelly family, and others—all need to know there is a God who loves them and cares for them."

Robert finished reading his notes and opened his Bible. "Lord, there are many needs here in this territory. You know each heart and the obstacles involved. I commit each one to You and pray for leading and guidance in the work before me. Give me the words to say to these people. May they see You, lifted up and exalted, the only answer to the needs of their hearts. Thank You, in Jesus' name. Amen."

Wearily Robert undressed and climbed into bed. "I'll write Emily as soon as I have more news to tell her," he muttered. "She will pray with me for these dear people."

Chapter 9

Emily threw herself wholeheartedly into her studies. She must keep her mind busy, she decided, so as not to dwell upon her painful separation from Robert. "We will talk through our letters," he told her. "Be assured, darling, our love will overcome any distance between us." Oh, how she longed for Robert's first letter. She forced herself to be patient, for she knew it would come as soon as he had news to share with her about his work. The waiting would have been unbearable without the demands of the rigid schedule of her college classes.

Louisa, on the other hand, seemed unusually happy. She often hummed little tunes and always had a smile on her face. "It's good to see someone in such a cheerful mood." Emily sighed. "Is there something I should know?"

"Things are happening," Louisa said mysteriously. "I feel happy all the time."

"Tell me about it," Emily begged. "I need some news on the brighter side. Things seem very dull right now with no news from Robert."

"You've been so busy studying you haven't missed me during the noon break. Guess where I've been?"

"Oh, Louisa, we're too old for guessing games. I've been in the library doing some research, and I assume you've been in the dining hall. Where else would you be?"

Louisa giggled. "I've been having lunch uptown with Dr. Matthews, at that nice little café on Main Street. You know the one."

"How? When?" Emily gasped, taken aback.

"It started when I went to his classroom during the noon hour to talk with him about my advanced Shakespeare class. He simply invited me to have lunch with him, and I accepted. We've been meeting for lunch several times a week."

"Louisa, is that wise? You don't know much about Dr. Matthews, do you? Would your parents approve?"

"That's no problem. We're just having lunch together, as friends. What harm can there be in that? We've found we have many things in common to talk about. He's a charming and interesting person. Anyway, I've invited him for dinner tomorrow evening to meet my parents, and he's accepted. That's one reason I'm so happy and humming little tunes all the time."

"Well, your parents must approve of the idea then."

"They didn't at first, but they do now." Louisa hesitated a moment, then continued, "I told them we both have him for a class, and you agreed it would be nice to entertain him."

"I never agreed!" Emily sputtered. "Why would you say such a thing, Louisa? This is entirely your idea. Just leave me out of it. I won't be a party to a falsehood."

"Please, Emily, don't tell them differently. It will go over better with them if they continue to think it's our idea, not just mine. I dearly want him to come."

Emily found it difficult to resist the pleading in her friend's eyes and, against her better judgment, finally gave in. "I guess it will be all right this once. But don't involve me in any further plans. If your parents ask me specifically, I will not lie, Louisa. It's important to keep everything honest and out in the open. You know that. A relationship must be built on trust. God hates lies."

"I know," Louisa said as she hugged her friend. "Thanks, Emily. I knew I could count on you. Once my parents meet James, they'll see what a fine man he is. I'm positive they'll agree to him courting me."

"Are you certain those are his intentions, Louisa? This could be only a pleasant interlude for him. I hope your expectations aren't set too high."

"You sound like a prophet of doom. I thought you would be happy for me, Emily. Of course he intends to court me. Why would he spend all that time taking me to lunch? Seriously, I believe he has marriage on his mind. After all, he's over thirty. He's ready to settle down. . . . You'll see."

Emily found herself thinking about Dr. Matthews's coming visit and wondered if Louisa was taking too much for granted. "Perhaps Dr. Matthews is really interested in her," she muttered aloud. "I mustn't be suspicious of his character. Louisa should know him fairly well by now. She is obviously taken in by his charming smile. Maybe I *am* a prophet of doom." She sighed. "I just don't want to see Louisa get hurt."

The Bradfords did not question Emily about their coming dinner guest, and Dr. Matthews arrived the following evening promptly at six. "Please greet Dr. Matthews and show him into the parlor, Emily," Mrs. Bradford called from the kitchen. "Louisa is still getting dressed upstairs, but she should be down shortly."

Reluctantly Emily did the formalities and led Dr. Matthews into the parlor. "Louisa will be down in a few minutes," she said stiffly and turned to leave.

"Please stay, Emily. I was hoping for an opportunity to talk to you alone. Can't we be friends?"

"Of course." Emily smiled, relaxing her tone.

Dr. Matthews moved closer, and his dark brown eyes searched hers. He took her arm in a firm grip, and she felt his warm breath against her cheek. "I agreed to this dinner invitation for one purpose, Emily," he said softly. "I'm very attracted to you, and I wanted to see you in an informal situation."

Trembling, Emily stepped back and pushed his arm away. She caught her breath and said shakily, "I'm practically engaged, Dr. Matthews, and I expect to be married next year."

"Are you certain about your feelings for this young man—this. . .this preacher? Perhaps you are not willing to admit that you are attracted to me? Don't fight any feelings you may have for me, Emily," Dr. Matthews said as he reached out and took her in his arms.

Emily felt heat rising in her cheeks as she pushed him away and turned to leave. "Mrs. Bradford needs me in the kitchen, Dr. Mathews." Her voice trembled with outrage. "And I believe Louisa and her father will be down presently."

Emily was quiet during dinner, trying to sort out her feelings, but the others seemed not to notice. She caught Dr. Matthews's questioning eyes on her several times, although he carried on a lively conversation with Louisa and her parents. "He can be very charming," Emily muttered under her breath.

Against Mrs. Bradford's protests, Emily insisted on helping her clear the table and do up the dishes, while Mr. Bradford, Louisa, and Dr. Matthews retired to the parlor. Later she joined them briefly and then excused herself to attend to her studies. "I have English exams tomorrow," she said in all honesty. "Please excuse me. Good night, Dr. Matthews."

Back in her room, Emily found it hard to concentrate on her lessons. Dr. Matthews's actions continued to haunt her again and again. "What a conceited man, to think I would forget about Robert and pursue a relationship with someone I barely know," she murmured. "Why doesn't Dr. Matthews understand the situation and let it stand? It seems he is deliberately trying to annoy me." Emily picked up her brush and brushed her dark curls vigorously. "I suppose I'm a bit flattered by his attention to me. But he's supposed to be interested in Louisa. She believes he is, and she is certainly interested in him. She has been taken in by all his charm and attention. From what he said tonight, he is using her as a ploy to be near me." She threw down the brush and flung herself on the bed. "Why are things so difficult, God? If I tell Louisa what Dr. Matthews did, she will be crushed! And yet she ought to know the truth about the sort of man he is."

Emily spent a lengthy time in prayer, asking God for wisdom and guidance. She prayed Louisa would realize Dr. Matthews was not the one God had for her. He was too polished, too charming, and she prayed for herself and Robert and their love for each other. "Please, God," she whispered, "keep us close to each other, no matter how far apart we are. And most of all, keep us close to Yourself."

Chapter 10

The following days fell into a pattern for Robert. Thomas Whan supplied him with the use of a horse and buggy, and he acquainted himself with the area. He visited the Davidson and Wilson families, the regular attendees at the Bible study held by Thomas. They were fine Christian folk and eager to see a church raised up in the area. Robert checked the Whan School where Sunday services would take place and was pleased. Space was ample for a growing congregation, and he liked the proximity of it.

The Whan children were delighted with their houseguest, and Robert quickly became attached to them. He proved quite a storyteller, and the youngsters begged him for stories and involved him in their games. They were energetic and abounding with enthusiasm, yet well behaved and careful not to disturb his study periods. Samuel designated himself as guide whenever possible, and Robert often depended on his help. Robert spent his mornings in study, prayer, and preparation. Then after school, he and Samuel set off together and called upon a prospective family before the evening meal.

"Why does Samuel always get to go with Pastor Harris?" William protested one evening before dinner.

"I'm the oldest," Samuel said with an air of importance. "The pastor needs my help, William. I'm a go-between for him with the neighboring families."

"Why can't I go, Pa?" William begged. "I could help Pastor Harris. I'd be a good helper."

"No, William," Thomas Whan said as he tousled his son's dark, unruly hair. "You're needed here to help with the chores. I can't spare both my boys. Samuel is a young man now and ready for adult duties. He knows the families living in the outer areas and can prepare Pastor Harris en route for what to expect. You'll need to do double duty after school, William, as my right-hand man."

"Yes, sir," seven-year-old William said reluctantly. "I'll do Samuel's chores and mine, too. You'll see I'm a good helper, Pa."

Thomas chuckled. "I know you are, son. I'm glad I can depend on your help. Little Robert is just a babe. . .he won't be doing chores for quite a while yet."

The first Sunday services went as well as expected. The only attendees were the three regular families involved previously in the Bible study group. Robert felt a pang of disappointment that no newcomers came except the schoolteacher, Miss Johnson. She arrived late, sat in the back, and gave the impression she had come to observe, not participate. Robert hoped to talk with her after the service, but she left hurriedly during the closing song.

Robert and Samuel made two important calls during the following week. Their first visit was to Olivia Mayer, whose husband had been killed in the Civil War. A young mother, pushing back wisps of light brown disheveled hair, answered their knock at the door. Weariness etched the otherwise pretty face, and sadness veiled the wide-set brown eyes. Three youngsters, stair steps in height, crowded around her.

Robert introduced Samuel and himself and invited them to the newly established community church services. "We'd be mighty happy if you'd join us," Robert said.

"God did me a bad turn, Preacher, and I don't fix ta come ta no church."

"I heard about your loss, Mrs. Mayer. I'm truly sorry. War is a terrible thing. But God can fill the void in your life with His love. We'll be starting Sunday school classes next Sunday. Won't you bring your youngsters so they can learn about Jesus?"

"I wanna go, Ma," the oldest child, a daughter, said, pulling at her mother's skirt. "Can we, please?"

Olivia Mayer bit her lip and gazed at her daughters, ages eight and seven, and her six-year-old son. "It's been downright hard without my man. He didn't hafta go ta war. . .these young'uns were babies when he left. Jess said he had ta go, couldn't stand the idea of slavery. . .one man bein' owned by another. He was proud the day he joined up with a Pennsylvania regiment. 'What kinda world would this be, Liv?' he asked me. 'I don't want my babies gowin' up thinkin' some folk better'n others. All folks is created equal, and it's what they does with their life what counts.'"

"Your Jess was a wise man, Mrs. Mayer. I think he'd want you and the children in church."

"I'll think on it, Preacher. I might bring the young'uns Sunday, but I'm not makin' any promises."

Robert glanced around at the sagging porch and noticed the house badly needed repairs. "Our church folk would like to help out with some chores around your place, if it's all right with you. Samuel and I will split and chop some wood for you today, and our menfolk will take turns helping out whenever possible."

"Bless you, Preacher!" Olivia exclaimed. "My Jess didn't leave us destitute. His folks lived with us when he left fer the war. They helped me with my babies and helped run the place. Jess knew we'd be in good hands. But his ma passed away last year with the croup, and his pa died six months later. Heart attack, the doc said. 'Twas a sad time fer us. I know the place is run-down, but I jest can't keep it up."

Robert laid his suit coat in the buggy and rolled up his sleeves. In no time he and Samuel had split a nice pile of wood, and the widow's young son and two daughters had stacked it neatly on the porch. Mrs. Mayer kept a supply of cold water handy, and the job was completed in short order.

Robert and Samuel bid the Mayer family farewell and turned the horse homeward, as it was nearing supper time. Robert was hopeful. "I'd say that was a promising call, Samuel. I think the widow has a tender heart underneath that somewhat bitter and weary exterior."

Later that week, Samuel directed Robert to the Larson homestead. "This'll be a scary one, Pastor. Old man Larson is an ornery critter."

"It will be a challenge then, Samuel. We can handle it. We have nothing to fear, because God is with us."

Robert guided the horse about three miles south of the Whan homestead before coming to the narrow lane that led to the Larson property. The log home was massive and hidden by trees until they reached a large clearing. Children scrambled in the yard everywhere. "This must be a big family." Robert chuckled. "How many children do they have?"

"Nine, I reckon," Samuel replied. "I know all the Larson youngsters who attend school."

"What a wonderful addition they could be to our Sunday school!" Robert muttered as he climbed down from the carriage and found himself surrounded by bubbling, chattering children. "Are your parents at home?" Robert asked. "We've come to call on them."

"What's it about?" asked one of the larger boys. "My pa doesn't like strangers. He don't take ta them one bit."

"You know me, John," Samuel spoke up. "We're in school together, so it's not like we're strangers. We just came to make a friendly call on your family."

"This man who's with ya. . .what's he sellin'?"

Robert stepped forward and held out his hand. "I'm Robert Harris, the new pastor in this territory, John. We've started a church in the Whan School, and we came today to invite your family to join us for worship services."

"Whoo—ee!" John shouted. "Wait'll Pa hears who ya are. Ya best leave right now!"

Just then the door to the house opened and a middle-aged man stepped out on the porch. He wore bib overalls and had a red bandanna tied around his throat. His graying hair was long, and he sported a full beard. "Who is it, John?" he shouted, squinting into the sun. "We ain't buying anythin'."

"It's not a salesman, Pa," John shouted back. "It's the new preacher come ta call!"

Mr. Larson swore. "We don't want no preacher varmints visitin' us, no time. So git yerself outta here."

Robert walked toward the older man on the porch, but Samuel lagged behind by the carriage. "Please, could we just talk a bit, Mr. Larson?" Robert asked. "This was intended to be a friendly call. We'd like to get better acquainted."

Mr. Larson grunted, swore some more, and ran into the house, returning with a shotgun. He pointed the barrel directly at Robert. "Yer not welcome here, Preacher. Now git afore I use this gun on ya!"

The younger children screamed and scattered. Frightened, they ran toward the back of the house where a tall, thin woman was removing clothes from the line. She gathered her children to her as a hen gathers its chicks.

"I'm sorry, Mr. Larson. I didn't mean to rile you," Robert said. "Could we just pick up your children for Sunday school on Sunday?"

"Ya must be deaf, Preacher. I said to git, and I meant it. Now git!" He cocked the shotgun and held it on Robert. "My young'uns don't go to no Sunday school."

"Please, Pastor Harris, let's go," Samuel called. "We aren't wanted here."

Robert backed up and joined Samuel at the buggy. "I think you're right, Samuel. We're obviously not wanted here. Too bad. . .with all those children."

"Guess they would fill up our Sunday school fine, wouldn't they, Pastor Harris?"

"That they would, Samuel," Robert said as he turned the horse around and they headed back down the narrow, wooded lane. "But most importantly, they would hear about Jesus, something that could change their entire life."

That evening Robert wrote his first letter to Emily. It was lengthy because he had much to tell about the Whan family. He described the well-behaved children and how much he was enjoying them. A word picture of the attractive log home and his fine accommodations was included, as well as descriptions of the beautiful, rolling countryside. He told about the first Sunday services, a partial disappointment, but also expressed his high hopes for what could happen in the future. When he gave her an account of his calls thus far, he omitted nothing. "And, dearest Emily," he said in closing, "I miss you and think about you every day. Let me know how things are going in Waterville. I long to see your dear face and sweet smile. I keep all our special times together stored in my memory, which brings you close. Please pray for the work here and for these very needy people."

Chapter 11

Peter McClough had become a regular attendee at the little Waterville Community Church. He seated himself where he could obtain the best view of Louisa without being too obvious. Although she ignored him completely, he clung to the hope she would one day acknowledge him with a smile. The Mason family was delighted with his sudden interest in church. They had not prodded him unnecessarily, but they'd felt certain all along that he would eventually join them for worship services. The people of the congregation welcomed Peter wholeheartedly. Their expression of friendship was heartwarming and a completely new experience for the lonely young man.

"Why such a long face?" Emily asked Peter one balmy Sunday shortly after the morning service. Peter stared forlornly at the departing Bradford carriage as it rambled down the roadway. "It's Louisa." He sighed. "She won't give me the time of day."

"So that's it." Emily laughed. "There are many other available young ladies, Peter. Just glance around you."

Peter shook his head. "Not anyone like Louisa."

"Louisa is lovely," Sarah agreed as she and Fred joined them. Looping her arm through Frederic's, she smiled up at her husband.

"But not as lovely as you are, Mrs. Mason," Frederic said, tenderly pulling her body close to him. "You are the loveliest creature on earth."

Sarah blushed profusely, pleased at her husband's attention. Married less than two months, they were more in love with each passing day. "Come home and have dinner with us, Peter," Sarah said gaily. "We'll drive your gloomies away."

"Thanks, but not today, Sarah. I appreciate the offer, but I need to be alone with my thoughts. I just can't figure Louisa out. She won't give me a chance to be friends. I'd feel a lot better if she'd talk to me. Maybe I've done something wrong—something I don't know about. If so, I'd like to apologize.

"Guess I'll walk a spell and stretch my legs. It may clear out the cobwebs and settle some things in my mind. I might stop in at the Bradfords' and make a social call, if I get up enough nerve. Louisa might be more receptive with her parents present."

"That's a fine idea, Peter," Emily agreed. "Louisa hasn't had any opportunity to talk with you. I'm sure the Bradfords would welcome such a visit."

Peter spent the next two hours walking the streets of Waterville. It was a peaceful afternoon, late in May, and warm breezes caressed his face. The trees that lined the streets were in full leaf, and flowers poked their heads through the rich, moist soil. He pulled off his suit coat and laid it carelessly over one arm. Pushing dark locks of hair back from his forehead, he took a deep breath. "What a perfect day it would be if Louisa were only here by my side."

Hunger pangs gnawed at his stomach. He'd eaten little breakfast that morning, and it was now long past the lunch hour. Deciding against a cold supper of leftovers at home, he turned toward Main Street, heading for the common and Castonguay Square. Peter knew the Elmwood Hotel served fine food in its dining room. Then he remembered the small restaurant near the Waterville Hardware. "I don't need a big meal," he murmured. "Just a bite to hold me over. They'll have everything I need."

As Peter walked down Main Street, he noticed a young lady, by herself, gazing through the window into the eating establishment. "That looks like Louisa," he muttered to himself and hastened his step. "I wonder why she is in town alone. Something inside seems to have captured her interest. Maybe I can talk her into joining me for something to eat."

Louisa Bradford had walked uptown on an errand and happened to glance into the window of the restaurant on Main Street. Her face turned ashen as she stared at the couple seated nearest the window. There was no mistaking Dr. Matthews. He sat with a lovely young woman, both his hands on the table upon hers. He was smiling warmly at her, gazing intently into her eyes. The look on his face communicated deep feeling and emotion. Then he leaned toward her and kissed her lightly on the lips. Louisa's heart beat wildly. *I sat in that very seat with him many times when we dined here together. James Matthews spoke words of love and led me to believe he cared deeply. How could he toy so with my affections?* Bursting into tears, Louisa whirled around, wanting to get as far away from him as possible.

Blindly she entered the roadway, covering her face with her hands. A horse and carriage, out of control, was barreling toward her. Peter heard the roar of the carriage wheels as the horse bore down upon the unsuspecting figure. "Dear God, she'll be killed!" he shouted. Flinging his coat aside, he dashed into the road after her. He hurled himself in front of the horse, thrust Louisa aside, and managed to push her free of the carriage. She hit the ground hard and tumbled over and over in the dusty roadway. Unhurt except for bumps and bruises, Louisa picked herself up and turned to thank the one who had saved her life. A crowd had gathered around a young man lying on the ground. He had not been so fortunate, for he had taken the full brunt of the horse and carriage. Louisa pushed her way through the crowd just as a few men rolled the crumpled and battered body over. She took one look and screamed.

"Do you know the man?" someone asked her.

"It's Peter McClough," she whispered and fell in dead faint.

When Louisa next opened her eyes, she was at home in her own room and her mother was fussing over her. She struggled to sit up, then fell back against the pillows and covered her eyes with her hands.

"What is it, dear?" Mrs. Bradford asked. "You took a bad spill, but you're going to be fine."

"Yes, I'm all right," she choked. "But Peter McClough died saving my life. I'll never be able to live with that!"

Mrs. Bradford gathered her daughter to her bosom. "Don't fret, child. Peter McClough is not dead. He is badly hurt, but he will live. We owe him a great debt of gratitude."

Louisa sobbed quietly. "It's all my fault. I didn't look where I was going."

"That's not like you, dear. You've always been such a careful person. You must have been distracted by something."

"Yes, I was." Louisa turned away and quickly changed the subject. "How badly is Peter hurt? Is he in the hospital?"

"He's in the hospital with a concussion and some broken bones. Fortunately he is a strong and healthy young man. He should heal quickly. When he comes home, he will need extra care. Probably Martha, his part-time housekeeper, will look after him."

"I think we should do something for him, Mother. Is there any way we can repay him? It was a great sacrifice he made."

"He doesn't need money, and I'm sure he wouldn't take it. We can be friendly and take food in. . .ask to help in any way we can. I think he would appreciate our friendship more than anything else. I know you've always avoided him at church. The Mason family says he has changed a great deal since he first came to Waterville. A little kindness on your part would help immensely."

During the next several days, Louisa thought long and hard abut her attitude toward Peter McClough. She had snubbed him, been indifferent, and been totally unresponsive to any offers of his friendship. "What a snob I've been," she confessed to Emily one afternoon. "I've been so captivated with Dr. Matthews's charm, and what a philanderer he turned out to be. I've treated Peter as less than a human being—certainly not a person of any worth. I hope he will forgive me and we can become friends."

"I'm sorry you had to find out about Dr. Matthews in such a hard way, Louisa," Emily consoled her friend. "I knew he wasn't the right person for you, so I prayed God would show you the truth about him. I am sorry it meant Peter getting hurt."

Peter McClough recovered completely from his concussion and returned home after two weeks. He had broken ribs and a broken arm, leg, and shoulder. While he was in the hospital, the Mason family, along with others from the church, visited him frequently and prayed for him.

"I think God was trying to get my attention," Peter said to Emily when she and Fred were visiting him after he returned home.

"He has a way of doing that, Peter. Have you considered turning your life over to Him?"

Peter's eyes grew moist with tears. "I have, and I did. I know you, Fred, and others have been praying for me. While flat on my back, I looked up to God. I've led such a worthless life, Emily. But God drew close to me, and I felt His presence. He seemed to say it didn't matter about the past. . . . He loved me anyway. It was a wonderful experience. I asked His forgiveness, and He accepted me. I belong to Him now."

Emily threw an arm around Peter's good shoulder. "That's the best news you could give me, Peter," she said excitedly. "I know Fred talked to you several times about God. . .and we've all prayed for you. You are one of God's family now, and there is great rejoicing in heaven."

"I'm anxious to get back to church. There's so much to learn. I've always listened, but it went right over my head. I'm such a dummy when it comes to the Bible."

"Start reading the book of John," Emily counseled. "That's a good place for new Christians to start. Do you have a Bible?"

"I have the one that belonged to my pa, your uncle George. It was left at the house when I moved in. I just never bothered to bring it to church with me."

Martha, Peter's housekeeper, entered the room and announced another visitor.

"Who is it?" Peter asked.

"Miss Louisa Bradford."

Emily stood up and tugged Fred to his feet. "We must leave now anyway, Peter. You and Louisa need some time to talk alone. You'll find her delightful company."

"She's only here because she feels indebted to me," Peter said gloomily. "I don't want her friendship on that basis—because she thinks she owes me something."

"You did save her life, Peter. Louisa is grateful, I know. And isn't this what you've been wanting—a relationship with Louisa?"

"I want her to care about me because of who I am, not for anything I've done," he insisted. "She just wants to show her appreciation, and that will be it."

"Shall I show her in?" Martha asked from the doorway. "She seems bent on seeing you today."

"Show her in, Martha," Emily said. "This fellow needs some cheery conversation and charming companionship. I think Miss Bradford is just what the doctor ordered."

Emily and Fred passed Louisa on their way out, and Emily greeted her with a warm hug.

"How is he, Emily?" she asked.

"He's doing fine. . .be his old self in no time. He's a bit edgy, but that's to be expected. Peter is an active fellow. He isn't used to being confined. I think you are just the one to cheer him up."

"I hope so, Emily. I'm nervous about seeing him. I really regret the way I treated him in the past."

Martha ushered Louisa into the parlor where Peter lay awkwardly on a sofa, his right arm and leg in a cast. His forehead was bandaged, and a shock of dark, wavy hair fell carelessly to one side. "Hello, Peter. I'm sorry about what happened," Louisa said. Her lovely face was pale against the mass of light blond curls, and her gray eyes registered deep concern. Shyly, she walked toward him, twisting her handkerchief nervously in her hands.

"Why'd you come?" Peter asked almost gruffly. "It wasn't necessary."

"Yes, it was, Peter. I needed to thank you. You saved my life."

"Your parents already thanked me. Anyway, it was nothing."

"Oh, but it was," Louisa said, moving a small stool close to him. She sat down and smoothed her calico skirts around her. "I wanted to thank you personally and let you know how I feel."

"You are not indebted to me, so don't worry your head about it."

"It was a brave thing that you did. You gave no thought for yourself when you pushed me out of harm's way. Now you are laid up with broken bones, and it is all my fault."

"I knew that was the reason you came. You felt sorry for me." He spat the words out bitterly. "Many times I've tried to talk with you and establish a friendship, but you ignored me. I don't want your sympathy, Miss Bradford. I did what I did because it was the decent thing to do. Believe me, I haven't done many decent things in my life. But I wanted to protect you. You are like a lovely and fragile porcelain doll. I couldn't bear to see you broken and destroyed."

Louisa dabbed her handkerchief at her eyes as tears filled them and spilled over, running down her cheeks. She jumped up and ran to the doorway, then turned to face Peter. "I know I don't deserve your friendship. I've been rude and acted like a spoiled child." Her voice broke, but she struggled to go on. "I hope someday, Peter, you will find it in your heart to forgive me."

Chapter 12

When Robert's long-awaited letters arrived, Emily clasped them eagerly to her bosom. Hurriedly, she entered her room and tore open the envelopes, reading the letters several times and lingering on every word. In his first letter Robert described Thomas and Elizabeth Whan and each of the children. Emily chuckled as she read about some of the younger ones' antics and noted their attachment to Robert. It gave her a deep satisfaction to know Robert was well, happy, and actively involved in his work. Emily gasped when she read about the angry Mr. Larson holding a gun on him and ordering him off his property. But Robert only considered it a challenge and looked forward to what God was going to do in the future. His letters always closed with endearing words of love. "I miss you, Emily," he wrote, "and wish you were here by my side. Please continue to pray for the Larson family and others. I feel confident God is going to do a work here."

Emily shared Robert's news and requests with her family, the Bradfords, and the church folk, and many prayers were uttered on his behalf.

Emily posted lengthy letters of encouragement to Robert in return. They included news of family, church activities, and her studies. She shared about Peter's accident and heroic effort in pushing Louisa out of harm's way. "He saved her life, Robert," she wrote, "and the wonderful news is that Peter is now a believer. He is excited about reading his Bible and fellowshipping with the believers. Pray for his growth as a Christian—it is all so new to him. And pray for Louisa. It was a shock to find Dr. Matthews with another woman in a seemingly intimate relationship. She realizes now that he is not the gentleman she thought him to be, nor was his attention to her sincere. She is unhappy and struggling with problems in her life. The fact that Peter saved her life—although she treated him so unkindly in the past—bothers her more than she lets on.

"I miss you so much, dear Robert, and long to feel your strong arms around me, drawing me close."

Louisa was indeed a very unhappy young lady. She missed a week of classes trying to pull herself together. Her return to college found her listless and on guard. She had no heart for her studies during the remainder of the semester. Returning to her advanced Shakespeare class was the most difficult. She had opened her heart to Dr. Matthews and thought he returned her feelings of love. Now she felt betrayed, for he was obviously involved romantically with another young woman. Emily did her best to raise her spirits. "Don't pine over him, Louisa. He isn't worth your concern."

163

Louisa turned on her friend. "You don't know how I feel, Emily! How could you? You've never had such an experience. You haven't loved someone who didn't love you."

Emily put a comforting arm around Louisa's shoulders. "You are right. I can't understand fully how you feel, because I haven't been through the same situation. But God knows. He cares, and He understands. He is able to work this all out for your good."

"It's all so impossible!" Louisa cried, tears welling up in her gray eyes. "Dr. Matthews trampled on my affections. He doesn't care about me, and I was certain he did. He's coolly aloof in the classroom, as though we never had a close friendship at all. And now Peter has rejected me. He won't forgive me for snubbing him in the past. I went to see him as a friend, and he turned me away." The tears were flowing freely now, and she buried her head on Emily's shoulder. "What can I do?"

Emily patted her friend. "This seems like such a big problem now, Louisa. But it will pass. Turn it over to God and wait patiently on Him. Remember He is still in control."

Louisa blew her nose and dabbed her eyes with her handkerchief. "I'm glad classes end next week. I can't stand much more of this."

"I'm really sorry, Louisa. I should have discouraged you right at the beginning of your relationship. I learned too late he was not the kind of man to become interested in. There is someone very special for you. God will reveal him in time."

"I wish I could be as sure of that as you are. I feel like God has forgotten me. My faith is a little weak right now."

Emily managed to change the subject and ease Louisa out of her doleful attitude. Eventually she had her smiling over some humorous things in one of Robert's letters. "He loves the Whan children, and they are a constant source of entertainment for him. Their games and antics are a cheery aspect of his work there in Pennsylvania. Robert has adjusted well to his change of location and the challenges of the ministry."

"How does he get anything accomplished with all those children around?" Louisa asked. "He must have nerves of steel."

"Robert welcomes their attention. Being an only child and raised by his grandmother, he feels he missed out on the joys of family life."

"Well, that will all change when you two get married next year, Emily, and start your own family."

"Yes." Emily sighed contentedly. "When I finally become Mrs. Robert Harris."

❧

The warm spring rains gave way to the warmer days of June. Trees were in full leaf, and flowers exploded everywhere. Emily inhaled deeply the sweet scents of the blossoms as she and Louisa left Colby College on the final day of classes.

"It's such a beautiful day," she exclaimed. "Let's walk over to Peter's and see how he is doing. I'm afraid I've been so busy finishing up my courses, I've neglected the poor lad. I'm sure he gets lonely being cooped up for such a long time. He's a very active fellow ordinarily."

"I don't think he will want to see me," Louisa said. "He treated me badly the last time I was there. You go on ahead, and I'll see you at home."

"Nonsense! He needs some cheerful conversation and friendship. Imagine how hard it is being confined for such a long while."

"I know, and it's all my fault. If I hadn't been such a foolish girl—lovesick over a handsome professor—this wouldn't have happened."

"Peter did what he needed to do at the time, Louisa. It was a gallant thing for him to do, but I'm sure he has no regrets. He's never mentioned any."

"Well, he doesn't want my friendship. He made that very clear. It might anger him if I call again. He sounded bitter, and I'd rather not antagonize him. He's suffered enough."

"It won't hurt to try again to be friends. You need to go the extra mile, Louisa. Peter is a new Christian and needs our encouragement. A bitter and unforgiving attitude, unless reconciled, will stunt his growth in the faith. Perhaps he sees things a little more clearly now. Anyway, you need to give him another chance."

"All right. After what he sacrificed for me, I guess I can swallow my pride. I do want to gain his friendship. I regret my former actions, when I treated him so shabbily. But if he rejects me again, I don't know what I'll do."

"You'll keep trying, Louisa, because you know it's the right thing to do. If you do your part, that's all God asks. You can't force Peter to have a right attitude. But you can be an example to him. And God can move in Peter's heart and show him how to react."

Martha answered their knock and greeted them warmly. "It's good ta see ya young ladies—and how lovely ya look. Peter will be cheered by yer presence."

"How is he, Martha?" Emily asked. "Is he in good spirits today?"

"That he is. Must be the lovely day and warm sunshine makin' him so chipper. Come right on through the house ta the backyard. Peter is relaxin' in the garden, partly readin', partly dozin'. I'm not sure which at the moment."

"Oh, we don't want to disturb him," Louisa said quickly. "Please don't wake him if he's asleep. He probably needs his rest."

"Land sakes, child, he'd never forgive me if I turned two lovely young ladies away because he was nappin'. He longs fer company and gits so bored sittin' around. Why, you are sure ta brighten his day."

As they stepped into the yard, Emily felt a pang of nostalgia. She noticed the trees, shrubs, and flower beds, so familiar to her. "Everything looks the same, Martha," she said softly. "Peter has kept Aunt Maude's garden just as lovely as when she was alive. How good of him."

"He likes workin' with the plants, but he didn't know much about yard work at first." Martha chuckled, remembering. "He couldn't do nothin' right. Guess he never had a yard when he lived with his ma growin' up. Yer aunt Maude's gardener, Zeke, gave Peter pointers and advice, lendin' his know-how. Since the accident, Zeke's been doin' it all—cuttin', trimmin', weedin', and transplantin'. Peter takes great pride in his garden and wants it kept nice, jest as yer aunt Maude and his pa kept it."

They walked toward the back of the yard toward a large elm tree. Peter was in the shade, sprawled on a long bench padded with blankets and pillows. His crutches leaned against the tree. The dark eyes were closed, and a shock of dark, wavy hair fell across his forehead. "He really is asleep," Louisa whispered. "Wouldn't it be cruel to wake him?"

"It would be cruel not to," Martha said in a normal tone.

Peter stirred briefly, but his eyes remained closed. Louisa noticed him as if for the first time. He seemed so vulnerable, so little boyish, yes, even handsome. Maybe it was the strong jaw, firm mouth, or tousled hair. Something tugged at her heart as she studied the manly features.

"Peter, wake up!" Emily commanded. "You can't sleep all day. You have company."

Peter opened one eye and grimaced. "It's you, Emily. Guess I fell asleep. The warm sunshine feels great on these old bones. I'm glad you came." Then he noticed Louisa standing a little to the back. "How are you, Miss Bradford?"

"Fine, Peter, er. . .Mr. McClough. Thank you."

"My, aren't we being formal today," Emily said. "I think you are well enough acquainted for first names."

Martha asked the girls to be seated and reached over to straighten and puff Peter's pillows. "Please excuse me because I have a kettle o' stew on the stove," she said, heading toward the house. "Can I get ya somethin' cool ta drink?"

"No thanks," the girls said in unison, sinking onto the wooden chairs. Emily proceeded to tell Peter the news from Robert's last letter, while Louisa listened quietly, her eyes upon Peter. "The Whan children sound delightful," Emily said, relating one unusually humorous incident. "And Robert is enjoying every minute of it."

Peter grinned, then burst into a hearty laugh. Louisa, caught off guard, felt a strange warmth come over her. She liked his deep robust laugh and the way he cocked his head to one side.

As Emily and Peter continued to carry on a lively conversation, Louisa remained silent, studying the features of this young man who had so bravely saved her life.

"When do you get rid of the crutches?" Emily asked. "I'm sure you are looking forward to that day. Will it be soon?"

"Another three weeks." Peter sighed. "And yes, I'm anxious to get rid of the crutches and get back to work. I feel so lazy, being idle. It has been an opportunity to read some good books, though. My pa and your aunt Maude had a fine library of books, which are mine now. I never had an opportunity to read quality books before. It has broadened my education immensely. My recovery time has served a good purpose in that respect. And the prognosis is good. The doctor says I'll recover fully and be good as new."

"Well, that is encouraging news, Peter," Emily said. "I'm glad there are no serious problems involved. Aren't you, Louisa?"

"Oh yes, indeed I am," Louisa faltered, color rising to her cheeks. "It would never have happened if I'd been more careful." Her gray eyes were pleading now. "I'm sorry."

Peter studied her intently with his dark eyes. "It was nothing," he said, giving her a little smile. "I would do it over again, Louisa. . .for you!"

Chapter 13

By June, Robert had visited all the families suggested by Thomas Whan, plus some others. The church congregation had expanded to include Olivia Mayer and her children; Miss Johnson, the schoolteacher; and more recently the Morrison family. Mrs. Morrison, a sweet-natured, heavyset woman, took Robert aside one Sunday after services. "We'd a come sooner, Preacher, but Richard weren't ready. Our son has been so hesitant since he lost his arm in the war. I know he feels less a person, though we've tried our best ta make him feel normal. It's his left arm, and he can do most everythin' still. He jest feels different. His friend, John, has been a great help ta all of us."

Robert had taken a special interest in Richard Morrison and his war buddy, John Smith. When he first met John, he thought John reminded him of someone—perhaps someone in his past. Both Richard and John had suffered trauma from the war. Richard lost his left arm, but John had amnesia and remembered nothing about his home or family. With no record of who he was, he assumed the new name and graciously accepted Richard's invitation to live with his folks. The Morrisons had a younger son, fifteen, and a daughter, nine, but they had welcomed John as one of their own.

"John is good therapy fer Richard," Mrs. Morrison continued. "John feels beholdin' ta Richard fer bringin' him home with him, but Richard depends on John—it's like he was a left arm ta him."

"I can see that, Mrs. Morrison. They depend on each other, and it's good for both of them. What will happen if John remembers who he is one day, and who his parents are?"

"He'll leave us, I reckon. It will be hard on Richard iffen thet day ever comes. They are sech close friends."

"But you want John to remember, don't you? I expect some mother is grieving over her boy. She most likely believes he is dead."

"Thet's a hard one ta answer, Preacher. We got our boy home safe, less a arm. It tears my heart ta think some ma is pinin' for her boy, not knowin' what happened. . .wonderin' iffen he's dead. Maybe she's still hopin' he's alive. She might be thinkin' he'll come back after all this time. Mas don't give up hope easily."

"Has John had a doctor look at him to see if there is anything that can be done for him? There may be some kind of shock treatment they could do. It would be worth checking into."

"No doctors looked at him since he left the hospital. They said they done everythin' they could fer him, and now it's up ta the Almighty. He was told it might come back gradjerly, a little bit at a time. Poor boy's not remembered a whit what happened afore. Iffen he did, he'd leave us fer sure. He seems a mite restless lately. I 'spect he feels he should be out on his own. He worries so about bein' a burden."

Robert started spending one afternoon a week at the Morrison home because Mrs. Morrison pressed him to take a meal with them every Thursday. It gave him a good opportunity to spend time with Richard and John on a friendly basis, away from church. John opened up readily and discussed his troublesome feelings about not knowing his identity. "I need to know who I am, Preacher. Where do I belong? Who are my folks? Maybe I don't have any, but if I do, I want to know who they are. Can you understand how painful it is, not knowing anything about my background?"

"I think I can, John. My parents died when I was very young, and my grandmother raised me. But at least I know who I was and who my parents were. I can understand your stress in not knowing, in not having a family to relate to."

"The Morrisons are wonderful to me—just like family." John smiled fondly at Richard. "Richard is the best brother I could ever have. And he always will be, no matter what."

Eventually Richard, quiet at first, let down his barriers and entered the conversation. "John is my best, my only friend, Preacher. Losing my arm wasn't the worst thing in the world. I get along pretty well without it. I'd gladly have given my life for the 'cause.'" I knew the price I might have to pay when I enlisted. But I have a problem with how folks look at me now, how they treat me. I'm different, handicapped, disabled, whatever. I can see the pity in their eyes, and yes, it bothers me. It bothers me a lot. Sometimes I want to hibernate. It was hard for me to start going to the church services, but I'm glad I did. It's been good."

"The people at church care about you, Richard. It isn't pity you see in their eyes—it's genuine love. You did a great service for our country, fought bravely, and sacrificed so we could be a united nation once again. Most people are proud of your great sacrifice. Yes, they are sorry you had to lose an arm, but they don't mean to show pity. Some folk don't know how to react, so they try to cover up their feelings. But I daresay it's love and concern more than anything else."

Robert's talks and visits had a decided effect on the two young men. Richard professed to be a Christian since childhood but admitted he had drifted away from the Lord. "God was watching over me on the battlefield. I lay unconscious for a long time after I was injured. If the medics hadn't reached me in time, I would have bled to death. Many soldiers did. I'm thankful I lost only my arm and not my life."

John was certain of his Christian faith but had no memory of the experience. "I believe in God, and I know He is real, Pastor," John said. "Although I can't tell you when, I know I have accepted Him into my life. I can feel His presence with me wherever I go."

Both young men grew in their Christian walk under Robert's leadership and began to take an active part in the ministry of the little church.

In a letter to Emily, Robert wrote:

The people here are a blessing and encouragement to my heart. God is moving among these people, and I am thankful to be a part of it.

We are still a small congregation, but Richard and John are becoming actively involved in the church's outreach. Their eagerness and zeal are a godsend. The children of the church families look up to them as role models. Richard and John symbolize war heroes, and as Christians they can inspire these youngsters to live for God. I study the Word with them every Thursday when I visit the Morrisons' home. By fall, they will be ready to have a ministry with the youth, and that is exciting to me.

The Whan family feels as though they know you because I speak of you so often. They are like family to me. The children are all fine and delighted to have the summer free from studies. I try to help Thomas and the boys with the farm chores whenever possible. It's a diversion for me and good therapy. Little Robert is talking more and more. He toddles after me and begs for a 'tory' out of his favorite book. The lad loves to go barefooted and constantly removes his 'hoos' and 'hocks,' as he calls them. Mrs. Whan worries that he is bothering me, but that is impossible. I adore the child and welcome any opportunity to spend time with him. Maybe, Emily, after we are married, we will have a little Robert someday.

How is everyone, and sweet little Rebeccah? From your letters, I can tell she is getting cuter every day, laughing, jabbering, and cooing.

I know she is a great joy to you and all the family. I'm sorry to miss all of her growth and development stages. Keep me posted on her activities.

It was great news about Peter. We rejoice in another wandering one brought into the fold. He seemed to be heading that way. I had a feeling it wouldn't be long until he made that decision.

I've been praying for Louisa and trust her problems will be resolved soon. She is hurting because she feels betrayed by one she loved. Through this difficult experience she'll find that God does work everything out for our good, in the long run. It doesn't seem at all good to her now. I know it's hard for her to be patient. But one day she will see that it is true.

I appreciate your prayers, dear Emily. This work cannot grow without the prayers of God's faithful people. You cannot know how much I miss you. I see your sweet face before me in everything I do. My arms ache to hold you, and I sometimes wonder why I am here, so far away from my sweetheart. If I could just see your smile and hear your soft voice and the special way you laugh. They are music to my soul. But I know God is working in this place and He wants me here for now. Remember, darling, there is a time for us, a time for our love in the future.

For now, I remain yours forever,
Robert

Chapter 14

Robert and other men of the church took turns each week helping Olivia Mayer around her farm. They mended fences, patched and rebuilt the sagging porch, and plowed her garden. The womenfolk passed on good clothing their children had outgrown and welcomed Olivia into their sewing circle. Olivia was genuinely pleased and began to show more interest in her hair and personal appearance. Gradually her sad countenance vanished. She greeted everyone with a smile that brightened her entire face and brought back the sparkle of youth. The loss of her husband, Jess, and then his parents had left her with a despairing heart and no interest in life. Now, back in fellowship with God and God's people, she rejoiced in each new day as a day to live for Him.

Richard and John were among those who spent many hours at the Mayers' farm. Soon they took over the work entirely and spent two afternoons a week cultivating the garden and doing odd jobs. "Let us handle it, Pastor," Richard said. "John and I, being single, have more time than the other men. They have their farms and families to care for. We can handle the work, can't we, John?" John nodded his agreement.

"That's good of you," Robert said, obviously pleased at this latest development. "This is the season the men are busiest, with new cattle, crops, and grain. They'll thank you for taking over this responsibility. It will make their own work a whole lot easier."

Olivia welcomed the two young men's assistance. Often she asked them to share supper with her and the children around the old oak table in the spacious kitchen. During the afternoon she kept refreshments handy and enjoyed serving them cool drinks and some of her freshly baked cookies. Sometimes she and the children carried the newly baked treats out to the field where the men were working. Then she and the men would sit in the shade for a spell and talk while the children romped nearby.

Robert became increasingly aware that a relationship was developing between Richard and Olivia. John was quick to keep him informed. "Olivia bakes cookies and brings them out to the field where we are working. Richard and I rest a spell and talk with her while we eat. It's kind of her to think of us needing some refreshments."

"They are a welcome treat, Pastor," Richard added. "Olivia thinks we're spending too much time on her place. . .says it keeps us from any social life. I told her John and I don't need any social life except this. Being at Olivia's is all the social life we want."

"Has Olivia said anything about leaving the farm?" Robert asked. "She has some kinfolk in Ohio, I understand. But her parents are dead."

"Olivia is so happy to see the place getting fixed up," John replied. "She says her heart never was in leaving the homestead. Her young'uns love the farm. They're settled in school, and they all favor the worship services."

"It's good to see the family in church," Robert said. "Olivia has changed a lot since I first met her. She was one very sad lady, trying to raise three young children by herself and run the farm. It's too much for a young woman."

"Yes, it is," Richard agreed, pushing back a lock of his sandy hair. His square, handsome face, bronzed from the summer sun, spread into a wide smile.

"I think Richard has been taken in by Olivia's brown eyes and dimpled smile," John said teasingly. "And I believe the feeling is mutual. After all, she is a very attractive woman."

"John. . .are you. . ." Richard hesitated a moment and then went on. "Are you interested in Olivia? I mean, if you are, I wouldn't hesitate to back away. Not that she'd be attracted to me anyway. . .a one-armed ex-soldier."

"She's a fine woman, Richard, but I'm not interested in her in a romantic way. I'll never get involved with anyone until I learn my true identity. I might have a sweetheart somewhere, or even a wife. Furthermore, Olivia has eyes only for you. It shows all over her face."

"Are you ready for a serious relationship and all its responsibilities, Richard?" Robert asked soberly. "There is an entire family involved here."

"I never thought I'd find anyone like Olivia, who would care for me, Pastor. When I lost my arm, I planned on being a bachelor all my life. Do you really believe she could learn to care for me, handicapped the way I am?" Richard's empty sleeve hung loosely at his side.

"That doesn't make you any less of a man, Richard," Robert stated. "Olivia has had heartache in her life, but she is beginning to fall in love with you. John and I see all the signs. So you can take it from there or let it drop. If you don't want to be involved, you'd best back off. No sense in her getting hurt again."

Richard felt a new warmth rising in his sun-bronzed face. "It's a pleasurable feeling just thinking about a possible relationship with Olivia Mayer. God is breaking down the barriers, Pastor. I built obstacles and barricades, but they seem to be crumbling around me. God is showing me I can have a normal life and even a ready-made family of my own."

"It's a breakthrough for you, Richard," John said, putting an arm around his friend's shoulder. "You can have a full life because you've faced your disability and accepted it. And perhaps you've found the person to share your life and your future. Olivia is quite a woman."

"Yes," Richard said with emotion, "Olivia Mayer is quite a woman!"

≈

The warm days of summer were passing swiftly. Emily welcomed the change of pace from her studies. The Mason household gathered the crops, and Emily and her mother prepared them for the long winter months ahead. Often, Cassie joined them, and they worked together as in days past. Little Rebeccah was a contented baby and played quietly with her toys or napped in the old crib upstairs. Peter McClough, fit as ever, was back to work at the lumber mill. Faithfully he attended church services and spent much of his time studying the Bible. He was like a young stallion, chomping at the bit in his eagerness to learn. Many weekends were spent at the Mason household or with Fred and Sarah at their cabin. He had a gnawing hunger to saturate himself in the Word and fired questions tirelessly.

"Whoa, man," Fred said one Saturday afternoon in August. Peter had come out to help with the harvest, but he constantly pelted Fred with questions about things he didn't understand. Frederic mopped his brow and squinted in the hot afternoon sun. "Some of your questions are beyond me, Peter. I'm not a student of the Bible like Robert. Perhaps you'd like to write to him or talk to Rev. Davis. They've been trained and are better equipped to delve into some of these deeper issues."

"Maybe I need some schooling myself, Fred. I have this desire to know all there is to know about God. My life up to now has been wasted. I did unspeakable things, used God's name in vain, and had no thought for anyone but myself. I'd like to make my life count for something—something worthwhile."

"That's a commendable goal, my friend. You've come a long way. Are you serious about this? Do you want to study for the ministry?"

"I reckon I couldn't be a good preacher, Fred. Not someone like me with my past starin' me in the face."

"Of course you could. God takes the weak things of this world—"

"And vile things, too?"

"Peter, God changed you already. You're a new creature. Forget your past. God forgives and buries it in the depths of the deepest sea. It's what you do from now on that is important."

Peter kicked at the dirt, as if to rid himself of thoughts of his past. "And I want to do things that count for God. Not necessarily as a preacher, maybe just a helper. If I could help folks like me—like I once was—trust God, then I'd be satisfied."

"You can do that, Peter, without going on to school. Just share your experience. Tell people about the changes in your own life."

"But some further study would help me, wouldn't it? I'd be in a better position to talk to people where they're at. Right now I can't put words together and have them make sense. I need a lot of help, Fred."

"The schooling would certainly be a big help, Peter. But it will mean dedicated study, time, and effort on your part. Even a short-term course would be worthwhile."

"I like the idea—it's a challenge," Peter said excitedly. "I'll see if I can take a couple of classes and still work part-time at the mill."

"You'll be busy, Peter. It will mean studying every night. There won't be time for much else. Do you think you can handle that?"

"I won't mind, because this is important to me. It will give me a feeling of self-worth, especially if God can use me."

Frederic chuckled and placed an arm around Peter's broad shoulders. "Is this the same pompous, brash individual I once knew in the army?"

"No, thank God," Peter said in a serious tone. "That scoundrel is gone forever."

The following Monday Peter checked out the curriculum at Colby College for the fall term. After considerable thought, he chose two classes: religion and English. This combination would be an excellent place to start, he determined. He desired a deeper knowledge of religion, and the English course would be helpful in honing his skills in grammar and speaking correctly. He found he could keep his job at the mill by working afternoons, Saturdays, and any extra hours he could squeeze in.

"You won't have much of a social life," Emily declared when she heard his proposed schedule. "Classes, homework, and your job will fill up all the weekday hours."

"That's fine with me. I'll socialize at church on Sundays and pop over to the farm occasionally, or to Fred's cabin. That will give me enough visiting to keep me happy. You don't have much time yourself, Emily. You seem to keep busy all the time."

"It's different for me, Peter. With Robert gone, I try to keep as busy as possible so the time will go faster."

"Isn't he coming back in September for a few days, as planned? I expected we'd be seeing him soon."

Emily tried to smile. "Robert can't leave right now. He hopes to come at Christmas for sure. I hope. . ." She faltered, then added wistfully, "I hope nothing prevents his coming then. He's already been gone almost five months, and it seems like a lifetime."

"Being separated has to be difficult when you care so much about someone," Peter said sympathetically. "But as least you know he cares and longs to be with you. He's longing for the day you can be together. Some people, like me for instance, don't have anyone who cares about them."

"Peter, you silly goose. Our entire family cares about you. You must know that. We've tried to make you feel like one of us."

"And I do, Emily. I appreciate the warm way your family has received me into their lives. They've shown their care and concern in so many ways. I meant. . .someone to care for me the way you and Robert care about each other—love between a man and a woman."

"That will happen one day, Peter. And it's worth waiting for the right person, the young woman God chooses for you."

"I'm not sure I'll ever find the right person—the one who feels toward me the way I feel toward her. It has to be both ways, you know?"

"Well, Peter, you need to start courting some nice young ladies from church. I think some of them have noticed what a fine young man you turned out to be. And church is a good place to find your special someone. Are you attracted to any of them?"

"I'm afraid I'm only interested in Louisa—and that's hopeless. She wouldn't consider letting me court her."

"Fiddlesticks! Ask Louisa to accompany you to a concert or to dinner sometime soon. She would probably be delighted."

"I've had too many insults from her in the past. She let me know how she felt about me every time I tried to approach her. Louisa Bradford is too high and mighty. She considers me a very low character, not in her class."

"I think you're wrong, Peter. I'm almost certain she would appreciate seeing more of you. Louisa made some changes in her life, just as you have. Try asking her to accompany you for dinner sometime and see if she'll accept."

"Louisa would accept out of gratitude, not because she really cares about me. She feels she owes her life to me. I don't want to court her under those circumstances. It wouldn't work, Emily. She'd be seeing me for all the wrong reasons."

"Louisa told me she hoped you'd forgive her for her rudeness in the past. I know she's grown up a great deal during the past months. Did you know she'd been seeing someone else?"

"I thought there must be another man. Louisa is beautiful and far too good for me. I'm nothing compared to her. I hope this man makes her happy," Peter said glumly.

"You don't know the entire story, Peter. Louisa thought this person cared deeply for her until she saw him that Sunday afternoon, the day you saved her life. She saw him in the restaurant with another young lady, holding hands and kissing. He appeared very devoted to her, and Louisa was crushed. That's when she ran blindly into the street and was almost run down by the horse and carriage. She will always be grateful to you for pushing her out of harm's way."

"What a cad!" Peter muttered. "I'd like to get my hands on him and punch him in the nose. That scoundrel needs to learn some manners on how to treat a lady. I'm just the man who can do it."

"That wouldn't help anything, Peter. Louisa has accepted the fact that this person was not honest and aboveboard with her. He tampered with her affections. Actually, he deceived her into thinking his attention was genuine, when it wasn't at all. She's learned a difficult lesson early in life."

"I hope this episode doesn't sour her on all men," Peter said thoughtfully.

"She'll probably need some time to get over it. It's bound to make her cautious from now on."

"Louisa didn't know enough about the man to begin with. She threw herself headlong into a relationship and expected it to end in marriage. She has led a sheltered life and was very naive about men of the world. He probably never intended her to take him seriously. Or if he did, he didn't seem to care."

"You are right, Emily. This man tampered with Louisa's affections and probably didn't even care. I know what I'm talking about, because I've been a man of the world myself. It's something I'm not proud of. Most men without God are all puffed up in themselves. Selfishness and pride are what it's all about. It becomes a game to see how many women they can make fall in love with them. Then it's on to the next one, and the next. Guess I can't be too hard on the bum. I used to be just like him."

"But you're changed now, Peter. You're not a man of the world anymore. You don't have any regrets, do you?"

Peter relaxed, and a broad smile crossed his rugged face. "No regrets, Emily. I'm thankful for the new life I have in Christ. What does the Bible say? 'Old things are passed away; behold, all things are become new.'"

Chapter 15

Robert tore open Emily's letter and held it to his lips. A sweet scent floated from the envelope into his nostrils. He inhaled deeply and quickly scanned the letter's contents.

My dear Robert,

The days are shorter now, and the briskness in the air is refreshing. It's a welcome relief from those hot, hazy days of summer. Oh, Robert, how I want the days to pass swiftly until you return to me. My studies are going well, and they keep me busy, which is a blessing. But there are times at night when I lie awake and think of you. So many miles separate us, darling, but often I remember something you said, or the way you smile. Then I feel you close to me once again.

Peter has enrolled in two classes at Colby College—religion and English. He is a very determined young man and serious about his desire to learn more about God. He is so busy with studies and working at the mill, he has little time for anything else.

Louisa is still troubled with her emotions. I'm trying to pull her out of her melancholy, but I'm afraid it might take a little time. She's been through a difficult and embarrassing situation.

The family is all well and send their love. Little Rebeccah gets cuter every day. She is crawling now and getting into things, keeping Cassie busy. Her reddish gold hair has grown longer, and it's curly. You will be surprised at how much she has changed.

I am counting the days until Christmas. Let me know when you plan to arrive. Until then, my darling.

Love always,
Emily

Robert once again inhaled the sweet perfume from the letter and tucked it lovingly into his pocket. He would read it and reread it again and again.

❧

Richard and John had become coworkers at the little Wampum church and were reaching out to the youth. On Saturdays they planned organized activities for the youth that included fun times as well as a short gospel story. Enthusiasm mounted to such an extent that it enticed youngsters from unchurched families in the area.

Eventually some of these youth started attending Sunday school. Robert was pleased with the way the two young men had become heartily involved in the work.

"I'm grateful for your dedication to this ministry," Robert told the two men. "We'll have an opportunity to reach some of the parents through their children."

By mid-October it was obvious to the Wampum church folk that Richard and Olivia were in love. The congregation watched their relationship grow, slowly at first, then gently blossom and mature. Richard spent more and more time at Olivia's farm getting the house and grounds in shape. Each Sunday he sat with her and the children, while John sat on the other side of the church with the Morrison family.

Robert knew a wedding was forthcoming, and he grinned at the couple mischievously one Sunday after services. "Is there something you two want to tell me?"

Olivia blushed as she extended her hand. "Why, Preacher, what do ya mean?"

Robert chuckled. "Just thought you might have something on your mind." Richard cleared his throat and shifted from one foot to the other. "We do have something to tell you, but I didn't know it was so obvious."

"I'm afraid the folk here are a mite perceptive, Richard. We've seen all the signs. Now we're waiting to hear the big news."

Richard glanced at Olivia and grasped her hand tightly in his. "She has accepted my proposal, Preacher. I'll never understand why."

Olivia hugged his arm and looked up at him. "Because I love ya, Richard," she said quietly. "That's why."

Richard's eyes met hers and held them in a lingering gaze. "Dearest Olivia, that's all the reason I need," he said huskily. Then in a barely audible voice, he whispered, "I love you, Olivia."

"Ahem!" Robert said, bringing them back to the moment at hand. "When is the big day going to be? Have you decided on a wedding date?"

"Christmas," they said simultaneously. "It's such a beautiful season," Olivia added. "I can't think of a lovelier time to have a weddin'."

"It's a wonderful time for a wedding," Robert agreed. "But I'm afraid I have a problem with that date. I'm sorry."

"Why, Preacher? Is the season too busy?" Richard asked.

"No, that's not it. I'm planning to be away for Christmas, back in Waterville. It's my first opportunity to get back for a visit. I'd hoped you and John would handle things here for me while I'm gone. The other men of the church will help in any way they can."

"We'll gladly do that for you, Preacher. Can't blame you for wanting to be with your family for the holidays. I'm sure they've missed you all these past months."

"I don't have any family except the dear church people back in Waterville. But I do have a special young lady, whom I love very much, waiting for me."

"Then you must go, Preacher," Olivia said firmly. "Your young lady must be missin' ya somethin' dreadful. Why, ya been away sech a long time. Couldn't we be married at Thanksgivin' time, Richard?" she said, looking up at him. "Thet's a wonderful time fer a weddin', too, and we got so much ta be thankful fer."

Richard smiled broadly. "That's even better than Christmas," he said happily. "It's a whole month sooner. Would the Saturday after Thanksgiving be a good day for you, Pastor?"

"It's a fine day. I'll mark it on the calendar, and we'll let the church folk know. They've been anxious for a celebration. Your wedding will be a special occasion for the Wampum Community Church."

With little over a month until the wedding, Olivia was in a frenzy. She spent long hours fashioning an elegant pale yellow and lace frock for her wedding dress. The material had been purchased before her husband was killed in the war. She had put it away in the old trunk and not had the heart to make it up. Now was the right time, she decided. God had brought a fine man into her life, someone to share the future with. It would be appropriate to use the lovely material to fashion her dress. She made dresses for Abigail and Lydia in a pastel pink, while Jess's suit was a handsome blue serge. The three children would stand with her, sharing a part of the wedding ceremony. Richard planned to have John as his best man.

As the wedding day drew nearer, Robert noticed a decided change in John. He became aloof and distant, always seeming preoccupied. Hesitant to speak with him until he knew the problem, Robert drew Mrs. Morrison aside one Sunday morning. "Something is wrong with John," he said seriously. "Do you know what the problem is?"

"He's mournin' over Richard, Preacher. Oh, he's happy fer him and Olivia gettin' married and all, but it leaves him on the outside, don't ya see? John's allus been Richard's left arm. They been best friends since the war. Now John feels useless, in the way even."

"But he mustn't feel that way. I'll talk to him. He's needed more than ever in the work here. He and Richard have done a fine job with the youth, week by week. There's no reason that can't continue."

"We been talkin' ta him, Preacher, but he don't listen. He'll be here fer the weddin'—says he wouldn't miss it fer anythin', but then he's goin' away. He plans ta search the country till he finds his kinfolk. They hafta be out there somewhere, he figgers."

"Where will he go? He has no inkling of where to start. John doesn't know anything about his background or where his family is. Perhaps he has no family, no relatives at all. He mustn't go off by himself."

"We allus knew John would leave us one day. I'm glad we had him with us as long as we did. He's sech a fine young man. We'll all miss him terrible. Maybe if ya talk ta him, Preacher. Maybe he'll listen ta ya. Anythin' is worth a try."

Robert decided to wait until after Richard and Olivia's wedding to talk to John. He needed time to think through his thoughts and come to a conclusion. *Show me what to say, God,* he prayed. *John is Your dear child, and I know You care about what happens to him. He's at loose ends and doesn't know what to do with his life. Give me wise counsel that only You can give.*

Thanksgiving at the Thomas Whan household was a joyous occasion for Robert, although he missed Emily and the folk back in Waterville. The children were delightful, and he entered their games wholeheartedly. At the dinner table Thomas drew him into conversation. He sensed Robert's eagerness to return to Waterville for the Christmas holidays. "How long will ya be gone from us, Robert?"

"About two weeks, Thomas. I'm working it out so I will only miss two Sundays. I thought Richard and John could handle the services while I'm gone. Of course I'm depending on you and some of the others to oversee things and help whenever you can. Would that be an agreeable arrangement?"

"That will work out fine. Richard and John are very responsible young men. They know they can call on the rest of us if they need anything. We'll pull together and all help in whatever way we can."

"John may not be here. According to Mrs. Morrison, he plans to leave after the wedding. He's decided to search out the past—find where he's from and who his folks are. The fact is, he doesn't feel he's needed anymore, with Richard getting married."

"That's nonsense. We need him here. He's been a great help in the growth of the church. John would be sorely missed by everyone."

"I agree, and I plan to have a talk with him. I'm not sure he will listen, but it's certainly worth a try. Pray that I'll have the right words to convince him to stay."

"If anyone can change his mind, it's you, Pastor. I'll let some of the others know so we can all pray. There's power in prayer."

❧

It was a crisp but sunny November afternoon for Richard and Olivia's wedding. The small schoolhouse had been decorated in pastel bows by several ladies of the church. They planned to serve punch and cookies outside after the ceremony. Elizabeth Whan, Thomas's wife, created a three-layer wedding cake for the occasion.

The ceremony was sweet as the couple stood side by side, with Olivia's children beside them. John stood tall beside Richard, dressed neatly in a dark suit. His dark, wavy hair had been slicked back, but a few unruly strands insisted on curling over his forehead. John was smiling, but his blue eyes seemed veiled in sadness. He gave the appearance of being in another world, far away from the festivities.

"There is something about John," Robert muttered under his breath as he studied the young man's face. "There is definitely something about him, but I don't know what it is. Could I know him from somewhere in my past?"

The final vows were spoken joining Richard Morrison and Olivia Mayer as husband and wife. They kissed shyly, and Robert introduced them to the church family. "May I present to you Mr. and Mrs. Richard Morrison."

There was a rush to congratulate the couple and wish them a lifetime of happiness. Children hurried outside for the cake and cookies. In the midst of the excitement, Robert drew John aside. "I need to talk to you, John. Can we be alone for a few moments?" The two men walked toward the front of the church, away from the crowd, and sat down.

"I know what it's about, Preacher, but you can't change my mind. I've made my decision, and I believe it's the right thing to do. I plan to leave Wampum as soon as possible. It's time I got out on my own and searched for my family. I've been extra baggage to the Morrison family for quite a spell."

"Why leave, John? Your friends are here. The Morrisons are like family to you, and they don't feel you've been a burden to them. On the contrary, they've appreciated your help. None of them want you to go."

"I know. They've been wonderful to me and treated me as a son. I care about them deeply and always will. But I need to find out who I am, who my real family is. My future seems so uncertain because I don't remember my past. I need to find some roots."

"This is a big country, John. Where will you go? Do you intend to just wander around until you find something familiar? That could take years. We need you in the work here. You've grown in your Christian faith, and you are serving God."

"And I want to serve God wherever I am. You can count on that. I've appreciated your ministry, Preacher, and your wise counsel."

"Will you come back someday, John? A lot of folk here are going to miss you. I'll miss you." Robert put an arm around John's shoulders. "We pray God will go with you."

"I'll be back. Whether I find my parents or not, I'll return someday. Part of my heart will always be here, tied to these people in Wampum, Pennsylvania."

Chapter 16

In December, colder, brisk air penetrated the little Pennsylvania valley. The days became shorter as snowflakes sifted and swirled, softly icing the trees and stone fences. Robert welcomed the change in the weather but determined to make his calls earlier, during the warmer hours of the day, rather than wait until young Samuel Whan returned home from school. Besides, this would give him the opportunity he needed to detain John's departure. By involving John in visitation and the work at hand, the young man felt a renewed sense of usefulness. John was quick to remind Robert, however, of his plans to leave in the near future.

"Richard and Olivia are very happy, Preacher," he said one afternoon as the two men set forth in the buggy. "I'm glad they got together. They make a fine couple. It makes it easier for me to leave now. I've known I should leave for a long time, but I've just kept putting it off. The Morrisons begged me to stay. They seem to appreciate an extra hand on the farm, and I enjoy the work. But Richard's younger brother is almost sixteen, and he's a big help. I don't feel I'll be leaving the family in the lurch. Ever since we came back from the war, Richard has depended on me. I knew he counted on me more than he needed. It gave me a good feeling, a kind of importance, knowing I was needed and essential to his well-being. Perhaps I was wrong. Maybe I even hindered his progress. Was I wrong, Preacher, to always be there for him?"

"I understand where you're coming from John, but no, I don't think it was wrong of you. Your motives were pure. After all, Richard did you a good turn by inviting you to come home with him. It was your way of showing your appreciation for the family's kindness. Mrs. Morrison expressed how grateful the family is for the relationship you and Richard shared. She said you depended on Richard and he counted on you. It was give-and-take all the way and a healing time for you both."

"Richard is healed, all right. He's faced the world and is ready to go on with his life. With Olivia and the children by his side, he'll make out fine. I wish I could say the same for myself."

"Richard faced up to his responsibilities, John, but he credits the Lord, you, and Olivia for making it possible. Don't ever forget that."

"God did a work in both of our lives, and we have you to thank, Preacher. You spent time with us, drawing us out, and set us on the right track. It's good you came to Wampum when you did. The folk here needed you more than they realized. Richard and Olivia, myself, and others, we've all changed for the better.

What I mean is, we appreciate you."

Robert cleared his throat self-consciously. "Thanks for the encouragement, John. I've counted it a privilege to be here, because this is where God wanted me. I'm just a tool in His hand. The experiences I've gleaned will prove invaluable in my ministry. My faith has been stretched, as well as yours. I've grown right along with the rest of you." Robert snapped the reins and turned the mare down a narrow, wooded country lane.

"Who are we visiting today, Preacher? I've never been down this way before. Is there a house at the end of this road?"

"The Larson family lives down here. I've been here once before with Samuel Whan. Mr. Larson told me to 'git' and said I wasn't welcome. We only planned on a friendly visit, but he got so angry he turned his shotgun on me."

"What makes you think he's changed? Another visit might make him angrier than ever. Let's hope he doesn't decide to pull out his gun again."

"I think the shotgun was just a big bluff. Mr. Larson has a reputation for being a grumpy individual. It's his way of putting up a front. Anyway, I heard through the schoolteacher that the children haven't been in school lately. She told me Mrs. Larson is ill and the children must stay home and help with the chores."

"So you're thinking Mr. Larson might be reachable now? His heart might be a little more tender if his wife is ill?"

"Maybe we can help in some way, John. We can offer our assistance. If so, Mr. Larson might be more receptive to us. It's worth a try."

The house seemed unusually quiet as Robert pulled the buggy into the spacious yard. Suddenly the front door opened and several youngsters, two dogs, and a cat rushed onto the large porch. Robert could see smoke curling and snaking its way from the chimney as he and John climbed down from the buggy.

"Who is it?" a hoarse voice called from inside the house.

"It's the preacher-man, Pa," one of the older children called back. "The one who was here before."

Robert heard loud cursing as the disgruntled man pushed his way out the front door. "Didn't I tell ya before, Preacher? Ya ain't wanted here. Now git!"

"Mr. Larson, I understand the missus is ill," Robert called back. "Is there any way we can be of help? Has the doctor been here to see her?"

"Don't need yer help nor anyone else's," Mr. Larson snarled. "Now jest leave us alone."

The oldest daughter ran down the steps and grabbed Robert's arm. "Ma's bad, Preacher, real bad. She needs a doctor or somethin' ta help her. She coughs and spits a lot. Ma can't hardly breathe, and I'm scared fer her."

"Ellie Mae," Mr. Larson bellowed, "ya get back on the porch. We don't need no help from nobody."

Ellie Mae cowered under his gaze. "Yes, Pa," she mumbled, tears splashing down her cheeks. "I'm comin'."

"Mr. Larson," Robert called, "you're doing your wife an injustice. She obviously needs a doctor. We'll be glad to contact Dr. Williams for you."

"I s'posed ya'd be prayin' fer her. Ain't yer church in the prayin' business?"

"Yes, we are. And we will definitely pray for your missus, Mr. Larson. But may I see her now and speak with her?"

"She ain't up ta no visitors. We 'uns be a hardy bunch. We allus take care of ourselves and don't bother nobody."

"We'll be praying for Mrs. Larson, sir, but she also needs medical attention. The doctor has the medications to help in times like this."

"So yer God cain't handle it by Hisself, is thet it? What kind o' God is thet?"

"Our God is able to cure your wife, but He often uses medical doctors to carry out His work. Mrs. Larson needs prayer and medicine both."

"Jest git yerselves outta here, pronto. My Libby don't need yer help, nor any doctor's. Iffen ya want ta pray fer her, thet's yer business."

Robert sighed as he and John turned back toward the carriage. "My hands are tied, John. I feel like I'm up against a stone wall. Mr. Larson's wife apparently needs medical help, but I can't get through to him. He's an ornery individual."

"He's what I'd call stiff-necked and hardheaded, Preacher. Too proud, I reckon, to accept help. What are we going to do?"

Robert untied the mare and climbed into the buggy. Soft snowflakes were tumbling down, and a light sprinkle covered the ground. "We can pray hard, John, for Mrs. Larson's healing, according to God's will. And we'll continue to pray for the entire Larson family. They all need God."

That evening, Robert shared the Larsons' situation with the Whan family, while John related the circumstances to the Morrisons. Urgent prayers were offered in behalf of the needy family.

During the night the Whan household was awakened by incessant pounding on the front door. Hurriedly, Thomas lit a lantern and pulled on his clothes. When he threw open the door, he found young Luke Larson, the oldest son, gasping for breath. "What is it?" Thomas asked, pulling the lad in out of the cold.

"It's Ma," Luke panted. "She's dying; Pa's sure of it." By this time, Robert had bounded down the stairs, fully dressed. "I got Doc Williams in the buggy, Preacher," Luke said, looking past Thomas at Robert. "Pa wants ya ta come, too. He wants ya ta pray fer Ma."

"I'll get my coat," Robert said, tucking his Bible into his pocket.

Mr. Larson was pacing the floor and wringing his hands when the trio rode up. Robert surmised he had been up all night, for his face was pinched and haggard. Helplessness etched the lined face, which only yesterday afternoon had been cocky and arrogant. "Please, Doc, can ya heal my Libby?" he asked, pulling the doctor toward the bedroom. "And, Preacher," he said over his shoulder at Robert, "maybe ya can put in a prayer or two."

Several minutes later Dr. Williams retuned to the front room and faced Robert. "Mrs. Larson is dying, and there is nothing I can do for her. Perhaps if I'd seen her earlier, I might have been able to save her. She has double pneumonia and has had it for weeks. . .with no medication. This is a sad situation. It's difficult to see cases of neglect like this, where medical help was available and not taken advantage of. Mr. Larson will regret this as long as he lives. Would you like to go in now?"

Robert felt his stomach lurching, and he felt sick inside. He entered the cluttered bedroom and found Mr. Larson kneeling by the bed, sobbing uncontrollably. He held his wife's hand tightly in his. Mrs. Larson, pale and thin, coughed and choked spasmodically. "Don't leave me, Libby," he sobbed. "Don't leave me."

"I want ta. . .ta talk ta the preacher, Jared," she gasped. "Is he here?"

"I'm here, Mrs. Larson," Robert said, drawing nearer and grasping her free hand. "We've been praying for you and your family."

Libby Larson held Robert's hand tightly as she talked in jerky sentences, telling him the things resting heavy on her heart. "I know 'bout prayer and God, Preacher. My folks took me ta church—as a child." After a fit of coughing, Libby continued. "I knowed what was right 'cause Jesus come inta my life. I jest been away from Him all these years." She choked and wheezed, her thin, frail body fighting for strength to go on.

"Don't try ta talk, Libby," Mr. Larson begged hoarsely. "Save your strength."

Libby let go of Robert's hand and patted her husband on the head. "Don't fret so, Jared. I'm—I'm gonna go ta Jesus soon. I learned 'bout heaven when jest a girl. It's a wonderful place." The slight body wracked once again in a fit of coughing.

Robert opened his Bible and read from John, chapter fourteen. "Jesus said, 'Let not your heart be troubled: ye believe in God, believe also in me. In my Father's house are many mansions: if it were not so, I would have told you. I go to prepare a place for you. And if I go and prepare a place for you, I will come again, and receive you unto myself; that where I am, there ye may be also.'"

"Thet's it, Jared. The Bible describes heaven as a wonderful place. I want you and the youngsters ta come there, too. Ya need ta accept Jesus. Promise me ya'll take our young'uns ta Sunday school and church," she gasped. Taking her husband's face in her two hands, she looked deeply into his tear-stained eyes. "Please, Jared, make me this one promise."

"I promise, Libby," he sobbed as he gathered the slight body into his arms and rocked back and forth. "I promise."

Robert prayed softly, committing Libby to God as the couple held each other. *And, Lord, do a work in Jared's heart. . .and the children's.*

Chapter 17

Emily clasped Robert's letter to her heart as she ran into the Bradford home. She and Louisa had just returned from Colby College. She threw down her books and stamped the snow from her boots. It had been snowing heavily, and she brushed the snow from her coat and hat. A few snowflakes lingered on her hair and eyelashes.

Louisa smiled at her friend. "Good news, I hope," she said, following Emily. The girls quickly removed their wraps and headed for the parlor. "Will you share it with me?"

Emily sighed audibly as she sank into the plush sofa. "Only parts of it, Louisa," she said, tearing open the envelope. She smiled mischievously. "Parts will be too personal." Quickly she scanned the letter, then shouted joyfully, "Robert is coming for Christmas! He's really coming. Everything is working out so he can make the trip."

"I'm glad," Louisa said honestly. "You and Robert have been apart too long. When does he arrive?"

"Here, I'll read parts of his letter to you, Louisa." She smoothed the pages of familiar writing.

I will arrive one week before Christmas, darling, and we will have two weeks together. How wonderful it will be to see you again.
We have much catching up to do. I've missed my saucy little sweetheart.

Emily paused, reading silently. "Wait, Louisa, there is more," she said after a moment.

I am bringing a young man with me who was injured in the war. I'm sure I told you about John Smith in a previous letter. He has amnesia and doesn't remember anything about his past or his family. John's best friend, whom he'd met in the hospital where both were recovering from war injuries, married recently. Now John feels like he needs to get away and search for his relatives. He's a pretty stubborn fellow, but I finally convinced him to visit with us over the Christmas holidays before setting out on his quest.

"How sad!" Louisa cried. "I wonder if he'll ever remember. I've read about people with amnesia who go for years and then suddenly remember, through some circumstance or incident. Others never recall their past and must make a new life for themselves. It must be very difficult, not knowing who you are."

Emily continued to read.

Fred and Sarah have already invited me to stay with them at their cabin. Do you think it would be possible for John to stay at the farm with your folks? He may feel a little strange, and I would like to be close by.

Emily glanced up from the letter. "Oh, I know my folks will be glad to have Robert's friend over the holidays. Ma loves having extra guests." Emily frowned as she continued to read her letter to herself.

"Bad news?" Louisa asked. "Sorry, Emily, I'm being very nosy. But your face changed from pure joy to very serious and solemn. I hope nothing is wrong."

"A sad thing happened to the Larson family in Wampum. They are a large family Robert tried to reach with no success. Mr. Larson swore and cursed Robert when he called on the family awhile back. He even grabbed a shotgun and turned it on him."

"What happened, Emily? Did someone get hurt?"

"Mrs. Larson became ill, and Mr. Larson declined help, stubbornly refusing a doctor. When he got desperate and finally called for a doctor, it was too late. The doctor could do nothing to help her. Mrs. Larson passed away last week, and the family is devastated. There are nine children, ranging in age from seventeen on down."

"How tragic!" Louisa whispered, visibly moved. "All those children and no mother to care for them."

"It is tragic," Emily agreed. "Robert talked with Mrs. Larson before she died, and she was a Christian but away from the Lord. She pleaded with her husband to take the children to Sunday school and church."

"How did her husband respond to such a request? He sounds like such an ornery and bitter man. It's his own fault his wife died."

"Before she died, Mr. Larson promised. He sobbed his heart out and could hardly talk, but he gave her his promise."

"I wonder if such a man will keep his vow," Louisa said. "He could have agreed just to please his wife during the final hours of her life. Mr. Larson may have wanted to salve his conscience with no intention of carrying out her wishes."

"Robert says only time will tell. Mr. Larson did permit him to have the funeral service. It was well attended by the church folk, and they have all pitched in to help the family. But the man is so grief-stricken he seems in a trance."

"He probably feels guilty about not getting a doctor sooner. A doctor and medication may have saved his wife's life. No wonder he appears to be in a trance."

"Indeed it will be a heavy burden on his shoulders," Emily said. "He will have no peace until he gives his burden to God, the One who takes all our burdens on Himself."

"I'm certainly grateful I can lay all my burdens on Him." Louisa sighed. "It's so comforting to know He forgives me when I do foolish things, and He cares about every part of my life."

"So what foolish thing have you done now, Louisa?" Emily teased good-naturedly.

"I'm realizing how mixed up life can get, especially when it's my own doing."

"Referring to what?" Emily asked as she folded Robert's letter and placed it back in the envelope. "What phenomenal mix-up have you accomplished now?"

"It's a vicious circle, don't you see? Life can be so exasperating at times." Louisa sighed heavily and then continued. "Peter McClough seemed to genuinely care about me at one time, and I would have nothing to do with him. I was rude and unkind. Now, when I'm experiencing certain, uh, feelings toward him, he's not interested."

"Louisa!" Emily cried excitedly. "When did this happen?"

"I'm sure it started when he saved my life. But my feelings aren't just out of gratitude as he thinks. They are something much deeper. When I see him on campus or at church, my heart leaps within me. Is that true love, Emily?"

"Only you know the answer to that, dear friend," Emily said as she gave her a hug. "But it sounds like the symptoms, all right."

"How can I know for certain? I thought I was in love with Dr. Matthews, but I know now it was only an infatuation. He wasn't the right man for me at all. When did you know you were in love with Robert?"

A slow smile spread across Emily's face. "Remember that winter day in town when I slipped and sprawled awkwardly on the ice? I'm sure I told you about it when it happened. My packages flew in every direction."

Louisa giggled. "I remember. Robert happened to be right there and was kind and attentive, wasn't he?"

"Yes. He helped me up and gathered my packages, but he had a silly grin on his face all the while. I was angry at myself for being so clumsy and angry at him for being so condescending. I acted very childishly and went off in a huff."

"I know it took you awhile to get over feeling awkward around Robert, but he seemed interested in you from the beginning. You may have fallen on the walkway, but I think he fell hard for you the first time you met."

"Actually, I was attracted to Robert's teasing green eyes and silly lopsided grin from the start. But I wouldn't admit it. I was too high-and-mighty for my own good. Fortunately, it didn't drive him away."

"You finally came to your senses, Emily, and realized you and Robert were meant for each other. That's when you fell in love. It must be a wonderful feeling to love someone and know, without a doubt, that he loves you."

"Love is such a special feeling between two people, Louisa. You know it's real because you care and want what's best for him rather than thinking of yourself. Warm, exciting, inner emotions are steady and lasting. There is a deep longing within when circumstances separate one person from the other for any length of time. It's a gnawing, achy feeling of being incomplete, only half a person, because your heart's love is not there. Oh, Louisa, you will recognize true love when it comes to you."

"Peter became a kind and caring person, but I couldn't see it. I only saw him as he used to be and let his background stand in the way. He thinks of me as a self-righteous snob, and I don't blame him. I'm only getting what I deserve." Tears trickled down Louisa's cheeks, and she dabbed at her eyes with her lace handkerchief.

"Peter will come around, Louisa," Emily comforted. "He's too fine a Christian not to forgive your past actions. I know it cut him deeply and his pride is involved. But I also know he still cares for you."

"How can you know that? Has Peter told you?"

Emily smiled, not wanting to betray Peter's confidence. "I'm sure he cares about you. Why else would he ask about you in roundabout ways sometimes, trying to seem nonchalant? Underneath, he's eager for any information that relates to you."

"Do you think there is hope for us, Emily? It would help if I thought we might get together someday. I could face every tomorrow gladly. It wouldn't matter how long it took, if I just had hope."

Chapter 18

Wearily Robert settled himself in the train for the trip home to Waterville. Lines creased his forehead, and his eyes were heavy from lack of sleep. The past weeks had been hectic and taken their toll on the young preacher.

"It's been a trying time, Preacher," soothed John Smith, who was seated next to him. "What with the funeral for Mrs. Larson and helping with the family, it's no wonder you're exhausted. I know you've been talking with Mr. Larson, spending hours with him, trying to get him over his grieving. Seems he can't pull himself together."

Robert sighed heavily. "I'm worried about him, John. I'm afraid he might harm himself while I'm away. He wants to be with Libby, but the children need their father more than ever now. Jared Larson needs to accept his wife's death, stop blaming himself, and go on with his life. I can't get through to him. He will listen when I tell him the good news of the gospel, but it's like he's in another world."

"He's a broken man," John said. "All the orneriness is gone, and he's like an empty shell. Do you think he'll ever be stable-minded again?"

"I pray so," Robert said quickly. "I've asked Thomas Whan and some of the others to keep an eye on him, but they can't watch him all the time. The ladies will continue to bring food and help with the children. I'm glad Richard and Olivia are keeping the two youngest Larson children for a while. Jared's oldest daughter, Ellie Mae, is a very capable young lady. She will probably want the children returned in time for Christmas."

"I agree, Pastor. Ellie Mae is an able and caring person. She won't let those little ones stay with Olivia and Richard any longer than necessary. Right now it's a big adjustment for the family and it's good to have their help. Olivia and Richard have big hearts, and they love the Larson children. The baby and the three-year-old need a lot of tending, though."

"The older Larson children are very self-reliant," Robert said. "The girls cook and sew, while the larger boys handle the farm chores. They should make out fine. It's their pa, Jared, who concerns me the most."

"Try and get some sleep, Preacher. You've told us not to worry, because then we're not trustin' God. I guess He knows all about this sad situation."

Robert relaxed, leaned back, and closed his eyes. "God knows. . .and cares, John. I guess I can leave it in His hands. By the way, please call me Robert—at least while we're away from the church." The rhythmic *click-clack* of the train on the rails had a calming effect as Robert committed his concerns to the Lord. With release came peace, and soon he drifted into a deep sleep.

John heard his heavy breathing and sighed. "Sleep well, my friend," he whispered. "You've earned a good rest."

~

Emily flitted back and forth nervously from the kitchen to the living room. "Where is Fred, Ma?" she asked impatiently. "We need to get to the train station now."

"There's plenty of time, Emily. Don't fret so and git yerself in sech a dither. Land-a-Goshen, Fred knows what time the train comes in," Mrs. Mason said. "He'll git ya there on time."

"I want to be there early, Ma, so I can greet Robert as soon as he steps off the train. He mustn't be kept waiting." Emily twisted her handkerchief as she looked through the window toward the barn. "Fred doesn't even have the sleigh hitched up yet."

Grandpa was sitting at the kitchen table sipping a mug of warm cider. He peered over his glasses at his youngest granddaughter. "Emily, what's got into ya? Yer actin' like a high-spirited filly pacin' back and forth like thet. Set a spell and have some hot cider. It'll warm ya up inside afore ya go out inta the cold."

Emily came up behind her grandfather and kissed him on the cheek. "No time for cider, Gramps. Fred will be coming with the sleigh anytime now. I must be ready to go."

"Wonder iffen Robert knows what a lucky man he is," Grandpa said, smiling as he patted her on the cheek. "We're all kinder anxious ta see him. It's been a long time."

"Don't fergit, Emily," her mother warned, "that John Smith will be stayin' at Fred and Sarah's cabin along with Robert. Make him understand thet we wanted him ta stay with us. But with cousins Amos and Sophie comin' fer Christmas from Portland, our rooms will be filled up. Robert and John can share Fred's extry bedroom and take their meals with us."

"When are Amos and Sophie coming, Ma?" Emily asked. "It will be wonderful seeing them again. It's been a long time. It's been ages since that part of the Mason family came for a visit."

"They arrive on Christmas Eve day," Grandpa volunteered. "This be their first visit since afore the war. It's been a mite hard on them. . .what with losin' Samuel and all. After he died at Bull Run. . ." He shook his head. "Not everyone's been as blessed as us, with our Frederic come home ta us after the war. It's been a grievous thing fer them, and we been beggin' them ta come fer quite a spell."

"Oh, this will be the best Christmas ever!" Emily exclaimed, joyfully clapping her hands together. "All the Mason clan together sharing the Christmas spirit of peace and goodwill." Suddenly her face grew serious. "But we'll miss Samuel something dreadful, Gramps. He and Frederic were such close cousins.

And I was always trailing after them whenever Samuel visited here."

"We hafta keep our spirits up fer Amos and Sophie's sake," Emily's mother insisted. "It will be good fer them to git away from Portland fer a spell."

Emily smiled. "I'm feeling pretty excited today, Ma."

"It's a certain young man who has you excited, I'm thinkin'," Grandpa teased. "Why, yer face is so flushed ya might faint dead away on us."

Emily threw her warm wrap around her shoulders and pulled on wool mittens. "I hear Fred coming, Grandpa. It's time to go."

"Be careful," her ma called. "The porch is a mite slippery."

Emily wanted to run down the steps, but she walked cautiously, planting one foot before the other. Fred drove the sleigh up beside her, and she climbed in, pulling the warm lap robes snugly about her body. "Fred, it's a glorious day!" she exclaimed. "I'm so happy."

"I wonder why," Fred teased. "Can it be a certain preacher?"

"You know it is, Fred." She laughed. "My heart is pounding so hard I'm afraid it will burst. I can hardly wait to see Robert."

"I'm sure Robert is feeling just as excited, after all these months of being away. I wonder what his companion, John Smith, will be like."

"That's the only sad part of Robert's visit. Since his friend can't remember his past or his people, maybe we can make him feel a part of our family. Christmas is such a magical time."

"People are different at Christmas, Emily. It's too bad the feeling of love and goodwill doesn't last. God, through His great love, gave us the gift of His Son. He wanted folks to communicate love toward one another all year long."

The horses trotted along the snow-packed road as snowflakes started falling softly. Emily started to hum, then sing the Christmas carols. Frederic soon joined in with his rich baritone, and they continued singing until they reached the train station in Waterville. "Whoa!" Frederic shouted as he reined in the team and headed for the hitching post.

"I'll get out here," Emily called as she scrambled from the sleigh.

"Land sakes, Emily, can't you wait until we're completely stopped? You could get hurt jumping out like that."

"I'm in a hurry, Fred," she exclaimed from the ground. "I can see the train is already in. Robert might be waiting, and I'm anxious to greet him."

"The train just pulled in, Emily, and it takes awhile to get out and pick up the luggage. You've got plenty of time."

Emily ignored her brother's remarks and hurried toward the platform, where a few passengers were exiting the train. She stood on tiptoe, searching each person for sight of Robert's face. Passengers filed down the steps from several coaches until there was a multitude of people thronging together. Emily strained her eyes as she darted among the masses. "There are so many people," she said in dismay. "Seems everyone is traveling home for the holidays."

Suddenly strong arms grasped her by the shoulders and spun her around. She looked into Robert's green eyes as he pulled her close. "Darling Emily," he whispered with emotion against her dark hair. "I've waited so long to hold you like this." Gently he turned her face toward him and looked deeply into her blue eyes. Ignoring the crowds of people, he kissed her hair, then her cheek, and finally her lips, in a sweet and tender kiss.

"Robert!" Emily said breathlessly as he released her. "You are actually here. You've come home at last. Just let me look at you."

Robert took her arm and steered her away from the masses toward a clearing. Then he kissed her again and held her close. "Darling, I'm home," he said huskily against her dark tresses. "And there is someone I want you to meet. He's here somewhere, probably picking up our luggage."

"Your friend, John Smith, of course," Emily said. "I'd almost forgotten about him. I hope he isn't lost in the crowd." Robert leaned over and kissed the top of her head. "It's a wonder I remember anything when I'm around you," he whispered.

"Ahem!" a man's voice spoke behind them. "I've got the luggage, Robert, and I see you've got the girl."

Robert spun around quickly and faced his friend. "John, I want you to meet my special young lady—Emily Mason."

Emily turned toward John and held out her hand. Suddenly she gasped, and her face turned ashen. "I—I—" she choked.

"What is it, darling?" Robert asked. "Is something wrong?"

Emily stood staring at John Smith with parted lips, unable to speak.

John shifted from one foot to another, uncomfortable and obviously embarrassed under Emily's constant gaze. "I'm happy to meet you, Miss Mason," he stammered. "I've heard so many good things about you from my friend."

Tears trickled down Emily's cheeks as she threw her arms around John. "Samuel!" she cried. "You've come back to us from the dead!"

John Smith stood awkwardly, his arms at his side. "Do I know you?" he asked, dumbfounded. "I don't remember ever seeing you before."

Robert stared in unbelief at the scene before him. "Emily, do you know who John is? Do you have some link with his past?"

Emily released her grip on John Smith and wiped at her eyes. "John is Samuel Mason, my cousin from Portland. We were told he was killed at Bull Run in July of 1861. Samuel and Frederic are the same age, and Sam spent many summers at our farm over the years. His last visit was in April, just after the war began between the North and South. Only seventeen at the time, Samuel came to bid us farewell before he joined the Union forces. He couldn't wait until he was older, he said. The country needed him, and he was anxious to go and fight for his country. Then"—she faltered, and her voice broke—"we heard he had fallen at Bull Run and was killed. That's when Fred determined to join up the following year, as soon as he finished school."

"Did I hear my name mentioned?" Frederic asked, coming up beside them. "Welcome home, Robert. And is this your friend, John—" Frederic broke off his sentence and gaped at the young man before him. "Can it be possible?" he cried. "Can this be Samuel?" Awkwardly he threw his arms around John Smith's shoulders. "Are my eyes deceiving me, or is it really you?"

Robert stood back and surveyed the two men standing side by side. "I think so. Emily says this is your cousin Samuel, and the resemblance between you two men is uncanny. Same build, same dark, curly hair and blue eyes. You have a mustache, Fred, but the likeness is still there. Ever since I first met John—er—Samuel, I knew he reminded me of someone. I thought it was someone from my past. But then I didn't even know you had a cousin."

John Smith cleared his throat. "I'm sorry, but I don't recognize you or these surroundings. All I remember is being in the hospital. They told me I was wounded at Bull Run and left for dead. When they finally brought me in, I had no identification on me, nothing to show who I was. Mine was a head injury, and I remembered nothing—no name, no family."

"You have a family, all right." Fred smiled. "And we're part of it. If Robert hadn't gone to Pennsylvania, we might never have found you. Let's get your luggage, Sam, and head on home."

Chapter 19

During the ride to the Mason homestead, John Smith pumped Fred and Emily with questions about his parents and background. "It's all so strange," he said, "not remembering anything about my past. I feel numb, like my life is a blank sheet of paper. My mind strains to see something familiar or hear words with some meaning to them. Even you, my own cousins, have made no impact on my memory. Maybe I'll never feel like I belong anywhere."

"It's amazing how God works things out," Fred said. "Your folks are coming from Portland for a visit the day before Christmas. We've invited them many times, but this will be their first trip to Waterville since before the war. Maybe seeing them will jar your memory. I stayed at their home two years ago when I visited Portland."

"Were they well?" John asked.

"They were fine. Your pa's been a seaman all his life, and it seems the cold and dampness have taken their toll on him. I knew they grieved for you, their only child. They talked about you but kept their grief inside. I loved your ma's cooking, and your pa and I had some good talks. There were important decisions I needed to make in my life, and I appreciated his wise counsel."

"I won't know what to say to them," John faltered. "They will be strangers to me."

"You'll love them, Samuel," Emily said. "You'll find you can't help yourself. They are homey, down-to-earth folk. Your pa spins exciting yarns of his adventures at sea. Growing up, we couldn't get enough of his stories. And your ma is a sweetheart. She cooks as good as our ma, and that's saying a lot."

"I'm sure my parents are fine people," John said thoughtfully. "I have such mixed feelings inside: excitement over having a family, and apprehension at meeting them. To be honest with you, I'm scared stiff."

"Don't be afraid, John," Robert said as he placed his arm around Emily and grinned at her. "I'm marrying into the Mason family, so I should be the fearful one."

"Robert!" Emily cried excitedly. "When are you marrying into our family?"

Robert leaned over and nuzzled her hair. "How about next June, darling?" he whispered. "I'll be back from Pennsylvania by then."

Emily leaned against him contentedly and sighed. "June. . .a time for brides. . .a time for love. I'll hold you to it, Robert." She laughed. "I have witnesses!"

"Well, Robert," John said, "I can see your future is sealed. There is no backing out now. Tell me, Fred, did I have a special girl, anyone you know about, when I entered the army? I've often wondered about that."

Fred chuckled. "Growing up, you always said you wanted to marry Emily someday. I don't know about any other young ladies in your life. Maybe your folks can shed some light on the subject."

John Smith glanced across at his cousin. "I don't remember a thing about it, Emily, but I can certainly understand why. It's easy to see that you could turn a man's head."

Emily blushed. "We were just kids, Samuel. I must admit I adored you and looked up to you. I think you liked me because I was a tomboy and joined right in with you and Fred. We went horseback riding, climbed trees, and built a tree house back by the creek."

Sounds as though we had some fun times together," John said. "I hope I helped with the chores to earn my board and keep."

"Grandpa and Pa kept us busy most of the day," Fred added. "You helped with the garden, the animals, and the haying. Our free time was after the chores were done. That's when we whooped it up. On hot days we swam in the creek and pulled some fish out of it, too. Those were some good times we had, the three of us. Our sister, Cassie, was much too ladylike to join in our escapades."

"I thought farming came quite easily to me out in Pennsylvania," John said thoughtfully. "Now I can see why. Spending summers with you on the farm introduced me to the farming way of life. It's something I really enjoy. You mentioned a sister, Cassie. Are there any other brothers or sisters?"

"Just the three of us," Fred answered. "I'm the oldest, then Cassie, and Emily is the baby." Fred smiled at Emily with a teasing grin. "But she sure kept up with the two of us and sometimes led us on a merry chase."

Emily noticed Samuel's eyes upon her for the remainder of the trip to the homestead. She tried to avert her eyes and watch the snow-covered landscape. Time after time, something compelled her to glance at Samuel, and she found him gazing steadily into her face. It was as if he was reaching back into his memory for something to take hold upon, some remembrance of his past.

Emily finally broke the silence. "Samuel, don't be too concerned with the past. We hope you will remember everything someday. But if you don't, at least you know about your family and who you are. It will be important to go forward in your life and start anew. There may be things in your past, especially about the war, that you'd rather forget. And forgetting might be a blessing."

"I would like to forget the war years," Frederic said soberly. "The horrors of war are etched clearly on my mind—beastly, unspeakable pain and suffering. My best army buddy died in my arms at Appomattox. It was terrifying."

Samuel cleared his throat. "I don't remember the bloody battle at Bull Run where I was injured and so many died needlessly. But I did see the aftermath of it, those broken and battered bodies in the hospital. Others lost both arms, or legs, or eyes. Some never recovered—they just didn't make it. I can still hear the cries and moans of the wounded in the hospital. Maybe it's better if I don't remember all that took place on the battlefield."

As Frederic turned the team up the long, winding drive to the Mason home, Samuel exclaimed, "What a beautiful spot for your farm. No wonder I loved coming here as a boy. It makes me wish I were a child again. I can see there is much to do here: working the ground, tending the animals, roaming the fields and woods. It is a perfect place for a young lad."

"It was a special treat for us farm youngsters to visit you in Portland, Samuel," Emily said. "Your folks live on the seacoast. You are their only child. We gathered shells, walked the beach, and splashed in the surf. Sometimes your pa took us out in his skiff. Can you imagine how exciting that was?"

"It's hard for me to visualize, but yes, it does sound exciting," Samuel said. "I hope I can be useful during my stay with you over the holidays. I'd like to split and stack wood or something, whatever needs to be done."

"We always appreciate an extra hand, Samuel," Fred assured as he halted the team by the house. "Emily, run in and prepare the folks for the good news about Samuel, while we men unhitch the horses and put them in the barn. The folks might need a few minutes to catch their breath."

Robert helped Emily down from the sleigh, and she ran eagerly into the house. No one was in the kitchen, but she could smell the delicious aroma of the evening meal coming from the cookstove. "Hi, everyone!" she called. "We're back!" She could hear giggles and talk coming from the parlor. The family had gathered there and were being delightfully entertained by little Rebeccah, who clapped her hands, laughed, gurgled, and cooed. Mr. and Mrs. Mason, Grandpa, Bill, Cassie, and Sarah sat in a semicircle enjoying the little tot who was almost a year old. She was walking now and said a few words. As Emily entered the room, Rebeccah clapped her hands and said, "Hi." Emily snatched her into her arms and gave her a big hug and kiss. "How's my precious little niece?" she asked.

Remembering her errand, Emily put the child down. "I have some wonderful news. It's about our cousin Samuel."

"What can thet be?" Grandpa asked. "Our Samuel was killed at Bull Run."

"Robert's friend, John Smith, is actually Samuel, Amos and Sophie's son," she said breathlessly. "He has amnesia and doesn't remember anything prior to waking up in the hospital."

The family sat speechless until Grandpa finally spoke up. "God be praised," he said, wiping a tear from the corner of his eye. "Where is the lad?"

"They'll be right in," Emily explained. "They are putting the team in the barn. Fred thought you might need a little time to get used to the idea. Samuel looks fine, same as he always did, just a bit older."

A shy, hesitant John Smith followed Frederic and Robert into the house.

He lagged behind as they entered the parlor, and he heard the family greeting Robert. "And this is my friend from Pennsylvania, John Smith," Robert said. "As it turns out, he is related to you."

Mrs. Mason hurried to John Smith and gathered him to her bosom. "Samuel, lad, you've come home. We're jest so happy ta see ya alive and well. Yer lookin' fine, jest fine. What a welcome surprise ya'll be fer yer folks."

The rest of the family welcomed Samuel with such warmth and sincerity, he began to relax and feel comfortable. Confusion occurred when some called him John and others Samuel. Chase Mason, Emily's father, cleared his throat to get everyone's attention. "There will be no more usin' the name John Smith," he said. "It's a nice name, but 'tain't his. This be our relative, Samuel Mason, and we best call him by his rightful name."

Grandpa came up behind Samuel and clapped him on the shoulder. "Many's the summer ya spent with us on the farm, my boy. Why, ya can hay right along with the best o' them. I 'member you and Fred jumpin' in the haystack and skeerin' the chickens. Ya were quite a pair, ya were. Seemed like a pair o' brothers. What one didn't think o' doin', the other did. " 'Course Emily was always follerin' ya around, like a little puppy. She didn't want ta be left out."

Fred introduced Samuel to Sarah. "This is my bride," he said, hugging her close.

Sarah's red gold hair bounced around her shoulders as she laughed gaily. "We've been married since last April, Samuel."

"She will always be my bride," Fred insisted, giving her a tender look.

"I must have known you, Sarah, in the past," Samuel said. "Everyone says I spent a lot of summers here. Were you around then?"

"My family's farm is adjacent to this one, and I do remember seeing you occasionally, mostly on Sundays at church. You probably never noticed me. Fred didn't in those days."

"Sarah is much younger than us," Fred added. "Cassie's husband, Bill, is her older brother. I'm afraid I robbed the cradle when I married Sarah. But she is the joy of my life!" His eyes met hers in unexpressed emotion.

Sarah blushed under Fred's gaze. "I had turned sixteen by the time we married, Samuel, so I wasn't a babe. And I knew what I wanted!" Teasingly she reached up and tousled a lock of Fred's dark, curly hair, twisting the locks gently through her fingers as she spoke. "I knew what I wanted—I just needed to convince Fred!"

Chapter 20

Louisa Bradford pulled gown after gown from her wardrobe and laid them gently on her bed. Gingerly she picked up one at a time and held it to her, surveying her image in the mirror. "Nothing looks right," she mumbled forlornly as she tossed each dress aside. "What am I to do?" Impatiently she pulled combs from her hair and let the golden tresses fall in masses around her shoulders.

Emily, who had arrived earlier at the Bradford home, knocked on Louisa's door. "Is everything all right, Louisa? I hope you are ready, for the men will be here soon."

"Come in, Emily," Louisa called. "I have nothing appropriate to wear to the concert tonight," she said sadly, "and I know Colby's Christmas concert is a special affair."

"You're just excited about going with Samuel. He's never seen any of your lovely gowns, Louisa. Whatever you choose will be beautiful."

Louisa grabbed her hairbrush and brushed her long hair vigorously, forming a cluster of yellow curls at the nape of her neck. "Emily, I've tried on all my frocks, and not a one is suitable."

Emily glanced at the careless pile of dresses on Louisa's bed. "The problem is, you have too many to choose from. They are all very attractive and perfectly suitable for the concert tonight. Just select one and get dressed. You don't want to keep Samuel and Robert waiting."

"I can't choose," Louisa wailed. "You decide."

Emily pulled out a cranberry velvet gown with lace collar and cuffs. "This seems appropriate for the season. It's very flattering and will look lovely with your golden hair."

Louisa reached for the dress and gave Emily a hug. "I don't know what's wrong with me. I'm excited about going. . .and I'm not. I seem to be all in a dither."

"You're just nervous about attending with Samuel. After all, you hardly know him. This will give you a fine chance to get better acquainted."

"I remember when he used to visit your family in the summers. Sometimes I would be at the farm with you. But that was a long time ago." Louisa hesitated, then went on. "There is another reason."

"Do you want to tell me about it?" Emily asked. "Sometimes it helps to talk things over with someone."

"You have probably guessed. It's Peter McClough. I'm sure I'm in love with him. At least I'm experiencing certain feelings that lead me to believe I am."

"That's wonderful." Emily gave her friend a little hug. "Louisa, get changed into your dress. You are attending the Christmas concert with Samuel tonight, who is just a friend. I'm sure you will have a good time."

Louisa sighed as Emily left the room, then she slipped the cranberry gown over her head. She smiled at her reflection in the mirror. The dress did look striking against her fair hair and pale complexion. "I wish," she said aloud pensively, "I wish I was attending the concert with Peter, Emily's other cousin!"

Robert and Samuel arrived promptly at seven, and Mrs. Bradford ushered them into the parlor. "Emily and Louisa will be down in a moment," she explained. Turning to Samuel, she expressed her delight in seeing him again. "I've told Louisa," she continued, "to invite you all back here after the concert for hot cider and Christmas tea cakes. The invitation is meant to include Fred and Sarah and any other young folk you would like to bring. Mr. Bradford and I enjoy having young people in our home."

Expressing their thanks to Mrs. Bradford, they turned to greet Louisa and Emily, who had entered the room. Louisa's pale face was flushed, and she walked shyly toward Samuel and extended her hand. "I'm very pleased to see you again, Samuel. It's been a long time."

Samuel stared openly at the fascinating creature before him. "They didn't tell me I'd be escorting anyone so charming," he mumbled. "Are you certain we've met before?"

Louisa blushed and lowered her eyes. "Yes, Samuel," she said softly. "But we were younger then. It was long ago."

"We'd better be on our way," Robert said, preparing to leave. "Concerts usually start on time, and Fred and Sarah will be wondering where we are."

The musical instruments were tuning up when they found their seats at the concert hall. Peter McClough had come with Frederic and Sarah, and they stood up to greet the new arrivals. "This is Samuel Mason, our cousin," Frederic told Peter. Briefly he explained the unusual situation of Samuel's amnesia and his return with Robert from Pennsylvania. "I believe that makes him your cousin also, Peter."

Peter extended his hand in a hearty handshake. "Glad to meet you, Samuel. I guess we are shirttail cousins of a sort. But I'm the black sheep of the family."

Samuel chuckled. "It's nice to know I have a family, Peter. You can't imagine how distressing it is not knowing anything about my past." He turned toward Louisa, who stood just behind him. "Are you acquainted with Miss Bradford, Peter? I'm a fortunate fellow. She agreed to attend the concert with me this evening."

Peter glanced past Samuel at Louisa with a wistful look, his eyes reflecting pain as they searched hers. "Yes," he said finally, "I am acquainted with Miss Bradford."

Louisa smiled brightly at Peter and held out her hand. She could feel the color rising in her cheeks and her heart beating wildly within her breast. "Peter and I are good friends, Samuel. He saved my life once."

"I would like to hear about that," Samuel said, "when we have more time to talk. It sounds like an exciting experience."

"It was nothing," Peter mumbled as the auditorium lights dimmed. "I just happened to be there at the time."

The concert was well-balanced and filled with classical as well as Christmas melodies beautifully done by the choir, soloists, and orchestra. The artistic musical arrangements were breathtaking, emphasizing the joy of the Christmas season.

During the concert's intermission, Emily and Louisa left the others and headed for the ladies' powder room. When Louisa saw Peter in the hallway later, she called to him. "Peter, my parents have invited everyone back to the house for refreshments after the concert. Will you come and join us?"

"Don't feel it's necessary to include me," Peter said soberly, "just because I'm with Fred and Sarah. I don't mind going on home."

Louisa moved closer and put a hand on Peter's arm to detain him. "Please," she said softly, "I want you to come."

Emily could sense the strong emotions passing between Louisa and Peter as they looked at one another. Peter's voice sounded husky when he spoke. "I'd be an extra person, Louisa. I don't have a young lady with me."

"That's all right," Louisa insisted, letting her arm rest on his. "It's just a friendly get-together for the holidays. You'll be able to get better acquainted with your cousin Samuel."

"Do come, Peter," Emily added. "It will be a fun get-together. You've been so busy with classes and working, you've not had much opportunity to socialize."

Peter swallowed hard as he looked at Louisa. The desire to hold her in his arms was almost greater than he could bear. Going with the others would give him an opportunity to be near her, even though she had been escorted by another. "I'll come then, as long as it's all right with your folks. Thank you, Louisa." Peter stood watching the two young ladies move away. "Darling Louisa," he muttered under his breath. "I wish you were my darling, and mine alone."

Louisa smiled radiantly as she and Emily walked toward the auditorium. Her face was flushed, and excitement was building inside her. "Peter has agreed to come! Oh, Emily, it will be his first visit to my home—something I've dreamed about. Perhaps after this first time, he will feel free to visit often. Maybe he will call on me and invite me out to dinner or a concert."

"I'm sure there is a great possibility that he will," Emily said. "I saw the look on his face. There was a kind of magnetism between the two of you. I don't think Peter even noticed I was there."

Back at the Bradford home, the group carried on the Christmas spirit by singing the traditional Christmas carols. The huge mantel was decorated with pine boughs and bright, cheery bows. Fruit and pinecones in a large wooden bowl adorned the large dining room table, which was covered with a delicate lace cloth. In the corner of the main hall stood a magnificent pine tree decked in holiday trimmings. Artificial birds, colored bulbs, and candles peeked out from beneath its branches.

When Mrs. Bradford and Louisa served hot mulled cider and Christmas tea cakes, the young folk relaxed in the parlor and kept up a lively conversation. Samuel seated himself next to Louisa on the love seat and was very attentive. Emily noticed it seemed impossible for Peter to get near enough to talk privately with Louisa. She could see him watching Louisa across the room as she smiled and laughed at something Samuel said. A few times Emily thought she saw Peter look at Louisa with an urgent appeal, but Louisa seemed compelled to stay by Samuel's side.

Peter was the first to leave, insisting he preferred to walk the few blocks to his home. "A walk in the cold air will do me good," he said. After thanking the Bradfords for their hospitality, he headed for the hall to pick up his warm coat and muffler. He didn't realize Louisa had followed him until she touched his arm. "Will you come again, Peter?" she asked. "We didn't have an opportunity to talk this evening."

"You were obviously too preoccupied to pay any attention to me," he said curtly.

Louisa looked hurt. "Samuel was my escort, Peter. It was my place to be with him this evening. Surely you understand that."

"Why did you invite me then? You knew I'd be at loose ends."

"We all wanted you to come. I thought you would enjoy being with everyone. Why didn't you talk to Samuel yourself? Don't you want to know him better?"

"Sure, but he was all taken up with you. It's obvious he's fallen for you. He never left your side for a moment. And he didn't seem to talk to anyone but you."

"Since he was my escort for the evening, he probably felt it his duty to stay close to me. He was just being a gentleman."

"Oh, so he's a gentleman—and you probably think I'm not. Is that the way it is?"

"Oh, Peter, don't be so difficult!" Louisa cried with a flash of temper. "After all, you didn't invite me to attend the concert with you. You could have, you know. Then I would have been your companion for the evening—not Samuel's."

"Invite you so the high-and-mighty Miss Bradford could turn me down and put me in my place? You'd enjoy that, wouldn't you?" With those words, Peter went out the door and slammed it behind him.

Louisa rushed to the kitchen as tears overflowed and ran down her cheeks. Emily was there helping herself to another mug of cider.

"Why are men such beasts?" Louisa fumed when she caught her breath.

"Why, Louisa, Samuel seems the perfect gentleman," Emily said soberly. "What did my cousin do?"

"Oh, it's not Samuel, Emily. He *is* a perfect gentleman. It's Peter!" She dabbed at her face with her lace handkerchief. "He is absolutely impossible. I'll never understand why he is so contrary."

"This sounds like a lovers' quarrel, Louisa. If you are in love with Peter, maybe you need to let him know how you feel. Men are not mind readers, you know."

Louisa stamped her foot haughtily. "In love with Peter? Ha! I wouldn't give him the satisfaction! He's an ill-tempered boor!"

Emily smiled knowingly, comforted her friend with a warm hug, but said nothing. Louisa splashed her face with cool water, pinched her cheeks for color, and returned to her guests.

Chapter 21

The following day was a joyous occasion at the Mason household. Robert and Frederic took the team into Waterville to pick up Sophie and Amos, who arrived on the afternoon train from Portland. Frederic greeted them warmly and introduced them to Robert. "This is Robert Harris, our young pastor, who is raising up a mission church in Pennsylvania. He is also Emily's beau," he said slyly, grinning at Robert.

The two young men helped Sophie and Amos into the sleigh, wrapping warm lap robes around them to ward off the chill. As simply as possible, Frederic prepared them for the meeting with Samuel. He told them their son was alive and well, waiting for them at the house.

"He is a fine young man," Robert added. "I met him in Pennsylvania where he lived with a family whose son was also injured at Bull Run."

A soft snow was falling, covering the fields, trees, and stone fences with a delicate icing of pure white. During the ride over snow-packed roads, Robert explained how Samuel's war injury had caused amnesia, which he still had. He then related the fortunate coincidence that brought the young man to Waterville. "Samuel wanted to find his family. He didn't have a clue where to start. I'm thankful I finally convinced him to come here with me for the holidays before he began his search."

The older couple could hardly contain their joy. "Praise God!" Amos said with emotion, placing an arm around his wife.

"Can it really be our boy?" Sophie said, crying softly. "Can it really be Samuel?"

The reunion with their son at the Mason farm was so heartwarming it left them speechless. Tears flowed freely as they embraced Samuel again and again.

That evening, Christmas Eve, the entire Mason family gathered around the fireplace with thankful hearts for this time together. Samuel rehearsed all that had happened to him since his stay in the hospital. "If it weren't for the preacher, I wouldn't be here," he told his parents. "I was determined to find my roots but didn't know where to start. Robert insisted I come home with him for the holidays—and here I am."

"God brought yer son home ta ya, Amos and Sophie," Grandpa said thoughtfully. "And thet's a mighty fine Christmas gift."

Sophie and Amos sat on the large camel-back sofa in front of the fireplace with Samuel between them. "I jest can't hardly believe it's true," Sophie said.

"Our boy is alive! He's here in this place, and he's alive!"

Someone started to sing one of the Christmas carols, and they all joined in. High and low voices mixed and harmonized as sweet melodies filled the air. The house and tree were decked in their holiday finery, while the fire snapped and crackled in the fireplace, casting a golden glow over each happy face.

When the song ended, Robert cleared his throat and said seriously, "This is indeed a joyous occasion. Sophie and Amos have their son, who was lost to them, back from the dead. And we are celebrating the birthday of God's Son, born that first Christmas day so long ago. To add to the joy of this evening, Emily and I have an announcement to make, which will be no surprise to you. We would like to formally announce our engagement. Mr. Mason, if we may have your approval, and Mrs. Mason's, we will be a very happy couple."

Chase Mason chuckled. "We been 'spectin' this fer quite a spell, Robert. And ya have our blessin'. The Mason clan approves wholeheartedly and offers congratulations ta ya."

Everyone started talking at once, asking when the big event would take place. Emily laughed gaily, looked at Robert, and tousled a lock of his sandy hair with her fingers. "In June, when Robert returns to Waterville for good."

"Yes, darling," Robert said, kissing her cheek lightly. Then he whispered in her ear, "Our time. . .a time to love."

"As long as we're making happy announcements, we have one also," Frederic said as he pulled a giggling Sarah onto his lap. "Sarah and I are going to become parents."

"A baby!" Ma cried. "Land-a-Goshen!"

"How exciting!" Cassie said, hugging little Rebeccah to her. "Oh, Sarah, how I long to have another child. When will it be?"

"Around the middle of May," Sarah said, "if he's on schedule. You've probably all noticed I'm getting a little chubby."

"Why, yer purty as can be, Sarah," Grandpa Caleb said with a sly grin. "I allus said ther's nothin' purtier than a lady who's expectin'."

"Are ya feelin' well, child?" Mary Jane Mason asked. "Ya must take keer o' yerself so's ya'll have a healthy young'un."

"I'm fine, Mother Mason," Sarah said. "No morning sickness even. It appears I'm healthy as a horse—and I probably eat like one."

"I make sure she eats right, Ma," Fred added. "And I try to make her rest. But this bride of mine is a mite headstrong!" Fred laughed and gave Sarah a playful squeeze.

"Fred babies me too much," Sarah insisted. "He thinks I'm helpless now. Women have babies all the time. I feel good, and I'm always hungry. I know it's important to eat the right things. I'm probably eating more than I should." She patted her midsection. "Little Junior will be a chubby one."

"Have you decided on any names?" Cassie asked. "I know you mentioned

Junior. Did you mean that?"

"Oh yes," Sarah said quickly. "He'll be Frederic Jr. if it's a boy. We've already decided we want a little Fred. We're not agreed on a girl's name yet. There are so many we like."

Cassie stood up and handed a sleepy little Rebeccah to Bill. "I think Bill and I need to get back to our cabin, Ma. Tomorrow will be a big day for our little girl—her first Christmas. But I'll come over early in the afternoon to help with the dinner."

"No need o' thet," her mother insisted, giving Rebeccah a big hug. "Dinner is at three, Emily and Sophie are here ta help, and Sarah is close by. We have lots o' helpin' hands. Ya jest enjoy yer first Christmas with yer little one. It be a special time fer ya."

Fred pulled Sarah up and placed an arm around her. "Time for us to go, too, Sarah. We need to get you to bed on time, little mother," he said, grinning.

Sarah grabbed a pillow and tossed it at Fred. "Wait, Cassie," she called. "We'll walk out with you. I want to kiss that sweet little niece of mine."

The two couples said their good-byes, and one by one the older family members slipped upstairs to bed. Emily, Robert, and Samuel were left alone with their thoughts, each staring deeply into the fire. "I've been doing some thinking since last night," Samuel said in a serious tone. "There are some straight answers I need from you."

"Is it about your parents, Samuel?" Emily asked.

"No, nothing like that. It's about Louisa and Peter McClough. I sensed some problems there. He seemed almost antisocial at the Bradford house. Then he left abruptly."

"Peter did seem a bit edgy," Emily agreed.

"Was it because I was Louisa's escort?" Samuel asked. "Is Peter jealous of me? Has he been courting Louisa?"

"Hey, one question at a time, friend," Robert said.

"I guess I'm the one who should answer your questions, Samuel," Emily said thoughtfully after a moment. "Peter has not been courting Louisa, although he cares for her and has for a long time."

"Why not?" Samuel asked.

"When Peter first came to Waterville, Louisa ignored him and would have nothing to do with him," Emily said. "Peter was a rather crude and raucous individual and didn't present a good image. He was very conceited, self-centered, and opinionated. Even after he changed his ways and became a nicer person, she avoided him. In the meantime Louisa had a relationship with someone else that turned sour, leaving her brokenhearted."

"Does she care for Peter now?" Samuel asked. "I thought I detected something between them."

"Yes, she cares for him a great deal. Louisa regrets the way she treated him in the past and longs to be forgiven. He's nursing his pride, so he avoids her. Last night brought them together, but I'm afraid it opened new wounds. Peter left the house angry because she spent all her time with you. He wouldn't consider the fact that you were her escort. Louisa was in tears after Peter left so abruptly. I talked with her briefly, alone, before we left last evening."

"Should I say something to Peter tomorrow?" Samuel asked. "I understand he will be joining the family for Christmas Day. I'd like to have a good relationship with him, if possible. Louisa is a lovely person, but we are friends and nothing more. Peter probably thinks I'm horning in on his girl. That's the farthest from my mind. I'll be leaving Waterville for Portland with my folks in a couple of days. I may not see Peter again."

"You might befriend him tomorrow and let him know the situation in an indirect way. Peter is really a likable fellow when you get to know him," Emily said.

"Will you be staying in Portland, Samuel?" Robert asked. "I know you want to be with your parents, but I was counting on your coming back to Wampum eventually. We need you in the work there."

"I'm not certain what I'll do. My folks are happy to have me back, and I won't leave them right away. My father would like me to take over the fishing business. It's getting too hard on him, at his age."

"Would you like to make fishing your livelihood, Samuel? Didn't you take a liking to farming while you were in Pennsylvania?" Robert asked.

"Yes, I did, and I'm not sure about the deep-sea fishing. I don't remember a thing about it. My father insists it will come back to me. But I do want to go back to Wampum later, if only for a visit. There is someone I want to see again."

"I understand," Robert said. "You've been so close to the Morrison family, especially Richard. You will want to see all of them again."

"The Morrisons and Richard, of course," Samuel said. "They will always be very dear and special to me. But there is someone else also. A young woman."

Robert jerked and sat upright. "What young woman, Samuel? I didn't know you had an interest in anyone. You certainly kept it well hidden."

"Ellie Mae Larson," Samuel said, smiling. "She and I had a fine talk the day of her ma's funeral, and we talked together several times since then. Ellie Mae's a right nice person."

"Isn't she quite young?" Robert asked.

"She's seventeen—oldest of the nine children. But she's very mature for her age and levelheaded. Ellie Mae has carried a lot of responsibility, being the oldest child, and I guess it caused her to grow up in a hurry."

"As I recall," Robert said with a chuckle, "she's a pretty girl, too. Did you happen to notice that, Samuel?"

Samuel gazed into the fire dreamily. "Ellie Mae has hair like fine corn silk, Robert, and her blue eyes are clear as the sky. She takes all her looks from her ma.

I love the way she smiles at me and wrinkles her nose. It makes her freckles go all over." Samuel sighed contentedly. "I'm thankful I don't have a special young woman who I was involved with before the war."

"Ellie Mae Larson!" Robert exclaimed. "You sure had me fooled. I had no idea you were seeing that pretty little lady."

Emily jumped up, stretched, and covered a yawn. "Guess I'll head on upstairs and let the two of you continue your discussion of Ellie Mae." She laughed. "Sounds like you are wound up and might talk all night."

Robert and Samuel stood up. "We'll be heading out to Fred's cabin," Robert said as he walked her to the stairway. "Good night, darling," he whispered, taking her in his arms. He could feel her body tremble as their lips met in a sweet and lingering kiss.

Emily hurried to her room, undressed quickly, and snuggled under the warm, handmade quilts piled high on her bed. *Thank You, dear God for such a wonderful family reunion on this special night, Christmas Eve! Sophie and Amos have their son back once again. That is a joy to all our hearts. Fred and Sarah are expecting a new little one in the spring—how exciting! And Robert and I are to be married in June. I'm so happy. My cup is full and running over. You are a great and marvelous God, and my heart is filled with Your love.*

The moon cast a ray of light across her bed through a crack in the curtain. She glanced up and saw a myriad of stars flickering in the inky blackness. As she snuggled deeper into her covers, she whispered, "One of them is the star of Bethlehem."

Chapter 22

Snow fell steadily Christmas Day and decorated the landscape. By three o'clock the entire Mason family had gathered together under one roof. Cassie, Bill, and Rebeccah arrived by horse and sleigh at the same time Peter arrived from town. They were laden with packages, and Rebeccah, peeking from beneath her warm wraps, clutched a rag doll tightly to her chest.

"Let me carry this cute little cherub," Peter said, taking Rebeccah and handing Bill his packages. Rebeccah giggled and snuggled in Peter's arms as he bounced her while carrying her up the steps. "How's our sweet girl today?" he asked. "Did you get a new dolly?"

Rebeccah laughed, nodded her head, and hugged the homemade doll. It had yellow yarn hair, blue bead eyes, and a pink calico dress. She held the dolly up so Peter could see it better, and he kissed the doll with a loud smack on the cheek. Rebeccah giggled some more and then was taken from Peter by Mrs. Mason, who was waiting eagerly at the door for her granddaughter.

Dinner was a gala feast, turkey and ham with all the trimmings. The light conversation was interspersed with laughter and pleasant reminiscing. Emily joyfully displayed her engagement ring, a gift from Robert that morning. The stone was a large opal surrounded by tiny diamonds. "It belonged to Robert's mother," Emily said, holding it up for all to see. "Isn't it beautiful? I love it, and I shall treasure it always."

There were many oohs and aahs by the womenfolk as they examined the ring's delicate beauty. "My grandmother gave me my mother's ring before she died," Robert said soberly. "Grandma impressed on me the fact that it was meant for a very special young lady." He grinned his crooked grin and took Emily's hand, and his green eyes searched hers. "Grandma would be pleased," he said huskily. "I wish she was alive today to meet this wonderful young woman who has promised to be my wife."

After dinner the men gathered by the fireplace while the womenfolk cleaned up the dishes. Little Rebeccah, thrilled with several new toys, played quietly on the floor, talking and jabbering to her doll.

Later the four younger men, Bill, Peter, Robert, and Samuel, joined Fred for the evening chores. "Many hands make light work," Bill said as they donned warm outer garments.

"After that fantastic meal, we could all use a little exercise," Robert agreed, pulling on heavy boots.

In the barn, Samuel managed to draw Peter aside. Robert, while working in another stall, prayed silently for the two young men.

"I'm sorry about the other night at the Bradfords', Peter," Samuel said. "I didn't realize Louisa was your girl."

Peter laughed sarcastically. "She's not, Samuel. You own me no apology. I was the one who was out of line. I'm afraid my actions were inexcusable. I have no claims on Louisa."

"But you do care for her," Samuel persisted.

"My feelings don't matter much," Peter said. "Louisa has never cared for me, never given me so much as a thought. It was obvious she enjoyed your attention."

"I hope she regarded me as a gentleman and a friend," Samuel said seriously. "And you are wrong about her not caring for you. I have it on good authority that she does."

"She told you so?" Peter asked hopefully. "Did you talk about me the other night?"

"No, we didn't have to. I understand Louisa shed some tears after you left so hastily. I think she was feeling quite let down."

Peter sighed. "I was upset and rude when I left. The 'old' me isn't a very nice person. I'm sorry if Louisa cried on my account. I wish I hadn't been such a cad."

"Go see her and talk with her," Samuel suggested. "I think Louisa would welcome an opportunity to clear the air. Don't let a silly misunderstanding go on for any length of time. She is probably hoping you will call."

Peter eyed Samuel squarely. "You're on the level, aren't you? Don't you care about Louisa yourself? Would you be interested in her if I wasn't around?"

"Louisa is a lovely young lady," Samuel said. "But she is already enraptured with you. And anyway, there is a certain young lady in Pennsylvania who I have my eye on. She doesn't know it yet. We've only talked together a few times. But I have a little hope there."

Peter slapped Samuel on the back. "You're a good friend, Samuel. You bring everything out in the open and face things fair and square. I admire you for that. Thanks for the advice."

"Don't mention it." Samuel laughed. "Remember, though, advice is no good unless it's heeded. Go visit Louisa soon and get things straightened out. Then everyone will be happy."

The two men joined the others and helped carry water and haul in hay and corn for the animals. Laddie followed close at their heels, barking playfully. Occasionally one of them tossed a stick or small stone and the dog dashed after the object, retrieving it in his mouth. It was a game he never tired of playing.

As the family gathered around the fire that evening, they shared stories of experiences and past Christmas celebrations. "We'll be a mite sorry ta leave day after tamorra," Amos said, "but we best be gettin' on home ta Portland."

"We be sad ta think o' yer leavin' us so soon," Grandpa Caleb said. "Ya jest got here, after sech a long time."

"Gettin' Samuel back ta our place could help his memory a mite," Sophie added. "Iffen he sees some familiar things an' places, it's likely ta come back ta him." She patted Samuel's arm fondly. "Yer sech a blessin', son. We're thankful ya come back from the war."

"I'm grateful I found my family after all this time," Samuel said. "It's good to know I have a home—a place where I belong. I've been like a ship adrift on the sea, not certain where I was headed."

"Ya were seventeen, jest a boy, when ya left us," Amos said thoughtfully. "Now yer twenty-three and a growed man. We're hopin' yer port o' call will be Portland, leastwise fer a spell."

"I do intend to stay in Portland for a spell, folks. But I have ties in Pennsylvania now also. Eventually I'll want to go back there."

"Do ya mean ta live?" Sophie asked in dismay. "Will we be losin' our boy agin, after we jest found him?"

"I don't have any definite plans at this time," Samuel said. "Things are too unsettled. I'm still hoping to get my memory back. And maybe when we get home, in Portland, it will happen. Something from my past, in the familiar surroundings, could draw me out."

"We gotta give the boy some time, Sophie," Amos said. "He's not used ta us yet—or Portland. He's got a heap o' adjustin' ta do afore he knows what he means ta do with his life."

"I liked working with Robert in the little church in Wampum, Pennsylvania," Samuel said. "It's a needy area, but the work is growing. I felt useful and grew close to many of the church folk there."

"We appreciated Samuel's help in the ministry in Pennsylvania," Robert added. "He was a real asset to the church. We'll all miss him while he's away."

Emily jumped up from her spot next to Robert. "The time is going too fast," she wailed. "I don't want to think about it. In another week Robert must return to Pennsylvania! I'll be alone again." She rushed over to the piano and started to play softly. "Let's get back into a joyful mood of the holiday season. We won't talk about people going away—or things changing. Let's just enjoy our wonderful blessing of right now!"

At once the voices joined in with the piano and the house was filled with the lovely melodies. Some crowded around the piano, while others remained seated. All sang heartily, harmonizing and lifting their voices in praise. Little Rebeccah rocked back and forth, chattering and enjoying the music. She pulled herself up and stood by the sofa, bouncing up and down, smiling at the joyful people around her. A sweet spirit of love, peace, and goodwill filled every corner of the room, while the light from the fireplace cast a bright glow over the happy faces. There could be no hint of sadness or feeling of separation while singing the glorious anthems of Christmas.

Chapter 23

Emily glanced out her bedroom window at the scene below. Snowdrifts painted the landscape, and the trees were bent down under their heavy burden. Some of the stone fences were completely covered, and small tunnels had been dug to the barn and outbuildings. She could see Robert helping Fred hitch up the team for the trip into town. His luggage was sitting there ready to be loaded. The days had passed so swiftly until there were none left. Amos, Sophie, and Samuel had returned by train to Portland earlier that week.

Now Robert must go. These separations are so difficult, God. I'll do my best to be brave and not cry. Please help me to be strong. I want Robert to remember me with a smiling face, not a tearful one.

With trembling lips she lifted her chin and surveyed her image in the mirror. The soft blue wool dress, one of Robert's favorites, peeked out from beneath her winter coat. She tucked her dark curls under a warm bonnet, tied it securely, and hurried downstairs.

The pure, cold air whipped at their faces on the way to the train station, and Emily snuggled against Robert's strong body. They could see steam rising from the horses' breath as the horses clip-clopped along the snow-packed road. Emily sighed contentedly.

"You'll be back in June, Robert—when we get married. They can't make you stay any longer. You won't let them dictate your future, will you?"

"Of course not, darling. They aren't dictators who rule over me. They might prefer I stay for the good of the people, but they know my contract is for one year. They will honor it if it's my desire to leave."

"I'm glad there won't be any problem about you leaving the first of June. Rev. and Mrs. Davis will be through here at the church in Waterville, and we will have the parsonage for our home."

"I have mixed feelings about that, Emily, but I know your heart is set on it. It will be difficult leaving the folk at Wampum."

"You left the people at Waterville, Robert. Isn't it the same thing?"

"The church here was established when I came. The congregation was already built up and faithful. In Pennsylvania we've started a new work with just a few families. The work is growing, and the people are groping for answers. It's a difficult decision for me. I'm praying God will guide me in making the right choice."

"Robert!" Emily gasped. "You sound like you might not come back to our church here. I thought you made a decision long ago. What about us?"

"We would still get married in June, darling," he said. "Nothing will change that."

"We might go back to Pennsylvania after our wedding?" she asked in disbelief. "Where would we live? Oh, I can't bear the thought of leaving family here, Robert. Waterville is our home!"

"Don't worry about it," Robert said, kissing her lightly on the cheek. "I've asked for a replacement. Let's wait and see how the Lord leads."

Peter McClough met them at the train station to bid Robert good-bye. There was a veil of sadness overshadowing his ruggedly handsome face as he shook Robert's hand.

"Why are you so downcast, Peter?" Emily asked. "With Robert leaving, I'm the one who is sad. And if Robert decides to stay in Pennsylvania after this one year, I'll be a very unhappy lady."

"It won't matter where you and Robert live, Emily, as long as you are together. That's all that matters."

"I know you're right, Peter, but it would be very difficult to leave all my loved ones here. I'm not sure I'm a strong enough person."

"It's painful being apart from the one you love. I went to see Louisa today, and she is in Augusta visiting relatives. I'd hoped to clear up our differences and set things straight. Mrs. Bradford said she isn't returning to Colby for this semester. She may be gone for months."

"I won't be returning to college for the winter term either, Peter," Emily said. "I have my one year in, and that is all I planned to do. There are many things to get done before the wedding in June, like dresses, curtains, and quilts. My time will be spent sewing and writing letters to Robert."

As he pulled Emily close, Robert winked slyly at Peter. "Emily is well prepared to be a preacher's wife. She's had enough schooling. But don't give up on Louisa, Peter. She may be feeling as miserable as you are. Call on her when she gets back from Augusta."

The train, like some huge, black monster, snorted and spewed steam. "All aboard!" the conductor shouted as smoke belched from the smokestack. Robert picked up his satchel momentarily and drew Emily close again. "Good-bye, darling," he whispered, lightly kissing her upturned face. "I'll write often," he called as he hurried to board.

Emily watched, waving her lace handkerchief, until the train was out of sight. *God, don't ask me to leave home and loved ones. I can't. It's different for Robert. He doesn't have parents or any family. It's all an adventure to him. Help him understand my situation, my feelings. Oh, he says he does—but how can he really know how difficult it would be? Doesn't he know my heart? I love him, but I love my people here, where I've lived my entire life.* Emily glanced around her. Frederic was talking to Peter as he waited for her by the sleigh. *Sweet Waterville, I would miss you too much.*

Emily had not shed a tear in front of Robert, but now they came, tumbling down her cheeks as she fought to control her sobs. Dabbing her eyes with her handkerchief, she bid Peter good-bye when he helped her into the sleigh for the return home.

"Parting isn't easy, is it?" Fred asked as he snapped the reins. "But in a few months you and Robert will be married. That should be a comfort to you."

"It is, Fred," she said, wiping her tear-stained face. "Robert and I will both keep busy during the coming months. The time will pass."

Robert settled himself for his lengthy trip with many stops, a change of trains, and little sleep. Although parting with Emily was difficult, he eagerly antici-pated the return to his work in Wampum, Pennsylvania. He could not help but wonder how things had gone without him. Jared Larson had been in such stress over the loss of his wife. Oh, the people were in fine hands, he knew, but still an uneasiness crept over him. He tried his best to shake off disturbing thoughts, but they seeped into his mind, nagging and annoying, time and time again. Rather than brood over what might have happened, Robert left his seat and walked the aisle. He was jarred from side to side as the train lurched and swayed on its seemingly endless journey. His heart ached concerning Emily's attitude. *Dear God, give me strength to make the right decision about staying in Wampum. And change Emily's heart, please. Let her be willing to go if that is where You want me to serve.*

Exhausted after his two-day trip, Robert welcomed the sight of Thomas Whan, who was waiting at the station with his carriage. The two men greeted each other warmly, and Robert told Thomas there was good news about John.

"Did he get his memory back, Pastor?"

"No, not yet anyway. But it turned out he is Emily's cousin—quite a nice surprise for all the family." Robert continued to relate the details about John's exciting meeting with his parents. "His name is Samuel Mason, and he is the only child of Amos and Sophie Mason of Portland. They had been notified their son died in battle at Bull Run. Samuel is happy to have found his roots, and Amos and Sophie are very grateful to have their son home again."

"A happy ending for all three of them," Thomas said as they headed for the Whan homestead. "Would you say it was a coincidence bringing them together? A one-in-a-million chance?"

"I'd say it was the hand of God, Thomas. It's nothing short of a miracle."

"How was your trip?" Thomas asked. "You look tired."

"It was long, Thomas, and yes, very tiring. I'm afraid I didn't sleep much. Too excited about getting back to the work here probably."

"And your Christmas holidays with your special young lady and her family? How were they?"

"Fine, Thomas. It was wonderful to be back with Emily and other loved ones.

I gave Emily an engagement ring, and she has promised to marry me in June."

"That's good news, Pastor. Congratulations. We can sure use some good news. I have some bad news for you, so I'm glad the good news came first."

"What's the problem, Thomas? Is anything wrong with your family?"

"No, nothing like that. The family is fine—'cept maybe a cold or two among the young'uns. It's Jared Larson. He hung himself in the barn a few days after you left, right before Christmas."

"Dear God, how terrible!" Robert exclaimed. "I shouldn't have gone away. Jared needed me, and I wasn't here. I failed him."

"No, Pastor. He'd have done it even if you were here. We all knew he was bent on joining Libby, so we kept an eye on him. We tried to reach out to him, but he pushed everyone away. He sorta lost touch with the world."

Robert bent forward, his head in his hands. Tears welled up in the corners of his eyes and streamed down his face. "God, help those children," he murmured. "They must be devastated."

"It was a terrible sight," Thomas added. "Jared tied a rope to one of the barn beams, stood on a stool, and must have kicked it over. Young Luke found him hanging there and kept the others away. It was a hard thing to face, for a youngster of sixteen. Guess it's the hardest thing that's happened in these parts, as far as I can remember. It was difficult, but Richard and me done the funeral service best we could."

Robert pulled out his handkerchief and blew his nose hard. "How are the children making out?"

"People are helping whenever possible. But that Ellie Mae is something else, all right, for her seventeen years. She's like a little mother to the young'uns and does all the cooking and laundry. She even brought the two youngest children home from Richard and Olivia's in time for Christmas. She wants to keep the family together. Says her ma would want it that way."

"That's a big order for a young lady, Thomas. Eight children younger than her. What a weight on her shoulders!" Robert shook his head. "Such a tragedy—all those children alone to fend for themselves. Can they handle it?"

"Luke and the older boys can run the farm. They did it when Jared was alive and out of touch with the world around him. Ellie Mae has help with the housework from the older girls. They're good attending to the little ones. They seem to be doing fine, and they know we are ready to help if they need it. We keep an eye out for them. I wish they had some grandparents or other relatives around, but they don't—nary a one. Ellie Mae says the church folk are just like family. They send over food occasionally and are always ready to lend a helping hand." Thomas fell silent, and his face grew serious. "Pastor. . .is Jared Larson lost forever?"

"Only God knows the heart, Thomas. We have no way of knowing if Jared accepted Jesus in the moments before he died."

A TIME TO LOVE

It was late by the time Robert and Thomas reached the Whan homestead, and the children had been bedded down for the night. Elizabeth met them at the door and insisted they eat a bowl of warm soup before retiring. Although grieved by the Larson tragedy, Robert ate hungrily of the warm beef soup and homemade bread. He had eaten very little since his departure from Waterville two days earlier. After a brief discussion about the Larson children's welfare, Robert retired to his room to read and pray.

Chapter 24

Early the next morning Robert penned a letter to Samuel explaining the tragic circumstances of Jared Larson's death.

"I was certain you would want to know," he wrote, "especially for Ellie Mae's sake. Since you two had some lengthy conversations together before you left Wampum, perhaps you would like to write her a letter of sympathy and encouragement." Robert went on to add that the family was holding up well and Ellie Mae had the situation well in hand.

Immediately after breakfast, Robert hitched up the sleigh and headed toward the Larsons' log home. Mrs. Whan loaded him with supplies for them—homemade bread, two pies, and a kettle of vegetable soup. He found Ellie Mae and Luke alone with the two youngest children. All the others were in school. Robert marveled at how well kept the house seemed. Ellie Mae was mixing biscuit dough while the two youngest Larsons played together quietly on the floor.

"Good to have you back, Preacher," Ellie Mae said, wiping her hands on her apron and pulling a chair out for him.

Robert took her hand and patted it gently. "I'm so sorry about your father. I should have been here."

" 'Tweren't nothin' anyone coulda done. Guess Pa just loved Ma so much he didn't want ta live without her." Ellie Mae wiped a tear away with the corner of her apron. "Luke and me and the children are gettin' on fine."

Robert glanced around the room. "I can see that you are managing very well, young lady. Mrs. Whan sent a few things along to help out."

"Everyone is so generous, Preacher. I never knew folks could be so kind."

Luke came in from the barn and greeted Robert heartily. They talked for some time, and Robert felt satisfied the two young people had everything under control.

"Let me know if there is anything you need, anything I can do," Robert said kindly. "Don't try to handle more than you can bear. Remember, we are to share one another's burdens."

"Jesus takes care of us," Ellie Mae said. "Luke and me, we know He loves us and cares about what happens. Since we gave our hearts ta Him right after Ma died, He's been our helper."

Robert encircled both young people with his arms. "Indeed, as God's children, God will be watching over you."

"Preacher," Ellie Mae said shyly, "is John ever comin' back? We got acquainted at Ma's funeral, and well, I was just wonderin'. . ." Ellie Mae blushed and turned away.

"Yes, Ellie Mae, I think John will be back someday and maybe soon. I mailed him a letter today about your pa's death." Robert explained the exciting news about John finding his family and that his real name was Samuel Mason. "He is a cousin to the young lady I plan to marry. Samuel told me his plans to come back to Wampum. I think he had a special reason why he wants to return." Robert smiled slyly at Ellie Mae.

Ellie Mae's face reddened from her hairline down to her throat. "Samuel is a nice name," she said thoughtfully. "I'm glad he has a family, but I hope he comes back here."

Robert prayed with the brother and sister, then left to call on others of the church membership. His final call was to the Bishop family, who had moved into the Wampum area the past October. Mr. Bishop had been a thorn in Robert's flesh, insisting on his own way and stirring up dissension among the brethren. Robert had tried to deal with Jim Bishop in a kind and loving way, but the man was bullheaded and set in his ways. He had been head deacon at his former church in Ohio and was used to running things his way. There were certain changes he wanted to make at the Wampum church that Robert did not feel would be beneficial. When Jim Bishop found he could not control Robert or dictate to the church board, he became sullen and belligerent.

"I wonder what kind of a mood Jim is in today," Robert mused as he guided the horse and sleigh in front of the Bishops' residence.

Mrs. Bishop, a quiet woman domineered by her husband, greeted Robert with a smile. "Hello, Pastor," she said, pushing back a stray lock of brown hair. "Jim is out at the barn. Did you want to talk to him?"

"Yes, Mary. I'll head on out there. How is everything with you today?"

"Just fine, Pastor. We missed you while you were away."

"Thanks," Robert called as he walked toward the large, red barn.

Jim Bishop, a tall, heavyset man in work clothes, was cleaning out cattle stalls and turned quickly when he heard Robert approach. "Well, if the preacher ain't back!" he said in a disgusted manner. "It's about time you returned. Old man Larson hangs himself in the barn, and where are you? Off joyriding somewhere when you shoulda been here."

"I regret not being here, Jim," Robert said. "But my trip over Christmas was planned, and I had no way of knowing what would happen."

"You left people in charge who know nothing about running a church," Jim Bishop insisted. "I tried to tell them what to do, but they wouldn't listen. I practically ran the church single-handed back in Ohio. Jim Bishop's word was law."

"No one person runs the Wampum Community Church," Robert stated firmly. "As pastor, I seek God's direction and the direction of my deacons. We have church doctrine and a constitution that we go by. If changes are to be made, the membership votes on it."

"You're pastor now, but you may not be for long. I've been talking to a lot of folk and letting them know my views. We'll see what happens," Jim Bishop said with a smirk, turning his back on Robert. "I'm too busy to stand here wasting time. I have to get my work done."

"I'm sorry you feel that way, Jim. I'd like to be your friend."

There was no answer, and Robert started back toward the horse and sleigh. He could hear Jim Bishop mutter to himself. "Need a new pastor—one who will listen to me—someone who will do it my way!"

Robert thought about his meeting with Jim Bishop all the way home. *What am I doing wrong, Lord? Somehow I'm not getting through to Jim. He's cantankerous and creating a real problem in the church. Please show me how to deal with this man. If I leave in June, what will happen to the church? I'm torn between staying and leaving. Emily will be unhappy if I change my mind and plan to stay in Wampum. She won't understand, and I can't disappoint her. Help me to make a wise decision, Lord, one that is pleasing to You.*

❧

When Samuel received Robert's letter early in January, he was distressed to hear of Mr. Larson's tragic death. Because his parents were so joyful to have him home in Portland, he felt he could not leave them at this time. Samuel posted a letter immediately to Ellie Mae Larson and expressed his condolences to the family. Ellie Mae penned a letter in return, and they began writing regularly. She informed him about the children and the happenings at the Wampum church. Samuel related information about obtaining a job as a clerk in a watch shop and about his parents, whom he had grown to love. He told her he still had no recollection of the past, but he felt comfortable with Amos and Sophie and his surroundings.

In a later letter to Robert, he wrote:

Gradually little things from my past are coming back Snatches here and there flash before me. I strain to recall bits and pieces as they tumble into my mind, taunting me, teasing me. My room, with all the familiar books and treasured keepsakes, pulls at me, beckoning me to remember. Pa and I walked along the coast and examined the fishing boats in dry dock for the winter. My pa pointed out special places we had been and told me about them.

One afternoon I visited my old schoolhouse on the hill and sat at one of the desks. I felt a strong pang of nostalgia in that place, as if I'd been there many times before. School was out for the day, and the students were gone. As I sat, striving to reach back and pull out the lost pieces of my school years, a woman appeared and asked if I needed help with anything. Robert, it was my former schoolteacher, Mrs. Lewis.

She looked much the same. Her dark brown hair was pulled back into a bun, and her dark eyes had the same snappy look. I remembered her! My memory is coming back—piece by piece.

When I told her who I was, she remembered me. Mrs. Lewis heard I'd been killed, so I had to explain about my amnesia and where I'd been living. She said I was one of her prize pupils. Imagine that!

She offered to work with me after school hours, with review and tests, so I could qualify as a high school graduate. I'm very grateful for the opportunity.

My folks are excited that my memory is coming back. It's been like a puzzle where the pieces are strewn all over. I've been fitting them into place, and eventually I should have the entire picture. Locked in a web these past years, I am finally breaking free. More and more I'm beginning to feel like Samuel Mason, and it's a good feeling!

How is everything there in Wampum? Ellie Mae and I write often, and she keeps me pretty well informed. I miss everyone.

Sincerely,
Samuel

By April the snow had melted and spring was struggling to blossom forth. Samuel finished his studies and passed his exams with flying colors. Mrs. Lewis was pleased.

It became evident Amos would not be able to handle his fishing boat alone. Samuel questioned whether sailing would be good for his father, in any case. At times Amos was prone to pains in his joints, due to many years as a seaman in all kinds of weather. Sophie had confided to Samuel that she wished Amos would give up the sea and take life easier. "Ev'ry year, when spring comes, yer pa's rarin' ta go." Sophie sighed. "He says he has ta do it ta survive. Ther's money in the fishin' business."

"Sure there is, Ma," Samuel said—calling them Ma and Pa came easily to him now. "But Pa shouldn't be doing such hard work at his age. He doesn't need to jeopardize his health. And anyway, I'm working."

"We can't let ya do all the workin' and providin', son," Sophie said, gazing fondly at her son. "Yer gonna want a life of yer own with a fine young lady someday."

"Ma, I've met a fine young lady out in Wampum, Pennsylvania. I want to go back there and marry her if she'll have me."

"Thet's so far away, son. Is she the one sendin' them sweet-smellin' letters?"

"Yes, Ma, she's the one. Her name is Ellie Mae Larson, and she's a fine person. You and Pa would like her. We met only briefly and had some long talks before I left Wampum to come to Waterville with Robert. But we've been writing, as you know, and we've learned much about each other. I feel so comfortable with Ellie Mae's letters. I feel like I've known her all my life."

That evening, around the fireplace in their cozy cottage, Samuel shared an idea with his parents. He related the situation with the nine children of the Larson family. He told them about the mother's illness and death, and the father's tragic death. "Ellie Mae, the young lady I'm writing to, is seventeen and the oldest child. Her brother Luke is sixteen. I understand Ellie Mae and Luke are managing their farm very well, besides caring for the younger children. I know Ellie Mae will not leave those children, and I want to marry her. If things work out for us, would you consider selling the place here and joining us in Wampum? There are many things to do on a farm, Pa. I think you might like the change. And, Ma, you could help with the cooking and the children."

"They wouldn't want us imposin'," Amos said. "They have too many people now. We'd jest be in the way."

"Their log house is huge, Pa. Mr. Larson made it very ample. And I think you're wrong about them not wanting you. I'd find out, of course. But they are so alone. They miss having folks—no parents, grandparents, or other relatives. I think they'd like the idea fine."

"I allus wanted more young'uns, Amos," Sophie said excitedly. "I'd be so pleasured ta tend ta the little ones and help with the cookin'. It would please me ta help out."

"I'm planning to go next week, Pa. I know this is sudden, but I've given it a lot of thought. I've already given notice to Mr. Clark at the watch shop. He understands because he hired me on as temporary help back in January. I'll see how things go in Wampum with Ellie Mae. It will give you time to think over what I've proposed. I don't want you to move if it would make you unhappy. You are too dear to me. This has been your home for many years, and I understand your feelings.

"But the fishing business is too much for you, Pa. I know farming is hard work also, but you could do as little or as much as you pleased. You deserve to take life easier now. There will be a lot of us to handle the chores at the Larson farm. And maybe this will be just what you need. It might prove to be challenging to you. We'd sell this place and move you in the summer. Will you consider it, Pa?"

" 'Course we will," Sophie said eagerly. "Won't we, Amos?"

Amos was quiet for several minutes. "Not certain I can leave the sea, Samuel. It's in my blood. I chose it over farmin' years ago. But I'll pray about it, son. We had hoped ta spend the rest of our days with ya close by."

Chapter 25

Jim Bishop continued to be a disturbing factor in the little Wampum church. Robert tried very hard to smooth over the difficulty, but Jim's outspoken forcefulness was overwhelming. He attempted to stir up the congregation into a feeling of discontent. The harder Robert tried to befriend Jim and dissuade him of his underhanded tactics, the more Jim deliberately went out of his way to be obstinate. Many of the church family were disgusted with Jim's brash disregard for the pastor's feelings and told Robert how they felt.

"Don't worry none, Pastor," Thomas Whan assured Robert one afternoon when they were alone. "No one with any sense will listen to Jim Bishop and his ranting and raving. He wants to run everything his own way, or he's not happy. I know you won't give in to his demands, but many of us are concerned about you leaving in June. Would you consider staying on, at lest for another year, until we get better established? Your replacement might not stand up to Jim. What if the new pastor can't handle the situation?"

Robert placed a hand on Thomas's shoulder. "I've been giving it a lot of thought, my friend, and a lot of prayer. I'm torn between staying and leaving. I know God wanted me here to start this new work. If I stay another year or longer, it will tear Emily and me apart. She is so insistent that I return to the Waterville church. I know God brought Emily into my life, and I love her dearly. I don't want to lose her, Thomas. Can you understand how I feel?"

"Of course I can, Pastor. You must do whatever your heart tells you. I know you are praying for God's direction. He will show you the answer."

During the following days Robert spent much time in Bible study and prayer, seeking God's answer to his dilemma. When news came that the young man who was to replace him had become seriously ill, Robert realized that he could not leave at this time. He felt confident it was God's will for him to continue as pastor of the Wampum church, and he had complete peace about his decision. *Surely Emily will understand that it is God's will for us to return to Pennsylvania after our marriage. She may even recognize it as a new adventure—coming to a new area and meeting new people. This will enable me to work with Jim Bishop and eventually bring things into harmony at the church. I will write Emily immediately and tell her of the change of plans.*

❧

Emily pressed Robert's latest letter to her heart, then tore open the envelope.

My dearest Emily,

Much has happened since I last wrote. Perhaps you know your cousin Samuel has gradually received most of his memory back. He is back in Wampum, staying with the Morrison family. Samuel is courting Ellie Mae Larson, and they appear deeply in love.

I'll be having a wedding ceremony when Sophie and Amos come for a visit in May. If all works as Samuel hopes, he will move his parents here in the summer. Samuel's plan is for them to all live together in the Larsons' large log home. It is certainly adequate. Amos would help with the farm, and Sophie could help with the cooking and little ones.

Ellie Mae and Luke love the idea. That way the Larson family can stay together and also have a set of parents in Amos and Sophie. Samuel says his ma is excited about the idea, but he's not sure whether his pa can be convinced to make the move. Time will tell.

Richard is grateful to have his best friend back. He and Olivia and her children are doing well.

The remainder of Robert's letter touched on a delicate subject.

The church board has given me bad news about my replacement here. The young man selected has contracted a serious illness and will be unable to minister for some time, if at all. They have asked me to remain until they locate another replacement, and after much prayer, I have agreed to do so. It could be another year, more or less. The church board tells me Rev. Davis has agreed to stay on at the Waterville church for the time being. I will return for our wedding in June, darling, and we will still take our honeymoon to Portland as planned. We will have three glorious weeks before returning to Pennsylvania. I've located a small, furnished cabin, in good condition, that we can rent here in Wampum. It belongs to a family in the church. I am convinced this is where God wants us to be, at least for now. Only a short while, darling, until we are together for a lifetime.

Emily burst into tears, crumpled Robert's letter, and threw it on the floor. "I won't go!" she exclaimed aloud in her room. "I told Robert I wouldn't leave loved ones here, yet he deliberately plans to go back. He doesn't care about my feelings!" Filled with self-pity, Emily fell sobbing on her bed. "You can just take your ring back, Robert Harris. There isn't going to be any wedding!"

As soon as Emily could compose herself, she posted a letter to Robert. It was short and to the point.

Dear Robert,

I have removed your ring, and it is my desire to break off our engagement.

Your letter tells me you are not concerned whether I am happy about your choice to remain in Pennsylvania. You told me the position would last only one year. Now you are extending it another year and possibly longer. It is obvious you do not love me enough. I'm thankful we found out now, before we were married.

Sincerely,
Emily

The days dragged for Emily while she waited for Robert's answer. There was a glimmer of hope he might change his mind and put her wishes above all else. If he didn't put her desires first, there would be no relationship between them. She walked about in a daze much of the time, moping around the house with a sad face. The family tried to cheer her up, thinking her moodiness was due to the lengthy separation from Robert.

"Ya'll be fine, dear, when Robert gits back fer yer weddin'," her mother ventured one morning at the breakfast table. "We understand how ya miss him, but he'll be a-comin' soon. The time will pass fer ya."

Emily raised sad eyes that were red and puffy from crying through the night. "Oh, Ma, you just don't know what's happened. Pa. Gramps. You all might as well know there isn't going to be any wedding. I've written to Robert breaking off our engagement. In his last letter he told me his replacement was seriously ill and unable to come to Pennsylvania. Robert has agreed to stay on until they find another person to take over the work in Wampum. It could take a year or more. He insists on going back to Pennsylvania after the wedding, and I refuse to go. It's too indefinite when we will return. I will not leave loved ones and friends, and I told him how I felt."

"Thet's a serious decision, Emily," Chase Mason said. "Are ya willin' ta forfeit yer happiness fer sech a foolish reason?"

"It isn't foolish, Pa. You don't want me to live far away, do you? I want to be near you and Ma and Gramps, Fred and Sarah, Cassie, Bill, and Rebeccah. Family and friends are special to me—they are my whole life."

" 'Course we don't want our girl far away," Gramps said, putting a big, gnarled hand on her small one. "But ya didn't mention checkin' with God 'bout yer decision. What does the Almighty want ya ta do?"

"I don't want to check with Him about my decision," Emily cried, jumping up from the table. "I've already made up my mind! I've made the only choice I can be happy with."

"Ya don't give the appearance o' bein' happy," Pa said. "Maybe ya jest better think on it some more, Emily. Ya act like yer suffrin' a mite. We don't like seein' our girl suffer so. 'Specially when ya can change the situation. Talk ta God and see what He says. Ya don't have ta be so headstrong and have yer own way all the time. Cain't ya jest bend a little?"

"Bend a little?" Emily cried tearfully. "You don't understand, do you? Robert apparently doesn't care how I feel about his decision. It's proof to me he doesn't love me enough. I can't be happy with a man who won't honor my wishes."

The family watched in the days ahead as Emily became pale, withdrawn, and aloof, avoiding conversations about Robert. She had completed her wedding gown, veil, and the other items in her wardrobe long ago for the wedding. They hung or lay neatly in her room, a constant reminder of what might have been. Each day she retreated to Fred and Sarah's cabin, where she spent long hours helping with little Frederic T. Mason Jr. He had been born ahead of schedule on April 16. Although he weighed barely six pounds at birth, he was gaining rapidly, and the doctor assured the parents they had a healthy son. Emily loved to cuddle the little dark-haired bundle and rock him to sleep before placing him in his wooden cradle.

"You're spoiling him for us, Emily," Sarah teased one afternoon. "He thinks he's supposed to be rocked all the time now. How will I get any work done?"

"Just you wait," Frederic warned, laughing, "until you and Robert have your first child. Sarah and I will come over and spoil him for you. Then you'll see what we mean."

Emily kept her head down as she rocked the baby, tears welling up in her eyes. "There isn't going to be any wedding," she said flatly. "I thought Ma had told you."

"She did, Emily," Fred replied. "But we thought it was just a lovers' quarrel and would be over soon. Those things happen. You and Robert are so much in love—you can't just break off the wedding. Can't this be patched up?"

"I won't leave Waterville. It's my home. All my loved ones are here. Robert plans to stay in Pennsylvania, even though he knows how I feel. He will come for the wedding but says we must go back. If he really loved me, he wouldn't ask me to give up family and friends. He wouldn't expect me to go to some forsaken place in the middle of nowhere." A tear slipped out of the corner of her eye, and she quickly brushed it aside. "All our plans and dreams are shattered."

Fred and Sarah did their best to comfort Emily, but she would not be comforted. "Pray about it, Emily," Fred counseled. "You mustn't bear this burden alone. Before we ask, God hears us. He will give you peace about your decision or change your heart."

"That's what I'm afraid of, Fred," Emily said, letting the tears trickle down her flushed cheeks. "I don't want to change my decision; it's as simple as that. Robert needs to stay here where we'll both be happy. He was content in Waterville before. I keep praying he'll change his mind."

Later that week Emily paid a visit to Cassie's cabin and received more unwanted advice. "You mustn't let this quarrel bring an end to your relationship, Emily," Cassie said. "Robert is a fine man, and he loves you dearly. Don't you love him enough to follow him wherever his ministry leads?"

Emily looked up from her position on the floor where she was playing with Rebeccah. She remained silent a few minutes as she stacked homemade wooden blocks higher and higher. "Whee!" Rebeccah cried as she knocked them all down. "Moe," she cried. "Moe!"

Emily started rebuilding the tower and said thoughtfully, "I've given it a lot of thought, Cassie. You say Robert loves me dearly. I don't think he loves me enough to change his plans, and I won't settle for less."

"But you are unhappy," Cassie said, "and I hate seeing my sister unhappy—especially when the situation could be changed. Write Robert again and tell him you've reconsidered. He'll understand."

"And let him have his own way!" Emily exclaimed. "That is exactly what he expects me to do."

"It isn't letting him have his own way, Emily. The circumstances regarding his replacement changed, and he had to make a decision. I'm sure he prayed about it and felt God leading him to stay. Have you prayed about it, too?"

"I should be hearing from Robert any day now." Emily sighed. "Since I've been praying God will change Robert's mind about staying, perhaps He will. I'm really counting on Robert to have a change of heart and see things my way."

Chapter 26

When Emily received Robert's answer to her letter, she hurried upstairs to the privacy of her room. The hope that raged within her breast kept conflicting with the doubts in her mind. Would Robert give up the ministry in Pennsylvania and return to Waterville, for her sake? Did he love her enough to respect her wishes and put her desires first? Breathlessly she tore open the envelope and clutched the letter with trembling hands.

Emily, darling,

I read your letter with mixed emotions, and it left me cheerless and with a heavy heart. I try to tell myself this is only a bad dream and will pass. Can two people who are in love turn their back on that love? I still believe you are the woman God has chosen for me, the one I hoped to love and cherish for a lifetime. Is it possible that I will never claim you as my beautiful bride?

God has called me to this place and to these people. I strongly believe it is His will for me to serve here until He raises up another minister in my place. And there are other problems here that I need to deal with. One man in the church is causing disunity and creating havoc.

I cannot, in good faith, leave the church without a pastor at this time. Can't you trust God to make this your calling also?

There will not be time for another of your letters to reach me before I leave to return to Waterville. I am praying, dear Emily, that God will change your heart. I have purchased my train ticket and will arrive in Waterville on June 3 at 1:30 p.m. If you do not meet me, I will know there is no hope for us. After a brief stay I will return to the ministry in Pennsylvania, where I am badly needed. Please remember, darling, how much I love you.

Forever yours,
Robert

Emily made an attempt to read Robert's letter over again, but tears blurred her eyes until she could not see the pages. She ate little supper and retired early that evening. The letter rested under her pillow so she could read it first thing in the morning. "Robert says he loves me, but he won't change his plans," she muttered as she lay awake, brooding. "I thought everything was settled for us. We were the perfect couple and would stay in Waterville, close to loved ones and friends. Robert doesn't have any family, so he can't know how I feel. He's insensitive to my needs and desires. Perhaps he isn't the man I thought he was. If he loved me, I would come first."

Mrs. Mason tapped softly on her daughter's bedroom door. "Are ya asleep, Emily? Can I come in and talk to ya?"

Emily hastily wiped her tear-stained face. "Sure, Ma," she called. "Come on in. I'm awake."

Mary Jane Mason entered in her nightclothes and sat on the edge of the bed. Then she leaned over and gave her younger daughter a hug. "Yer hurtin', child, and I wish I could make all yer pain go away. Mas hurt jest the same when their children are achin'. Ya won't understand till ya become a ma yerself someday."

"I'll be all right, Ma. It's just hard knowing Robert doesn't love me as much as I thought he did. He won't change his mind about returning to Pennsylvania."

"Did he say he doesn't love ya in his letter taday?"

"No, he says he loves me. But if he loved me enough, he'd be willing to stay here in Waterville, wouldn't he? He knows this is where I want to live."

"He cain't stay here iffen God wants him in Pennsylvania. Robert has a callin' ta follow, and thet comes first. Cain't ya see thet, Emily?"

"Don't you want me nearby, Ma? I always thought I'd grow up and get married but live close so our family could be together. We need one another."

"Emily, yer pa and I allus prayed fer each o' you children. God protected Frederic and brung him home safe from the war. God watched over Cassie and brung her through a difficult childbirth. And God blessed Fred and Sarah with a healthy little Fred. And now we're prayin' fer ya ta make the right decision about Robert. Yer jest so miserable, child. Talk ta God about it, won't ya? Let Him be the decidin' One."

Emily sighed but pulled her mother down and kissed her lightly on the cheek. "I'll pray about it, Ma. I confess I haven't been praying to God lately except to tell Him what I want."

"Jest talk ta Him, dear, but don't fergit ta listen," her mother cautioned. "Sometimes we tell God what we want when He has somethin' else planned fer us. He'll show us what's best if we'll jest listen."

❧

By the end of May, spring was in full bloom. Soft, warm rains permeated the earth until flowers burst forth in their bright array of colors. The budding trees, bare and desolate through the long winter, carried themselves loftily, stretching toward the heavens. Lingering scents from the blossoming trees and bushes filled the clean, pure air with their delicate fragrance.

Sophie wrote the Mason family, bringing them up-to-date concerning Samuel's marriage to Ellie Mae Larson.

We come by train ta Pennsylvania so's we could be here fer Samuel's weddin'. His Ellie Mae is a sweet young thing, and Samuel dearly loves her. It makes Amos and me glad ta see the two of them so happy. Ellie Mae's folks had built a large log home, and Samuel's plan is fer us ta move there. He says iffen we like, he and the Larson boys can build us a separate cabin on the Larson property so we can be a mite private. Amos had a hard time thinkin' 'bout movin' here but now says we can give it a try. I think it's a fine idea. We'll be goin' back ta Portland soon and stay until we sell our place. Whenever our house gits taken care of, we'll move down here.

Pennsylvania is a purty state and has a lush, green, rollin' countryside. There are hills and valleys and little creeks here and there. Amos can fish in the creeks right from the bank, ta his heart's content. Don't even need a boat. The scenery don't match the seacoast with all its huge granite rocks, rollin' waves, and poundin' surf. But it's pleasing ta the eye and should be a mite warmer in the winter fer us. Those old Maine nor'easters are bitter cold and blustery. We spent all our lives there with no regrets, but the winters have taken a toll on Amos and me.

I have me a little flower garden ta dig around in and call my own. The Larson children are all so lovable, and the little ones call us Grandma and Grandpa. It's a joy ta our hearts.

Sophie's letter went on to say they appreciated Robert's fine preaching while in Wampum, and they could see it was a warm and growing church. She inquired about their health and closed with love to all the family.

"It sounds like Amos and Sophie are making a big change in their life," Emily commented that evening at the supper table. "They lived by the sea so many years, it must be a difficult decision for them."

"Wal, they want ta be near Samuel, and he plans ta stay in Pennsylvania," Ma offered. "I can understand thet."

"Yep," Chase said. "Samuel bein' their only son, I don't blame them a mite. Their boy, who was lost ta them, has been found agin. It's right normal fer them ta want ta be near him."

"But Amos and Sophie love the sea," Emily said quickly. "They will miss the seabirds, the rocky cliffs, and the pounding surf. How can they just pick up and leave?"

Grandpa Caleb laid down his fork and became thoughtful. "The place isn't what's important, Emily. It's where their heart is. Amos and Sophie know Samuel won't come back ta Portland, 'ceptin' maybe fer visits. He and Ellie Mae have a bundle o' responsibilities. They'll stay in Pennsylvania because the farm is there and it's a mighty fine place ta raise the young'uns. Yep, Amos and Sophie felt it tuggin' on their hearts ta go where Samuel is."

"It still seems cruel," Emily said, "moving them from the only home they've known since they were married. You'd think Samuel would understand how difficult it will be for them. Wampum, Pennsylvania, is a remote area and will be entirely different from Portland. It will seem almost like another world."

"Sophie says in her letter thet it's purty country, Emily," Chase said. "It's rollin', lush, and green countryside, with springs and creeks fer fishin'. And Robert told us hisself 'bout the beauty of the land, thet its rich, fertile fields make fer good farmin'. I think it was a fine idea fer Amos and Sophie ta visit Wampum and be there fer the weddin'. Thet way they can kinder get used ta the idea o' movin' there. And I think Amos realizes, though he loves the sea, he can't manage his fishin' boat anymore at his age. A change will be best fer his health and could be a little excitin' ta boot. Sophie seems pleased 'bout the move, and Amos will come around."

Emily sighed heavily. "Changes! Changes! Changes! I hate changes! I wish everything could stay the same—the way it is right now."

"Life isn't like thet, Emily," Grandpa said. "People grow up and move on. It's what life is all about—a series of changes and decisions."

"But you've lived on this farm, Gramps, ever since you and Gram first got married," Emily protested. "Ma and Pa moved in after their marriage and stayed on to help run the farm. Fred is on the same property in his own little cabin with Sarah and little Fred, so he can help farm. Cassie, Bill, and Rebeccah are nearby. It's all been so perfect for our family until now."

"We been blessed," Ma said, "ta have our young'uns close. And Amos and Sophie will be happy ta settle near Samuel. It's fittin' they be near their only son."

"Maybe it's right for them," Emily said gloomily, "but it's not right for me. I want to be here, not in Pennsylvania." Emily jumped up to clear the dishes. "Why is life so difficult and unsettling? Why can't everything go according to plan?"

The following day Emily rode into Waterville with Fred, who was picking up seeds and garden supplies. Since Fred would be in town a few hours, Emily planned to pick up some personal items and visit her friend Louisa. She and Fred would meet later for the trip home.

Emily took deep breaths of the sweet, fresh air as she walked down Main Street and purchased her packages. It was a bright and cheerful afternoon, and for several moments she forgot the deep ache in her heart as she took in the beauty around her. Colorful flowers bloomed everywhere, in little gardens by well-kept houses, in flower boxes underneath curtained windows, and in bright rows along the common.

"Waterville is so lovely this time of year," she muttered. "How could I ever leave it?"

Louisa answered her knock at the Bradford home and was delighted to see her friend. "Come in, Emily," she said cheerily, giving her a hug. "I haven't seen you in ages. And you look pale. Have you been ill?"

"No," Emily said as she sank down on the richly covered sofa. "I know Peter has been courting you, Louisa. Is it going well?"

"At the moment, yes." Louisa laughed. "We have some disagreements at times, and he stays away. I miss him dreadfully during those days. But we've found it's wonderful making up. I think our relationship just needs a little time. He's still afraid I care about him out of a thankful heart because he saved my life. It probably started then, but I'm certain about my feelings for Peter. They are real! I hope I can convince him of that."

"I'm glad you and Peter are getting together. You are a dear and special couple. I won't be surprised to hear about a wedding in the near future."

"I'll be ready whenever he is, Emily. But I'm excited for you and Robert. He arrives next week, doesn't he? Mother has finished my dress for your wedding. It turned out lovely."

Emily's face clouded over. "Robert is coming next week on the afternoon train. But I've told him the ceremony is off. I'm sorry about your dress, Louisa. There isn't going to be any wedding."

"Oh no, Emily!" Louisa gasped. "What's wrong?"

"Robert insists we return to Pennsylvania and live in some small cabin after the wedding. He says he can't leave the work now. He's putting his work ahead of me. I refuse to leave family and friends here in Waterville. It's as simple as that!" Tears began to trickle down Emily's fair cheeks.

Louisa reached out and put her arms around her friend. "Oh, Emily, I don't want you to move away. You're my best friend, and I would miss you dreadfully. But you can't give Robert up if he feels Pennsylvania is where God wants him to be. His first answer is to God. You must go wherever he goes."

"Would you follow Peter to some distant, forsaken place far away?" Emily asked. "I'm sure I would hate it there!"

Louisa was quiet for a moment. "Emily, I love Peter, and I hope in time we will be married. It is wonderful living here in Waterville near so many family and friends. But if Peter proposed and wanted to leave this area after our marriage, I would follow him. Yes, I would follow him anywhere on this earth, as long as he loved me."

At those words, Emily burst into tears and sobbed uncontrollably. "It's—it's easy for you—to say, Louisa. You don't have to leave."

Louisa patted her friend's shoulder as she hugged her close. "Who knows what the future holds, Emily? Only God. I know I would be willing to go, rather than be here without the man I love."

Emily was quiet and thoughtful on the way home as she considered all the advice given recently by those who loved her. Fred, acquainted with her moods of late, hummed softly as he drove the team homeward. Once home, Emily went immediately to her room and opened her Bible. She read the entire book of Ruth and then read it over again. God spoke to her as she read the heart-warming story, and Ruth's words to Naomi, recorded in chapter 1, verse 16, brought conviction to her aching, broken heart. "Intreat me not to leave thee, or to return from following after thee: for whither thou goest, I will go; and where thou lodgest, I will lodge."

Falling upon her knees by the side of her bed, Emily cried out to God with a broken and contrite heart. "Dear Father, forgive me for my selfishness in wanting my own way. I have not been in tune with You and Your desires. I've been asking You to answer my prayers the way I wanted them answered, instead of seeking Your will. I love Robert, and You've shown me that You want me in Pennsylvania. Together, we will serve You in the little mission church. Help me to be a good wife and helpmate for him as we both seek to do Your will. In Jesus' precious name, amen."

Emily got up from her knees, her eyes wet with tears but with a smile on her face and a peace in her heart. "Thank You, Lord," she exclaimed aloud, "for being so patient with me." She hurriedly opened her top dresser drawer and placed the beautiful engagement ring Robert had given her back on her finger. "This is our pledge of love and commitment," she said, turning the ring toward the light. "My dear Robert, with God to guide us, our love will last forever."

In the days that followed, the Mason family was delighted with the change in Emily. She had done a complete turnaround. Gone were the sad eyes and sorrowful look. She laughed merrily and danced around the house as would a child having her first party. Her sweet soprano voice filled the air as she did her chores. In her spare time she sat at the piano and played some of her favorite hymns or compositions.

Chapter 27

Robert went about his duties in Wampum halfheartedly, with thoughts of Emily ever on his mind. He knew this was the place God had for him until another preacher could take over, even though it could mean the end of their relationship. She had been adamant in her letter, refusing to leave family and friends. The wedding was off unless he returned to Waterville to preach. "And that is out of the question." Robert sighed. "I cannot leave these dear people without a shepherd."

The work in Wampum had flourished and grown. It was apparent that soon the little schoolhouse would be unable to accommodate them. Robert had visions of a new church building more adequate for their needs. The thought was exciting, and he had discussed it fully with the church family. The men themselves wanted to build the church with wood from their properties. Many of them had built their own homes and seemed very capable. The building could be started in the fall, after harvest, when the men had more time. With many hands helping, it could be completed before the bitter thrust of winter set in. A larger building would provide more room for Sunday school classes, fellowship dinners, and other activities. Rough sketches had been pored over by several of the men who were most qualified. It was a challenge for the people to take on such a commitment. After a great deal of prayer, the church body voted to step out in faith, believing God was guiding the decision. The families were eager to go forward with these plans, and Robert shared their excitement and enthusiasm.

The problem with Jim Bishop had not diminished, but Robert stood firm when the man pushed for his own way. He dealt with Jim gently, in a loving manner, and encouraged him to participate at the church in team activities. The congregation became accustomed to his pushy ways and tended to overlook his outspokenness. Robert hoped to eventually win Jim's confidence and support. "Jim would make a fine leader," Robert mused, "if he would only get himself out of the way."

Robert continued to pray for Emily's change of heart as he went about his pastoral duties, teaching, preaching, and visiting the sick and elderly. He had ably prepared Thomas Whan, Richard Morrison, and Emily's cousin Samuel Mason to preach during his absence and handle the duties at the church. All three were capable men. "The Wampum Community Church will be in good hands while I'm away," Robert said aloud as he packed clothing into his valise for the trip to Waterville. "I'm thankful to have godly men to leave in charge." His eyes moist,

Robert slipped to his knees. "I may be gone a week or a month, depending on how things work out with Emily," he whispered. "I'm torn apart, God. I don't want to lose Emily. Our love seems so right, so real. But I will return, with or without her, to the work You have given me here in Pennsylvania."

Dark clouds gathered overhead the next morning as Robert prepared to leave for Waterville, Maine. "What a gloomy day," Robert muttered to himself as he loaded his gear onto Thomas's wagon. "It's quite fitting for the way I feel."

"Pastor, you've not been yourself lately," Thomas Whan said as he and Robert headed for the train station. "I know you must be plumb excited about your weddin'. But is somethin' botherin' you?

"It's good having Samuel back. He and Richard have a fine work with the young'uns. Those youngsters look up to them. Now that Samuel and Ellie are married, they bring the children regularly. Samuel's parents, Amos and Sophie, will be in regular attendance once they get moved. And we have plans to build a new church. It's been a good year, Pastor. We look forward to you comin' back with your missus."

Robert hesitated, searching for the right words. "I know I've been distracted lately, Thomas. My heart hasn't been in the work. I'm making this trip to Waterville but may return in a few days without a bride. Emily has broken our engagement, and I am heartsick."

"Why, I had no idea you were carrying such a load, Pastor. Guess that's why you've been so quiet and stayed to yourself. Shoulda sensed there was a problem. The folk here enjoyed gettin' the Richardsons' cabin all prettied up for her. What happened?"

"Emily says she cannot leave her family and friends in Waterville. The Masons are a close-knit family and depend on one another. She expected me to return to the little church in town where I preached previously. It was my intention to go back when I first came to Wampum. I do love the people there and had claimed the sweet town of Waterville as my home. They are good people and have a special place in my heart. But I care about the dear people in this place who need me. Emily counted on us sharing the quaint, clapboard parsonage and serving in a ministry where all her family and friends are. Waterville is the only home she has ever known."

"Does she understand there is no preacher to handle the ministry here if you leave? Jim Bishop might try to take over the church if he's given a chance. He's forceful enough. It would leave us in dire straits. I daresay the church might fall apart if left to itself."

"Emily knows, Thomas. I've told her God wants me in Wampum, at least for now, until He directs differently. This has been a matter of prayer for quite some time. I've asked God to show her it's her calling, too."

At the train station, Thomas Whan helped Robert with his valise and shook his hand. "We'll be praying about this situation, Pastor. God can ease the pain in your heart. We trust He will work this together for good and give you His peace."

Robert grabbed the older man in a warm embrace. "Thank you, Thomas. You're a good friend. I'll need your prayers to get through this. It's not easy to follow God's leading when it means giving up someone I love with all my heart."

Robert's thoughts were on Emily during the long train trip from Pennsylvania to Maine. He remembered dark, curly tresses framed around a fair, oval face. Her deep blue eyes, full of fire, could melt his heart at a moment's notice. "She's like a sweet yet high-spirited filly," Robert mused, "and she wants her own way. She won't be tamed!"

As the train drew closer to his destination, fear gripped Robert's heart. "What if she isn't here?" he whispered to himself. "I may never hold her in my arms again and feel her soft body close to mine. How can I forget the way she laughs as she caresses my cheek with her fingers and tousles my hair? I can't, God, without Your help."

"Waterville!" The porter called loudly. "Next stop is Waterville, Maine!"

Robert hastily gathered his belongings, smoothed back his unruly, sandy hair, and prepared to leave the train. The aisles were filled with anxious people, and he moved along slowly, a few inches at a time. He tried unsuccessfully to calm the excitement rising within his chest.

When Robert reached the train's steps, he paused a moment before descending and scanned the platform. Amid the thronging, struggling mass of people, there was no familiar face. His heart sank. "Emily's not here!" he murmured under his breath. "She evidently refuses to be my wife if she must move to Pennsylvania!" With slow steps and aching heart, Robert gathered his luggage and sat down on a bench in front of the train station. *Maybe she's late. I'll wait for her.* His heart soared at the thought.

Gradually the thronging mass of people dwindled until no one was left. Still Robert waited, hopeful, expectant. He took out his pocket watch and studied it through blurred eyes. *Emily is an hour late. She isn't coming, Robert. Stop fooling yourself.* With a deep sigh that shook his entire body, Robert entered the train station and bought his return ticket to Pennsylvania. Glancing around outside, he scanned the area once again for a glimpse of Emily.

"It will be three days before I return to Wampum," he said halfheartedly. "Since Mr. and Mrs. Meade have invited me to stay with them, it will give me a good opportunity to see some of my friends, some of the fine people of Waterville while I'm here." Shouldering his load, Robert started to whistle as he headed toward town. But the merry tune fell flat and could not overcome the ache in his heart.

Chapter 28

I t's nice to see our girl so happy," Grandpa Caleb said at the breakfast table as he sipped his coffee. "We're glad ya got yer life turned around and back on track with Robert."

"I'm so happy, Grandpa," Emily said, beaming, as she sat down at the old oak table in the kitchen to join him. "Everything is perfect again. I finally had that talk with God that everyone suggested. You all had good advice for me, but I was too stubborn to listen. When I prayed before, I told God what I wanted. I didn't listen to Him or try to seek His will for my life. I just wanted to go my own way and do my own thing."

"Ya allus was strong-spirited, Emily," her mother said as she placed ham and eggs before them. "But I was sure ya'd come around, with everyone prayin' fer ya."

"Thanks, Ma. I needed all those extra prayers. I know now that God wants me to follow Robert wherever he goes. It will be a big change for me, and I'll miss all of you very much—more than you know. But Robert and I will be together, and that's what counts."

"I look forward to walkin' my little girl down the aisle on Saturday," Chase Mason said as he joined them and began to butter a biscuit. "I'll probably choke up a bit, this bein' our last young'un to marry off. Are all the plans ready fer the weddin', Emily? I know yer ma has my best suit all pressed and steamed."

"The ceremony is back on schedule with Rev. Davis and all the church family, Pa. My wedding gown and other things were completed long ago. Ma and I and some of the other church women are cooking and preparing for the dinner afterward. I get so excited every time I think about Saturday, and today Robert arrives on the afternoon train. I can hardly wait to see him. He'll stay with the Meades. He lived with them, remember, when he was our pastor, and they want him to stay with them again, until the wedding."

"Wal, it's good to hear music and harmony in the house agin," Grandpa said as he leaned over and kissed Emily on the cheek. "I reckon I'm gonna enjoy this weddin' more than any, 'ceptin' my own with yer grandma."

Emily took special pains as she dressed that afternoon and prepared to meet Robert at the train station. They had been apart since Christmas, and her heart jumped within her at the thought of their reunion. She carefully slipped a soft blue dress, one of Robert's favorites, over her head and surveyed herself in the mirror. Her dark, curly hair had been brushed until it shone, and she tied blue ribbons to secure the curls back from her face. She smiled impishly at herself as she placed her bonnet over the dark tresses. "Robert Harris," she said aloud, "I cannot wait to see you again. Soon I will be Mrs. Robert Harris, and we will be together always!"

Frederic was waiting with the carriage to take her to town, and she climbed in, humming a little tune. "It's a beautiful day, Fred." She laughed. "I hope it's like this on Saturday for my wedding."

"Ah, Emily, it's good to see you happy again," Fred said as he snapped the reins and headed the team down the gravel drive. "You seemed so miserable and lost for a while. It cheers me to see you this way."

"I certainly wasn't very pleasant to be around. I'm sure it was hard on all the family, me being weepy all the time. But that's in the past, Fred. Today, everything is beautiful!"

About two miles down the hard clay road, the carriage lurched suddenly, throwing Emily and Frederic to one side. "Whoa! Whoa!" Fred shouted as he pulled hard on the reins and brought the team to a quick halt.

Emily was all disheveled and tried to straighten her dress and rearrange her bonnet. "What happened, Fred?" she asked shakily. "Will everything be all right?"

Fred had already climbed down and was examining the carriage. "We lost a wheel!" he shouted. "I don't think I can fix it without some tools. The wheel must be laying back a ways by the side of the road."

"Oh, Fred, I'll be late to meet Robert's train," Emily said in despair. "He'll think I'm not coming. He specifically said if I wasn't there to meet him, he would know I didn't plan to go through with the marriage. What shall we do?"

"We could leave the carriage here until later and each ride one of the horses back to the house. Then I can hitch up the wagon and we can take that instead. It's not as comfortable, but it would serve our purpose, Emily. And time is so important right now."

"I wish someone would come along and take us back, Fred," Emily said forlornly. "I'll be a mess if I have to ride bareback in my good clothes. I wanted to look special for Robert. He hasn't seen me since Christmas."

"We can wait awhile if you'd rather. But you know how it is on this country road. Sometimes it takes forever for someone to come along."

"I really don't have time to wait," Emily said as she jumped down from the carriage. "I must get to Robert as quickly as possible. Unhitch the horses, Fred, and let's get going. I don't understand why this had to happen just when I thought things were going so perfectly."

Emily pulled her skirts around her, and Fred helped her onto the horse's back. She loved riding bareback and had done it often, but not when she was dressed in her best clothes. With her bonnet tied securely, she galloped, along with Fred, back to the farm. The dust from the road swirled around her, getting into her face and eyes.

While Frederic explained to his parents what happened to the carriage,

Emily quickly washed up and changed into fresh clothes. She tried to brush the dust from her hair and coax the dark curls into place. *I spent all that time trying to look my best, and now look at me. Robert hasn't seen me in months. I did want to make a good first impression.* Emily sprinkled her arms and throat with some sweet-smelling scent and replaced her bonnet. "This will have to do." She sighed, viewing her image in the mirror.

As soon as Fred hitched the horses to the wagon, he and Emily started for town once again. Emily fussed and fumed most of the way, twisting her lace handkerchief into knots. "We'll be so late, Fred. What will Robert think? When I'm not there to meet him, he'll believe I'm still being difficult—stubborn and selfish. Robert will think the wedding is off. I don't want to lose him, not when I've finally come to my senses. What if he turned around and went right back to Pennsylvania? What will I do?"

"If I know Robert, he'll be waiting for you, Emily. He wouldn't leave to go back immediately. He would want to talk to you and try to change your mind. And Robert wouldn't leave without seeing his friends and the church folk. Don't fret so, Emily. I'll get us there as quickly as possible. The four miles into town takes longer with the wagon, though."

"Robert will think I don't want to marry him." Emily sighed, tears starting to trickle down her fair cheeks. "He may not want to talk to a self-centered young woman who wants her own way all the time. I made it pretty clear in my letter how I felt."

When the Waterville station loomed in the distance, Emily strained her eyes to see if anyone was outside waiting. It had been an hour and a half since Robert's train had pulled into the station. As they drew closer, she could see the area was deserted. Emily jumped down from the wagon as soon as Frederic pulled the horses to a halt.

"Maybe he's waiting inside," Emily exclaimed. "I'll ask the ticket master if he's see a young man fitting Robert's description."

Emily returned to the wagon, her face lined with concern. "The ticket master said a young man waited for about an hour before leaving. He said the fellow seemed very depressed and bought a one-way ticket back to Pennsylvania. When he tried to engage him in conversation, the man just stared at him with a dazed expression, then left abruptly. That's not like Robert at all. Oh, what have I done to him, Fred? He won't want to marry me now. He doesn't want a spoiled child for a wife."

Frederic reached down a hand to help Emily into the wagon. "Don't get so worked up, Emily. As soon as we find Robert, this will be straightened out. He's probably at the Meades' right now getting settled in. We'll find him, I promise."

Emily sat in a half trance as Frederic headed the horses toward town. "Please be there, Robert. Please be there," she kept muttering.

The Meades greeted them warmly and invited them in to have tea. They were surprised Robert wasn't with them.

"No, Robert isn't here yet," Mr. Meade said. "We thought his train must be late."

"His train came in over an hour and a half ago," Frederic said. "We were late getting to the station to pick him up. A wheel came off our carriage, and we had to go back to the house for the wagon. It was a long delay, and we missed him somehow."

"You can visit here, Fred," Emily said hastily, "while I run uptown and see if I can find Robert. He has to be somewhere!"

"Maybe he's at the church," Fred suggested. "Do you want me to look there?"

"I'll try the church on my way," Emily called as she hurried off.

"I think she wants to meet Robert alone," Fred said to the Meades. "Thank you, I will accept that cup of tea now."

Emily rushed to the church and the parsonage, but Rev. and Mrs. Davis had not seen him. As she walked uptown to Main Street and the common, she pondered where Robert might go. Maybe he needed something at the clothing store, or perhaps he was hungry. He always said the long train trip made him hungry. She looked in each store as she went along, including the restaurant, but found no sign of him. As she looked ahead toward Millers' store, the ladies' hat and piece goods shop, she saw a figure standing there, just looking inside. Her heart beat rapidly and did flip-flops.

"Can that be Robert?" she muttered. "What would he be doing by a ladies' shop?"

The figure turned, and she recognized him. "Robert!" Emily called. "Robert!"

Robert started quickly toward her, his face wreathed in his lopsided grin. His heart pounded within his chest as he ran. Emily gathered her skirts above her ankles and rushed forward into his open arms. Robert pressed her body close, then, laughing heartily, he lifted her off her feet and swung her through the air. Her bonnet fell backward, held only by its ribbons.

"You came," he whispered against her dark, curly hair as he drew her close against his broad chest. "Does this mean you will marry me and go with me to Pennsylvania?"

"Yes, Robert! Oh yes!" she cried, her blue eyes lost in his. "I've changed. I'm not a spoiled little girl anymore. I'll always want to go with you—wherever you go, wherever God leads you. I'm late because we lost a wheel on the carriage. But that's not important now. You're here, and we're together."

"I thought I had lost you, Emily. I've been standing in front of Millers' store for a long time. It's where we met, remember?"

Emily giggled and looked up at him. "Yes, I fell in a very unladylike way on the ice, and you recovered my packages. I acted like a snob. It's a wonder you ever looked at me again."

"I fell in love with a saucy young lady that day, darling," he said, looking deep into the blue of her eyes. "But are you sure about returning to the Pennsylvania church with me? I want you to be certain of your decision. I want you to be happy."

Emily sighed contentedly and reached up and touched his cheek. Then she pushed a tousled lock of sandy hair back from his forehead. "I'll be happy, dear Robert, as long as I can be with you. As long as we're both where God wants us."

Completely unaware of people milling around them, Robert pulled her close. "We'll serve God together, darling," he said huskily as his lips found hers. "And we'll have our time to love."

Epilogue

The sun did shine on Emily's wedding day, and the Waterville Community Church was bedecked with flowers, ribbons, and candles. Family and friends filled the little sanctuary to its capacity. Emily's attendants, Cassie, Sarah, and Louisa, wore pale blue gowns and matching headpieces. Robert stood at the altar, dressed in his finest dark suit, with his groomsmen: Frederic, Bill, and Peter. Nervously Robert watched as Emily walked down the aisle on her father's arm. He had never seen her look more beautiful. Her satin and lace gown billowed gracefully, and she had an angelic air about her.

As Robert took her hand, she looked up into his eyes with her sweet smile. He knew it was a smile of promise, a smile of commitment. After their honeymoon they would return to Pennsylvania as a team, to serve God as long as He needed them there. Robert tucked her arm into his and flashed his wide, crooked grin. As he listened to Rev. Davis present the beautiful words of their wedding ceremony, his heart overflowed and he marveled at the goodness of God.

The Best
Laid Plans

God has blessed my husband Herb and me with four children.
This book is dedicated to our wonderful children:
Cynthia, Mark, David, and Kimberly; their dear
spouses and our precious grandchildren.

I have no greater joy than to hear
that my children walk in truth.
3 JOHN 4

Chapter 1

1868

Louisa Bradford hummed a little tune as she walked quickly along Main Street away from the shops in town. She carried a light package under one arm, and a smile played about her lips as she considered the new frock she had just purchased. It was a mint green satin with delicate lace and tiny buttons. The dress made her feel special, and the saleslady insisted the color was right for her because it accented the gray of her eyes. Louisa gave a little skip as she contemplated how the dress would affect her beau, Peter McClough. They had been seeing one another for some time, but she sensed tonight would be different. Peter seemed rather eager when he mentioned his plans for the evening, and the glint in his eye lent an air of mystery. He had hinted it would be a special occasion, and Louisa felt this particular event warranted a new gown. Excitement mounted within her breast as she thought about Peter. He was tall and muscular, not overly handsome, but with rugged good looks. She loved the way a shock of his dark hair occasionally fell across his forehead. His dark eyes held her attention and gazed deep into her soul. At times he knew what she was thinking and what she was about to say. Their friendship, rocky at first, had grown into a sweet and caring relationship.

It was a warm August afternoon in Waterville, Maine, and Louisa reached up with her free hand and loosened the ribbons on her straw bonnet. A slight breeze toyed with her pale, golden tresses as they cascaded around her shoulders. She hoped her new dress would impress Peter as much as it had her. Anxious to inspect her purchase once again, she hurried down a side street and turned in at the Bradfords' large two-story home. Her banker father would be at work, but she was eager to show her mother the gown and seek her approval.

"Mother, I'm home," she called as she placed her bonnet on a hook and dropped the package on a pine bench by the front door. "Where are you?" Dead silence met her repeated calls, and then she remembered. Her mother had a ladies' meeting at church and wouldn't be home until later. "Oh, fiddle! I so wanted Mama to see my beautiful gown right away," she muttered aloud. Louisa grabbed the package, untied the string, and held the satiny frock against her body. "It's exquisite!" she exclaimed as she viewed her image in the mirror over the bench in the entryway. "I must find the appropriate jewelry to go with it—something very special."

Louisa dashed up the stairs and in a very short time stood, dressed in her new gown, before a full-length mirror in her bedroom. She emptied her jewelry box and tried on several necklaces. "None of these are right with this dress," she moaned. "I should have purchased something new to complement the gown." She tossed her jewelry back into the case and headed for her parents' bedroom. She was sure her mother would gladly loan her a piece of her jewelry. Elizabeth Bradford had often suggested that her only daughter should wear one of her necklaces or a particular brooch for a special occasion. Louisa lifted her mother's case from the top of her dresser and pulled out several pieces of jewelry. She held each piece up to her throat and gazed into the mirror. A deep sigh escaped her lips as she decided nothing seemed suitable. She was about to replace the several items when she noticed a false bottom with a little ribbon pull tab in her mother's jewelry box—something she had never seen before. Usually her mother brought pieces of jewelry to Louisa's room for her to try on. Louisa pulled on the ribbon and found it opened to display a beautiful gold locket nestled in old satin. Excitement mounted within her as she tenderly lifted the lovely piece and held it to her throat. It was the perfect accompaniment to set off her gown. She turned it over in her hands and found the initials L.A.M. engraved on the back. When she opened the locket, she found a picture of a lovely young woman. Eagerly she placed the locket around her neck.

"Maybe it's my great-grandmother," she whispered as she whirled around the room. "It can't be my grandmother's. Her name was Abigail."

Louisa decided to keep the necklace on until her mother returned home so she could see how beautiful it looked with her new gown. She pulled the satiny cloth out of the box to straighten it and found a faded picture underneath. It was a picture of two young ladies with their arms around each other's waists. "The one on the right is my mother," Louisa said audibly, "when she was about fifteen or sixteen years old." She turned the picture over and found inscribed in her mother's handwriting, "Louisa and I, best of friends, June 1847." Louisa puzzled over the picture and wondered why her mother had never mentioned her dear friend of long ago. Obviously Louisa had been named for this person. Why had her mother never told her? Was there some reason she kept the locket and picture hidden?

When Louisa heard the front door open, she rushed to the top of the stairs with the picture clutched in her hand. "Mother!" she cried. "I'm upstairs. Come up and see my new gown. I hope you will like it. It's beautiful!"

"I'll be right up, dear, as soon as I remove my hat and gloves. I'm sure the dress is lovely. What time is Peter calling for you?"

"About six o'clock. I have plenty of time, so I'll change my gown and help you prepare dinner for you and Father. But you must see my outfit first. And may I wear a piece of your jewelry? I've found just the right necklace to give it a perfect touch."

"Of course, dear. You know I like to share my jewelry with you," Elizabeth Bradford said as she climbed the stairs and eyed her daughter's new gown. She leaned over and kissed Louisa's cheek. "You are right; it is indeed beautiful. You have excellent taste. Peter will be overcome."

"And the locket, Mama. I found it at the bottom of your jewelry box hidden underneath. It complements the dress so well. I hope you don't mind if I wear it."

Elizabeth Bradford glanced at the necklace for the first time, and her face turned ashen. "Why—how—," she stammered.

"The initials, Mama, are L.A.M. on the locket. And this picture"—Louisa still clutched it and held it out to her mother—"is a picture of you and your very dearest friend, Louisa. Why did you never tell me about her? Is she the one you named me after?"

Elizabeth Bradford grabbed the picture from Louisa's hand and hurried into her room with Louisa right on her heels. "What's wrong, Mother? Didn't you want me to see the picture?"

Tears trickled down Elizabeth Bradford's fair cheeks as she sat down on her bed. For a few moments she was unable to speak. "No, Louisa," she said, "I never wanted you to see the locket or the picture. That is why I kept them hidden in the bottom of my jewelry case. I thought they were safe there—safe from your eyes—safe from questions and answers."

"I'm sorry, Mama," Louisa said as she sat next to her mother on the bed and hugged her close. "I didn't think you would mind. You always want me to wear your jewelry, so I took the liberty of going into your jewelry case. I realize now it was wrong of me. But what is wrong with my seeing these things? Why did you keep them from me?"

Elizabeth Bradford wiped her tears on her lace hanky and blew her nose. "Your father always thought I should tell you, Louisa, but I was afraid to. Afraid it would alienate you from me. Afraid I would lose your love."

"Tell me what, Mother? Is it something so secret that I cannot know?"

"Now there is nothing else to do but to tell you the entire story. I hope you will accept what I have to say and not be angry with me."

"Never, Mother! I love you! I couldn't be angry with you. I'm grown up. I hope I'm mature enough to understand whatever you tell me."

Elizabeth Bradford patted her daughter's hand and spoke softly. "Louisa Ann McKay was my dearest friend. Our families lived near one another in Augusta. We went through grade school together and into the higher classes as soul mates. The two of us were inseparable, always together." Elizabeth hesitated briefly and looked away from her daughter's intense gaze. A deep sigh escaped her lips. "The picture you found was taken when my friend and I were both sixteen—still very close after all those childhood years. When I met your father, we fell in love and not long after were married. Louisa and I were still the best of friends and pledged our friendship to one another. Louisa became pregnant and refused to tell me who the father of her child was. I begged her to tell me, but she was stubborn and would not divulge her secret. The McKays, wealthy people and high on the social roll, insisted she give the baby up for adoption. They wanted nothing to do with the child. Before you were born, Louisa pleaded with me and your father to adopt her child. It was a planned-ahead transaction. I wanted to do it for Louisa's sake, although I wondered how difficult it would be for her to know her child's adoptive parents."

Louisa's face turned ashen with shock as she grasped the meaning of her mother's words. "I—I am Louisa McKay's child, born out of wedlock?" she asked. "And no one knows who my real father is?"

"No one," Elizabeth answered as she pulled her daughter close to her breast. "That is one reason I didn't want you to know about this. I couldn't bear to lose your love. You are my daughter—our daughter, your father's and mine—as much as our own flesh and blood would have been. We wanted other children, but it was not in God's plan for us. We love you, Louisa."

"I know, Mama." Louisa sobbed lightly against her mother's breast. "And I couldn't love you and Father any less because of this. You are the parents I've always known and will always love. But what about Louisa McKay? Did she ever marry? Did she want to see me? Did she care about me at all?"

"Louisa died in childbirth, dear, and I was heartbroken. She had always been rather frail, and something went wrong with the birth. It was tragic to lose my dearest friend. She was so young and full of life. But it was a blessing for me to have you, a part of her, to care for and raise as my own. Louisa never got to hold you or name you or care for you. I wanted to name you after her, and your father agreed. Louisa Ann Bradford. Only your last name is different. A lovely name for a lovely girl."

"So I have grandparents, the McKays, in Augusta? Didn't they care about me after I was born? Didn't they want to see me?"

"I regret that they did not. The McKays could not bear the embarrassment. They moved out west somewhere after Louisa died and built a new life. It was as if you never existed to them. They were glad your father and I adopted you, but they wanted to be out of the picture entirely. They instructed me to keep everything secret and raise you as my own. That was part of the agreement. It's their loss, Louisa. You are so like your real mother. The McKays will never know the lovely granddaughter they could have shared their life with. And your father and I thought it best to move from Augusta to Waterville. A change of scenery, all new people. No one here knew that you were not our own child by birth."

Elizabeth Bradford held her daughter against her bosom for several moments as Louisa sobbed quietly. She stroked her daughter's hair and sang a song from Louisa's childhood in her sweet soprano voice. The words had a soothing effect for each of them as they clung to one another and rocked gently back and forth. Several moments passed before Elizabeth Bradford relaxed her grip on her daughter. "We don't want to wrinkle your new gown, dear. This is an important evening for you. Go ahead and wear the locket. It's yours to keep and someday pass on to your own daughter. Your birth mother," Elizabeth said, choking on her words, "would have been so proud of you."

Louisa straightened her frock, dabbed at her eyes, and stood up. "I feel so strange, Mama. It's like a story being told, but it's not fiction. Instead, it is about me. I'm not sure I can fathom this all at once. Do you have other pictures, or memory things, from my. . .birth mother? If so, I want to see them. I hope you will understand, but I must see them."

"I understand, dear. And I do have pictures from our early days and high school years. Also a few mementos in my old scrapbook. I'll show them to you another time." She held up the picture Louisa found with the locket. "This one of my friend and me together was my very favorite. That's why I kept it with the locket."

❧

Peter McClough arrived promptly at six, and Louisa descended the staircase in her new gown. She could feel his eyes upon her and hoped no trace of her former tears lingered. Her gown, pressed to perfection, accented the gentle curves of her slender body. The sweetheart neckline of her frock fell just below the lovely gold necklace. Her pale gold hair, brushed and shining, fell in a mass of curls around her shoulders.

A soft whistle of appreciation escaped Peter's lips, and he reached for her hand. "You are a beautiful vision, Louisa," he said huskily. "I need to touch you to be sure you aren't just a dream."

Louisa's dimpled smile spread across her face as she gazed into his dark eyes. "I'm real, Peter, and very much alive." She reached up and touched his cheek. "I must say you look very handsome, sir, in your dark suit and striped tie."

Peter took her arm and tucked it into his as he escorted her across the hall-way. "I'm taking you to a special place tonight because this is a most important evening. I hope," he said mysteriously, "it will be the best of my whole life."

They called their good-byes to Louisa's parents with promises to be home at an early hour. Mixed emotions filled Louisa's mind as they headed down the road toward Main Street in Peter's carriage. She wondered where he was taking her. They had visited every restaurant in town several times. Why was Peter being so secretive? She loved him and had for a long time—this man with the boyish face and shock of dark, unruly hair. He had never proposed and often said he wanted her to be sure of her feelings before they made a commitment to each other such as marriage. She knew it was due to his background and the kind of life he had led. But God had changed him—changed him from a loud, raucous, self-centered young man into the caring man he was now. It was a change of heart, a change of his former type of life. Peter McClough had repented of his sins and had accepted Jesus Christ as Lord of his life. The change in Peter delighted Louisa, but now she must tell him about her secret—her background—especially if he planned to propose. The news she had so recently learned was too important to keep hidden from the man she loved. Peter must know the details. She was a child born out of wedlock—adopted by the Bradfords. Louisa shuddered slightly as she wondered if her birth news would make a difference to him.

Peter maneuvered the reins with a flip of his wrist on a pair of bay horses and glanced at Louisa. She had pulled a white shawl across her shoulders. "You are very quiet this evening," he teased. "Is anything wrong?"

Louisa leaned her head against his shoulder. "I'm excited, Peter," she said, evading his question. "Where are we going?"

"You'll see soon enough. It's a new place out of town on the old Webb Road. I've heard some good comments about the food. I thought we should try it and see for ourselves."

Shortly thereafter, they arrived at a small but quaint restaurant nestled in a grove of pine trees. From the number of carriages tied at the hitching post, Louisa realized it must be a popular spot. They were soon inside and settled at a table set very privately in a back corner away from the eyes of the other clientele. The wall paintings, candles, colorful tablecloth, and pink flower centerpiece caught Louisa's eye.

"It's lovely," she said, glancing around her. "You are right, Peter. It's a very special place."

"The food will tell the tale. I'd heard this place was decorated nicely, but let's hope the food is as good or better than the rumors I've heard. I'm starved. How about you?"

Louisa studied the menu and fumbled with her napkin. Actually, the news she received earlier in the day had ruined her appetite, but she determined to make every effort to disguise her feelings. "I'm anxious to see how delicious the food is, Peter. I'm sure it will be as excellent as the decorations."

As the couple ate their dinners, Louisa tried to form in her mind the right words to tell Peter about her past. Should she just blurt it out or work up to it in some way? She didn't want to spoil the evening, with all its glamour and beauty, too soon. *Maybe after dessert would be a good time. Peter will be fully satisfied with his meal and in a good mood.*

Louisa was not prepared when the waitress brought a small cake and placed it on the table before her. "I understand this is a very special occasion," the waitress said with a smile. "I hope you like the cake. It was special ordered." The white cake had a tiny layer on top, and the waitress cut it out and put it on a plate before Louisa. "Enjoy!" she said with a sly glance at Peter and walked away.

"Go ahead and eat," Peter said with a grin. "I'll help myself to a larger piece."

"I'm so full, Peter. I'll save it and take it home with me. I can eat it tomorrow. I'll enjoy it more then. The rest of the cake isn't that big. Why don't you eat all of it?"

"No, you don't, Louisa!" Peter insisted. "You must eat your piece now, and I'll eat the rest. It's part of our celebration."

"What is the celebration?" Louisa asked as she dug her fork into the piece of cake. But the fork hit something hard and brittle. "Something is wrong with this cake, Peter!" Puzzled, she pushed the cake apart with her fork and exposed a small jeweler's box. "What's this?" she asked, wide-eyed with excitement.

"Open it and see, darling," Peter urged as he handed her his napkin. "Wipe the box off first."

With trembling hands, Louisa wiped the cake from the box and opened it. "Peter!" she cried as she examined its contents. "It's a ring—a beautiful ring!" She lifted it out and studied the magnificent piece of jewelry. In a gold setting nestled a large diamond surrounded by about eight smaller ones. "I've never seen such a beautiful diamond ring," she said in a hushed tone.

Peter reached across the table and took it from her hand. "I love you, Louisa. Will you marry me, darling? I've waited a long time to ask you this important question. I want to marry you, with God's blessing, and love you forever."

Louisa sat speechless for several moments and then burst into tears.

Chapter 2

Peter jumped up and moved his chair closer to Louisa. "Darling, I thought you would be happy," he said, putting his arm around her. "Why are you crying?"

"I am happy, Peter. I always cry when I'm happy."

"Then you will marry me? Please say yes."

Louisa lifted her face to Peter and smiled through her tears. "Yes, yes, yes! I've waited for this moment for a long time."

Peter slipped the ring on her finger and brushed away her tears. Then he cupped her face in his hands and kissed her—a sweet, lingering kiss to seal their words of commitment.

" 'Grow old along with me. . .the best is yet to be,' " he whispered huskily against her hair as he quoted from Robert Browning. "Darling, this is the best day of my life so far. It will only be better when you are Mrs. Peter McClough."

"Mrs. Peter McClough," she echoed. "It sounds wonderful to me."

"How soon, dearest?" he asked. "How soon can we be married?"

Louisa held up her hand and turned it over and over to see how the diamonds in her ring sparkled. "It takes time to plan a wedding, Peter. I'll have to talk with Mother. She'll want to sew my wedding gown and gowns for my attendants."

"And I must ask your parents for permission, Louisa. Do you think they will consent and trust their only child to me? They've known me for a long time now and have seen the changes in my life. Surely they knew my intentions were serious."

Louisa smiled up at Peter and said softly. "I think they've wondered if you were ever going to ask me. They know pretty much how I feel about you."

Peter stood up, his face flushed and excited. "Let's go home so I can talk to them. I'll ask for your hand in marriage, and with their permission, we will set the day."

As the horses trotted toward the Bradford home, Louisa listened to the familiar *clip-clop* of their hooves on the hard clay road. It was a lovely evening and glistening stars dotted the magnificent heavens. She felt comfortable with just a shawl about her shoulders to ward off the chill in the night air. Although elated over Peter's proposal, her happiness was overshadowed by the news about her birth. She wasn't really a Bradford after all, and she didn't have any knowledge of her real father. Why had this happened today of all days—to mar such a special occasion? She must tell Peter and get it out in the open. He, of all people, would surely understand.

"Peter," she said, clutching his arm, "I have something to tell you about my past, and I want you to listen. It's important to me that you hear the entire story."

Peter guided the horses at a slow gait and headed toward town. "Of course, darling. What is so important about your past that you must confess it now? Have you kept a big, dark secret from me?"

"You may consider this a big, dark secret, Peter, but I only learned about it today by accident. I couldn't have told you or anyone else the circumstances earlier."

Louisa took a deep breath and started. She repeated every detail of the afternoon—her shopping trip, the way she found the locket and picture in her mother's jewel case, and her mother's dismay when she arrived home. When she related the part about her birth mother, she choked up and could not go on.

Peter reined in the horses and pulled off to the side of the road. He turned to Louisa, drew her close, and held her in his arms. "It's all right, darling. I understand. I'm sorry you had to find out that way. But it doesn't matter. Your folks, the Bradfords, are your real parents. They've nurtured you, taught you, guided you, and given you so much care all these years. We know they love you as their own, and that is what counts. Don't you agree?"

"Yes, Peter, but do you mind about the fact of my birth? I have no knowledge of my birth father—who he is or where he is. Does this bother you?"

"I love you, Louisa. These incidents could never change that. Besides, you have not been concerned about my past, which was colorful to say the least." Peter flipped the reins and headed the horses back to the roadway. "Let's get on home and talk to your folks. I want their permission to marry the girl who will share my future!"

It was a happy scene at the Bradford home when Peter obtained permission to marry their daughter. A wedding date was set tentatively for mid-October or November to give ample time to sew Louisa's wedding gown and other articles of clothing. The remaining weeks of August found the couple deliriously happy as they courted and planned for the future. They would live in Peter's fine home, the one he had inherited from the widow Maude McClough, his father's second wife. Peter gave Louisa free rein to replace a few pieces of furniture in the large home, and she and her mother sewed new curtains for each of the rooms. By mid-September the house was completely redone to suit her taste and met with Peter's approval. The couple discussed several fall wedding dates, but a definite date had not been established.

❧

"Peter McClough left town this afternoon," Jack Bradford announced to his wife and daughter as they sat at the dinner table one September evening. "I saw him at my bank this morning, and he said he was leaving on the one o'clock train."

The trio sat around the walnut dining table in their large brick home. Jack Bradford, a banker, was a tall man of medium build with dark hair and eyes. His spectacles sat low on his nose as he studied his daughter's reaction.

"Why, Father?" Louisa gasped as she dropped her fork with a loud clatter on her delicate china plate. "Where is he going?"

"Didn't say," Mr. Bradford said and helped himself to another slice of ham. "Peter seemed distracted and appeared to be in a great hurry. He didn't stop to talk but said to tell you good-bye."

Louisa pushed back her chair and stood up—her face ashen. A frown knotted her forehead above her wide, gray eyes. Nervously she pushed back a lock of pale, honey gold hair and secured it with the tortoiseshell comb holding the mass of curls around her shoulders. Her slender build and tiny waist lent an air of frailty.

"Nothing else?" Louisa demanded as she twisted her lace handkerchief into knots. "When is he coming back?"

"I have no idea." Jack Bradford paused and dabbed at his dark mustache with his napkin. "Peter actually ran out of the bank with a wild look on his face. He had an air of mystery about him and didn't want to stop and chat. I must say, Louisa, your fiancé seemed a bit strange today."

"I don't understand, Father!" Louisa exclaimed. "We've just completed all the work at the house, and Peter loved every detail. It's beautiful and ready for us to move into as man and wife. Why would he leave town without telling me his destination? It doesn't make any sense!" Louisa blotted her eyes with her handkerchief and blew her nose.

Elizabeth Bradford stood up and reached to comfort her daughter. "There, there," she soothed as she pulled her only child against her ample bosom. She stooped slightly as she wrapped long, fleshy arms around Louisa. Honey blond hair, somewhat darker than her daughter's, was coiled neatly into a bun at the nape of her neck. Her green eyes, although clouded now with concern, bore a mischievous twinkle at times. "Everything will be all right, dear," Mrs. Bradford murmured. "It must be something important. Wait and see."

Louisa welcomed the comfort of the large arms wrapped around her for a few moments. The soft plumpness of her mother's body proved a soothing escape from the news of Peter's departure. Suddenly she jerked away. "Men! I'll never understand them! One moment Peter talks of our wedding day, and the next moment he is off somewhere on a trip. Why are men so difficult?"

Elizabeth Bradford smiled slightly as she glanced at her husband. "I know you are upset with Peter, Louisa, but aren't you judging him prematurely? And I don't think we can consider all men the same or bunch them together. Many men, like your father, are steady and dependable. I'm sure you will find Peter is also."

"Of course, Father," Louisa said, running to him. "I didn't mean you." She planted a kiss on his cheek, knocking his spectacles awry. "It's men like Peter. He's so unpredictable. One minute he cares about me, and the next minute he's off somewhere."

Jack Bradford cleared his throat and adjusted his spectacles, which had a tendency to slip down on his nose. "I admit Peter seemed in a big rush and not willing to talk, but let's give him the benefit of the doubt. He's been going to Colby College and using his father's money wisely that he inherited. Perhaps he's checking out another college somewhere. Isn't that a possibility?"

"It could be another college, Father, but why didn't he share his plans with me? After all, we are engaged to be married. And surely he would have talked about another school if that were a possibility. We've spent so much time together lately redoing the house and picking out fabrics. He's never mentioned going away—for any reason. In fact, it sounds like an unstable thing to do. I wonder if Peter has changed his mind about getting married. Perhaps he is having second thoughts about his freedom and doesn't want to be tied down."

"Why don't you finish your dinner, dear?" Elizabeth Bradford suggested. "You're making too much out of this. Perhaps it's school as your father suggested. Or it could be another job somewhere with challenging possibilities. Wherever he is, he probably has you foremost in his thoughts. If ever I saw a man in love, it's Peter McClough!"

"All my friends are married," Louisa moaned. "My dearest friend, Emily Mason, is now Mrs. Robert Harris. Wasn't it a strange coincidence when we found out Emily's uncle George was Peter's father? So she and Peter are cousins."

"Peter served at the same army base as Frederic, Emily's brother, didn't he?" Jack Bradford asked. "They were actually war buddies and didn't realize they were cousins."

"According to Peter, they were together for a short time during the war. But Peter despised Frederic because of his Christian stand. He swore at him, called him a goody-goody, and tried to pick fights with him. Peter regrets his actions, and he and Fred are close friends now." Louisa paused, her brow furrowed. "I wish Peter were more predictable."

"Peter changed for the good, Louisa," her mother said, "and we've all noticed the difference. I believe you are just overanxious, dear. Have a little patience."

Louisa sighed audibly. "I haven't heard a word from Emily since she and Robert married three months ago. I hope I get a letter soon so I'll have her complete address. I'm sure she'll have a lot to tell me about her life as a pastor's wife in Pennsylvania."

"You'll need to let her know as soon as your wedding date is finalized," Elizabeth Bradford said. "Does she know about your engagement?"

"I sent word to her through her parents, so I should be hearing back soon. She will be happy for us, but now maybe there won't be a wedding. Peter is off somewhere, and I don't have the slightest idea where he's gone. Perhaps I'll end up an old maid, Mother."

Jack Bradford choked on his coffee and sputtered, "You're not an old maid, Louisa, so don't act like one. Peter will probably be back by the end of the week."

Louisa twisted her napkin and glanced at her mother. "I'm twenty years old and not married yet. How old were you when you and Father married, Mother?"

"You are not an old maid, Louisa," her mother insisted. "Twenty years of age doesn't make you an old maid. Be a little patient with Peter. He's the one who has been anxious to consummate this marriage. Something evidently came up, and he needed to leave town."

"How old were you when you got married, Mother?" Louisa repeated.

"Age is not important. The important thing is to marry the young man God has prepared for you. And it seems that young man is Peter McClough. When he returns, all will work out for the best."

"I know you were barely seventeen, Mama, so I'm much older than you were when you and Father married. Do you want me to live with the two of you forever?"

Jack Bradford threw up his hands, and his mustache twitched above a slight smile at the corners of his mouth. "Such a thought!" he joked. "How could we bear it, Elizabeth?"

Elizabeth Bradford poked her husband playfully. "Be sensible, Jack. Louisa may take you seriously. You know how serious-minded she is. And right now she is upset about Peter's departure."

"You are joking about a very touchy subject," Louisa said as she picked up her plate and started toward the kitchen. "I have no desire to discuss this conversation further. Peter McClough is a complete cad and inconsiderate of my feelings. He didn't have the decency to stop by and say he planned to leave town. We were together yesterday, and he never mentioned a thing. In fact, we had an engagement for tomorrow evening. He planned to take me for a carriage ride by the river and then out to dinner."

"Perhaps that will still come to pass," Mr. Bradford said matter-of-factly. "Peter may return in time for your meeting tomorrow night, although it doesn't seem likely. Don't panic over something when you don't know the details. Give him the benefit of the doubt."

There was a long pause as Louisa considered her father's words. "I can't sit around and wonder when and if Peter means to return, Father! We are betrothed, and I should know about his plans for the future. He can't tamper with my feelings and expect me to ignore his neglect. Peter should have taken time to come by today and explain the circumstances surrounding his trip. He wasn't very considerate of my feelings. He could have sent a message with you when he saw you at the bank. Instead, he hurries off like a house on fire!"

Louisa reflected for a few moments on the night Peter proposed. She remembered the eagerness in his boyish face as he vowed his love for her and asked her to be his bride. A quiver of excitement mounted as she mentally pictured herself once again in his arms—their lips touching in a gentle kiss. Life seemed so perfect then, as they made plans for their future together as man and wife. Her heart constricted within her breast. Why had Peter left so quickly and without a word? Had something come up from his past that could interfere with their marriage? Was there another woman somewhere, someone he was involved with before he met her? She glanced at her parents, who seemed deep in thought. Bless their hearts, they liked Peter and were encouraging and supportive. She appreciated their care, but a strange fear gripped her thoughts. *What if Peter never returns?*

Louisa frowned and shook her head, as if to clear her mind of such thoughts. "You're right," she said to her parents and forced a smile. "I am making too much of this. Surely I'll hear from him soon. *However*," she said with emphasis, "Peter McClough will have a lot of explaining to do when he gets back!"

Chapter 3

Peter McClough hurriedly covered the distance from his house to Front Street and the Somerset and Kennebec railway station. His ticket had been purchased earlier in the day, soon after he received the wire. A frown knotted his forehead, and his lips pursed together as he let out a deep sigh. It had been a hectic morning. He took large funds out of the bank for his trip and engaged Martha, his part-time housekeeper, to watch after things at his house. He stopped by Zeke's, his occasional gardener, and requested he look after the grounds. Then he gave notice of his departure to Mr. Turner, his boss at the lumber mill.

Peter pushed back locks of dark hair that had fallen over his forehead and ran his hands across his brown eyes as if to clear his vision. His many hasty errands had tired him, and he groaned inwardly as he found a seat in the coach next to the window. Anxiously he pulled the crumpled wire from his coat pocket. It had been read and reread so many times it was barely legible. He fumbled with the crumpled piece of paper and smoothed it with his hands so he could read the words once again.

"Peter. Come at once. Important news about your brother."

It was signed by the distant cousin of his mother who had notified him during the war of his mother's death. She had taken care of the burial arrangements. Simply *Annabelle Hayes*. The address enclosed was a small suburb of Boston, out in the country, a place unfamiliar to him. Peter shook his head as he studied the crumpled message. He knew it by heart but needed something tangible to hold in his hands. *What is this about a brother? As far as I know, I never had a brother. Unless he was born after I left for the army. Why wasn't I told, if that were the case? Ma died in 1864. He'd be just a little chap about four years old. Whatever would I do with a kid? Who is his father? And where has he been all these years?*

Peter recrumpled the message and stuffed it back into his pocket. It puzzled him. He felt weak thinking about it, but he couldn't ignore the wire. It was important to go to the Boston area immediately and find out the details. He recalled his brief encounter with Mr. Bradford that morning and felt ashamed at his haste and mysterious attitude. But it was nothing he desired to discuss—at least at the present. He had too many questions himself and could hardly explain it to others. *What must Louisa be thinking? We had an engagement for tomorrow night for a carriage ride by the Kennebec River and dinner at our favorite restaurant. I'd planned a wonderful evening. I'll not be able to keep it, and she won't understand. Louisa, my darling, I do love you, and I'll be back.*

THE BEST LAID PLANS

Peter had wired the cousin explaining he would meet with her at her address on the outskirts of Boston the following day. His hand trembled as he took out his gold pocket watch—one he inherited from his father, George McClough. It was something he cherished deeply since it belonged to the father he never knew. "It's especially dear to me since I learned what a respected man my father was," he muttered, noticing the time. He pocketed the watch hastily. "The train seems to be right on time. Good! I need to get this brother business settled once and for all."

Peter planned to arrive in Boston and take a room for the night before meeting the cousin on the morrow. A good night's sleep would help settle his nerves and prepare him for the encounter with Annabelle Hayes—and his brother. "I can never expect Louisa to marry me until this part of my life is cleared away," Peter mumbled aloud. "It wouldn't be fair to involve her. I don't know any of the details, but I may have to raise this child. He's my brother and my responsibility, but I can't ask Louisa to be strapped with a child. She may want to break our engagement when she finds out."

Peter leaned back and tried to relax as the train sped down the tracks with a rhythmic *clickety-clack*, *clickety-clack* past the lush countryside. He took off his suit coat and laid it on the empty seat next to him—thankful to be alone. Worried, anxious, and somewhat depressed, Peter preferred not to engage in conversation with anyone. The coach looked barren—virtually empty with only a few passengers scattered here and there. Weariness overtook him as the train swayed from side to side. The methodic hum of the wheels on the track pulled at his tortured mind, and he slept fitfully for a short time. Peter smiled in his sleep during a brief dream about Louisa. They sat together in the parlor of the Bradford home. She smiled at him with her lovely smile and teased him with her wide, gray eyes. He reached for her, but a small child moved between them. He tried to reach past the child, but Louisa evaded his embrace and seemed to melt into oblivion. Peter ran after her, calling her name. His legs felt heavy, almost glued to the spot, and would not cooperate. He couldn't move! Frantically, with all his strength, he reached for her again and woke up in a deep sweat.

Peter took a room in a modest but clean boardinghouse and went to find a decent meal. His stomach growled loudly because he hadn't eaten since breakfast. "At least I had breakfast before the wire came," he muttered. "Otherwise, I couldn't have eaten a bite." He settled himself in a small café on the main street and ordered a light supper. Although hungry, he ate little and turned in early—planning to eat a good breakfast the following day.

After a restless night, Peter ordered a hearty breakfast at the same small café where he had eaten a light supper the evening before. His mouth watered at the tasty food, and he managed to down two mugs of black coffee, pancakes, and sausage. Fully satisfied, Peter set out for the livery stable on the corner. He rented a carriage and team of horses, and with directions from the stable boy, he started for the country and his cousin's address.

The September air felt warm and balmy as he drove the horses along the dusty roadway out of town. Horses and cattle dotted the countryside where wide, open fields of oats and alfalfa blew in the soft breeze. Beyond the fields, wooded areas of tall trees beckoned as their lofty branches stirred and bent toward him. Peter appreciated the fresh, sweet smells around him and took long, deep breaths of air. The farms and surrounding areas reminded him of the Mason farm back in Waterville, Maine. He always loved working with his friend Frederic and Fred's father and grandfather around the farm. Many chores awaited, and the Mason family appreciated an extra hand with the plowing or harvesting. They welcomed Peter as one of their own. Peter especially enjoyed the horses and became quite adept at riding and herding the cows into the barn. Harvesttime proved busy for everyone. The men brought in the crops so the womenfolk could prepare them for the long, hard winter. Jams and jellies often bubbled on the cookstove as the women ladled them into their proper containers.

Peter enjoyed none of this growing up with his mother. They lived in a small flat over a grocery store in the city of Boston. It was always hot in the summer and cold in the winter, and there was never enough food for a growing boy. But his mother always had her drinks—and reeked of it. He shuddered as he envisioned the smell—and the way she looked when drunk. Lucinda Graham, the name she went by, was a pretty woman when sober, but she neglected her son and left him alone most of the time. Evenings she dressed up in gaily colored clothing, bid him good night, and went out on the town with her men friends. Many nights he cried himself to sleep and never heard his mother come home in the wee hours of the morning.

"I couldn't wait to get away," Peter stated loudly. One of the horses jerked his head and snorted, as though Peter had given him a command. "When the war broke out between the states, I joined up with a Massachusetts regiment," Peter continued, talking audibly. "They needed every man they could get their hands on to enlist. I wasn't a very nice person in the army, but I learned some things. I obeyed the rules. I didn't desert the military like a lot of the men I knew. The army learned they could depend on me. For the first time I felt my life had a purpose—serving my country. The killing was terrible—the pain and the dying. I don't ever want to go through that again. Some of my buddies fell beside me, downed by a reb's bullet. I can still hear their anguished moans of pain as they suffered on the battlefield, bled, and died." Peter brushed a hand across his forehead as if to blot out the memory. "There was nothing I could do—nothing anyone could do to save them. Both the North and the South suffered through those bloody battles. But, God, I know You protected me through the war. Rotten as I was, and not worth a cent, You kept me alive. I'll be forever grateful, Lord. There must be some purpose for my life. Show me what it is. My highest desire is to have my life count for You."

Peter studied his directions from the stable boy, ones he had hastily scribbled on the back of his wire. "Ho there, boys," he shouted to the horses while pulling on their reins. "We need to make a turn here and go yonder down thataway."

Annabelle Hayes's address led him to a small, white cottage with green shutters and trim. It looked very neat and inviting as Peter stepped down from the carriage and secured the horses to the hitching post. It lay at the side of the house with ample grazing area and a water trough for his team. At his knock, a middle-aged woman appeared—her dark hair pulled back at the nape of her neck in a bun. She was pleasantly plump, with a round, jolly face and big smile. Her eyes rolled up at the corners with delight when she spied Peter.

"Peter!" she cried, throwing her arms around the tall young man. "I'd know you anywhere! It's so good to see you."

"But—," Peter sputtered at this sudden show of affection. "I don't know you, do I? Have we ever met before?"

"I'm Annabelle Hayes, your mother's second cousin. I've seen glimpses of you through the years, Peter. Your mother would never let me visit, but I caught sight of you at times whenever I could without your knowing I was kinfolk. Once in a while I happened to see you in town—from a distance. Other times I viewed you playing with friends behind the store where you lived. You do bear a resemblance to Lucy. I'm her only kinfolk except for you. . .and Thomas."

"I don't understand why she never allowed you to visit us," Peter said. "I would have welcomed a visit to you and your quaint little cottage in the country. It's so different from my mother's stuffy flat over the grocery store. And who is Thomas? Is that my so-called brother?"

"Come inside, Peter, and we'll talk," Annabelle said, leading him inside the neat dwelling. "I have some lunch prepared and a cool drink. You must be hungry."

"Thank you, Mrs. Hayes."

Annabelle Hayes laughed a hearty, rippling laugh that went on and on. "It's so good of you to come. I feared you wouldn't. And please call me Annabelle. We're kinfolk, you know."

Peter glanced around the well-kept cottage at the plain but sturdy furniture. His eyes lingered on a large oval portrait of a young man and woman. It hung prominently above the small stone fireplace. The face of the young woman looked vaguely familiar. "Is this you in the portrait, Mrs. Hayes—er—Annabelle? I believe I see a likeness there."

Annabelle Hayes's laugh tinkled merrily once again. "Yes, Peter, that's me and my husband, Thomas Hayes, when we were married some thirty-five years ago. I'm surprised you recognized me, though. I've put on so much weight since then."

"You haven't changed much, Annabelle," Peter said kindly. "I see the same sweet smile and merry glow about the eyes. I'm sure your wedding was a happy occasion."

"Indeed it was," Annabelle agreed. "There's a bowl and pitcher in the back room so you can freshen up, Peter. Meanwhile, I'll get our meal on the table."

After Peter refreshed himself, he returned to the kitchen and sat down at the small pine table. Annabelle busied herself putting out plates of ham, cheese, preserves, and huge chunks of homemade bread and butter. Peter noticed there were only two places set at the table.

"Where is your husband, Thomas?" he asked. "I would surely like to meet him."

Annabelle ladled out two bowls of chicken soup and two mugs of cool apple cider. "I have much to tell you, Peter," she said, taking his hand. "Would you mind if we return thanks for our food first?"

Peter smiled broadly and squeezed Annabelle's hand. "Not at all. I'm happy to hear you want to thank God for our food."

Annabelle murmured a soft prayer of thanks for Peter's safe arrival, for God's goodness and daily benefits, and for the food. When she glanced up, her eyes were moist.

"Peter, you must be a changed young man. From things your mother told me about you before her death, I understood you hated God with a vengeance—as she did."

"I did, Annabelle," Peter said, buttering a large chunk of homemade bread. "Mother brought me up to be bitter against God. She said He had ruined her life and that was the reason we had nothing, not enough food or clothing at times. She always looked out for herself, though. She had enough money for drinks. . .and clothes to entice her men friends."

"What happened, Peter? Did you accept the Lord on the battlefield? I've heard many young men turned to God during wartime, especially in the southern ranks. General Robert E. Lee and other leaders in the North and South were fine Christians. Many of the Southern camps held special evangelistic meetings. That was such a tragic war between the northern and southern states. Brother against brother sometimes." Annabelle's face gathered into a frown, and she shuddered slightly.

"No, I didn't meet God on the battlefield, Annabelle. I should have. God certainly looked out for me and kept me safe. I was a wretched individual in the army, crude and miserable to most of the people around me—especially if they believed in God. It happened when I went to Waterville, Maine, to claim my inheritance left to me by my father, George McClough."

Peter continued, between mouthfuls, to explain the influence the Mason family had in leading him to the Lord. He told Annabelle he mistrusted their kindness at first and thought they wanted part of the inheritance. "Originally it went to the Mason family because George's second wife, Maude, was Mr. Mason's sister. It was when Maude died, several years after my father died, that his lawyer located me as sole heir to George's estate."

"Did that upset the Mason family?" Annabelle asked. "It seems an unexpected loss might anger some folk."

"They were wonderful about it. At the time, it seemed unreal to me. How could anyone be nice to someone who took away their inheritance? But their attitude was so kind. They are Christians and treated me like family. Frederic, the son, is my dearest friend. He and his young wife, Sarah, cared about me and my future even though I had treated Fred rotten in the army. I grew to love the entire Mason family. I owe them a great debt of gratitude. Because of their example, their lives of faith, I eventually found peace with God by trusting Jesus as my Savior."

"Praise God," Annabelle whispered. "My prayers for you have been answered after all these years."

"Annabelle," Peter said with emotion, "you prayed for me all these years? I never knew I had anyone who cared about me, let alone who prayed for me, except for the Masons during these later years. Did you pray for my mother also?"

"Yes, I did. Your mother was a lovely person at one time. We were close growing up, but we had different ideals, different views on life. Lucinda was the pretty one. I was plain beside her. She desired money, clothes, entertainment—anything this world had to offer. She changed from a sweet young girl to an aggressive, greedy woman of the world. Her values and her morals were warped. But all I could do was pray. She wouldn't listen."

"If she had only stayed with my father," Peter said thoughtfully, "our lives would have been so different. I understand he was a fine Christian man and well respected as a doctor in Waterville."

"He certainly was," Annabelle agreed. "I knew your father well when he had his medical practice here in Boston. I was never able to have children, and I doctored with Dr. McClough for several years."

"Did you finally have a child, Annabelle?"

"I was never able to conceive my own child," Annabelle said sadly. "But Dr. McClough was not to be faulted. There seemed to be no explanation for my lack of childbearing. It was in God's hands, and someday I'll understand. He knows what is best."

"I'm sorry, Annabelle. I'm sure you would have been a wonderful mother."

"Your mother met George when she accompanied me on my many visits to his office in town. They talked together often, and Dr. McClough started courting her soon after. The couple didn't know each other well when he asked her to marry him. Your father was such a fine man. I assumed Lucy would change. My heart sank when Lucy told me she'd married him because he had more money than any other man she knew. And he was well respected in Boston. It was a big step up for her, she said. Now she would be somebody!"

Peter rested his elbows on the table and bent his head into his hands. When he looked up, his eyes were moist. "What happened, Annabelle? Why didn't my mother stay with my father?"

"George McClough, a fine Christian, did not tolerate drinking, not even socially. He saw what it did to people—especially some of his patients who drank all their lives and ended up with liver problems. Lucinda drank. She never let go of it for him or anyone else. God never entered the picture. 'Why would God want to keep me from having fun?' she'd ask. Lucy hid drink around the house, drinking when George was away at his office or on calls. I never knew where she got it, but she had connections, certain friends who kept her supplied."

"Didn't things change when I came along?" Peter asked. "Was my mother happy about my birth?"

"I'm sorry, Peter, but that's when the marriage fell apart. Your mother didn't want to be tied down with a child. She resented you, but she wouldn't let George McClough have you. She seemed to go out of her mind with hatred toward him. She said he'd ruined her life. Lucy expected to have a soft life as Dr. McClough's wife. 'I'll be queen of the social world when I marry George McClough,' she told me once. 'We'll be wining and dining all the important people of Boston, Annabelle, and you'll be so envious of me.' I tried to reason with her, but to no avail.

"Your father was delighted with your birth and expected Lucy to stay home, give up her drinking, and tend to their son. They were from two different worlds, Peter. It's very sad. George McClough could never visit or see his only son. Lucy didn't want you, but she refused to allow your father the privilege of raising you. She moved the two of you out of the large brick house he'd provided and moved into the cheap flat above the grocery store."

"I wonder about the divorce lawyer," Peter said thoughtfully. "Didn't he know the kind of woman my mother was? It's obvious my father should have raised me. How different my life could have been."

"George McClough said nothing against Lucy to taint her character. I'm sure the lawyer, a new man in town, knew nothing of her past. The divorce was a mutual agreement between them. Your father agreed to give Lucy a large sum of money and send a very substantial monthly support payment until you reached age eighteen. Dr. McClough left Boston soon afterward and took up his medical profession in Waterville, Maine. Boston lost a good doctor, and Waterville gained a fine one. Lucy could have lived well with the money George gave her and his monthly support payments. Instead, she fell into a life of drinking and degradation. She held on to you so she could count on George's support money. It was a good amount of money on the first of each month, but she frittered it away. Lucy wasn't concerned with your best interests, Peter. I'm sorry to be the one to tell you. It's sad but true."

Peter pounded his left hand with his right fist. "Why did I have such a rotten mother?" He pounded his fist once again. "Why couldn't I have had a mother like you, Annabelle? You wanted a child desperately and couldn't have one. My mother didn't want me but kept me as a hold on my father's pocketbook. Life seems so unfair sometimes."

"Don't be bitter, Peter," Annabelle soothed, patting his arm. "We'll never understand the why of everything in this life. All life's trials can be turned into good by resting them in God's hands. He knows about our heartaches, and He cares."

Peter's face relaxed. "I know, Annabelle. I'm still learning about God and His ways. I've been studying religion at Colby College in Waterville. I should probably go to a Bible school, but I haven't wanted to leave the area. I work at the mill in Waterville and go to Colby part-time. I'm unsure about my future. I'd like to be involved in the Lord's work somehow. I'm just waiting on Him for direction in my life."

"That's commendable, Peter. It makes me happy to hear you talk about God and a desire to serve Him in some way. He will use you mightily if you'll follow His leading."

"But, Annabelle, you never answered my question about your husband, Thomas. Where is he? And I need to know about my brother. Do I really have a brother? I'm anxious to meet him. He must have been born while I was at war. I'd guess he's about four years old. Where is the little fella?"

Annabelle's eyes widened, and her mouth dropped open; then her round face broke into a merry laugh that went on and on, crinkling up her eyes in the corners. "Oh, Peter," she said as her face grew more serious. "Your brother is not here at this time. Come, let's get more comfortable on the sofa. There is so much I've yet to tell you."

Chapter 4

Annabelle settled down on the mohair sofa and folded and refolded her hands. "It's quite a story, Peter. I hardly know where to begin."

"I want to hear everything," Peter said seriously, sitting beside her. "This part of my life is a mystery to me. It's important to know all the facts, because they are part of my heritage. Don't hold anything back."

Annabelle glanced upward as though uttering a silent prayer, took a deep breath, and began to speak softly. "Lucinda, your mother, had a baby boy before she met your father. Your half brother is not a mere child, Peter. He is a grown man. Your mother was not married at the time, and the baby's father did not stay around to see his child."

Peter gasped slightly as he took in everything Annabelle said. "What happened to him? Didn't my father know about this child when he married my mother?"

"No, he never knew Lucy had a son. He was only a babe in arms when she accompanied me on my visits to Dr. McClough. She always left him with one of her so-called lady friends."

"But my father had to know later, Annabelle. She couldn't hide him from my father after they were married."

"She could and she did, Peter. When Dr. McClough showed interest in Lucy, she decided it was her big chance. Through marriage to an important doctor in the community, the upper class would welcome her into Boston's social arena. This meant a great deal to Lucinda. She begged me to take the child and raise him as my own. Dr. McClough was never to know my foster son was hers. It would ruin her chances for a better life, she said. The boy was too young to know what was happening. She said if I took him, it would be better for all concerned."

"How could she do that, Annabelle? How can a woman give up her child and not care deeply?"

"I think she honestly hoped to start over and make a new life for herself with your father, but she fell back into her old ways and ruined your father's life, as well. Lucy made Thomas and me promise, if we took the child, to never come around them or tell anyone whose child it was. Eager to have a child, I didn't hesitate at her offer. We agreed to take the little tyke and raise him as our own. We loved him dearly, Peter. A delightful child, he grew in our hearts. We named him Thomas after my husband. He is only a year and a half older than you."

Peter's brow knitted into a scowl. He spat out angry words. "The more I hear about my mother, the more I hate her. She was the worst kind of a mother. I knew she never cared about me, but to give up her first son without a backward glance is too much."

"Don't harbor hate, Peter. It eats away at your insides and makes you a bitter person. You don't want to go through life with a bitter spirit."

Peter bent forward and placed his head in his hands as he struggled to control his emotions. "Life is full of surprises, Annabelle. Just when I thought my life was all straightened out and going well, this happens. Now the old feelings toward my mother are alive again and real. They cut into me like a knife. I dealt with them long ago and put them behind me. But today they taunt me again. Is there more to this story?"

"There is, Peter, but let's take a walk first. It will clear your mind to get out in the fresh air, and I need some exercise. The doctor tells me to walk a little every day."

Peter jumped up and stretched. "I'm sure a walk will be good for both of us. Are you quite well, Annabelle? It sounds as though you are under a doctor's care."

"I'm fine," she said, pulling off her apron and hanging it over a chair. "It's this roly-poly body of mine." Annabelle patted her midsection, smoothed her full calico skirts, and placed a bonnet on her head. "The doctor tells me I mustn't gain any more weight, or I'll waddle like a duck. He's a young whippersnapper, but a fine doctor. And he's right, of course. I need to lose some weight and keep active."

They went out the kitchen door, and Annabelle closed it tightly behind her. Peter went to the pump and drew fresh water for the team of horses. The horses snorted and stamped their feet as he approached and poured water into the trough. "Thirsty, aren't you, fellas?" Peter asked, and he watched them as they took long drinks and jerked their heads up and down. "Mind if I give them a few of your apples, Annabelle?" Peter asked, gesturing toward the apple tree nearby. "They must be hungry by now." When Annabelle nodded her okay, Peter picked some juicy red apples from a nearby tree. "Here you go, boys," he said, cupping his hands, which were full of apples. The horses shook their heads up and down and neighed when they saw the fruit. Peter patted their heads for a few moments as they ate heartily, chewing and drooling apple juice. Deep in thought, Peter mulled over all the latest details about his mother.

Finally, Annabelle approached him and took his arm. "Come with me, Peter," she said as as she guided him away from the horses. "It's time for our walk."

The couple followed the gravel road several hundred feet and then turned onto a country path. It was quiet and still, but Peter noticed a farmhouse in the distance and the cattle and horses grazing in the pasture. Although the path rolled gently over hill and vale, Annabelle walked it with no difficulty. Peter followed the short, stocky figure ahead of him, amazed at her quick and determined pace. A small creek ran alongside the trail, gurgling merrily as it bubbled over rocks and tree roots. Overhead a flock of geese honked noisily as they gracefully headed south.

"This is a shortcut," Annabelle stated.

"Where are we going?" Peter asked. "Anywhere in particular, or just a leisurely stroll on a warm September afternoon?"

"A grove of trees lies up ahead, and then you'll see the church. It's nestled into the countryside yonder just beyond a bend in the trail. Our little country church, the one Thomas and I attended with little Thomas, is very special. I remember many happy years of fellowship with God's people in this place."

Peter looked ahead and spotted a sharp bend in the path. The trail was well worn, and he decided Annabelle must walk it often. It was a shortcut, she'd said. It would be nice to see the church his brother attended with Annabelle and her husband. *My brother must be a Christian. I'm sure Annabelle and her husband saw to that. Wonderful! We'll have something in common besides having the same mother. I wonder if Thomas knows Annabelle isn't his real mother.*

"Is your husband, Thomas, the pastor of the church, Annabelle? I'm looking forward to meeting him."

Annabelle stopped abruptly. They had rounded a bend in the trail. Peter saw the little white church up ahead, complete with steeple and bell. The church stood near a grove of trees, and next to the church, shaded by some of the trees, lay a small cemetery. It was fenced on all sides with a gate at the front. The cemetery appeared very neat and well kept.

"My husband, Thomas, is here," Annabelle said, pointing toward the little cemetery. She noted the questions in Peter's eyes and hastened to explain. "He died several years ago and was buried in the little graveyard next to our church."

Peter's face registered pain, and he reached out to her. "I'm so sorry, Annabelle. I—I don't know what to say."

Annabelle smiled up at him. "It's all right, Peter," she said, patting his arm. "Of course I miss my husband dearly. We had a beautiful life together. But Thomas suffered so much with his illness, it was heartbreaking. His death ended all that. And he isn't here, actually, you know. He's with Jesus, which is far better."

"Yes, Annabelle," Peter agreed as he swallowed the lump in his throat. "Far better."

Annabelle led Peter through the little gate and down one of the long rows. She stopped in front of a plot with a small stone marker. Flowers still bloomed on the grave.

"I come here every day," she said softly, "unless I am ill or snowed in. I need the walk, and I feel closer to Thomas. . .even though I know his spirit is with God."

"It's a peaceful setting for a cemetery," Peter said as he took in the beauty of the surrounding area. His eyes lingered on the hills and valleys that were dotted with contented cows and grazing horses. "It seems so restful here."

THE BEST LAID PLANS

The couple stood quietly for several moments before Annabelle tugged at his arm. "Your mother is buried here, Peter. Would you like to see her grave?"

Peter grimaced. He felt the old bitterness fill his spirit and weigh him down. Tempted to refuse, he hesitated until Annabelle broke into his thoughts.

"You'll feel better if you see where we laid her. I was able to bury Lucy here because she is a relative of mine. I asked her many times, but she never did attend our little church."

Quickly Peter pushed the ill feelings out of his mind and followed Annabelle down another path. She stood before another small plot, well kept and complete with flowers and headstone.

"I keep Lucy's grave just as I do Thomas's. Lucy didn't treat me well in later years, but we were close growing up. I have fond memories of our early years together. I tried, but I could never reach her with the gospel." Annabelle sighed heavily. "This is my one regret concerning our relationship."

Peter stood spellbound and gazed at the tombstone. LUCINDA GRAHAM, 1820–1864. "My mother was only forty-four years old when she died," he said softly. Suddenly his shoulders convulsed as tears flowed down his cheeks. With head in hands, he sobbed uncontrollably for a few minutes. Annabelle moved toward him and placed an arm around his waist.

"It's good for you to cry, Peter. Let the tears come and get it out of your system. God washes away the dross and bitterness in our hearts. We need His cleansing power every day. Without it, we'd lose our sweet fellowship with Him."

Peter pulled out his bandanna and wiped away tears from his reddened eyes. A few deep shudders shook his body. "I needed this, Annabelle, and I feel better now. When I saw my mother's grave, I felt anger rear its ugly head inside me again. But I refuse to harbor bitterness. I will not let anger get the best of me or control my life. I make this promise to you, and to God, here and now."

Annabelle showed her delight at Peter's promise with a bright smile as they walked arm in arm toward the little church. They went inside the small building and sat quietly on one of the benches for a few moments. A few chairs sat on the platform at the front. The wooden stand, built to hold the pastor's Bible, was centered on the platform. Just below the platform, a large Bible rested on a table covered with a white linen cloth.

"I come here often and just sit for a spell. I feel close to God and to Thomas. It isn't a fancy church, Peter, but it's God's house, and we worship here."

Peter closed his eyes for a few moments. "I can picture you and Thomas, with my brother Thomas, worshipping here. I wish I'd attended with you, Annabelle. If only my life had been different."

"We can't live in the past or on the 'if onlys,' Peter. The past is over and done. We must see what God has for us in the present and then look to the future."

"You're right," Peter said eagerly as he stood up. "I need to meet my brother, Thomas, and see what the future holds for us. Is he anxious to meet me, Annabelle? Where do we go from here?"

Annabelle remained unusually quiet on their walk back to her cottage. She led Peter at a fast pace along the well-traveled path. Back at the house she dropped breathlessly onto the overstuffed, mohair sofa and motioned Peter to do the same.

"Is something wrong with my brother?" Peter asked as he settled beside her. "Is that why you asked me to come?"

"Yes and no," Annabelle said, searching his face. "Thomas visited me a month ago and seemed fine. But he took off without saying where he planned to go, and I haven't heard from him since."

"But, Annabelle, if he isn't here, why did you send for me?"

"Selfishness, I suppose," she answered, her face downcast. "I thought perhaps you could locate him for me. And I also wanted to see you, Peter. I didn't think you'd come to see a distant cousin of your mother unless you had a good reason. Would you?"

Peter's brow knitted as he glanced at his newfound cousin. "Probably not, Annabelle. I'm involved in college classes and work some days at the sawmill. I'm also courting a lovely young lady, and we are engaged to be married."

Annabelle's face drooped, and her eyes blurred with tears. "I'm sorry," she whispered, patting his hand. "But I did so want to meet you."

"Don't be sorry, Annabelle. I'm glad I came. I'd never have met you otherwise. You've helped me get over the bitter feelings I felt toward my mother."

"Thank you, Peter," she murmured softly. "Now I'll share some things about your brother. Thomas lived with my husband and me until he was ten. At that time my husband became ill with a serious lung disease and needed my full-time care. Lucinda decided to take Thomas away from us. She used my husband's illness as an excuse, but I believe it was the Christian training he received while in our care. Young Thomas had received Jesus into his life and knew many Bible verses. Lucy visited one day to see the extent of my husband's condition while you were at school. She didn't want you to know anything about Thomas. Lucy stayed for tea and remained long enough for the lad to return from the little schoolhouse up near the church. He only knew Lucy as a visiting friend at that time, not as his birth mother. Thomas was an outspoken child, and he talked to her about Jesus. This infuriated Lucy. A week later she arrived with a friend, and they took your brother away. He cried and clung to us, but Lucy forced him to go. My husband and I cried but could do nothing. We didn't have any right, actually. We had never signed any papers. He wasn't legally ours. Thomas was her child. She waved his birth record in our faces and left." Tears flowed freely down Annabelle's cheeks as she recalled the incident.

Clumsily Peter reached for her. A few shudders convulsed her body.

Suddenly she straightened up, wiped her eyes, and blew her nose. "I'm all right now," she whispered.

"Did you ever find out what happened to him?" Peter asked. "My mother never brought him home. As far as I knew, I was her only son."

"Lucy visited me again several months later." Little sobs caught in Annabelle's throat as she fought for control. "Lucy's friend took Thomas and moved back to the South where her parents lived. Your mother insisted he was well taken care of. The woman's family lived on a large plantation that boasted many slaves. Thomas would be brought up as a Southern gentleman and never need for a thing. A poor boy turned rich, your mother said."

Peter shook his head. "Didn't it make you angry, Annabelle? You must have hated my mother at that time."

"No, my husband and I didn't hate her. We were sad, though. Thomas the boy and Thomas the father were very close. They had a special relationship that only happens between a father and a son. We both loved him dearly and felt a tremendous loss. But we also felt sad for Lucinda. She continued to seek her own way in the things of this world. Instead of becoming bitter, my husband and I prayed for her. It's the only way, Peter. Otherwise, our lives become a poor testimony to His grace."

"Of course, Annabelle, you're right. I can't imagine you being bitter toward anyone."

Annabelle stood up and dabbed away at her teary, red eyes. "I'll fix us some tea and continue my story. Do you have to get the team back to the stable tonight?"

"Yes. I have my room reserved for one more night."

"Why don't you move your things out here tomorrow, Peter? You can have your brother's old room. It's just the way he left it when he was ten years old."

Peter hesitated and rubbed his chin thoughtfully. "It won't hurt to stay a few days, Annabelle. I'd appreciate being your guest."

Annabelle beamed, and her merry little laugh echoed forth. "You aren't a guest, Peter. You're kin, remember?"

While Annabelle continued her tale, they sipped the brewed tea and ate homemade sugar cookies. She told him her husband died without seeing young Thomas again. It had been such a difficult time for him, being ill and missing the lad so much. Annabelle felt it hastened his demise.

"Lucy refused to give me young Thomas's address in the South. When my husband died, I begged her to release the information, and she finally agreed. He was fifteen by this time. I sent a letter explaining my husband's death and asked Thomas to write me."

"Did he write you?" Peter asked eagerly.

"He didn't write at first. But I wrote him again and reminded him of some things from his childhood. I hoped this would spark his interest, and it did. I received a brief note. He hardly knew what to say. After all, it had been five years.

But he told me about the plantation and all the slaves who worked for them. He didn't go to a school but had a teacher at home instead. He had a special slave his own age, Ben, assigned to him who did all the menial tasks. Although Ben waited on him, Thomas said Ben was his friend. He spoke highly of him. They fished together in the creek, rode horses around the plantation, climbed trees, and spent much of their time together."

"That sounds like another world, Annabelle. Did Thomas ever come to see you during that time?"

"He was twenty before he looked me up. I was delighted. It was early in 1861 before the War between the States. Thomas couldn't understand all the fuss about slavery. He was very confused. He thought war was inevitable, though, because there was so much dissension among the plantation owners. Their anger against the Union had reached a new high. The North felt slavery had to be dealt with, and the South rebelled.

"It was a sweet reunion for young Thomas and me after ten years, Peter. He'd grown so tall and handsome. Thomas feared the slavery problem would separate the country because the South felt so strongly in favor of it. He said the South was ready to pull away and build their own government. I tried to impress him with the evil of slavery according to the Bible. I reminded him that all God's people are equal and precious in His sight."

"Did he agree with you? What was his reaction?"

"He'd been away from Bible training and church a long time. But Thomas agreed keeping slaves was wrong. He felt bad for them, especially when they were disciplined or separated from their family. His friend Ben's parents had been sold to another plantation owner, and Ben grieved for them. Whenever Thomas mentioned these things to the plantation owner, his foster father, the man laughed at him. The master argued that his father had slaves before him and his father before that. 'Who'll do all the work?' the master asked Thomas. 'No, lad, we've always had slaves and always will. We'll fight the North and win!' Thomas didn't agree with him, but there was nothing he could do. The master of the plantation had been Thomas's foster father for ten years. He had a certain amount of love and respect for the man. The Civil War started a few months later."

"Did my brother go to war, Annabelle? Surely he wanted to save the Union and fight for the North. He'd want his friend free to reunite with his family and break the bonds of servitude."

"I received a letter from him after the war started. Thomas felt a sense of duty toward his homeland, the South, even though he despised slavery. He enlisted with the Confederates and fought bravely with the men from Tennessee. The South believed in their cause just as the North did. Of course I never saw Thomas during the war. He wrote me a few other times and revealed the hardships. There were too many to describe. When the men marched, some had no shoes. The conditions were deplorable. They had a shortage of food, and men nearly starved to death. A great number died from disease and dysentery. It was a terrible war."

Peter frowned. "My brother was a reb! I fought this war against my own brother! I probably faced him across the battlefield! We might have killed each other, Annabelle!"

"I prayed for you both. You didn't know it, of course, but I prayed. And Thomas knew because I wrote him often and told him so. I reminded him of his Christian background and his decision as a child to follow the Lord. Although he had to kill or be killed, I urged him to stay close to God."

"If you saw him a month ago, God brought him through it—just as He did me. I'm thankful I didn't know I had a brother fighting for the South. I couldn't have faced each confrontation on the battlefield knowing my brother might be fighting in the field across from me. It would have been more than I could have borne."

"God knows how much we can bear, Peter. Perhaps that's one reason He kept you and Thomas apart all those years."

"Did Thomas go back to his plantation after the war? What happened to the slaves? They were given their freedom, weren't they?"

"Thomas went back to Tennessee in 1865 after the war ended. John Berringer, the master of the plantation, had passed away. Thomas's foster father went quite out of his mind when the war didn't go well for the South. His wife had passed away earlier. From then on, he went downhill and finally died. Your mother's young friend, the one who took Thomas away from us, had married and left the plantation several years before her parents' death. Thomas said the house, neglected and run-down, appeared almost haunted. All the slaves, free at last, had scattered except for his friend Ben. Ben married after Thomas left for the war, and he and his family settled in one of the small slavers' cabins. Faithful to his friend, Ben wouldn't leave without seeing Thomas again. Their friendship went too deep. He determined to help Thomas repair the big house and make it livable once more. The two friends worked side by side on the house and replanted some of the fields. Then the two men built a much larger cabin for Ben and his family."

"It sounds like my brother is a nice fellow, Annabelle. He showed concern and appreciation for his friend. I'm glad to hear good things about Thomas."

Annabelle glanced away, and Peter noticed a sadness cloud her eyes. "Thomas is in deep trouble, Peter. That's another reason I asked you to come. I hoped you could help him."

"What is it? Does he need money to get his plantation going again? My father left me well-off. Of course I'll help him!"

Annabelle blurted out the next words. "Thomas killed a man in Tennessee and fled the area. He stopped here last month and told me about the incident. I asked him to stay here with me until we could decide what to do. After a few days, he left secretly during the night, and I haven't heard from him since. He worried about getting me involved in his problem, Peter. That's why he left. He wanted to spare me any trouble."

Peter let out a low whistle. "Thomas killed a man! But, Annabelle, there must have been a reason!"

Chapter 5

"Why, I declare!" Louisa announced as she fumbled with the mail. "It's a letter from Emily out in Pennsylvania. Isn't that grand?" She waved a pink envelope for her mother to see, then hastened to tear it open. "I've been waiting for this!"

"Your friend has been busy, dear, getting settled," Mrs. Bradford said. "They've only been married a short time. What does she have to say?"

The pair settled themselves on the plush damask sofa in the parlor, and Louisa read her friend's letter aloud.

Dear Louisa,

We are still getting settled, but I wanted to write you as soon as possible. Robert and I are living in a sweet little cottage that belongs to a family in the church. It is small but adequate for our needs. The cottage has two bedrooms and is furnished with sturdy and comfortable furniture. Windows are decked with gay calico curtains, which makes the place seem bright and cheery. It's almost hard to believe I am finally married. Remember what a difficult person I was? I didn't want to come to Pennsylvania at all, and it almost prevented our marriage. I'm thankful Robert's patience held out long enough for me to come to my senses. Wampum is a lovely rural area and reminds me much of where I lived on my family's farm outside of Waterville. The countryside is lush and fertile. Wide, green pastures are dotted with cattle and horses, and you know how much I love horses. I should be able to ride to my heart's content. Beaver Creek is bigger than our creek at home, and fish are abundant in the stream. We are very happy, Louisa, and I heartily recommend married life. I like being a pastor's wife. Robert is such a dear, a very caring and helpful husband.

The women at the church are so kind. They held a reception for us and showered us with wedding gifts. Many gifts are homemade, charming, and special. Their expression of love made me feel accepted as one of them. I appreciate their friendship. As a pastor's wife, everything is new to me. Pray that I will be a good pastor's wife. I want to be a helpmate to my husband as he cares for the flock here in Wampum.

There is a troublemaker in the church, Jim Bishop. He is a thorn in Robert's flesh. Mr. Bishop tries to be in control. He is a very manipulative person. Everything must be done his way. Mrs. Bishop seems sweet. She is

*very quiet and shy. I'm afraid her husband domineers her also. Their two
children fear their father. I can see it in their eyes. Please pray about this
situation. Robert needs wisdom to deal with this problem.*

*How is everything in Waterville? I miss you, my family, and friends.
But this is where God wants me—with Robert and the ministry in
Wampum. Can you believe I said that, when I was so opposed to it at one
time? But I am content, dear Louisa, and at peace. Have you and Peter set
the date for your wedding yet? Robert and I rejoiced when we heard the
good news about your engagement. I remember Peter seemed very dreamy
and nostalgic when Robert and I married. We thought that young man had
some serious thoughts going on in his mind. The two of you make a charming couple. I will love having you as mistress of Peter's house, the home that
previously belonged to my aunt Maude and uncle George. When I lived with
Aunt Maudie before her death, I grew to appreciate her fine taste in furniture,
china, and paintings. It gives me joy to know you, my dear friend, will be
taking care of them. Peter does well enough for a man, but my aunt's home
needs a woman's touch. Don't you agree? Let me hear from you soon.*

With love, your close friend,
Emily

Louisa quietly refolded the letter and tucked it back into the envelope.
"Emily sounds blissfully happy in her new home, Mother. I knew she'd be content once she arrived. She really balked at the move. . .away from family and
friends in Waterville. But as long as she and Robert are together, nothing else
matters, does it?"

"Emily's learned to be satisfied in a new place with her new husband,"
Elizabeth Bradford agreed. "She's started a new life in Pennsylvania and has
adjusted well. It was a good letter. She sounded cheerful and content. I'm glad,
aren't you?"

Louisa looked down at her lap for several moments. When she lifted her head,
tears stood in the corners of her eyes. Quickly she brushed them away. "I am happy
for Emily. She and Robert are together—married—and everything worked out
well for her. Why can't things go smoothly for me? Here I am, with my best friend
married and living far away. To make matters worse, Peter deserted me without a
word. Emily asked if there is to be a wedding soon. What do I tell her? 'No, Emily,
Peter is gone, and no one knows why or when he plans to return.' "

"He'll be back, Louisa," Mrs. Bradford said, rising from the sofa. "His home
is here. He enrolled at Colby College again this fall, and there is his job at the
mill. He won't neglect his commitments."

"He neglected his appointment with me," Louisa said angrily. "Evidently
Peter thinks I'm not important. He didn't send a note or stop by to explain. It
seems there are more interesting things to occupy his mind."

THE BEST LAID PLANS

"What's all the fuss, Louisa?" Jack Bradford asked as he entered the room. "You sound as though you are in a foul mood today."

"Hello, dear," Mrs. Bradford said as she rose and kissed her husband briefly on the cheek. "How was your day at the bank?"

"Fine as usual, Elizabeth. But I overheard a little of your conversation with Louisa. Are things not going well at home?"

"Everything's fine, Jack. Louisa is still a little upset with Peter. Nothing serious, though."

"It is serious, Father." Louisa pouted. "I don't like being neglected by Peter. Today I received a nice letter from my friend Emily in Pennsylvania. She asked me if Peter and I had set a wedding date, and I don't even know where he is."

Jack Bradford loosened his necktie and took off his suit coat. "Well, I have a little news for you. Not much, mind you."

Louisa's face brightened. "What is it, Father? Do you know where he is?"

"He's in Boston visiting a distant cousin. His housekeeper came into the bank this afternoon. I noticed Martha from my office, thought she might have some news, and went out to greet her."

"What did she say? Why did he go? When is he coming back?" Louisa cried, somewhat breathlessly.

"Martha received a wire from him this morning. She doesn't know any details. Peter said he will not return for a while and asked her to mind the house. It sounded as though he will be gone indefinitely."

"That is so inconsiderate!" Louisa exclaimed. "He hasn't notified me at all! I must not be very important!"

Mr. Bradford cupped his daughter's face in his hands and looked into her wide, gray eyes. "You are very important to your mother and me. As our only child, you've been our whole life. Don't let this young man upset you, Louisa."

Louisa laid her blond head against her father's shoulder, and he gathered her close. A few sobs escaped her lips as she spoke. "You and Mother have always been here for me to lean on. I appreciate your love and care. Forgive me for being such a silly goose."

"I've a great idea," Jack Bradford said. "Let's pack up and visit my brother's family in Augusta next week. They've invited us several times. I'll send them a wire tomorrow. A change will do us all good."

"But, Jack," Elizabeth protested, "are you able to leave the bank at this time? Aren't you being a little hasty about all this?"

"Not at all," Jack Bradford said, adjusting his spectacles. "Remember the new assistant I told you about? The young man started work two weeks ago and has proved a fine worker. He has taken to the business extremely well, and I wouldn't hesitate to leave him in charge for a time. How does a trip away from here sound to you, Louisa?"

"It sounds wonderful, Father, thank you. I'm sure it will chase away my gloominess to see Cousin Clara. And it's always fun to visit Uncle Phil and Aunt Lydia. I wish they didn't live so far away."

"Then it's all settled," Jack Bradford said. He picked up his coat and tie from the chair and paused. "I'll pick up our train tickets tomorrow, and we can leave on Monday. We can stay all week if you like."

Louisa whirled about the room a few times. "I haven't seen Clara in ages, Mother. It should be great fun to be together. We'll have so much to talk about. When we visit one another, we talk nonstop!"

Elizabeth Bradford smiled as she watched the change in her daughter. Louisa's once pouty and downcast face was alive again. Her gray eyes twinkled with anticipation, and her face stretched into a wide smile. She twirled around the room a few more times until she fell on the plush sofa, completely out of breath.

"I'm glad to see you cheerful once again, Louisa," her mother said. "But, Jack, are you sure about this new assistant of yours? He's only worked for you a short time, and you know nothing of his background. Did he have any references for you?"

"Not really," Jack Bradford admitted as he headed for the stairway. "But he served in the Civil War, and that's enough of a reference for me. He's only done odd jobs since then until now. He'd like very much to be settled here, and he seems likable enough."

"Oh, please, Mother," Louisa begged. "Don't discourage Father. This trip will be so good for me. I need to get out of Waterville for a spell. And if Peter does contact me, I won't be sitting around moping over him."

Elizabeth looked from her husband to her daughter and knew she was outnumbered. "Well, dear, if that's what you want. You and Clara have always been close even though we don't see the Phillip Bradford family very often. I suppose it's because you are the only cousins in the family and practically the same age. Isn't Clara only six months older than you are?"

"Yes, and she's not married yet either. It's sad her friend Douglas Meakin was killed in the battle at Gettysburg during the war. They weren't really engaged, but they had an understanding. Douglas felt they should wait to declare their engagement. Clara knew they were in love and would marry after the war was over. She told me in a recent letter she is not interested in meeting other men. She is still in love with her memories."

"But she needs to get over Douglas," Elizabeth Bradford said seriously. "She mustn't live in the past. Clara is a sweet, lovely young woman. I thought she would surely be over him by now. It's been years. She must realize Douglas is gone and won't be coming back. It's a matter of accepting the fact. I believe it will be good for us to go to Augusta after all. If anyone can help Clara, it is probably you, Louisa. Perhaps you can help her accept the fact that Douglas is dead and put it behind her."

Louisa slouched on the sofa, her face pensive. "I'll try. I truly will. If I possibly can, I'll help Clara work through her loss of Douglas. It's devastating to lose the one you love. I'm finding out just how it feels." Louisa's face clouded as she stood up. "And I may need Clara to help me forget Peter McClough, Mother! He's shown himself to be irresponsible and inconsiderate!"

❧

Jack Bradford's new assistant offered to take the family to the train depot the following Monday. Louisa extended her gloved hand as her father introduced the young man to his wife and daughter. Tall and broad-shouldered with dark hair and blue eyes, Roger Evans grasped Louisa's small hand in his larger one. The tanned face revealed a satisfied smile as his gaze swept over her figure and lingered. His direct approach, when he looked deeply into her eyes, left her blushing and unsure of herself. Louisa watched him closely as he loaded their luggage onto the carriage. He appeared rather handsome, she decided, and very sure of himself. His hair was not as dark as Peter's, but then neither was it as unruly. Roger's hair, slicked neatly into place, gave him a debonair appearance. And his brown suit, neatly pressed, looked perfect with highly polished brown shoes.

When Roger helped her into the carriage, she felt a warm sensation within her. Somewhat befuddled, Louisa murmured a low thank-you, blushed, and turned her eyes away. Roger grinned his self-satisfied grin and climbed into the driver's seat. Louisa wondered if the young man was married. Her father had offered no information about his new assistant, and she had not inquired. She'd been too taken up with her sadness over Peter's departure.

The short trip to the train station ended before she had time to gather her thoughts. Roger Evans lifted her down with little effort and smiled as his blue eyes searched hers. "I'm glad I met you today, Louisa. I didn't know my boss had a daughter. He's kept you as a big, dark secret, and I can understand why. Lovely daughters need to be protected."

Louisa's face flushed, and she glanced away. Amused, Roger turned to Jack Bradford. "Have a safe trip," he said in his deep voice. "And don't worry about the bank, Jack. I'll take care of everything."

Jack Bradford extended his hand. "Thanks, Roger. I know the bank is in good hands. You have my brother's address if you need to get in touch."

"Good-bye," Roger said to the three of them. But his eyes lingered on Louisa.

Louisa and her parents settled into adjoining seats on the coach and relaxed. "Why haven't you told me about Roger, Father?" she asked eagerly. "He's quite handsome, isn't he? And he must be an able assistant for you to go off to Augusta for a week and leave him in charge. Is he married?"

"Uh, no, he isn't," Jack Bradford said absentmindedly. "But why are you interested? You are engaged to Peter, young lady. Have you forgotten?"

"No, Father, but Peter may be too undependable for me. Perhaps I was too hasty in accepting his ring. We may mutually agree to call the whole thing off.

And if so, your assistant could be the one to help me forget Peter McClough."

"Louisa!" Elizabeth Bradford exclaimed. "You are so changeable! First you are in tears over Peter's departure, and now you want to forget him. When you are in love with someone, you don't get over him so easily."

Louisa twisted in her seat and pulled some handwork out of her handbag. Memories of times shared with Peter flooded her mind, and she felt color rising in her cheeks. She did love him—or did she? No, she was angry with him. Maybe she still loved him. Maybe not. Sometimes she felt so confused she didn't understand her own feelings. Roger Evans, with his self-assured ways, could help her get over Peter. She glanced at her parents and sighed. They hadn't a care in the world. Jack Bradford read the morning paper, and her mother thumbed through a magazine.

"Your life is so settled, so happy, Mother. You and Father never had any problems in your relationship, did you?"

Elizabeth Bradford chuckled. "Of course we did, Louisa. All couples run up against problems. Your father and I had our share."

Louisa gasped in disbelief. "What happened? When did you have a problem? I can't remember a thing."

"Your father and I have had our differences of opinion through the years and still do. No two people always agree on everything. But that's a minor thing. It's a part of life. We work it out because we have God in our marriage to guide us. But we did have a large problem once."

"Tell me about it. I find it hard to believe you and Father ever had a big problem. Did it almost wreck your marriage?"

"We'd only been married about a year. I don't remember what the argument was about now, but it caused such stress I packed a valise and went home to my parents. You remember your grandparents' house, where they lived before their deaths. I was so angry I walked the few blocks in a very short time."

"What did Grandma and Grandpa say? Were they glad to have you back home?"

Jack Bradford glanced up from his newspaper and snorted. "No, they weren't! They told your mother to go home to her husband where she belonged."

Elizabeth Bradford giggled. "Your father was very upset, Louisa, and stubborn."

"Did they really tell you to go home to your husband?"

Elizabeth's face became serious. "Eventually they did. I was with them a few days and expected your father to come by and beg me to come back. He never came. His stubborn pride wouldn't allow it. Finally, my parents suggested I go home. As Christians, they reminded me God would not be pleased at our separation or a divorce. My place, as a Christian wife, was with my husband. I dishonored my wedding vows, 'till death do us part,' by leaving your father over such a small matter."

"And you went home? Back to Father?"

"I went home and settled in. When your father came home from the bank that day, he was delighted to see me. He had been under a strain. We both realized how foolish we'd been. Our marriage could have ended before it had hardly gotten started. And you came to live with us shortly afterward. God blessed our home by allowing us to adopt you, a precious little girl."

"I—I almost can't believe it, Mother. You and Father quarreled over a small thing, enough to cause a separation. It seems impossible."

Jack Bradford folded his newspaper and eyed his daughter. "When young people get married, there is an adjustment. Your mother and I were very young. She was seventeen. I was nineteen. I worked at my father's bank back then. We needed some time to grow up. Being Christians from Christian homes helped. The entire episode made us realize we needed God in control of our lives in every situation." Jack Bradford patted his wife's arm and gave her an affectionate smile. "Your mother is a wonderful woman, Louisa."

"I know," Louisa said softly. "You are both very special people. Thanks for telling me about that part of your lives. It helps to know others have weathered storms and had victory over their problems. Life isn't a fairy tale or a smooth sailing trip like the books tell us. I've found that out during courtship with Peter. I wonder if I'm even marriage material."

"Of course you are, dear," Elizabeth Bradford said. "To the right man. . .at the right time."

Her mother's advice seemed so glib. Louisa already knew the pat answers, and they didn't satisfy her anxious feelings. She picked up her handwork and worked quietly the balance of the trip. She had much to occupy her mind. Perhaps she and Peter could make a go of it. Or maybe God had brought Roger Evans into her life for a purpose. He almost seemed too sure of himself. A very smooth character. His smile was captivating, and his eyes told her he was interested in her. But he could be interested in all young women—a playboy of sorts. She would have to be careful. Well, the week at her cousin Clara's home might solve some problems. Hopefully Clara would come out of her shell and reenter the real world. She had been a recluse too long. And perhaps by chance Louisa would get over her anger toward Peter. Surely she would hear from him soon, and he would explain everything!

As the train pulled into the station in Augusta, Louisa questioned her parents. "Do Aunt Lydia, Uncle Phillip, and Clara know that I am adopted?"

"Lydia and Phillip know, dear," Elizabeth replied. "They were with us when we got you. But they've never told Clara—didn't feel it necessary. You and Clara are as much cousins as if you were born to us. I don't think you could feel any closer than you do now."

❧

"Louisa! Am I glad to see you!" Clara Bradford exclaimed as she threw her arms around her cousin. Clara, a little taller than Louisa, had the same slight build.

Her honey-colored hair, darker than Louisa's blond tresses, framed an oval face and hazel eyes. The two young ladies laughed and talked as they walked toward the waiting carriage. Both sets of parents followed them, talking rapidly.

"It's good to hear Clara laugh," Lydia Bradford said. "She's been such a moody person since she got word about Douglas's death. It's been several years since he was killed in the war. I know Louisa will be good for her. Listen to them. It's just like old times."

"Clara will be good for Louisa also," Elizabeth Bradford insisted. "Her fiancé, Peter McClough, left town abruptly without a word, and she is angry at him. Peter missed an appointment with her and hasn't written to explain."

"But your last letter said the wedding plans were almost settled," Lydia protested. "Are you saying it's all over between them?"

"I hope not. I'm praying this week will be a healing time for both of our girls."

Chapter 6

A nnabelle!" Peter exclaimed. "Tell me what happened! Why did Thomas kill a man? I know he killed during the war. We all did. We had to follow orders. But this is different, isn't it? Did my brother actually kill someone after the war was over? Was he defending himself?"

Annabelle pursed her lips and looked at Peter through clouded eyes. She pushed back strands of loose, graying hair and tucked them into the bun at the nape of her neck. "This is a difficult story for me, Peter, but I'll spare you no details. I'm sure you've heard of the Ku Klux Klan. It was organized in May of last year in Nashville, Tennessee. They assembled to form an organization, an 'invisible empire,' against the blacks. Former Confederate General Nathan Bedford Forrest accepted the leadership as Grand Wizard of the Empire."

"I've heard of it, Annabelle. It's a secret terrorist society, isn't it? Tell me more about it."

"The secret Ku Klux Klan society wears white robes and masks with pointed hoods and terrorizes blacks by flogging and beating them. Sometimes they plant crosses on hillsides near the homes of those they hope to frighten. They have burned down the homes of some and have even instigated a number of lynchings."

Peter slammed his arm down on the table with a loud crash. "This is despicable! Where is the law? What is the reason for these terrible acts? Is my brother a member of this society, Annabelle? I have to know!"

"No, Thomas isn't a member. He abhors the society. The group justifies their actions as necessary in defense of what they call white supremacy. They aim to keep black folks from voting or holding office."

"If Thomas isn't a member of their group, why are you telling me about this?" Peter asked.

Annabelle sighed audibly, her eyes glazed with pain. "It all happened when Thomas left his plantation for a couple days. He hoped to locate some cattle and put in a bid for them. He and Ben had made a partnership. They fenced in several acres of pastureland. It was to be a co-ownership deal between the two men. Thomas felt it would be a profitable business for the two of them. Ben and his wife had two small children. Thomas was courting a young lady from a nearby plantation, someone he knew before the war. He planned to marry her but felt he needed to get financially stable first.

"When Thomas completed his business in Nashville, he started back to the plantation. The night was dark, and only a few stars dotted the heavens. As he

283

neared his home, a huge fire lit the sky ahead of him. Thomas thought his barn was on fire. He galloped his mare at the highest possible speed and arrived in time to see several men in white sheets and pointed hoods involved in a lynching."

Peter stared openmouthed, and Annabelle's voice caught in a little sob as she struggled to continue. "After the war, Thomas always carried his rifle at his side as he rode. It had become a habit with him. He wanted to be prepared in the event of danger. Thomas jumped from his horse, grabbed his rifle, and ran shouting toward the group of men. The blaze from the fire illuminated the face of the man hanging from the tree."

Peter pounded his right fist into his left hand, again and again. "It was Ben!" he shouted. "They murdered his friend! I know it was Ben!"

"Yes, it was Ben," Annabelle said quietly. "Thomas shouted at the group, but they galloped away toward the woods without a backward glance. Your brother took aim and fired. One of the horsemen fell. Thomas quickly took Ben down from the tree, but he was already dead. The fire raged through Ben's house. The structure tumbled to the ground before him, and Thomas could do nothing. Ben's wife and two little children died in the fire. Thomas's heart ached at the loss of his friends. He prepared a burial spot for them and went to check on the man he shot. The man lay facedown, dead. So Thomas dragged his body to the burial spot and buried him also. Thomas wept here in this room when he told me about the incident. Outraged and angry, he feared for his life. He had killed a man and would be wanted by the law. Thomas couldn't think straight. Instead of telling the authorities, he left early the next morning before sunup. He needed to get away from the place. Too many memories depressed him. Thomas and Ben owned four other horses, and they were safe in the barn. He brought them along and sold all four of them on his way north to see me last month. Depressed and agitated, he only stayed a few days. I'm worried about Thomas, Peter. He was so distraught."

"And you have no idea where he went? How can we help him if we don't know where he's gone? Thomas could be out of the country, Annabelle. Maybe he went into Canada. The Underground Railroad helped many escaped slaves reach Canada during the war. Would Thomas feel compelled to go there?"

Peter and his cousin continued to discuss some possible ideas of Thomas's whereabouts. They had no clues to go on, and after a light supper, Peter hooked up the team.

He needed to get them back to the stable in town, but he promised Annabelle he would return the following day. Then they would discuss the situation further. Dusk fell quickly as he headed toward the outskirts of Boston. The horses trotted at a fast pace, anxious to get back to their stable and to bed down for the night. The rhythmic *clip-clop, clip-clop* of their hooves on the hard clay roadway had a soothing effect on Peter. He watched the roads carefully as dusk settled around him. A wrong turn could delay his arrival back at the livery stable. His mind lingered on the many things he had gleaned from his cousin. It was rather overwhelming. The fact he had a brother had been good news. But his brother had killed a man in Tennessee and fled the state. Would the law convict a man if they knew all the circumstances? Thomas was in trouble, and he and Annabelle wanted to help him. Could they even locate him? All these things preyed on his mind as he traveled the several miles back to Boston.

Peter guided the team and carriage down the side road leading to the livery stable. The young lad was not there, but an older man with gray hair helped Peter unhook the team.

"And how was yer day?" the older man asked. "Did the team suit yer needs? These are two of my finest horses and never give us any trouble." He patted their noble heads and led them toward their stalls in the barn. "Can we help you out again tomorrow with the same team?"

"They are a fine pair of horseflesh," Peter agreed, following the man into the stable. "They didn't give me a bit of trouble. But I've decided to buy a horse, as I'll be around for a while. Do you have any horses for sale?"

The stable master showed him several available horses, and Peter selected a spirited black stallion with a white face. After riding him on a short jaunt, he paid the man and reserved the horse for the following day. "I'll pick him up in the morning, sir, if that arrangement is agreeable with you."

The old stable master smiled. "You've made a good choice, young feller. I kinder hate to let Thunder go, but I have to think of my business. He's got too much spirit to pull a wagon or carriage. Some folks are afraid of him. Thunder likes to run with the wind. I could see you were able to handle him. The two of you will make a fine pair."

Satisfied with his selection, Peter patted the horse's flanks and stroked the fine head. Then he walked briskly down the road toward the inn. He liked Thunder, and the feel of the horse blended with his own body. They would make a good pair. He could travel to Annabelle's cottage quickly, and she had a small barn with stalls to house the animal. All the hay he needed could be purchased from the neighboring farm.

Peter undressed quickly and fell into bed. Exhausted from his busy day, he expected to fall asleep immediately. Instead, he lay wide-eyed and stared at the ceiling in the darkness. All the activities and discussions of the day controlled his mind and thoughts. Suddenly he climbed out of bed and knelt beside it. "Lord, I don't know what to do about Thomas," he prayed aloud. "Somehow I feel responsible for him since he's my brother. You alone know where he is and whether he plans to return to this area. Annabelle is so worried about him. Please give me wisdom and guidance so I'll know what to do. I don't know where to begin, but I long to meet him. . .to know him. Thomas and Annabelle are the only family I have. And, Lord, would You help Louisa understand about my absence? Let her know I would never disappoint her on purpose. I don't want to burden her with my problems—at least not yet. I love her, Lord, and believe marriage is in our future. Please keep her in Your care. She is very special to me. Thank You for all You've done for me already. In Jesus' name. Amen."

Rejuvenated from his prayer time, Peter stretched and yawned as he stood to his feet. He pushed back a shock of dark hair from his forehead and ran a hand across his eyes. They felt weary and bloodshot. A small light filtered through the window on the far side of the room. He walked toward it, pulled back the calico curtain, and gazed toward the heavens. The sky was dark, but the few visible stars twinkled. "God's up there in His wonderful heaven," he whispered softly, "and He knows all about my problems. I'll just leave them with Him." Peter headed back toward his bed with a broad grin on his face. He felt God's presence and His peace. "Now I can sleep!" he said. And he did.

Chapter 7

Let's go shopping, Clara," Louisa said eagerly in an attempt to get her cousin out of the house. Louisa and her parents had been visiting the Phil Bradfords in Augusta for almost a week. Louisa had tried in vain to interest her cousin in some semblance of a social life. She and Clara sat in the parlor while they worked dutifully on embroidery and other handwork.

"We must leave in a few days to go back to Waterville, and I've not had much opportunity to see the town," Louisa said as she placed her handwork on the sofa next to her. She stood up, stretched, and patted her pale gold hair, which fell in a cascade around her shoulders. "I'm bored with handwork. We need to get some excitement into our lives."

Clara grimaced. "Like what, dear cousin? I'm content to work on my pillowcases and dream thoughts of Douglas. We would have been married by this time and perhaps had a child. Why did that terrible war happen anyway? It ruined so many lives."

Louisa grabbed Clara's handwork from her cousin's lap and pulled her to her feet. "I've been patient with you long enough, young lady. It's a lovely day, and we need some fresh air. We are going out on the town!"

The Phil Bradford home, a large brownstone house just off the main street, was in close proximity to many interesting shops. Louisa felt the outing and exercise would do them both good. Since their arrival in Augusta, the only place they had visited was the church. It was bigger than their church in Waterville; but the people seemed friendly, and the pastor preached the Word of God. One gentleman in particular seemed very attentive to Clara. He talked to them at great length after the morning service.

"Doesn't Sam Burns work at the pharmacy?" Louisa asked, referring to the young man from church. "Let's stop by and see him when we're out."

Clara eyed her cousin carefully. "Why, Louisa? Do you find Sam attractive?"

Louisa blushed under Clara's scrutiny. "Why, yes, I do. Don't you think Sam is handsome? He has such broad shoulders and a manly build."

"Not to mention his blue eyes and sandy-colored hair." Clara laughed. "I'd say you were over Peter McClough, Cousin, if you can find another interest so quickly."

"I'm interested in Sam for you, Clara. I saw his attentiveness to you in church. Didn't you see the way he watched you? That young man is in love with you, or close to it."

287

"Fiddle!" Clara exclaimed. "He's just being friendly. Sam was Douglas's best friend. The two men did everything together—played sports, went fishing and hunting. They went off to war and were in the same unit. Sam came back wounded. Douglas was killed. It all happened in the same battle." Clara pulled her lace handkerchief from her bodice and dabbed at her eyes.

"Do you hold that against Sam?"

"What—what do you mean?" Clara stammered.

"Sam came back, and Douglas didn't. Do you think it's unfair for Sam to be alive? Is this the reason you can't recognize that the man loves you?"

"Nonsense!" Clara said, blowing her nose.

Louisa put an arm around her cousin. "I'm sorry, Clara. I didn't mean to upset you. Dry your eyes, and we'll go to town. You need to get out of this house!"

After a light lunch with their parents, the two cousins, decked with bonnets and parasols, started for town. Phil Bradford took some days off work at his bank so the two brothers and their wives could visit. Other days Jack Bradford accompanied his brother to his bank while the womenfolk busied themselves at the house.

The sun shone brightly upon the girls as they walked uptown. Clara, quiet at first, relaxed under Louisa's constant chatter. "Oh, look, a millinery shop!" Louisa squealed. "Let's go in and try on hats!"

Louisa's excitement caught on, and the two entered the shop with enthusiasm. A nice-looking, middle-aged woman approached them with a smile and nodded at Clara. "Hello, Clara. What can I do for you young ladies? Is it time for a new bonnet?"

"My cousin, Louisa Bradford, is visiting from Waterville, Miss Martin. We would like to try on some hats."

"Of course. Nice to meet you, Louisa. Just help yourself and let me know if you find something you like. I have another lady trying on hats at the moment."

Louisa and Clara settled themselves by a mirror and selected several hats to try on. They giggled and laughed at some outrageous ones, overdone with extravagant plumes, artificial birds, and flowers. Louisa watched her cousin with amusement. Clara was definitely coming out of her shell. They looked across the room and saw a tall, thin, sophisticated woman trying on hats. Each hat she chose was tall and thin like herself. Louisa and Clara had a difficult time as they struggled to control their laughter. "Why do tall, thin people pick tall, thin hats?" Clara whispered as she giggled quietly. Presently the woman purchased her hat and left the store.

The bell on the millinery shop door tinkled merrily as another customer entered. This lady was short and stout with several packages in her arms. She plopped herself into a chair on the far side of the room, and Miss Martin hurried to wait on her. All the hats Miss Martin brought she refused to try on. They were stylish and complemented the lady's figure and coloring. "No! No! No!" she insisted. "They are all too tall for me, Miss Martin." Instead, she chose a small, round hat—one that matched her well-rounded body and did nothing to enhance her appearance.

"Did you see the hat she chose?" Clara asked quietly as she suppressed her giggles with her hand. "Why didn't she take Miss Martin's suggestion?"

"It would have been a much better selection indeed," Louisa agreed with a smile as she placed a large, wide-brimmed hat on her golden head. "I like this, Clara. What do you think?"

"It's lovely. I like the pink flowers and ribbons. It becomes you."

"Are you sure? It isn't too wild, is it? I probably don't need a new hat, but this one is different. I brought enough money with me to purchase it. This is the kind of hat I've always wanted. It will lift my spirits and help me forget Peter."

Louisa made her decision and purchased the hat before she could change her mind. An elderly lady, who entered the store while they were still at the counter, tried on a brilliantly deep pink hat, complete with plumes and feathers. It fit nicely over the gray hair piled high upon her head. "Tell me, girls," she called to them. "Am I too old for this kind of hat? Miss Martin says it makes me look younger."

Clara and Louisa turned to face the elderly woman. The deep pink of the hat brought out color in her sunken cheeks and added a glow to her dark eyes.

"I like it!" Clara said. "Miss Martin is right. It makes you look younger. I'm sure heads will turn when they see you in it."

"Yes, indeed!" Louisa agreed. "The hat is very becoming. I think you will be happy with your purchase."

"Thank you, young ladies," the elderly woman said. "I've had my eye on this hat for a long while. It's been in the window enticing me each time I went by the shop. I just needed enough nerve to come in and buy it. I always appreciate an outside opinion." She turned to Miss Martin and smiled a mischievous smile. "Wrap it up! I can't wait until my husband sees me in this!"

Louisa and Clara walked leisurely down the main street and entered a few other shops. They purchased some new needles, embroidery thread, and ribbon at the variety store. When they came to the corner pharmacy, Louisa turned to go in.

"You were serious about visiting Sam, weren't you?" Clara asked as she followed her cousin. "Won't he think we're being a little forward?"

"I don't think so. I can purchase some small item if it makes you feel more comfortable. Sam will probably be delighted to see us."

The two cousins walked around the pharmacy and noticed Sam with a customer at the far end of the store. It was a young woman who giggled and gushed as she talked with him. Louisa and Clara busied themselves as they looked at the many items for sale, going from one aisle to another. Suddenly a deep, resonant voice behind them broke into their thoughts.

"Good afternoon, Clara, Louisa. How are you young ladies today? It's good to see you. May I assist you with something?"

The two cousins turned simultaneously. Clara's face turned dark crimson as she faced Sam. "Uh, no, thank you, Sam. We were just looking around."

Sam reached for her hand and held it briefly. "I see by your packages you and Louisa have been shopping. Isn't it a beautiful day?"

"It is a beautiful day, and we've enjoyed the walk and fresh air," Louisa said. She noticed Clara seemed at a loss for words. "Clara helped me select a new hat to take back to Waterville with me. It's somewhat daring, but it seems to lift my spirits."

"I'm sure it's a lovely bonnet," Sam said, "especially if Clara liked it. I've noticed she has impeccable taste in clothing and hats."

Sam's green eyes lingered on Clara's honey blond hair and hazel eyes as he spoke. She continued to blush, averting her eyes from his constant gaze. When she replied, it was with great effort. "Thank you, Sam, but I'm sure you are just being kind."

"I have a great idea," Sam said with a quick smile. "There is a concert next Friday at the Theatre House. Would you young ladies allow me the privilege of escorting you? It would give me great pleasure."

Clara stood quietly as though struggling for words.

"Thank you very much," Louisa said, breaking the silence. "But I cannot accept your generous offer. Our family is returning to Waterville in a few days. However, I'm sure Clara would enjoy going to the concert with you."

Sam's ruddy face broke into a wide grin. "Would you, Clara? Will you consider going to the concert with me?"

Clara hesitated as she glanced at her cousin and then at Sam. Why had Louisa put her cousin in this predicament? It would be rude for her to decline. "Uh, yes, Sam," she murmured breathlessly. "I'll go to the concert with you next week. Thank you for your kind invitation."

Louisa saw the look of pleasure that covered Sam's face at Clara's answer. What a fine and handsome young man he was! She hoped this was the start of a lasting relationship between them. It gave her a happy feeling to know Clara and Sam planned to attend the concert together. They would make a fine couple, and her instincts told her Sam could help Clara get over Douglas. She detected a certain magnetism between them.

When the girls left the pharmacy, they decided to stop at the nearby café for tea. Clara seemed unusually quiet, and Louisa hesitated to break into her thoughts. Finally, when they were settled with their tea, she reached out and patted her cousin's hand. "Clara, are you angry at me? I know I made it impossible for you to refuse Sam's invitation. I'm sorry if I've offended you. But I thought an evening at the concert would be a good change. You spend too much of your time at home with your handwork."

Clara remained silent and took small sips of her tea. She tucked a strand of gold hair back into her bonnet with her free hand. A few ringlets lingered about her fair cheeks, and her eyes were moist.

"Dear Clara, I'm so sorry!" Louisa exclaimed. "I've been such a fool! I forced you into an awkward situation you couldn't refuse. Please forgive me. I've been a meddling cousin and caused you unnecessary heartache."

Clara wiped her moist eyes with her lace handkerchief. "There's nothing to forgive, Louisa. I'm glad you meddled. It's time I accepted an invitation from Sam. He's invited me several times before, but I always refused. When I look at Sam, I see Douglas by his side. They were always a pair. When Douglas courted me before the war, Sam came along sometimes—on picnics or to church outings. I knew Sam was interested in me back then. It made me feel special. But he was always the gentleman. He never tried to move in on Doug's territory, and he seemed happy for the two of us. Sam was to be best man at our wedding."

"Will it be too difficult to be courted by Doug's best friend? I didn't realize the whole situation when I got you into this."

Clara smiled. "Actually, I'm looking forward to next week with Sam. He lost his best friend in the war. I lost my sweetheart. And Sam has been very patient with me. I can't expect him to wait around forever."

"Don't you think Douglas would be happy if his two favorite people got together, Clara? It almost seems like it was meant to be."

Clara toyed with her napkin. "Douglas wrote to me from the battlefield. He told me once, if anything happened to him in the war, he wanted me to consider Sam as a future husband. He believed Sam to be the finest friend a man could have on this earth. You see, Doug knew how much Sam cared for me. He also knew Sam would never attempt to court me while Doug was in the picture. I've kept all Doug's letters and reread them recently."

"Well, you certainly have Doug's blessing on a relationship with Sam through his letters, Clara. Sam cares deeply for you. It's evident in the way he looks at you. He seems such a fine person. Do you think you will ever grow to love him?"

Louisa was surprised at Clara's answer. "I think I've always loved him as a good friend. And today, for the first time, I felt the liberty to love him in a deeper way. Doug gave me that liberty through his letters, and you gave me courage to accept his invitation to the concert next week. Thank you, Louisa. I thought it was my duty to be faithful to Doug's memory and remain unmarried, but I see things differently now. I feel like a caged bird who has just been set free. It is the Lord's doing, and I praise Him for it."

Chapter 8

The week's visit with the Phillip Bradford family ended on a happy note. When Louisa bid Clara good-bye, her cousin bubbled with excitement. She no longer dwelt on the past but eagerly looked forward to the future. "I wouldn't be a bit surprised," Louisa told her, "if we receive a letter soon announcing your upcoming marriage."

"Louisa! Do you really think so? But it's too soon. We've not begun our courtship yet. Sam and I may find we are not compatible."

"No chance of that!" Louisa insisted. "Now that you are over Douglas, everything will fall into place. You are over him, aren't you?"

"I still have wonderful memories of my relationship with Doug, but I accept the fact he is gone. Sam Burns fills my thoughts and dreams now." Clara hugged her cousin. "You've been so good for me, Louisa. You are looking at the new Clara Bradford. I hope you and Peter get married when he gets back. You spoke so highly of him in your letters. I want you to be as happy as I am."

Louisa smiled wistfully. "I thought I would be the one getting married soon. I must admit I'm a little envious, Clara. When Sam looks at you, I see the love in his eyes. And actually, you've known him a long time. It isn't as though you just met. I've known Peter a long time also, but it seems he has tired of me. Perhaps I've taken our relationship too much for granted."

"Fiddlesticks!" Clara exclaimed. "You'll probably have a letter waiting when you get home that explains his absence. Or maybe Peter will be there in person. Wouldn't that be grand?"

Louisa smiled ruefully at her cousin's exuberance. "I might, Clara, and thanks for the encouragement. However, I'm so angry at Peter I'm not even sure I want to see him."

❧

Louisa worked dutifully on her handwork during the train trip home. Her parents dozed or read the morning paper, and she tried to keep her mind occupied between her embroidery and the scenery. But her thoughts constantly turned to Peter McClough and his whereabouts. *Perhaps there will be a letter waiting when I return home, as Clara suggested. Or Peter might be there in person to explain his sudden departure. But why would he leave so suddenly without a word? Was it something in his past? Something he was ashamed to tell me?* She felt concerned about Peter one moment and angry the next. *What if some harm has come to him? Could he have discovered a serious illness and gone to seek professional treatment not available in Waterville? Doesn't he realize I care about him and want to know what is going on in his life? I miss the closeness we shared. His dark eyes searching mine spoke of his love. I remember sweet and tender kisses as he bid me good-bye after an evening at the concert or a dinner engagement. A lock of his dark, unruly hair always fell across his forehead. I loved to push it back as I studied his firm jaw and wide grin. How I long to feel his strong arms around me once again. Oh, Peter, why don't you contact me? Whatever your burden may be, I want to share it with you.* The next moment her mood changed completely. *Peter McClough evidently doesn't care enough about me to share his secret. He is thoughtless and inconsiderate! If there is someone else, someone from his past, he should have told me. If I cannot come first in his life, there is no hope for us.*

As the Bradford family stepped down from the train in Waterville, Louisa spied Roger Evans waiting with the Bradfords' team and carriage. Jack Bradford had arranged earlier for Roger to meet their train and care for the team during their absence. Louisa noticed Roger's tall, muscular body and self-assured stance. He looked very debonair in a dark suit and tie as he approached the trio with a dazzling smile.

"How was your trip?" he asked.

"Fine, Roger," Jack Bradford replied. "How are things at the bank? Any problems I should know about?"

"Everything is in good shape at the bank, sir. I've handled everything. I'm sure you will be pleased."

Louisa detected a note of inflated ego, but the young man's smile pushed the thought aside. His next words took her by surprise.

"Mr. Bradford, may I escort your daughter to the concert at the music hall next week? It should be a most enjoyable evening, especially if Louisa could attend with me."

Jack Bradford studied the young man for a moment. "She is engaged to be married, Roger. I'm sure you didn't know."

"I didn't know the circumstances, sir. I suppose the concert is out of the question then." Roger Evans turned toward Louisa, and his gaze lingered as he took in her appearance. She wore a deep mauve traveling outfit along with her newly purchased hat. The ensemble brought out the gold of her hair and enhanced her fair coloring. "Who is the lucky fellow, Louisa, and when is the wedding?"

Color rose in Louisa's cheeks. "His name is Peter McClough. We planned to marry this fall, but Peter left town suddenly. I'm not sure where he is or when he will be back."

Roger Evans cleared his throat. "That sounds unusual for an engaged man— to go off somewhere and not tell his betrothed. Is there a possibility things may not work out? A broken engagement maybe?"

Louisa's cheeks felt hot as the color rose higher under his careful gaze and self-assured smile. She felt his eyes penetrating her very being. "I do not know, Mr. Evans," she said as she climbed into the carriage. "Only time will tell."

Roger Evans loaded the Bradfords' luggage and headed the carriage down Main Street. Louisa's thoughts centered around Roger during the short ride to the Bradford home. He seemed nice enough, she decided, but his self-confident manner took her off guard. He made it clear he would be interested in her if she broke off her engagement. Would she do that in the near future if there was no word from Peter? She mulled it over and over in her mind but was unable to arrive at a suitable conclusion.

There was no letter from Peter when Jack Bradford picked up the family mail the following day—nor was there any sign of his return. Louisa tried to give Peter the benefit of the doubt but grew more and more impatient with the passing of time. "I will blot Peter McClough out of my life!" she declared aloud in her room one afternoon. "He is not worth all my worry and concern! I'll show him I can get along fine without him! Roger Evans appears to be much more of a gentleman anyway. If he asks me out again, I may accept his invitation!"

Later that week Louisa stopped in at the bank and visited briefly with Roger Evans while there. He invited her again to attend a concert with him, strictly as a friend, since he knew she was engaged. "Since Peter is out of town, surely he wouldn't mind you attending a concert with a friend," Roger suggested. "You need to have a social life."

"I don't know—I'm not sure," she murmured. "It probably wouldn't be proper."

"Think of me simply as your father's business associate, Louisa. It will simply be a friendly evening out for both of us."

Louisa hemmed and hawed a bit but finally agreed—on a strictly friendly basis, nothing more. When her parents learned she planned to attend a concert with Roger Evans, they were dumbfounded and strongly advised against it. But Louisa held her ground and said there was no harm in it since it was just two friends who enjoyed music spending a little time together.

As Louisa dressed for the concert, she determined to look her best and enjoy the evening to the fullest. Deftly she pulled out one gown after another and tossed them on the bed. Not the blue satin, she decided. It was Peter's favorite. He always said it made her gray eyes light up with glints of blue. She held up the cranberry velvet but discarded it quickly. Another of Peter's favorites, it was more appropriate for the winter season. Finally, her decision fell on the light pink satin gown with lace, brocade trim, and tiny pink roses sewed onto the formfitting bodice. She grimaced as she viewed herself in the mirror and sighed. "Peter loves this dress also. He says it brings out the pale gold of my hair." Suddenly she cried out furiously, "Stop it, Louisa! Don't concern yourself with what Peter likes or dislikes. He isn't here, nor has he contacted you. Think instead about a casual but interesting evening with a friend. And that is all there is to it!"

THE BEST LAID PLANS

Roger Evans arrived at the Bradford home promptly at seven on the Friday evening of the concert. He wore a black suit, and his dark hair was slicked back from his broad forehead. When Louisa descended the staircase in her pink satin gown, Roger rushed to greet her. "How beautiful you look, Louisa," he said with glints of admiration in his blue eyes. "I'll be the envy of every man at the concert."

Louisa smiled and extended her hand, while hints of color tinged her cheeks. She felt a little guilty but dismissed the thought immediately. "Thank you, kind sir," she said demurely. "You look mighty fine yourself."

"There's a chill in the night air," Roger said as he helped Louisa pull her warm cloak around her shoulders. A hood fell loosely at the back, and he pulled the hood forward to cover the golden curls. "That hood will keep you warm and cozy."

The concert proved to be one of the better ones. The soprano, tenor, and baritone sang beautiful arias, sometimes together and sometimes interchangeably. Louisa felt herself being lifted to a higher plane of music appreciation as she listened wide-eyed with lips parted. "It's so lovely," she whispered to Roger. He leaned over, placed his arm around the back of her seat, and rested it on her shoulders. Louisa moved away slightly, but he only moved closer. His arm on her shoulder seemed too familiar, and his closeness unnerved her. She leaned forward in her seat and pushed his arm away with a smile. "Remember our agreement, Roger," she whispered. "This is just a little outing between two friends."

"Um. . .yes, it is." Roger's face registered disappointment, and he shifted in his seat. "But you are so lovely, my dear." His breath, warm and heavy on her ear, was too close for comfort.

During intermission Louisa excused herself to go to the powder room. As she glanced into the mirror, she noticed hot pink spots lingered on her cheeks. She fussed with her hair and tucked some stray ringlets behind her ears. Satisfied with her appearance, she turned to go. On her way out, a very attractive brunette, draped in blue brocade, approached.

"Isn't it a lovely concert?" the dark-haired woman gushed.

"Yes," Louisa agreed. "I've enjoyed it very much."

The young woman eyed Louisa up and down. "I see you are attending with Roger Evans. Isn't he dashing? He seems to be quite the man about town, doesn't he?"

"I—I wouldn't know," Louisa faltered. "I've not known him very long. We're just casual friends. I think he's only been in town a few weeks."

"Where have you been hiding, dearie? He's squired many women in the short time he's been here. I was one of his first. I still see him now and then. He seems to want variety and moves around rather fast."

Louisa frowned. The woman's chatter had a nauseating effect on her. "Please excuse me, miss. This discussion is of no interest to me." She deliberately passed around the young woman and headed out of the powder room door.

"Well, I never!" the woman exclaimed.

Louisa's skirts rustled as she hurried back down the aisle, the frown still on her face.

"What is it?" Roger asked as he stood to greet her. "You look angry about something."

Her face relaxed into a slight smile. "I met someone in the powder room who was not very pleasant. It's nothing to worry about. I've put it out of my mind already."

Roger pulled her down into the seat next to him but kept his distance. "Good. We don't want anything to mar this evening. And your pretty face looks so much better when you smile." He leaned close and whispered in her ear. "I'd rather watch you than the performers any day!"

When Roger took her home, he walked her to the door and boldly leaned to kiss her good night. Louisa, taken by surprise, pushed him from her. She couldn't deny the warm feelings she felt for this man, but she disliked the liberties he took with her person.

"Is something wrong?" Roger asked. "It was only intended to be a friendly kiss. Did I offend you?"

"No. . .yes!" Louisa faltered. "I mean, I'm engaged! Friendship does not include kisses. Besides, we hardly know one another."

Roger studied the uplifted face before him. "I intend to change that, Louisa." He looked deep into her eyes. "If Peter McClough doesn't return to claim his bride, I shall do my best to steal you away from him!"

Louisa felt warm inside and turned away. "Thank you for a lovely evening, Roger. It will take some time for us to get better acquainted. . .as friends. I don't know very much about you, your background, or your family. My life is an open book. You've met my parents. I've always lived in Waterville. There's not much else to know."

"You're sweet, Louisa. I admire your shyness. May I take you to dinner next week or call on you sometime soon?" he asked eagerly. "We need to spend a lot of time together. I can fill you in on my background if you wish. It's not very exciting."

"Would you like to attend church with our family on Sunday?" Louisa asked. "We attend the little Community Church here in town."

"Church?" Roger asked, taken aback. "I—I guess so. Why not? Especially if it will please you."

"Are you not in the habit of attending church on the Lord's Day?" Louisa asked. "The Bible instructs us to assemble ourselves together. I'm a Christian, Roger, and attending services is part of my life. What are your feelings toward God?"

Roger rubbed his chin as he thought for a moment. He realized this question was important to the young woman standing before him. "I believe there is a God up there somewhere. I just don't think about it much. I guess I'm a Christian, too."

"Christian means 'little Christ.' The only way one becomes a Christian is by trusting Jesus Christ, God's Son, as their Savior. Have you ever done that, Roger?"

"I think so, as a young lad. I can't remember for sure. My grandmother talked to me about it once. And I'll visit your church if you like. I'm sure it will be good for me."

As Louisa undressed for bed, her thoughts dwelt on Roger Evans. He was a bold one—but also very charming. She felt guilty about the warm glow she felt when she was with him. It seemed obvious he didn't know God in a personal way. But neither did Peter at first, and his life changed when he came to know Jesus. The same thing could happen to Roger, she reasoned. Louisa walked to the window and gazed out at the heavens. One star shone brightly and twinkled at her. "Star light, star bright. . . ," she started, then stopped. "Oh, I don't know what my wish would be if I could have one. Help me, dear God. Is Roger Evans just a playboy as that woman suggested at the concert tonight? And what about Peter? Where is he, and what is happening to him?"

Louisa knelt quietly by her bed and poured out her heart before God. Had she erred by attending a concert with Roger Evans—on a strictly friendly basis on her part? He hinted that he would like their relationship to be something more than friends. Perhaps it could be so, if Peter never returned. She didn't have any answers, but she knew the great God of the universe was in complete control.

Chapter 9

Peter had settled into his brother's old room at Annabelle's cottage. It had two cotlike beds and a single dresser. A small window with calico curtains that matched the bedspread completed the decor. It was homey and comfortable. Somehow it reached out to Peter and reminded him of the brother he had never known. Thomas had slept there, used the dresser for his clothes, and looked out the window. He could almost feel his presence.

His mother's cousin, due to her age, seemed more an aunt than a distant cousin to him. She hovered over him and cooked all his favorite meals—delighted to have someone to wait on. There had been no word from Thomas, and Annabelle grew more concerned as time went by. Peter busied himself around the cottage and outbuildings. He fixed the roof and made other needed repairs to the small home. When he mended the fences of the pasture, his horse, Thunder, followed him from place to place. The animal seemed to enjoy his new surroundings and showed his appreciation by nudging his new master. Peter rode the spirited animal at least once a day around the pasture or down the lane. It was the high point of his day as the two of them, the man and his stallion, blended as one and galloped across the valley at a magnificent pace. The high speed left Peter with a tremendous feeling of exultation and accomplishment. During these rides, Peter put his brother's problems out of his mind and thought only about Louisa. How he longed to see her and hold her in his arms. "I love you, Louisa!" he shouted to the wind. "I love you!"

When they returned to the barn, the beautiful animal panted and pawed at the ground. Peter, breathless and exuberant, jumped off his horse and removed the saddle and bridle. He led Thunder to his stall where he rubbed him down and brushed his black coat until it shone. Thunder nuzzled his master, and Peter patted his head, letting his fingers run through the thick, black mane. "What a beautiful animal you are. And you're hungry, aren't you, fella?" He reached for the pitchfork, went over to a mound of hay, and tossed hay into the stall. Thunder jerked his head up and down and quickly grabbed a mouthful of the feed. Deep in thought, Peter watched his horse munch quietly for a few moments before leaving the barn.

By the time he chopped some wood and carried water into the house, it was time for supper. After washing up, he sat down at the table and took a deep breath. The sumptuous odors coming from the woodstove filled his nostrils. "Annabelle, what smells so good? I'm so hungry, I could eat my hat!"

THE BEST LAID PLANS

Annabelle chuckled as she carried an iron pot of stew from the woodstove to the table. "Just stew and dumplings, my boy. It does my heart good to cook for someone who so thoroughly enjoys my cooking."

After the hearty meal, complete with blueberry pie, Peter leaned back and patted his stomach. "Annabelle, I'm getting fat. It's your wonderful home cooking. I'm afraid I'll resemble one of your neighbor's pigs if I don't watch myself."

Annabelle's merry little laugh tinkled forth. "Peter, you can't know how much it means to me having you here." Her face grew serious. "I worry so about Thomas. What will happen to him because he killed a man?" She shuddered as she spoke. "If he would only come back, we could work out a plan. Do you think he will have to pay for his crime?"

Peter frowned. "I don't know, Annabelle. But I've done a lot of thinking lately. Thomas might stay away until he thinks the episode has blown over. But who knows how long that will take? I can't wait any longer. I've decided to go to Tennessee and find out more about this incident. Maybe Thomas went back there and turned himself in. Do you think it's a possibility?"

Annabelle stared straight ahead, her face downcast. "I don't know, Peter. It is possible. He was in a terrible state when he left here. I just don't know what to think. It frightens me to think about it. Would—" Her voice faltered. "Would they hang him for his crime?"

Peter shoved back his chair and jumped up, a sick feeling in the pit of his stomach. "I can't sit around and do nothing! This matter needs to be dealt with! I'll leave early tomorrow morning for Tennessee. Try not to fret about it, Annabelle."

"When will you return?" she asked. "Could I go with you?"

"No, Annabelle. I'm not sure what I'll find or how long it will take. I'll need an address and directions to the Berringer plantation. Can you help me with that?"

"I have an address, and I know it's north of Nashville. If you go into town, someone will know the location."

"What name does my brother go by? Is he called Thomas Berringer, the name of his foster parents? Or does he carry your last name, Annabelle? It will help to know who I'm looking for."

"It pleased me to know he called himself Thomas Hayes when he joined the Confederates. When I wrote him in the army, I sent my letters to that name."

"Good!" Peter exclaimed, giving his cousin a little hug. "Then I'll search for news about Thomas Hayes, who happens to be my brother."

"God go with you, Peter," Annabelle whispered softly.

At first light on the following day, Peter saddled Thunder, tied his belongings to the back of his saddle, and headed toward Boston. Dark clouds dotted the horizon, and soft drops of rain dripped from his hat as Thunder raced toward town. He wasn't sure when he would see his lovely Louisa again, but he knew the task before him must take priority. It would consume his mind and energy for a time. When he resolved the situation with his brother, Peter planned to return to Waterville. Would Louisa wait for him? He prayed she would. His heart thudded inside his chest as he rode to the train station and purchased a ticket to Nashville.

For a small fee, the ticket master allowed Thunder to bed down in one of the empty freight cars. Peter tethered the animal, bought some hay and straw from the man at the livery stable, and made the freight car comfortable for his faithful charge.

As the train raced toward his final destination, Peter organized a plan in his mind. He would visit the town and casually inquire about the Berringer plantation. Surely someone could provide him with sufficient information—perhaps even the details of the tragic event. It must be done tactfully, he decided, especially since he was from the North. His speech would betray him immediately. He knew many Southerners carried a deep resentment toward Northerners, and it was understandable. The war, tragic to both sides, had left the South ravished in many areas. They lost husbands, sons, and other loved ones in bloody battles just as the North did. But many wealthy Southern folk also lost their homes and very existence. The cotton industry was their livelihood on the large plantations. With slaves set free, they had no one to work the cotton fields and care for their animals. Plantation owners faced a tremendous loss and difficult time as they strove to get their lives back together again.

Peter leaned back and tried to sleep. "I'm not certain what kind of a reception to expect in Nashville," he muttered to himself. "They may run this Northerner out of town—or tar and feather me." With eyes closed, a slight smile curved his lips. "Now wouldn't that be a sight to behold! Peter McClough, what are you letting yourself in for, anyway?"

When the train finally arrived in Nashville two days later, Peter grabbed his belongings and went to the freight car to get Thunder. The horse whinnied at the sight of his master, snorted and pranced, nodding his fine head. Peter removed the tether that held Thunder secure and examined the animal carefully. He seemed none the worse for wear.

Peter led him out of the freight car, saddled up, and swung his long legs over Thunder's sleek, black body. The horse, eager to run, started off at a rapid pace.

"Whoa, boy!" Peter shouted as he reined in the animal to a slow walk. "We're in town, not out in the pasture. I know you're anxious to run, fella, and we'll do that later. We need to mosey down the road first and get some information."

Peter noticed an attractive young woman watching him with a big smile on her face. She fluttered her fan back and forth and peered at him with violet eyes. "Do you always talk to your horse, sir?" she asked in a soft and delightful Southern drawl. "Is it just your way, or do all Northerners talk to their animals?"

Peter grinned as he reined Thunder to a stop. "I'm afraid my conversation gave me away already," he replied. "I don't know about all Northerners, but I like to talk to my animal. He's my friend."

As if he knew what his master said, Thunder nickered and jerked his head up and down. "Well, I can see your animal knows he's your friend. Good day to you, sir."

"Wait, miss. Can you give me directions to the Berringer plantation? I understand it's north of the city a small piece."

The young lady's face turned ashen, and she clutched at her throat. "Why do you ask, sir? Do you have business there?"

Peter quickly jumped down from Thunder's back. "Did I say something to disturb you, miss?"

"I—ah—no!" she exclaimed. "It's really none of my affair." She turned on her heel and started away. Her lovely yellow dress rustled as she moved quickly toward the town.

Peter hurried after her and blocked her way. "I'm sorry, miss. I'm not familiar with Nashville. Can you tell me the road that leads to the Berringer place? That's all I ask."

"Sir, you are blocking my path!" she said. Hot pink patches stood out on her fair cheeks, and her violet eyes displayed fire. "Ask at the ticket office," she flung over her shoulder as she marched away, her chestnut hair bouncing under her bonnet. "Or ask the sheriff over at the jailhouse. I'm sure he'd like to know about your interest in the Berringer place."

Peter watched the slight figure as she continued down the roadway. "Thanks, I will!" he called after her. But she did not look back.

The ticket master was closest, so Peter turned Thunder around and retreated to the train station. The ticket master was studying a schedule but glanced up as Peter approached. When he asked for directions to the Berringer plantation, the man's eyes narrowed. He looked Peter up and down several times before answering. "What's yer business here, mister?" he asked. "We don't cotton to Northerners in our parts. You'd best get back up north where you belong."

Peter flashed his friendliest smile. "I don't plan to stay in Nashville, sir. I'm only here for a short time, and I'll be on my way north. Could you tell me which road to take out of town and about how far it is to Berringers'?"

"The place is deserted, mister. Are you interested in buying the place? Old Man Berringer and his wife are both dead. Their only daughter married and moved away a few years ago."

"Wasn't there a foster son?" Peter asked, trying to sound nonchalant. "I heard he fought for the South in the War between the States."

The man's eyes narrowed into tiny slits, and his lips formed a tight line. Deep frown lines furrowed the wide forehead. "Take the main road through town all the way to the end. There's a road that winds north—can't miss it. The Berringer place is about three miles out on the left-hand side. It's a large, white house with pillars and sits back a piece from the road." The ticket master abruptly turned his back on Peter and moved to another part of the room.

"Thank you, sir," Peter called after him. "I appreciate your help."

Peter swung himself into the saddle once again and headed Thunder toward the town's main street. It was still early in the day, and he decided to ride out and see the plantation before dark. As the horse trotted through town, Peter noticed a small café on one corner and an inn on the other. Several horses were tied to the hitching post at the café, and throngs of people milled about on the roadway. "Must be good food there, Thunder. That's where I'll eat later and then stay overnight at the inn. We'll find a livery stable for you with lots of good hay and oats." He patted the animal's neck as he leaned over him. "As soon as we're out of town, we'll run with the wind!"

It was not difficult to locate the Berringer plantation, a magnificent antebellum estate, white with large pillars, set back from the main road, boasting of better days. An iron gate opened to a tree-lined roadway that led to the house. As far as Peter could see from the outside, the home was in good repair just as Annabelle had said. His brother, Thomas, and his friend Ben had taken care of all the renovations after the war. The home was locked, but Peter peeked through some windows and caught glimpses of beautiful furnishings. "This is quite the mansion!" he exclaimed, letting out a low whistle. "My brother has a fortune tied up in this place!"

Peter moved cautiously about the grounds. He examined the barn, which was also in excellent repair. The stalls were clean and well taken care of. Pasture and cotton fields extended as far as his eyes could see. At the back and off to one side, Peter came upon the rubble left from Ben's home. It was reduced to a pile of burnt boards in memory of the wife and two children who died there. Peter removed his hat and bowed his head. Farther back he stumbled upon the graves. Thomas had dug them hastily but carefully. Boards nailed together in the form of a cross stood by each grave. Somehow Thomas had managed to write their names, evidently burning the letters into the wood. Peter felt pain and despair wash over him as he read the names: BEN, MY BEST FRIEND; LILY, HIS WIFE; BEN JR.; and lastly LIZA. One other grave had a huge, empty hole. It had evidently been dug up and the body removed to another site. A wooden cross with no name stood by the empty grave. This was the burial spot of the man Thomas had killed in an angry rage. His family must have removed him to their own burial grounds. Thomas was justified in killing the man, wasn't he? After all, this man, together with his friends, killed Ben and his family.

Farther back, beyond the barn and off to one side, Peter discovered the Berringer family cemetery. It had an iron fence surrounding it and looked somewhat overgrown. The grayish white tombstones held many names of the descendants of the Berringer family. Peter felt a sense of urgency as he rode away from the cemetery. Would he be able to find his brother? In the stillness, as dusk fell, Peter looked heavenward. "I don't have the answers, Lord, but You do. Help me find Thomas soon."

Chapter 10

Louisa Bradford hummed a little tune as she carried the mail into the house. She had tried removing Peter from her mind during the past weeks as she involved herself in other interests. Roger Evans was close at hand, and she knew he desired to continue their friendship. It was awkward, her being engaged and her fiancé out of town. She didn't know where Peter was and when, or if, he planned to return. An evening out with Roger had been enjoyable, and she felt there was nothing wrong with attending a concert with him, especially since he worked for her father and they were just casual friends. Lately she realized her thoughts centered more and more around the charming Mr. Evans. It happened more often than she cared to admit. She chided herself at these times and vowed to discipline her mind and keep her distance.

As she flipped through the pile of mail, she discovered a letter from Peter and her friend Emily Harris out in Pennsylvania. Uncertain about which letter to open first, she carried them both into the parlor where her mother sat knitting. "I finally received a letter from Peter after all this time!" she exclaimed, handing her mother the rest of the mail. "Now maybe I'll learn some answers to his mysterious disappearance! And another letter from Emily."

Elizabeth Bradford laid her knitted sock in her lap. "Let's hear what Peter has to say, dear. I'm sure he'll clear up this mystery for you. You'll feel so much better knowing where he is."

"All right, I'll read his first. It's not a very lengthy letter. I wonder if he's breaking off our engagement. Perhaps he's found someone else, someone from his past."

"Louisa, you always jump to conclusions. Open Peter's letter, and let's hear what he has to say. The poor boy may be in some kind of trouble."

"Oh, Mother, you are right; perhaps he is in trouble," Louisa said as she tore open the envelope. "I wouldn't want anything to happen to him!" She cleared her throat and read aloud.

My dearest Louisa,

I am sorry about my hasty departure, but it was imperative I catch the afternoon train to Boston. A problem has arisen in my family, and I prefer not to go into detail at this time. I do not wish to burden you with my problems because I love you too much.

Please know that I think of you constantly and keep you in my prayers.

I'll try to keep in touch, although I'm not sure where I will be. I regret our wedding date must go on hold because I cannot give you any idea of when I will return. Postponing our wedding plans pains me very much. I trust you will understand.

I love you, my darling,
Peter

P.S. You may write to me at my cousin's address, and she will forward it to me if I have moved on. The address is on the envelope.

"Well, I don't understand!" Louisa said with a huff as she flung the letter onto her mother's lap. "How dare he speak of love to me!" She stormed across the room and settled in an overstuffed chair, smoothing out her pale blue calico gown and underskirts. "When you truly love someone, you don't keep secrets from them. You share everything! I can't see a life with anyone so mysterious about his wanderings as Peter. I might never know where he is or where he might go from one day to the next! What kind of a life would that be? As far as I'm concerned, it would be no life at all!"

"Really, Louisa, aren't you being a little melodramatic about this?"

"Oh, Mother, you always seem to be on Peter's side about everything. What about me? What about your daughter's feelings? Don't you even care?"

"Of course I do, dear, but you tend to get so carried away. And you're only thinking about yourself. Isn't that rather selfish? What about Peter's feelings? Will you answer his letter as he asked?"

Louisa snorted, jumped up, and grabbed Peter's letter from her mother's lap. "Yes, I'll answer it! I can't wait to write him! And I'll tell him a thing or two while I'm at it. Peter McClough is going to get a newsy letter about a new friend I have, Roger Evans. I'll tell him about a perfect gentleman who doesn't keep a lady waiting or wander around the country on mysterious trips! We'll see how Peter feels about that!" Louisa started toward the stairway with Peter's letter crunched in her hand.

"Wait!" Elizabeth Bradford called. "What about Emily's letter? Aren't you planning to read it to me? I'd like to hear all the news, Louisa."

"I'll read it at the dinner table, Mother, when Father is with us. He'll want to hear the news from Pennsylvania also. Right now I want to organize my thoughts and get a letter written to Peter. Maybe I'll be a little mysterious, too."

"I think it's best if you cool down some before you write to Peter. You may say something you will regret. We can't retrieve unkind words after they are said, or written. Bide your time for a few days. Maybe you'll feel differently by then."

Louisa walked slowly back into the parlor. "I won't feel any differently, Mother. But you're right. I needn't rush like a house on fire. My letter to Peter can wait. I'll be more objective if I give my letter a little more thought."

Elizabeth Bradford glanced through her mail and laid it aside. "Your father will be home early tonight. He seemed a bit nervous about something last evening and didn't sleep well. When I asked him about it this morning, he brushed it aside and said it was nothing. After all these years, I know your father pretty well. I can tell when something is bothering him. I hope it's nothing serious."

"What could it be, Mother?" Louisa asked, a frown knitting her brow. "He isn't ill, is he? He seemed so well and happy when we were in Augusta."

"He was indeed. . .very carefree and lighthearted. It did him good to get away for a week. He and his brother, Phil, have a lot in common. Your father made the trip for your sake, but it was good therapy for him also. He gets so wound up in his work at the bank."

"But Roger works for him now and takes over much of the responsibility, Mother. I've talked to Roger on several occasions at the bank. He tells me how many contracts he handles in order to make Father's job easier. He's glad to be so helpful and doesn't know how Father got along without him."

Elizabeth Bradford's face broke into a smile at her daughter's enthusiastic words. "That sounds like Roger, all right. I'm sure he feels he is the best thing that happened to the First Bank of Waterville—or even the whole of Waterville for that matter."

"Well, it's true, Mother," Louisa insisted. "I'm sure Father appreciates all his time and input. Roger deserves a promotion and larger salary."

"Did he mention that to you by any chance?"

"Well, he did. . .sort of. . .very casually one afternoon at the bank. He can't get by on the salary he makes now. He'd like to buy a home and make plans for the future."

"Roger hasn't been with the bank long enough to warrant a promotion, Louisa."

"How long does it take? If someone is as industrious as Roger, they should be able to move up in the company."

"Your father worked for his father for many years before he took over the bank. Your grandpa handed him the top job when he decided to step down and take life a little easier. Your father will do the same someday."

"Who will that be, Mother? Roger, maybe?"

"Since we didn't have a son, your father doesn't have an heir to carry on at the bank. He will groom someone for the position. And yes, it may be Roger Evans. Or whomever you marry, Louisa. Your husband may be the one to carry on the Bradford tradition. His name will be different, but he will be family."

Louisa's lips curved into a big smile. "Roger Evans—president of the Bradford family bank someday. Won't that be grand?"

The front door slammed as Jack Bradford entered the parlor from the hallway. "What's so grand, Louisa?" he asked as he pulled off his overcoat, hat, and gloves. "It's certainly not the weather. There's a misty rain in the air."

Louisa gave her father a hug and took his coat from him. "It's grand that you are home, Father." She smiled impishly, rubbing her hands across his knitted brow. "I have a letter from Emily Harris in Pennsylvania. I've waited to read it to you and Mother at the dinner table."

"And a nice letter from Peter also," Elizabeth Bradford added.

"Good!" he replied and bent to kiss Elizabeth. "I'll wash up and join you in the dining room shortly."

Louisa shared Peter's letter with her father during the meal but saved Emily's letter until they finished the main course. "Emily is my sweet friend," Louisa announced, "so I'll read her letter while we eat dessert. I've told her all about my friend Roger Evans, and I'm anxious to read her reply." Louisa opened the pale pink envelope and smoothed the letter with her fingers.

Dear Louisa,

It is always exciting to get your letters and hear all the news from back home. I'm very surprised about your friendship with Roger Evans, especially since you and Peter are engaged. From what you say, Roger sounds very nice, handsome, thoughtful, and a real gentleman. But you and Peter are the perfect couple, so I'm thankful your relationship with Roger is strictly platonic. We know Peter loves you very much. His sudden departure with no explanation has us all confused. We can't imagine what problem drove him away. Letters from my folks, Cassie and Bill, and Fred and Sarah have added no light to the problem. Peter did not confide in them, left abruptly, and sent no word as to his whereabouts. He loves Ma's cooking and often stopped by whenever he could. And Peter and Fred are such close friends. It seems he would have shared his problem with Fred even if he couldn't share it with you. Well, whatever it is, someday the story will come out.

The new church building is coming along well, and we hope to be in by Christmas. Robert and the men work long hours, every spare minute they can. I'm working on a children's Christmas program, and the young-sters are enthusiastic about it. I've coaxed Jim Bishop's two children into having parts, and they are coming out of their shells. The interaction with other children is good for them. Mrs. Bishop offered to help in any way she could. She is still very shy, but I can include her in small ways. I think it is good for her to feel needed. She seems happier when she works with the children. We're praying the program will have an impact on Mr. Bishop if he will attend. Jim Bishop is extremely bullheaded, and Robert grieves about his backbiting. Jim's antagonistic ways tend to stir up discord among the brethren. Finally, Robert and his deacons visited Jim at his home and approached the subject. They reprimanded him, in a kind and Christian manner, regarding his accusations. Jim was insulted. He threatened and did pull his membership out of the church. This seems to be best for everyone concerned. Thankfully he has allowed his wife and children to continue to attend and be involved. Please pray for Jim Bishop. He professes to be a Christian, but his actions surely must grieve the Lord.

Our ladies' guild meets once a month to sew baby layettes and make quilts. Samuel's wife, Ellie, comes and also my aunt Sophie. We bring our lunch and have a good time of fellowship and prayer in one of the larger farm homes. About ten ladies and several little children who are not yet school age attend. I know I haven't been married long, but I am eager to have a baby. All my family write to me about my niece, Rebeccah, and nephew, Freddy. They tell me all the sweet things the little ones are doing. Someday I hope to have a precious little child of my own.

Let me know any news you hear about Peter. He is very dear to our family. You asked about Christmas. We won't get home for the holidays this year. I'll miss seeing you, my family, and the old homestead. Waterville is so beautiful at this time of year, but it is our first Christmas since our marriage. It will be special to be together as husband and wife here in Pennsylvania. The lovely rolling hills and valleys remind me of my family home in Maine. It is beautiful country, and you must visit us whenever you can.

Love, your friend always,
Emily

Chapter 11

Peter mounted Thunder and headed away from the plantation toward the iron gates at the roadway. The warm and muggy night air closed in upon him as dusk fused into darkness. A moon sliver offered little light, and he strained his eyes in the vespertine inkiness around him. As Peter turned Thunder toward town, he heard hoofbeats coming from behind. He gave Thunder his head and urged him into a gallop. The hoofbeats following them grew closer as Peter bent low over his charge and allowed the animal to do what he did best—run like the wind. When a shot rang out in the night, Peter felt a chill run up and down his spine.

"Someone wants to kill me," he muttered. "Why? I've done nothing!" Another shot rang out loud and clear, but Peter realized it was high above his head. Thunder shook his head, whinnied, and picked up his already rapid pace. "Steady, fella," Peter whispered as they raced faster and the other hoofbeats grew dimmer. "I reckon whoever it is just wants to scare us. I get the feeling they don't like Yankees in the South."

When Peter realized the renegade was no longer tailing him, he pulled Thunder to a slow trot. "No use getting all sweaty in this heat, fella. We both need to do a little cooling off." Peter eased into town and located a stable about a block off the main street. After rubbing down his magnificent animal, he paid the stable master for Thunder's feed and overnight lodging. Thunder nuzzled his master, and Peter stroked the fine animal before heading toward town. He found the small café he had seen earlier in the day and ordered a hearty meal. The place was nearly deserted due to the lateness of the hour. A few people eyed him suspiciously and whispered among themselves; but no one gave him any trouble, and he left the café fully satisfied by the tasty meal. The inn on the opposite corner was clean and comfortable, and he purchased a room for one night. It was a relief to get out of his dusty clothes, wash up, and stretch out on the bed.

"What do I do next?" he murmured lazily. "Thomas isn't at the plantation, and people here don't want me to ask questions about him or the Berringer place." Peter yawned and felt himself drifting off to sleep. The trip had taken its toll on the young man. "Being tailed tonight from the Berringer place was"—a yawn broke into his musings—"exciting. Tomorrow I'll think about what to do next—tomorrow when my head is a little clearer."

Peter finished his breakfast at the café the following morning and lingered over his second cup of strong coffee. As he eyed the other patrons, he concluded the Southern folk were not that much different from the Northerners. *We are all created in God's image with a free will to choose God and His Son. We live, we work, we dream, we fall in love. We have families who we care about. It's too bad the Civil War had to happen and cause some to have bad feelings toward others. God tells us in the Bible to love one another.*

An attractive young lady and an older woman entered the café at that moment. Peter realized it was the same young woman he spoke to in town the day before. Quickly he stood up and caught their attention. "Pardon me, miss. We met yesterday when I asked for some directions. Won't you and your companion join me at my table?"

Genevieve Markam whirled around and faced Peter. Her violet eyes opened wide at his suggestion. A slight gasp echoed from the curved lips. "You are a stranger, sir, and we do not care to share a table with you. Come, Mother!" She reached for the older woman's arm and pulled her toward the far side of the room.

"Who is that young man, Genevieve?" Mrs. Markam demanded loudly. "I've never seen him before. He's obviously a Yankee by his speech. Where did you meet him?"

Peter watched as the café patrons turned in their seats and eyed the ladies as they settled into chairs at a small table in the rear.

"Where did you meet him, Genevieve?" Mrs. Markam demanded again, more loudly than before. Peter rose and moved toward their table.

"I didn't meet him, Mother," Genevieve said softly in an attempt to soothe her mother. She patted her chestnut tresses peeking from beneath her bonnet. "He's a Northerner, and I saw him in town yesterday. He asked me for directions. That's all. I don't even know his name."

"I can remedy that." Peter smiled as he reached their table, his mug of coffee in one hand. "May I sit down?"

"No!" Genevieve shouted. "Leave us alone!"

"Genevieve, that is no way to treat a stranger in town," Mrs. Markam insisted. "Where is your Southern hospitality? Forgive my daughter's rudeness, sir. Perhaps I can help you with directions. I've lived in this area much longer than my daughter."

"Thank you, but I received directions from the ticket master yesterday. My name is Peter McClough, and I'm from Waterville, Maine."

"My, you are a long way off, young man. I'm Harriet Markam, and this is my daughter, Genevieve. Won't you join us?"

"Thank you, Mrs. Markam," Peter said as he took a seat beside Genevieve. "I'm just finishing my second cup of coffee before I leave. May I ask you for some information regarding the Berringer plantation?"

Mrs. Markam gasped and caught at her throat. Her face paled as she slumped in her seat. Genevieve jumped up from her chair and put her arm around her mother. She patted her face and pushed back stray strands of gray hair. "Mother!" she cried. "Are you all right?"

Peter, brow furrowed, fanned Mrs. Markam with his hat and patted her hand. Genevieve pushed him away and cried, "Now look what you've done!"

"I'm so sorry," Peter cried. "Did I say something wrong?"

Mrs. Markam moaned, sat upright, and glared at Peter. "Young man," she said slowly, "why are you interested in the Berringer plantation? And what business is it of yours. . .a Northerner?"

Peter pushed back a shock of dark hair and let his fingers run through it. Should he tell these people his business? How else could he find out more about Thomas? Would it be hurtful to Thomas to confess that he was his brother? He hesitated, at a loss for words. Finally, with a prayer in his heart, he spoke slowly and softly. "I realize you are disturbed by my mention of the Berringer plantation, Mrs. Markam, just as Genevieve was yesterday. I am sorry. Thomas Hayes, the foster son of the Berringers', is my half brother. I came south to see if I could find him. We have never met. I only learned a short time ago that I had a brother. We fought on different sides during the war, but thankfully I did not know it."

Mrs. Markam looked at Peter through teary eyes. "Did you know, Mr. McClough, your brother killed a man at his plantation?"

Peter lowered his eyes. "I heard about it through a distant cousin of mine, Mrs. Markam. It was very sad news. But do you know the reason, the circumstances under which he committed this crime?"

"There is never a justifiable reason to kill someone, Mr. McClough," Mrs. Markham said, dabbing at her eyes with her handkerchief.

"Do you know my brother well?" Peter asked. "If so, you would be a better judge of his character than I."

Genevieve Markam held out her left hand and displayed a diamond on the third finger. "I know Thomas better than anyone else," she said with difficulty. "We are engaged to be married."

Peter's face constricted in pain. "This must be very hard for you, Genevieve. I wish I could make it easier. My cousin Annabelle, who lives near Boston, raised Thomas until he was ten years old. At that time he became a ward of the Berringer family. Annabelle and I are very concerned about him. I would give anything to find my brother and get his crime resolved."

"It's impossible!" Mrs. Markam cried. "He has to pay for his crime."

"Mother, don't excite yourself. You know what the doctor said."

"I know! I know! My heart could give out at any time. Well, I won't be satisfied until I see that young man pay with his life. He needs to hang for his crime."

"But why, Mrs. Markam? Why are you so bitter?" Peter asked. "The man my brother killed was one of a group of men who killed four persons, for no reason, on the Berringer plantation. They were Thomas's dear friends. Thomas reacted hastily out of anger, which was wrong. But I must find him as soon as possible. Due to the circumstances surrounding the crime, the law might be lenient if he turns himself in."

"He already did, Mr. McClough. Thomas came back to Nashville a few weeks ago and turned himself in. They are deliberating now what punishment he must endure," Genevieve said sadly. "We have a new sheriff since the incident happened. Perhaps you can talk to him on your brother's behalf."

"What are you saying, Genevieve?" Mrs. Markam cried, her face aghast. "Do you want Thomas to be acquitted of his crime? How could you?"

"I love him, Mother, and always will."

"Rubbish! Take that ring off your finger at once! My daughter will not marry a criminal!"

"I know it's a serious crime, Mrs. Markam, but God teaches us from the Bible about forgiveness. Jesus forgave all sinners—thieves, murderers, and tax collectors. Can't we do the same? The man Thomas killed was himself a murderer. He killed four of Thomas's friends. Put yourself in his place. Can't you forgive him for his crime?"

"Never!" Mrs. Markam ranted as the café patrons looked on. "I will never forgive him! Thomas Hayes killed Clay Prescott, my only brother, in cold blood!"

Peter sat spellbound, his mouth gaping, as one in shock. He let out a deep sigh and asked softly, "The man Thomas killed was your brother, Genevieve's uncle?"

Mrs. Markam cried softly into her handkerchief. "My only brother! He's been an anchor to me since my husband's death four years ago. Dear Clay was the only stability we had in our lives." Mrs. Markam blew her nose and struggled to continue. "Genevieve and I are completely alone in this world now. My son, Adam, died of battle wounds early in the war. It broke my husband's heart. He grieved for Adam until his death of consumption."

"I can't tell you how sorry I am," Peter said sincerely. "Is there anything I can do for you?"

"We'll manage, Mr. McClough," Genevieve said, "but thank you for your offer of help. Mother worries about losing our home. Our slaves left long ago, right after the war. My uncle Clay hired men to plant the fields, and Mother and I managed fine under his care. He had no family, so he moved into our home and took over where Father left off. We had no idea Uncle was a member of a secret terrorist organization. It gives me chills to think about the destruction and chaos this society causes. Mother and I need to beg Thomas's pardon for Uncle Clay's part in the deaths of his friends. We want no part of this organization."

"It is hard to understand the reasoning behind such a movement," Peter said. "And I'm certain most Southerners are not agreeable to their practices."

"If it is any comfort," Genevieve offered, "we found a handwritten note of my uncle's after his death. It must have been written right before the attack at the Berringer plantation. His exact words were, 'I am sick of this organization and its evil destruction. I will tell the men tonight that I want out. This will be my last escapade. Forgive me, God, for all the killing and havoc we have caused.' Finding this note was a great comfort to Mother and me. We believe my uncle misjudged the organization when he became involved. When he finally realized it before his death, he desired to leave the Klan."

"His note must be a great comfort to you both. I wish your uncle had retired before the escapade at the Berringer place, but we can't change the situation. I must talk to the sheriff about Thomas's crime. Perhaps he will listen. Good-bye, ladies. I'm sorry we met under such sad circumstances." Peter drank the balance of his coffee, which was already cold, stood to his feet, grabbed his hat, and left the café.

He went by the stable and paid for another day's lodging for his horse. His feet dragged as he headed toward the jailhouse located a few blocks away. Could he attempt to justify Thomas's crime? And how would Thomas react to a brother he had never seen? Was it a mistake for him, a Yankee, to come to this place and try to get his brother exonerated? The sheriff might throw him out—or worse yet, put him in jail. These thoughts permeated his mind until beads of sweat stood out on his forehead. He was unused to Tennessee's warm, muggy fall weather. As he hesitated before the jailhouse, Peter pulled his bandanna from his pocket and wiped the moisture from his brow and face.

Mustering all his courage, he pulled on the heavy wooden door of the jail-house and entered a small room. A medium-built man about forty years old sat at a desk just inside the door. He looked up as the door creaked to a close. "What can I do for you, stranger?" he asked cheerfully. "Are you new in town?"

"Yes, sir. I arrived yesterday," Peter replied, knowing his Yankee dialect would give him away. "I would like to have a word with you."

The sheriff folded the paper he had been reading, shoved back his chair, extended his hand, and smiled broadly. "Have our citizens been bothering you, or are you in some kind of trouble? I'll be glad to help in whatever way I can. Pull up a chair and sit down."

Peter grabbed a wooden chair from the corner and moved it closer to the sheriff's desk. "I have an unusual request, Sheriff. I understand Thomas Hayes is confined here because he killed a man on his estate, the Berringer plantation."

"That's right," the sheriff drawled. "Is he wanted for a crime somewhere else? Is that why you came?"

"Nothing like that," Peter said quickly. "I am Peter McClough, Thomas Hayes's half brother, from Waterville, Maine. I have an older cousin in Boston who informed me of the circumstances of the crime. It appears to us Thomas had every right to fire at the terrorist society band for killing his friend and his friend's family."

The sheriff eyed Peter keenly. "It is a sad situation, Mr. McClough. What happened at the Berringer plantation was a terrible atrocity. I have only been sheriff a little over a week. Your brother was already incarcerated when I replaced the former sheriff. Since my arrival, I have cracked down on this secret society. Notices have gone out over the county that I will not tolerate any terrorist actions. Any caught involved in such action will be punished severely."

"That's good to hear, Sheriff," Peter said. "But what about my brother? Must he pay for his crime under the unusual circumstances?"

"The killing of another human being is wrong, Mr. McClough, regardless of the situation. No one should take the law into his own hands. Justice must prevail."

"But, Sheriff," Peter blurted, "what will you do to him? Will my brother hang for his crime?"

The sheriff eyed the distraught young man before him. "No decision has been settled as yet, Mr. McClough. We are thoroughly investigating the death of the man killed. His niece brought in a note he wrote the night he died. . .before leaving for the Berringer plantation. It is evident he planned to leave the Klan that very night and informed them of his decision. I have some recent information that may put light on the subject, but I am not at liberty to discuss it."

Peter frowned. "It doesn't look good for my brother, does it, Sheriff? Could—could I see him for a few minutes? We've never met, and I think it's about time we do."

The sheriff pushed back his chair and stood up. "Of course you can see him. Take as long as you like. A visit from his brother will cheer Thomas up. We've had some fine chats, he and I. I like your brother, Mr. McClough. I like him a lot!"

Peter's face relaxed into a slight grin. "Thanks, Sheriff. And call me Peter, won't you? It seems friendlier somehow."

Peter followed the sheriff down a short passageway to a set of cells. Behind the first one sat a young man, head in his hands. He looked up as the sheriff and Peter approached, and Peter noticed the shock of dark hair, so like his own. Dark, sad eyes stared blankly from the man's unshaven face. The man blinked his eyes several times and pushed his dark hair back from his forehead. His eyes seemed sunken in the pale face, which registered despair. "Someone to see me, Sheriff?" he asked. "I hope it's not a lot of questions again about the shooting. That night stands out so vivid in my mind. I dread recalling it one more time."

"No, Thomas, no questions this time. You have a special visitor. He's come a long way to see you."

"Hello, Thomas," Peter said with emotion. "I'm your brother, Peter McClough. Annabelle told me all about you."

Thomas rushed over to the bars and stuck his hand through, which Peter clasped in his own. "And Annabelle told me all about you, Peter. I left Annabelle's place several weeks ago because I didn't want to get either of you involved. But

I'm glad you came. Thanks, brother." His eyes gathered moisture as he spoke.

The sheriff pulled out a key and opened the cell door. "Come out and visit with your brother for a while, Thomas. We'll put a couple chairs in the hallway so you'll be more comfortable. You two must have a lot to talk about."

"Aren't you afraid I'll make a break for it, Sheriff?" Thomas asked, his lips curled in a smile.

"My instincts tell me you won't try anything, Thomas. From all the talks we've had together, I think I know you fairly well. After all, you did return a few weeks ago on your own and turn yourself in."

"Maybe my brother came down here to help me escape. Did you consider that possibility? The two of us could overpower you easily," Thomas joked.

"Sure you could. But I don't think you will. I'm a pretty good judge of character. Now you fellows enjoy your visit together while I go back to my paperwork." The sheriff grinned. "And let me know when you want back into your cell."

Peter looked long and hard at his brother. Although their coloring was the same, Thomas was taller and a little thinner. There was no mistake about the resemblance, especially through the dark eyes and shock of unruly hair. They stared at each other for several moments without saying a word. Then Peter, his eyes moist with tears, threw his arms around Thomas's shoulders. The pair stood quietly for a time, too moved to speak.

An hour later they had covered every detail of one another's lives. Each had heard much of it from Annabelle but savored the stories firsthand. Peter assured his brother he would stay in Nashville until the situation was resolved. "I'll get the best lawyer I can find and get you out of here somehow!"

"Move out of the inn this afternoon and into my place," Thomas insisted. "The sheriff has the key to my plantation in the front office. Pick up your horse from the stable and mine also. I left my bay mare at the stable several weeks ago when I turned myself in. She's a beauty with white patches on her face. I call her Powder. The sheriff keeps tabs on her for me. He says she's still there—doing okay. The stable bill might be high, but I'll pay you back when and if I get out of here. If they hang me. . ." His voice drifted off, and he swallowed hard. "Anyway, if something happens to me, sell the plantation and all the furniture. I want you, Genevieve, and Annabelle to share the money."

Thomas talked about Genevieve, his betrothed, and about his great love for her. "Even if I could get out of this situation, it's all over for us, Peter. I killed her uncle, and she'll never forgive me."

"Don't be so sure of that," Peter said as he explained his earlier meeting with Genevieve and her mother at the café. "She is a lovely young woman, Thomas. And she declared emphatically, in the presence of her mother, that she still loves you."

Thomas jumped up and walked back and forth, his hands folded as if in prayer. "Could it be possible? Dare I hope that it is so?"

Just then they heard the jailhouse door open and a feminine voice speak. "Hello, Sheriff. I've come to see Thomas. I know his brother is here, but could I speak with him a few moments?" It was Genevieve's voice, and Thomas looked dazed. He started toward the office with Peter close behind him. They heard the sheriff speak.

"Of course, Miss Markam. I'm certain he would like to see you. Thomas speaks of you often. I understand the two of you are engaged to be married."

"Yes," she said softly. "I hope we can still carry out our plans."

Thomas rounded the corner at that moment and rushed toward his sweetheart. "Genny! I didn't think you would come after what happened to your uncle. I've longed to see you. . .to hear your voice."

Genevieve Markam walked boldly into Thomas's arms, and he pulled her close. His head bent over the chestnut curls as they rested against his shoulder.

"I didn't think there was any hope for us," he murmured huskily. "I'm sorry about your uncle." Then, recovering his composure, he introduced Genevieve to Peter. "But you already met my brother." He laughed. "Isn't it wonderful? Peter came all the way down to Tennessee to help me out of this mess. He thinks I should be exonerated because of the circumstances, but. . . ." His voice trailed off to a whisper. "I am still guilty, Genny. I was so upset about Ben's death, I shot and killed a man, a man who turned out to be your uncle Clay."

Genny put her fingers against Thomas's lips as if to quiet him. "Don't speak of it, Thomas. It was a tragic thing. My mother and I regret what also happened to Ben and his family. We never knew my uncle was involved in such a terroristic society. He planned to leave the Klan after that last evening. We found a note saying he was sick of their activities and wanted out. I gave the note to the sheriff a few days ago. He thinks it might have some bearing on the case."

"I didn't tell you, Thomas, because I didn't want to get your hopes up," the sheriff said. "Any information I can gather may help. But it's time to take you back to your cell. If the wrong person came in and found you in the front office, he'd be on my neck. Peter and Miss Markam can visit you in the back."

"I can't stay," Genevieve said. "Mother is so upset about this situation. I left her at home for a few minutes. She thinks I'm posting a letter and mustn't know about this visit. I need to get back to her. She's edgy these days and needs extra care."

The pair embraced, and Thomas kissed her lightly on the cheek. "Good-bye, my darling," he whispered. "I can face anything as long as I know you are on my side. Pray for me."

"Of course, dear Thomas," she whispered breathlessly as Peter and the sheriff turned away and tried not to listen. "I pray for you every day. I will visit you again tomorrow and the next day and the next. Until they let you out of this terrible place!" Turning to go, she asked, "Is there any hope, Sheriff? Dare I hope that someday Thomas will be free?"

"There is always hope, Miss Markam. I am investigating this case thoroughly. As I told Peter McClough earlier, I may have some further information soon, something I cannot disclose at present. Yes, Miss Markam, I assure you, there is always hope!"

Chapter 12

"Fantastic!" Louisa exclaimed as she waved her letter and whirled around the Bradford parlor. "Clara and Sam Burns are getting married over Thanksgiving weekend, Mother. She wants me to stand up with her. Our family is invited for Thanksgiving dinner, and the wedding is on the following Saturday afternoon. Of course we'll go, won't we?"

Elizabeth Bradford laid her handwork carefully on the cushion beside her. "I'm sure your father will want to go, dear. This is an important occasion. He will want to see his only niece getting married. I'll make a note of the date so we can plan on it."

Later, when Jack Bradford returned from his bank, Louisa greeted him and shared the news. "We must go, Father. Clara and her parents are our only living relatives. This is an important wedding for the Bradford families."

Elizabeth Bradford entered from the dining room. "Louisa is excited about the wedding, dear," she said, giving her husband a peck on the cheek. "I must confess I am also. I'm sure we are all thankful Clara gave up grieving over her lost love and reentered the real world. Sam Burns is a fine young man."

"Oh yes, Father," Louisa said. "Sam is quite the catch really. I found him a genuine and kind person. Clara and Sam will be very happy together."

Jack Bradford cleared his throat. "Ahem! Yes, yes, I agree. But most important of all, Sam is a fine, dedicated Christian. I talked with him after church at some length, and he appeared to have a heart for the Lord. That's more than I can say for Roger Evans. You talk to him a lot at the bank, Louisa. Why haven't we seen him in church lately?"

"Roger is busy, Father. He does so much extra work for you at the bank. I'm afraid you pile many extra duties on him that keep him after hours. Sundays he needs his rest. He reminds me how hard he works to keep the bank in good running order."

"Rubbish!" Jack Bradford exclaimed. "He has the same hours the rest of the employees do. I admit he's a hard worker. He spends a lot of time in the back room and goes over the files constantly, but it's his choice. I've reminded him it isn't necessary. I'll have an auditor come in before the Christmas holiday."

"Is anything wrong, Jack?" Elizabeth asked. "I thought the auditor didn't come until spring."

"No. . .no. . .of course not. Nothing is wrong. I merely decided to have an audit made earlier this time. I want to make sure all the accounts are in order before the first of the year."

"Well, dear, I have one of your favorite meals tonight. A beef roast with potatoes, onions, and carrots. And homemade bread."

"And fresh apple pie, Mother," Louisa added. "Don't forget Father's favorite pie."

Jack Bradford chuckled as he surveyed his wife and daughter. "It sounds like a feast fit for a king. I'm a little suspicious of my two girls, though. Is this special dinner a bribe to make sure I'll take you to Clara's wedding in Augusta? If so, you needn't have bothered. I wouldn't miss the wedding of my brother's only child. We Bradfords must stick together!"

⁓

When Louisa visited her father's bank later that week, Roger Evans asked her to attend another dinner and concert for a little outing together—as friends. Louisa, pleased at his offer, accepted—her face aglow with color. Her social life had been curtailed with Peter away, and she missed concerts and dinners out. Surely, she reasoned, it wouldn't be wrong to attend a casual dinner and concert with one of her father's employees. Their friendship had grown and blossomed through her many visits to the bank, and she accepted his invitation graciously. Although her parents seemed to disapprove, Louisa looked forward to the outing. She had received another letter from Peter that said he was in Tennessee. He still did not disclose any information about his mysterious trip. Upset and frustrated, Louisa penned a hasty letter in care of his cousin, Annabelle Hayes.

> *Dear Peter,*
>
> *I'm sorry to be so long in writing to you. I don't understand why you cannot confide in me about the mystery of your trip, especially since we are engaged. I thought when two people were in love, they would share everything with one another. I must tell you that I refuse to endure such secrecy.*
>
> *I also need to be honest with you and inform you I am seeing someone else. It is only a friendship, for now. His name is Roger Evans, and he works for my father at his bank. He is a fine young man who seems to care a great deal about me. It is nice to have someone take me to dinner and concerts. I don't know what the future holds, since I am seeing more and more of Roger Evans. Frankly, Peter, your brief letters are not enough.*
>
> *Sincerely,*
> *Louisa*

On the way to the restaurant, Louisa told Roger about her cousin Clara's upcoming wedding and how delighted her family was. She explained that she would stand up for Clara as her maid of honor.

"How nice," Roger said as the horses clip-clopped along the roadway. "And when will this wedding take place?"

"The Saturday after Thanksgiving. We'll leave by train on Wednesday and be there for Thanksgiving. Then we'll travel home on Sunday after church, so Father won't miss too many days at the bank."

Roger laughed. "Your father needn't be concerned about his bank. I'll be here, and I'll take charge! Jack Bradford can count on me to keep everything under control."

"I know you will, Roger. Father depends on you because you are devoted to your job. He mentioned how much time you spend reviewing the files." Louisa sighed. "I don't know what Father would do without you. But don't worry. Your workload will be easier after Christmas."

"Why is that?" Roger demanded as he reined in the team and brought the horses to a halt. They had arrived at the restaurant, and Roger climbed down to secure the team to the hitching post. Lanterns lit a pathway and illuminated the cozy eating establishment. As he reached to lift Louisa down, he asked once again, "Why will my workload be easier? Does your father plan to hire another assistant?"

"Mercy, no!" Louisa exclaimed. "He mentioned bringing the auditor in early because he wants to make sure all accounts are in order by the first of the year."

"But—but, Louisa," Roger faltered. His usually handsome face knit into a frown and looked agitated. "Why is your father changing the time schedule all of a sudden? I thought the auditor didn't come until spring."

Louisa's merry little laugh rang out clear as a bell. "Mother asked the same thing. Isn't that strange? But Father decided to have it done in December this year."

Roger, his lips pursed tightly together, steered Louisa almost roughly into the restaurant, and the waitress settled them at a small table near the back. He plunked himself down in his chair and stared at Louisa long and hard. "I don't like it, Louisa! I don't like it at all."

"What don't you like, Roger? The atmosphere here is lovely."

"No!" Roger snapped, rather loudly. Louisa, startled, looked at him wide-eyed, embarrassed as people near them turned in their seats. Roger lowered his voice and whispered harshly, "I mean about the auditor coming early. There is no reason for it. No reason at all."

Louisa reached over and patted his hand. "Don't fret about it, Roger. It isn't important. It has nothing to do with you."

"Of course not!" Roger's face relaxed in a slight smile, and his lips curled over his teeth. "It doesn't mean a thing."

Roger, quieter than usual, chewed his food thoughtfully. Louisa enjoyed each morsel and oohed and aahed over the tempting dessert. She tried to keep the atmosphere light and gay. It was unusual to see Roger in such a serious mood, so she shared humorous bits of news gleaned from letters sent by her friend Emily in Pennsylvania. Roger's occasional halfhearted response displayed a lack of attention. She could not understand his mood change but decided he suffered from overwork. His mood at the concert remained the same, and the ride home seemed dreary and uninteresting. Roger sat rigid, deep in thought. Usually a good conversationalist who kept her laughing until her sides ached, he was no longer a fun-loving companion. His tales of past escapades and jokes seemed forgotten. Louisa glanced sideways at his set mouth and knitted brow. What had happened to change his temperament?

Louisa sighed audibly. "Bother! I don't know what's troubling you, Roger, but you are out of sorts about something. Did I do or say the wrong thing this evening? If so, tell me, and perhaps I can correct it."

"No! No! It's nothing you did or said! I'm fine, just fine. My mind is on other things, that's all. Nothing of interest to you."

"I'm going to tell Father you are simply overworked and can't even enjoy an evening out with me. He mustn't heap bunches of accounts on you anymore. After all, you are only human. One man can do only so much!"

Roger feigned a little smile. "Don't worry your pretty little head about my problems, Louisa. And don't nag your father about overworking me. I only do what I have to do. Let's forget this conversation, shall we? Now then, shall we take a ride along the river tonight?" Roger pulled a blanket from under the seat and handed it to Louisa. "Wrap yourself in this. It will keep you toasty warm in the night air."

A little shiver escaped Louisa's lips as she took the gray blanket and wrapped it around her shoulders. She was glad she had worn a heavy wool skirt and warm boots. Her legs and feet were warm enough, but the chill reached deep into her back and shoulders. "This feels much better, Roger. There's a full moon, and I love to see the moonbeams dance on the river. We'll have snow before long, and it won't be as pleasant as it is tonight."

The ride by the river left Louisa breathless. A bright moon cast deep shadows from the buildings across the way. Fishing boats tied to the wharf bobbed up and down in the soft breeze. Some couples, bundled warmly, walked arm in arm along the riverfront or sat on benches. Louisa shivered from the cold, and Roger reached over and put an arm around her shoulders, drawing her to him. Louisa felt the warmth of his body next to hers and leaned against his shoulder. She felt warm and serene.

"Let's elope, Louisa!" Roger said impulsively. "I'll take you home so you can pack a bag. We'll leave tonight and go wherever you want. Just name the place!"

Louisa gasped and pushed Roger away. "What are you saying? We're only good friends, remember? I'm still engaged to Peter McClough! Where did you come up with such a ridiculous idea? And anyway, I want to have a church wedding. . .with family and friends in attendance."

"Peter's gone. Who knows where he is or when he will return, and you're beginning not to care anymore. Admit it, Louisa! You don't care if Peter comes back. And you care for me a whole lot more than you let on. I can see it in your eyes. All the time you've spent at the bank lately. . .just talking to me, laughing with me. You gave me hope. I thought sure, in time, you would break your engagement. Why did you encourage me?"

Louisa looked down at her gloved hands and wrung them together. A frown knitted her brow. "I—I do like you, Roger, very much, and I enjoy being with you. It was wrong of me to encourage you, especially since I'm wearing Peter's ring. I've told him about you, about our friendship in a letter, and I may break off the engagement in the near future. He's not being fair to me."

"Peter's gone, Louisa! I'm here!" Roger said brashly. "I want to elope with you tonight!"

"Take me home, Roger, right now!" Louisa drew the blanket closer around her shoulders. "I don't want to hear any more of this nonsense about eloping. It's out of the question!"

Roger Evans scowled. "I guess you are just a child after all! If you were a real woman, you would forget Peter and elope with me tonight! Well," he said as he snapped the reins over the team's flanks, "perhaps it is better this way!"

The ride to the Bradford home seemed longer than usual. Louisa noticed Roger's irate spirit and tried to carry on a conversation. He looked straight ahead and rejected her every effort to lighten the atmosphere. Grim-faced and brow furrowed, Roger sat in silence during the ride to her home. He brought the team to a halt in front of the large brownstone, glanced at Louisa, and nodded. He made no effort to help her down from the carriage. She removed the blanket from around her shoulders, folded it neatly, and climbed down by herself.

"Thank you for the lovely dinner and concert, Roger," she said softly. "I hope you feel better in the morning." He nodded his head, grunted some unintelligible words, and pulled away in a fury.

Chapter 13

Peter McClough whistled a familiar tune as he brushed down Powder and Thunder. The horses seemed to enjoy one another's company and the freedom to roam the large pastures during the day. He had cleaned their stalls and loaded in hay and water for the animals. It had been several weeks since he settled into the Berringer plantation, his brother, Thomas's, home. Peter felt almost lost in the huge estate. His own home in Waterville was large and somewhat elegant, but it did not compare with this. Thomas's beautiful antebellum home, nestled in a grove of trees, boasted a wide veranda across the front. Floors covered with wide-plank pinewood and expensive carpets met his eyes, while fine paintings and tapestries graced the walls. A brilliant mahogany spiral staircase led to the upstairs, which featured a number of bedrooms and dressing rooms. All were expensively furnished with luscious fabrics surrounding the tall four-poster and canopied beds. Peter spent time studying the family portraits lining the walls and the staircase. This estate would accommodate a wealthy Southern family with servants in the finest style.

After completing his tour of the house, Peter finally settled his belongings in the smallest upstairs bedroom available. It had a single canopy bed, dresser, commode, and washstand on the far wall. Pale yellow curtains dressed the windows and canopy enclosure, with matching pillows and coverlet on the bed. Peter appreciated the coziness of the smaller room and the family pictures that lined one wall. When he studied them, he found some contained pictures of Thomas at various ages of his life. Sometimes he lit the small fireplace on the far wall to ward off the chill. The days were still warm in Tennessee, but some nights became nippy as the temperatures dropped. And Peter enjoyed laying the logs, plenty of which were available on the property. Then he would sit in the old wicker rocker and gaze deeply into the crackling fire—his mind filled with thoughts of his dear Louisa. During these times he crowded out the despair of having a brother in jail, one he had just come to know, one who might be hung on the gallows for murder.

He had hired a lawyer for the case who seemed understanding and trustworthy, but as yet the lawyer had turned up no new evidence. Each day Peter rode into town, consulted with the lawyer, and visited his brother for several hours. He alternated riding Powder and Thunder in order to give each of the animals some exercise. Peter never mentioned the incident of his first evening to Thomas about the renegade who fired at him when he left the plantation. There seemed to be no reason to do so as there had been no mishap since.

Peter had written letters to Annabelle and Louisa and posted them earlier. He tried to give Annabelle hope, although he had no concrete evidence as to how the case would be settled. He assured her a lawyer was handling the case, and Thomas was well and safe in the county jail. In closing he said, "Thomas sends his love, Annabelle, and so do I."

⁓

Louisa wondered about Roger's change of character. She tried mentally to sort out her feelings for the man. She had to admit an attraction for Roger, but his moody character the other evening upset her. How could he be kind and attentive one moment and angry the next? If he cared about her in a proper way, wouldn't her desires matter to him? He had boldly suggested they elope, so he must care for her a great deal. But he only seemed concerned with himself, what he wanted, and not her desires. Her parents had warned her about his lack of interest in spiritual things, but she refused to listen. She had been caught up in his attentiveness at a time when she felt neglected and unloved by Peter. She realized Roger had fulfilled the selfish desires of her own heart by showering attention on her. The dinners and concerts filled a void and restored her spirit.

And what about Peter? His letters confirmed he loved her and missed her, but she felt letters were not enough to prove his love. What a foolish goose she had been! She had written him a letter and told him about Roger Evans. The letter intimated that Roger cared for her, and of course Peter would assume the feeling was mutual. What had she said exactly, and what would Peter think of her now? Would he think she was fickle and childish? She supposed she was, to a point. Could he forgive her foolishness and still love her? And was Peter the one she wanted—or Roger? These thoughts filled her mind constantly.

Louisa's skirts swished about her as she entered the parlor where her mother worked on her daughter's ice blue gown for her cousin's wedding. Elizabeth Bradford looked up from her handwork as her daughter settled herself across the room. "How was your evening with Roger, Louisa?" she asked. "Are you becoming serious about that young man? What about your relationship with Peter?"

"Roger and I are very good friends, Mother," Louisa said as she picked up her handwork. "He cares about me, and I enjoy our times together. Peter doesn't seem to care if I'm lonely. He never hints at when he'll return. I guess he expects me to enjoy a dull life. . .and be content with my embroidery. I'm not!"

"You are an adult, Louisa, and will make your own choices. But Roger doesn't seem interested in God or spiritual things. I truly believe he cannot be a Christian although he claims to be one. And the Bible cautions us not to be unequally yoked with an unbeliever."

"Mother! The Bible says we are not to judge one another!"

"I know, dear, but it also says in Matthew 7:20, 'By their fruits ye shall know them.' And we haven't seen any fruit in Roger Evans's life, have we?"

"Well, usually he's kind and attentive and thoughtful. Isn't being kind a fruit of the spirit? If it weren't for Roger, I'd be living a pretty colorless life."

"I know waiting for Peter to return is hard, dear. But I trust you will pray about any decisions you make. Marriage is a serious matter."

There was that word again: "serious." It unnerved Louisa. "Oh, fiddle!" she exclaimed. "I guess I'm a fickle person, Mother! I'm sure that's what you and Father must think. And maybe I am fickle. I cared—" She hesitated. "I loved. . . Peter at one time. But he's gone, and now I'm not sure about my feelings. Roger is here. I—I'm confused. I don't know who I care about anymore!"

During the following week, Elizabeth sewed furiously on the blue frock of satin and lace so it would be finished in time for Clara's wedding the Saturday after Thanksgiving. Louisa saw Roger briefly at the bank several times before her family's departure for Augusta. Each time he seemed his old self again, and she felt warm and happy during their talks. Why did he have to be so charming at times? His amusing ways tugged at her heart.

The Jack and Phillip Bradford families enjoyed a joyful and blessed Thanksgiving together in Augusta. Elizabeth Bradford helped her sister-in-law with the food preparations while Louisa and Clara set the table in a festive manner. Much to Clara's delight, Sam Burns, her prospective bridegroom, joined the two families at their Thanksgiving feast. Phillip Bradford prayed over the food and thanked God for all His benefits. "Truly we are a blessed people," he said in conclusion, "and You are a great and mighty God."

The afternoon went quickly as they talked about the upcoming wedding. When they sang around the piano, Clara and Louisa took turns playing the accompaniment. Their voices rang out with the wonderful hymns of the faith. Louisa tried her best to be lighthearted and had completely fooled everyone except Clara.

Later that evening, after Sam left and the family retired, Clara faced her cousin and countered, "Something is wrong, Louisa. You wrote so gaily about your new friend, Roger Evans. What has happened to your love for Peter? Do you plan to break your engagement?"

Louisa's face clouded as she turned toward her cousin. "I've been a silly goose, Clara. Roger seemed so attentive and thoughtful I've allowed myself to become involved. It's because I've been so lonely without Peter! I wondered if Roger might be the right one for me."

"What happened, dear cousin?" Clara asked.

"I must have encouraged Roger more than I realized, because he asked me to elope with him. He insisted I pack a bag so we could leave immediately."

"Elope!" Clara gasped. "Why would he expect you to elope? Of course you want a church wedding with family and friends. Weddings are important to women."

"Not to Roger. He said a church wedding is ridiculous. When I told him an elopement was out of the question, he got angry."

"Well, I declare! Mr. Roger Evans seems uncaring about your feelings in the matter. I always thought the bride planned the wedding. Anyway, you plan to marry Peter, not Roger."

Louisa shook her head. "I told Peter in a letter I was seeing Roger and that he cared about me. I intimated that I enjoyed our outings. . .and wasn't sure what might happen in the future. What will he think of me now, Clara?"

The Sam Burns, Clara Bradford wedding was a beautiful occasion. The church was filled to capacity with family and friends who witnessed the touching ceremony. Louisa walked down the aisle in her ice-blue frock followed by Clara on the arm of her father. Clara's gown, white satin trimmed with lace, boasted a fitted bodice. A crown of net and lace flowed out behind her from her golden head, and a smile touched her mouth as she looked toward her bridegroom. Sam stood sedately at the altar with the pastor and his one attendant. His eyes, glued upon his bride, reflected love and tenderness. Louisa, misty-eyed but composed, sang two appropriate songs chosen by the couple. Her lyric soprano voice rang out pure and sweet over the hushed audience.

When Louisa returned to her position next to Clara, she felt a sense of joy as she surveyed the couple. There was no question about Clara and Sam's love for one another. For herself, Louisa felt unfulfilled. She longed to be a bride. Would she ever know the true joy of sharing her life with someone she loved? Or had she, by her foolish, fickle nature, ruined her one chance for happiness?

Peter reflected on the days, which passed so quickly. Thanksgiving had come and gone and still no concrete news concerning his brother's crime. Several times, on visits to his brother, Genevieve Markam would be there also. He realized more and more that she was a remarkable and devoted young woman. Sometimes Genny brought food for both him and his brother. The Thanksgiving meal was especially delicious, and the three of them had a time of fellowship and prayer together. Peter made it a habit to stay only a short time after Genny arrived so the couple could be alone. He knew he would want privacy with his sweetheart if he were in Thomas's circumstances.

The week after Thanksgiving Peter received a letter from Annabelle. She wrote regularly, but this time she had enclosed a letter from Louisa. Peter's heart pounded within his chest when he saw her note. He tore open the sweet-smelling envelope and took deep whiffs. A heady feeling enveloped him as he remembered the sweet scent of his darling Louisa when he held her in his arms. Within moments he had finished reading her message. It was a short note and aloof. A fierce pain shot through his heart and mind as he reread her words. She had found someone else! Another man had entered the picture—someone who cared about her. He could understand that. How could any man help but care about Louisa? She was such a warm, vibrant, beautiful person. But did this man really love her as Peter loved her? Were his intentions serious? Peter groaned outwardly as his eyes reread the words that cut him the most. "He really cares about me. I don't know what the future holds." The balance of Louisa's letter was cool, and she signed it "Sincerely"—not "Love."

"I've been away too long," Peter moaned as he crumpled the letter and threw it on the table. "But I thought we had something special between us, something that would last. We made a commitment to each other when we became engaged. Why did this happen with my brother just at this time, Lord? Thomas needed me, and I couldn't let him down. You knew I would want to see this thing through, show him I cared, and be his support. Not just for his sake, but for Annabelle's. I don't understand why these things happen. I know You have a purpose behind everything You allow to come into my life. I really messed up because I didn't tell Louisa the entire story. Because I love her, I didn't want to burden her with my troubles. It's my own fault she is enamored with another man. I thought Louisa loved me"—Peter's voice choked as he mumbled the words—"as much as I love her." He pulled out his handkerchief and blew his nose. "There's no way I could be interested in another woman—not while I had Louisa." Peter thought about her laugh and the way her golden tresses framed her oval face. Her wide, gray eyes often sparkled with amusement, teasing him. Peter shook his head as though to clear his mind. "Help me to understand, Lord." He sighed. "I don't know the why of it, and I don't need to, but this is a tough blow."

Peter tried to hide his grief as he set out to visit his brother that afternoon. He rode Thunder hard toward town as dust from the road flew up into his face. It didn't matter. He wanted to put Louisa out of his mind for the moment and center his thoughts on his brother's situation. He went first to his lawyer's office.

"What is taking so long?" he demanded. "It seems you are dragging your feet. Why aren't you out searching for leads?"

The lawyer, a short, stout man with spectacles, leaned back in his chair and eyed Peter. "Y'all are in too much of a hurry," he drawled. "This kind of case takes time. We'll get you some answers soon enough."

"It's already too late for me!" Peter exclaimed. "I should have been out of here long ago!"

"Well now, Mr. McClough, don't y'all like our hospitality? We Southern folks pride ourselves on Southern hospitality."

"I do, sir," Peter said with a softened tone. "You've all been most gracious. But I need to get my brother out of jail, if possible. And I need to get back north to my home. I have some personal matters to take care of. My entire future is at stake. It may be too late already!"

Halfheartedly, Peter left the lawyer's office and headed toward the jail. Genevieve Markam entered just ahead of him. Peter greeted her and allowed her to go back to speak with Thomas while he talked to the sheriff. The sheriff, always friendly, smiled as Peter approached.

"I have a lead on something, Peter, and it's about to be finalized. It will give us some answers. I hope they clear up this situation, one way or another."

Peter caught his breath. "What do you mean, Sheriff? What kind of answers? Will it help my brother's case?"

"I sincerely hope so. Regardless of the outcome, it will settle the case once and for all, and that is important."

"How soon?" Peter demanded. "Will it be today or tomorrow?"

"There are two people I must interview, so it may take a few days. I'm trying to line up a time when they will see me. They have agreed to tell me all they know. I just hope they don't back down on their word."

"But it sounds hopeful, doesn't it, Sheriff? I'll pray about it along with my brother and Miss Markam. There is power in prayer, you know."

"Well, uh—we'll see. I've never been much on prayer—always worked things out by myself. Never felt I needed any help."

"Oh, but we do, Sheriff. We need God's help all the time. He's only a prayer away. He hears the prayers of His children, those who have trusted His Son, Jesus, as their Savior. God cares about us and every problem in our lives."

"What if we've never. . .uh. . .accepted His Son as our Savior? Does He still hear our prayers, Peter?"

"He hears the prayer of a repentant heart. I was once a lost sinner, Sheriff. Everyone is until they cry out to God as I did. The Bible is clear on that. Each person must confess he is a sinner and ask Jesus to come into his life."

"Wal. . .that's something I'd like to ponder for a while, Peter. But y'all go ahead and pray. It can't hurt none, and it sure will be interesting to see what happens."

Peter was optimistic as he shared the sheriff's news with Thomas and Genevieve. He needed, above all, to be an encouragement to the couple. He plastered a smile on his face to cover his own heartache. The smile didn't feel natural to him, but Thomas and Genevieve didn't seem to notice.

After a short visit and time of prayer, Peter took his leave, promising to return the next day. He bought a few groceries and stopped by the barber for a haircut. As he mounted Thunder for the ride back, the animal seemed ready to get moving. "You're anxious to get back, aren't you, fella?" he whispered in the animal's ear. "I don't blame you. Powder is a beautiful mare. She's not fickle like women are. I'm sure she misses having you at her side." Thunder snorted and shook his head up and down as if to agree. Peter sighed audibly, gave the animal full rein, and let him run at full gallop toward the plantation. The cool wind whipped color into his cheeks. He bent low over Thunder's back as the dust flew up from the roadway. It was exhilarating, and the cold air pushed thoughts of Louisa deep into the recesses of his mind.

Peter spent the afternoon cleaning the manure out of the barn. He spread fresh straw in the stalls, mended several loose boards, and oiled the saddles and harnesses. From there he went to the pasture and skirted the length and breadth of it. The horses trotted beside him and nuzzled him as he worked. Every so often he found a place that needed repair. He pounded almost fiercely in an attempt to ease the pain in his heart. When he finished his task, he saddled Powder to give her a run. They trotted around the pasture from one end to the other several times. Not to be left behind, Thunder followed at her side and stayed with them until they rode back to the barn. After Peter removed Powder's saddle and rubbed her down, Thunder whinnied and tossed his head. Powder responded with a whinny, and the two of them raced off to the pasture. Peter watched them go. The dark stallion with the restless nature led the way, followed by the lovely and gentle bay mare. They jerked their heads, snorted to one another, and raced the length of the pasture before stopping to graze, side by side.

"Sometimes horses have more sense than humans," Peter muttered. "Look how they stay together. That's what I hoped for Louisa and me. To be together always. . .side by side."

That evening Peter prepared a letter for Annabelle.

Dear Annabelle,

I know it's been a long time, and I wish I knew when Thomas's case would be settled. The sheriff informed me today about two people who are willing to talk. It seems they have information about what happened that night at the Berringer plantation. Whether it will help Thomas or convict him further, I do not know, but we must never give up hope. Thomas, Genevieve, and I pray together each day. You will love Genevieve. She is a sweet Christian, and she and Thomas love one another. When they marry, you will have her as a daughter. I know you always wanted a daughter. And just think, a special bonus! There will probably be grandchildren! What a blessing that will be! I will keep you informed of the outcome of the men's testimony. Keep praying, dear Annabelle, and looking up.

Love,
Peter

It was a short message, but it informed Annabelle of the latest news. She would know something could happen in the next few days. Peter pulled out another piece of paper and started to write Louisa. He wrote a few lines, crumpled the paper, and threw it on the floor. His second attempt turned out to be another disaster. He crumpled it and tossed it aside. After several unsuccessful attempts, Peter gave up. He wrung his hands and mopped his brow. "What's the use?" he shouted at the wall. "She's met someone else she cares about! And here

I sit in Tennessee! My hands are tied. I don't even know when I'll get back to Waterville!" Peter leaned forward and placed his head in his hands. "Oh, Louisa," he murmured. "If you only knew how much I love you!"

Chapter 14

Louisa and her parents attended church with the Phillip Bradfords the morning after Clara's wedding. Clara and Sam had already left on their honeymoon, a trip to the coast, and would be gone for one week. Louisa, anxious to get home to Waterville, ate little of the tasty meal prepared by her aunt after the church service. Phillip Bradford loaded their luggage into his carriage and drove his brother's family to the station, a short distance across town. The cold, brisk air whipped color into their cheeks as the horses trotted along the snow-packed roads. Large snowflakes cascaded down from the heavens. They sifted and swirled as they lit on everything—houses, roadways, fences, and people. The effect was breathtaking as the pure, white snow covered every dingy corner and provided a clean covering.

When the family reached the train station, Louisa climbed down from the carriage and lifted her face toward the heavens. Large flakes tumbled down and clung to her warm wraps and eyelashes. She laughed and whirled around in sheer delight. "Isn't this beautiful, Mother?" she asked. "I love the way the snow covers ugly things and makes them pure and white. Doesn't the Bible say something about 'Wash me, and I shall be whiter than snow'? I'd like my life to be pure like that. I've been selfish and self-centered of late. I wrote Peter and told him I cared about someone else. It was such a cold and distant letter. Whatever must he think of me now?"

Elizabeth Bradford smiled at her daughter. While Jack Bradford went to take care of their luggage, the two women had an opportunity to talk. "Yes, the verse you quoted is from the Bible, Louisa. Psalm 51, verse 7. And about Peter. I'm sure he felt pain when he read your note, but I believe Peter loves you. Does this mean you have decided Peter is the right one for you after all? What about Roger Evans?"

"I've been fickle, Mother. I admit it. Roger is handsome and charming. His attentiveness took my breath away. Against my better judgment, I allowed myself to become involved. But Roger is a controlling person. . .as you said. And he can't be a Christian. He doesn't care about my desires. Everything has to be his way, or he gets angry. I've seen another side of him of late. If we did marry, I'm not sure it would last. I want a marriage like you and Father have—one that endures."

Elizabeth hugged her daughter as the snowflakes continued to tumble down and lightly cover their bonnets. "It's good to hear you talk this way, dear. You've matured through your experience with Roger."

"I'm glad you and Father didn't give up on me. I was pretty hardheaded at times."

Jack Bradford, tickets in hand, rushed toward them somewhat out of breath. "It appears I missed out on some serious conversation between my two girls," he said. "Is there anything important I should know?"

Louisa smiled and glanced at her mother with a twinkle in her gray eyes. Elizabeth grinned, while an unspoken message passed between them. "Just girl talk, Jack," she said as she took her husband's arm and headed toward the train. "Just girl talk!"

Crowds of passengers thronged together as the engine spewed curls of dark smoke upward toward the heavens. The short, rotund conductor called, "All aboard!" loudly as he collected tickets from eager passengers pushing their way into the coaches. A sigh of relief escaped Louisa's lips as she settled into the seat beside her parents. It had been a busy, happy, yet exhausting few days in Augusta. A whirlwind of activities, including a bridal party at the church and a wedding rehearsal, had taxed everyone. Louisa knew her parents would doze on the trip home. She preferred instead to daydream about her own wedding, which she hoped would take place sometime in the near future. As she thought about Peter, she felt a deep pang of regret. He might consider her too fickle to be marriage material. Would he want to spend his entire life with someone so changeable, someone so childish? She wondered where he was, what he was thinking, and when he would return to Waterville. Eventually she felt a wave of drowsiness wash over her, and she slept the balance of the way home.

≈

"I cannot understand it!" Jack Bradford said, an annoyed edge to his voice. "I told Roger exactly when we would arrive back in Waterville! The train is only fifteen minutes late. He should be here waiting to take us home."

"Perhaps he was delayed, Father," Louisa said as she pulled her wraps closer about her body. "Roger is always working on something at the bank."

"Sometimes I wonder about that man," Jack exclaimed. "He's forever pulling out accounts and checking on them. There's no need for it. . .none at all!"

Elizabeth pulled on her husband's arm. "Let's go into the station and wait, dear. He'll be along in a bit. It's getting colder by the minute."

"Of course, Elizabeth. At least we have a warm place to wait. You and Louisa go on ahead. I'll locate our luggage and be right in. Roger will find us when he arrives."

The trio, alert since their naps on the train, sat close to the large potbellied woodstove while they waited. Time passed slowly as Louisa watched, her eyes glued on the regulator clock on the far wall. *Tick-tock, tick-tock.* A half hour passed—then an hour. Passengers came and went, and still no Roger Evans appeared.

"Something's happened!" Jack said as he stood up. "We can't wait any longer. I'll hire a carriage to take us home."

"Perhaps Roger is ill," Elizabeth said.

"He should have asked someone else to meet us," Jack said impatiently. "He appears to be a diligent worker most of the time, but he's lax in other areas. You'll probably think I have a suspicious mind, but sometimes I have doubts about his character."

Before long, Jack hired a carriage and the trio started for home. He directed the coachman to make a stop at Roger's boardinghouse. "I'll only be a minute," Jack said as he climbed from the carriage. "I need to find out why Roger failed to show up. Perhaps he is ill and in need of a doctor."

Several minutes later Jack Bradford reappeared with furrowed brow, his lips drawn into a tight line. Without a word, he climbed into the carriage.

"Is it serious, Father?" Louisa asked. "How sick is Roger?"

Jack Bradford frowned. "No, he's not ill, Louisa. He's not sick at all."

Elizabeth turned to her husband. "What is it, Jack? Something is wrong. Your expression gives you away."

Jack Bradford sat stunned for a few moments as the coach carried them toward home. "He's gone," he muttered. "Roger Evans checked out of his boardinghouse, paid his rent, and left."

"Where did he move, Father? He's been looking at other places. Roger was never happy at the boardinghouse. He had fine ideas of a big home somewhere in the area."

"No. . .no, Louisa. . .nothing like that. He left no forwarding address. His landlady, Mrs. Hogan, said he moved out Friday and planned to leave town on the evening train. When she asked him where he was going, he said he wasn't sure of his plans. But he was through here in Waterville. He had finished with this town. He completed what he came to do."

"What can it mean, Jack?" Elizabeth asked. "He's through in Waterville. He finished what he came to do. It doesn't make sense, does it?"

"No sense at all," Jack muttered. "I don't have a clue as to what Roger meant. Do you know anything about this, Louisa? You were close to Roger."

"No, Father," she faltered. "I had no idea Roger planned to leave town. When we were together last week, Roger asked me to elope with him that same night."

Elizabeth gasped and caught her breath.

"But I refused," Louisa said quickly. "When Roger couldn't convince me to run off with him, he grew angry. I realized Roger had another side to his character, and I knew I could never marry anyone so changeable—attentive one moment and angry the next."

"Well, Louisa," her father muttered, "I'm glad you're not all enthralled with Roger. Your mother and I knew he was wrong for you from the start. We've prayed you would see that for yourself, and it seems you have." Jack Bradford sighed. "I wish I'd been more careful in selecting him as my assistant. He produced all the right records. His military service during the war seemed excellent, but I've had some strange, mixed feelings about him of late. He did his work well, so I found nothing to fault him on. Now it seems he's left me in the lurch. I'll be doing double duty at the bank until I find another assistant."

"Could I help out, Father?" Louisa asked, a note of eagerness in her voice. "I feel so useless sometimes. I'm not in college anymore. I help Mother some with the house, but I'm tired of sitting home and working on embroidery. I've enough handwork stashed in my hope chest for two brides. And marriage seems out of the picture for me, at least at the present time. I could do some filing and handle some of the easier tasks at the bank. I did well in math. . .as far as I went with it. Could I help you out until you find another assistant?"

"Thanks," her father said absently. "I may take you up on it. You'd be an asset to the bank, my dear."

When they arrived at the Bradford home, Jack built a roaring fire in the large fireplace to ward off the chill. Elizabeth and Louisa prepared a light supper, and they carried it in by the fireside. The trio sat quietly for several moments as they watched the logs crackle and hiss. Elongated shadows stretched upward toward the ceiling and into other parts of the room. Louisa glanced sideways at her father. His eyes, glued on the fire, stared straight ahead. She noted the firm set of his jaw and furrowed brow. He wrung his hands, relaxed them, and wrung them again. Elizabeth reached for his hands and quieted them as she held them in her own. "Don't fret so, Jack. Everything will be all right at the bank. You've weathered difficult situations before."

Jack Bradford's face relaxed as he looked at his wife and daughter. "You are right, Elizabeth. We've had hard times in the past, but God always saw us through them."

"And He will again, dear," Elizabeth said.

Jack Bradford stared again at the fire for several moments, as if lost in thought. "I have a strange, uneasy feeling about Roger's sudden departure. He seemed edgy when he took us to the train station last Wednesday. Did you notice?"

"He was upset with me, Father, because I refused to elope with him," Louisa said. "I'm sure that was his problem."

Jack Bradford stroked his mustache thoughtfully. "No. . .no! I think it was more than that. I believe he planned his departure to coincide with our trip to Augusta. But I'll know the truth of the matter tomorrow when I open the bank. Perhaps he left a note of some kind or gave a message to one of the other employees. If he obtained a better position somewhere, he should have confided in me. I'm not an unreasonable person. I could have given him references and prepared for his resignation." Jack Bradford sighed heavily and stood to his feet. "Let's join hands and have a word of prayer before we retire. I want to turn this entire situation over to the Lord. He is our helper and comfort in times of trouble."

Chapter 15

The following day winds howled as they blew in a nor'easter. Snow no longer drifted down in soft flakes. Instead, it blew almost horizontally as the winds gusted and swirled. Jack Bradford arose early, but Louisa was up and dressed ahead of him.

"Breakfast is ready, Father," she said. "And I'm going with you to the bank this morning. Mother agrees with me. You need some support, and I'm prepared to do whatever I can to help out."

"But, Louisa, I don't even have the facts of the whole matter yet. Perhaps Roger will show up as usual, and all will be a misunderstanding. His landlady may have misunderstood Roger's intentions."

"That could be so, Father. But I intend to accompany you in the event he doesn't show up. I'm sure there are many things I can do to lighten the workload. In fact, I'm looking forward to it. It's about time I made myself useful and learned something about the banking business."

Jack Bradford looked from his daughter to his wife as a crooked smile tugged at his mouth. "Clearly I am outnumbered. I can see my wife and daughter have already made their decision. Elizabeth, if you want Louisa to go with me, I will not argue the matter. Perhaps it is indeed time for our daughter to learn how the family business operates. After all, the bank will be included in her inheritance."

Louisa's gray eyes sparkled, and she bubbled with excitement as she wrapped her arms around her father's neck. "Oh, thank you, Father!" It was a new adventure for her, and she welcomed the challenge.

After breakfast Louisa and her father set out for the bank, bundled warmly against the north wind. It whipped at their faces, and Louisa pulled her warm wool bonnet farther down over her golden curls. It was a relief when they arrived at the bank and were able to escape the cold blast of the nor'easter in all its fury. Mr. Bradford started the woodstove, and soon they were able to remove their outer wraps. He searched the office and front desk, but there was no note from Roger Evans. When he checked the vault, his countenance sank. Louisa heard her father gasp and mumble, "Oh no! It can't be!"

Louisa peered into the open vault. Her father's face paled as he wrung his hands. Louisa clutched his arm. "What happened, Father? Has someone tampered with the vault?"

Jack Bradford looked at his daughter through glazed eyes. Blindly he brushed a hand across his forehead as if to clear his vision. "It's all gone. The people's money—thousands of dollars—it's been stolen. I—I must tell the authorities immediately. Perhaps they can trace him. . .wherever he's gone. Dear God, I pray they can catch up with him."

"Who, Father? Who would do such a thing? Surely not Roger Evans. I found him self-centered and controlling, but surely he wouldn't stoop to this."

"Roger is the only one who could have done this, Louisa. No other person has access to the vault. And no one else knows the extent of the money stored there. Roger studied the accounts. He knew everything about our business here at the bank. Perhaps that's what he meant when he told his landlady he was through in Waterville. He had finished here. Roger may have a record of thievery, going from one place to another." Jack Bradford shook his head. "He seemed so sincere, so honest. His papers—records—seemed to be in order. And he told me he served in the Union Army during the Civil War. That carried a lot of clout with me. I like to give employment to our men who served so faithfully. Everything Roger showed me must have been a forgery. How could I have been such a poor judge of character?"

"Father, I'm so sorry. Don't blame yourself too much. Roger Evans is a smooth character. He fooled you and me, and I'm sure he fooled others. When you hired him, you believed he was an upright and moral person. Evidently he is not."

Jack Bradford put on his hat and boots and pulled his warm wraps around him. "I must go to the authorities, Louisa. You wait here, and I'll return as soon as I give them an account of the robbery. When my other two employees arrive, tell them the bank will be closed today and send them home. Don't give them any details about what happened. Tell them I'll stop by and explain everything to them later. They may have a clue to all this. I don't want to cause a panic among the people. The sheriff will know what to do. He'll want to question my employees, I'm sure. And he'll need a description of Roger before he can get the word out. Let's hope Roger Evans hasn't skipped the country."

Louisa busied herself in her father's absence. She found a cloth and dusted the counters and desks. Using a broom stored in a back closet, she swept the floor and tried to neaten the place. When her father's employees arrived, she told them the bank would be closed for the day. She also shared the fact that her father would visit their homes later and explain the situation. The employees, though puzzled over the circumstances, asked no questions and took their leave.

The bank was closed for an entire week, which made a hardship on some. The Bradfords discovered Roger Evans was indeed a thief. He had embezzled moneys before in various banks across the country and was wanted by the authorities. He never stayed longer than a few months in one place as he moved around from one state to another. Louisa gasped and clutched her throat when she learned he had several wives and a few children in various locations. If she had agreed to run off and elope with him, she would be counted as one of the unfortunate women. Thus far Roger Evans had escaped the law and continued his renegade lifestyle. There were few clues to go on, but one of Jack Bradford's employees had a bit of news. One week earlier he overheard Roger talking to one of the customers regarding Maine's frigid temperatures. The employee remembered Roger's comments word for word. "I'm not a Northerner at heart, ma'am. The weather in Florida is most appealing to me at this time of year." Whether the comment had any bearing on the case, only time would tell.

Phillip Bradford, Jack's brother, advanced him moneys so the Waterville bank could get back in business. The people of Waterville, for the most part, were understanding about the delay. It took time for the authorities to track Roger Evans's route from the time he left Waterville. They found he had taken the Kennebec train out of Waterville to Portland. From there they drew a blank, as there was no record of anyone securing a ticket under the name of Roger Evans. However, they knew he changed his name often—every time he hit a bank or business in a different state. Obviously he had changed it again. This made it difficult for the police, but they were dedicated to their task. Roger Evans, alias several other names, needed to be brought to trial and pay for his crimes.

Louisa went to the bank each day with her father and helped file records and fill in at the counter. She not only enjoyed the work; she brightened the atmosphere. When Louisa greeted customers, she always flashed her cheerful smile. Her father often praised her, saying he wondered why he hadn't brought her into the bank earlier. She needed to learn the business, he told her, in the event anything happened to him, especially since he had no son or son-in-law to carry on the work at the bank. And anyway, he had confessed, he enjoyed her company. Louisa knew that in his earlier years, Jack Bradford had longed for a son with a passion. But the good Lord had not seen fit to bless her parents with other children, and they had accepted the fact that God knows what He is doing and does all things well.

Louisa's cheerful attitude did not reach her heart. Deep down she wondered about Peter. There had been no more letters, and she hungered for one. Her short infatuation with Roger Evans had been a mistake. He had flooded her with attention, and she was ripe for it. She had a lot of time to think, and the more she thought about Peter, the more she missed him. Visions of his dark hair and the way a shock of it fell across his forehead crowded her mind. She longed to tease him and hear his hearty laugh as he reached for her. His dark eyes and tender glances always took her breath away. When he took her in his arms, she leaned against his shoulder and his manly scent filled every fiber of her being. "Foolish girl," she whispered to herself. "You gave up your handsome prince, and now you have no one!"

The days passed slowly for Louisa. She kept her mind occupied by serving at the bank, but each afternoon she looked for a letter from Peter. As the weeks came and went without a letter, she became depressed. What kept him away from Waterville so long? she wondered. She saw Martha, his part-time housekeeper, occasionally at the bank. But Martha had no news to tell her except what she already knew. Peter had business to take care of and would return as soon as it was finished. With this she must be content.

The Christmas season brightened Louisa's thoughts as she helped her mother decorate the house for the holidays. A special wreath topped with miniature bells and a cranberry velvet bow adorned the front door. Garlands and boughs dressed the fireplace mantel, interspersed with tiny candles. Bright velvet bows, placed here and there among the boughs, lent a festive appearance. The staircase, also embellished with garlands and bows, displayed a brass candlestick on each step going to the second floor.

On a Saturday afternoon, Louisa and her parents took the sleigh and set out for the farm of her friend Emily's parents. The Masons had given them a standing invitation to cut their Christmas tree from their woods each year. Louisa remembered how, as a child, her father carried her on his shoulders as they tramped through knee-deep snow to find just the right tree. With the tree tied to the back of their sleigh, Louisa and her parents sang Christmas carols on the way home. It lifted their spirits as they sang the familiar songs. Their voices rang out clear and strong in the cold, crisp air. Worries and cares seemed of no consequence as they rejoiced in the beauty of the season.

The authorities had various clues but had not yet located Roger Evans or the stolen money. Jack Bradford's bank was out of the red and doing well. It was only possible, however, due to the generosity of Phillip Bradford. Jack was deeply indebted to his brother, and Louisa knew the situation bothered him. Would his financial situation be cleared up soon so he could pay his brother back?

Louisa's concerns often turned to Peter. Her mind lingered on her memories of him. Would he come back to Waterville in time for Christmas? And if he did, would he want to see her? Her only letter to him, in all this time, intimated she cared for someone else. Should she write him again and explain what a foolish goose she had been? He hadn't written since he received her letter about Roger. Perhaps he had found a new love. Someone beautiful—someone who appreciated him—someone who wasn't so fickle. Maybe Peter McClough had written her off—and could never care for her again.

Louisa sang louder as she pushed these thoughts from her mind. Her sweet soprano voice echoed across the countryside as the horses clip-clopped along the roadway toward home. It was the Christmas season, and the beautiful message of "Silent Night, Holy Night" filled her heart with unspeakable joy.

Chapter 16

Peter McClough battled inner feelings of depression as he waited for answers regarding his brother's trial. It was the week before Christmas, and he longed to be back home. When he left so hastily back in September, it never occurred to him he would be gone such a long time. He knew Martha, his part-time housekeeper, looked after his house. She had written him on several occasions to assure him all was well. Her letters, written in care of Annabelle, had been forwarded to Tennessee.

Louisa had written no further letters, nor had he written any to her. Perhaps she and this other man, Roger Evans, were even married by this time. The thought caused Peter much pain, and he drew a hand across his brow as he pushed back the shock of dark hair from his forehead. Gloomily he glanced out the window and prepared for his daily trip into town. The skies, dark with ominous clouds, matched his emotions. "Surely the sheriff will get this thing settled before Christmas," he muttered. "I dread to think of Thomas sitting in that jailhouse during the holidays. This is the time we celebrate the birthday of our King. It should be a joyous time of remembrance." The frown left his face, and a shadow of a smile lit the corners of his mouth.

"Forgive me, Lord, for looking on the downside of everything. I will keep looking up!" Peter finished dressing, ate a light breakfast, and did a few chores. When he saddled Powder for his ride into town, Thunder threw back his dark head and nickered. "It's all right, boy! We'll only be gone a short time. I'll bring Powder back." Thunder seemed to understand, for he nuzzled Peter and let him run his hand through the thick black mane. It was a leisurely trip into Nashville until winds blew in a cold rain from the north. Peter drew his slicker closer around him as Powder ran at full gallop the remainder of the way. When he entered the jailhouse, he noticed two strangers seated with the sheriff. The sheriff smiled, reached out a hand to Peter, and pointed toward a chair.

"What's up, Sheriff?" Peter asked. "Do these men have any bearing on Thomas's case?"

"Yes, they do," the sheriff drawled. "I've waited a long time for them to be willing to testify. They were concerned about retribution from the Klan, but they've agreed to tell what they know. I've convinced them they have a debt of responsibility here. Your brother's life is at stake."

The sheriff introduced Peter to the two men who had taken on assumed names to protect their identity. They stood up and reached to shake hands with Peter. Their furrowed brows and tightly drawn lips lent an air of emotional strain.

Peter shook their hands warmly. "Thank you for coming forth with your testimony!" he exclaimed. "I appreciate any information you can give us about the killings. I hope it will help my brother's situation. But whether it does or not, we need to know the truth of the matter."

"Judge Barnhouse will hear the case at the courthouse this afternoon," the sheriff said. "Promptly at one o'clock. Miss Markam plans to be in attendance, and it is open to the public. These gentlemen will give their testimony then, under oath. Thomas will also relate his story of what happened at the Berringer plantation. What occurred was tragic and senseless. We'll have some answers for you today, Peter. This situation has gone on long enough. It's time to clear the air one way or another."

Peter spent the balance of the morning in conversation with his brother. He encouraged Thomas to hope for a quick settlement in the case, one that would be in his favor.

"I don't know how it can be in my favor, Peter. Facts are facts." Thomas drew a hand across his eyes as if to blot out the memory of that fateful night. "It was a heinous crime. They hung Ben on a tree at the back of the house. He must have been already dead when I arrived, because he didn't make a sound—he just hung there swinging from the rope. His cabin was enveloped in flames and past any hope of saving the house or his family. I was so angry I lost my head. I shouted at the men, but they jumped on their horses and rode away. When I fired my rifle at them, one of the Klansmen fell to the ground. After I took Ben down from the tree, I—I—" Thomas looked at his brother with moist, reddened eyes. "Ben was dead, Peter! My best friend was dead! I went over to the man I'd shot later. He was dead also. But you know all this. After I buried Ben, his family, and the Klansman, I left and went north to see Annabelle. My state of mind was desperate."

Peter agonized with his brother. His own troubles seemed unimportant compared to the hurt and pain Thomas experienced. "It had to be a terrible thing to witness. I'm sure I would have reacted in the same way. Hopefully the judge will take the entire story into consideration."

Though his eyes were still moist, a slight smile crossed Thomas's face. "You are a good brother, Peter, and a dear friend. I appreciate you more every day. You've been away from home for three months and never complained. I know you miss Louisa. You talked of her so often when you first arrived. Lately you haven't mentioned her, but I know you are anxious to get back to Waterville where your sweetheart lives. Let's hope this case gets settled today."

At noon Peter went to the small café on Main Street and brought back a lunch meal for the two of them. Then the brothers had a time of fellowship and prayer. They committed the outcome of the trial to the Lord and left it completely in His hands. Peter's heart felt lighter as he left the jailhouse and stopped by his lawyer's office for a brief meeting. The lawyer sounded optimistic about the case and felt Thomas had a good chance for a light sentence.

As Peter walked to the courthouse for the one o'clock session, he pondered what the outcome would be. Due to the circumstances of the situation, could Thomas receive a short jail sentence rather than a lengthy one? He refused to consider a death sentence. Surely the judge would never allow that to happen. And the two men in the sheriff's office. What testimony could they share that might have a bearing on the case? Peter quickened his step, entered the courthouse, and took a seat in the second row directly behind his brother.

The judge, an austere-looking man in his fifties, sat at a desk at the front. His long robe, gray hair, and thick spectacles added to the prestige of his office. A clerk sat directly in front and to the right of him, prepared to write down the course of action during the trial. The judge called Thomas to the witness stand first, and he related his story, word for word, as it happened.

"Where was the Klansman when you shot him?" the judge asked.

"He was riding away on horseback, Your Honor."

"Was he facing you?"

"No, sir. There was a group of them, and they were leaving in a hurry. I'm sorry to say I shot him in the back."

"Are you certain of that? Perhaps the man turned around toward you."

"No, sir. I fired at his back, and he fell to the ground. Then I went to get my friend down from the tree. I dragged him several feet away from the area, but he was already dead. It—it was very painful for me." Thomas pulled out his bandanna and wiped the moisture from his face before he continued. "I located a good burial spot out in back and buried him and his family. Then I went over to find the Klansman. His horse had run off. The man lay on his stomach—dead also. So I dragged him back to the burial grounds."

"And you buried the man along with your friends in a little burial plot, is that right?"

"Yes, sir, I did. I thought it the right thing to do. I marked the graves of my friend and his family, but the man's grave was left unmarked. When I came back in September to turn myself in, the grave was empty."

"I see," the judge said as he glanced at some papers in front of him. "The body had been removed from the grave sometime earlier. That agrees with information I have. You may step down, Mr. Hayes."

Thomas's lawyer gave a brief account of his client's deep sorrow over what had occurred. He reminded the judge that Thomas Hayes returned to the area by his own free will and turned himself in to the sheriff. "This fact needs to be taken into consideration, Your Honor."

"I believe our sheriff has two men who are here to enlighten us regarding this case," the judge replied. "I'll hear their testimony before I pass any judgment on your client."

Thomas sat in the first row with his lawyer with Peter just behind them. The first of the two men to give testimony moved forward and was sworn in. Peter tapped his brother on the shoulder and comforted him with a smile of encouragement. Thomas's face, tense and drawn, relaxed somewhat as he leaned forward to listen to the man speak.

The first man's testimony startled the judge and the many people seated at the trial. He revealed the fact he had been one of the Klansmen at the Berringer plantation on the night of the murders. Shortly thereafter he left the society because he could not continue in their evil practices. "What I am about to say," he said, "is true. I say so before God and all who are present in this building. This man"—he pointed at Thomas Hayes—"is not the murderer of my fellow Klansman."

There were several gasps in the audience as people shuffled their feet and turned in their seats. Loud murmuring issued forth until the judge ordered them to be quiet. Then he glanced at the witness and asked him to continue.

"There were about twelve of us gathered outside of town that fateful night. We knew Mr. Hayes was away, and the black folk were alone. Clay Prescott agreed to join the Klan one last time. He insisted this would be his final escapade with the group. He said he wanted nothing more to do with them from that night on. When the group heard this, they became angry and tried to dissuade him. But Clay Prescott could not be convinced to change his mind.

"The men shouted and worked themselves into a frenzy as they galloped hard toward the plantation. You may not believe this, but Clay and I hung back. We were there—we were in on it. . .but we only observed." The witness hung his head and wiped large beads of sweat from his brow. "Others grabbed the black man and set fire to his cabin, with the family in it asleep. Then they strung the black man up by the neck with a heavy rope and watched as he swung back and forth." The witness broke down and sobbed openly. He blew his nose loudly and struggled to continue. "That's when Mr. Hayes rode up and yelled at us. We rode off in a fury toward the woods. Clay and I were at the back of the group. I heard the rifle shot and saw Clay was hit in the back. But he stayed on his horse. One of the Klansmen turned toward him and shot him in the chest with a pistol at close range. I can honestly say I don't know which Klansman did this terrible thing. But that is when Clay fell from his horse, and I'm positive that is when he died."

There was another murmuring and moving about among the audience. "How can that be?" someone shouted. "Mr. Hayes said nothing about hearing a shot. He admits shooting Clay Prescott in the back. Let him pay for his crime!"

After the judge quieted the courtroom, he asked the witness the same question. "Mr. Hayes mentioned nothing about another shot. Why is that?"

"There could be several reasons," the witness said. "He was some distance away. He was concerned about his friend and his friend's family. The cabin fire was a roaring blaze, crackling and hissing while timbers fell all around the place. Maybe one of the crashing pieces of timber muffled the sound."

The judge directed a question to Thomas. "Mr. Hayes, did you examine the body before you buried it? Surely you would have noticed if there were two shots in the victim's body."

"Your Honor, I assumed I had killed the man, so I did not examine his body. He was over toward the woods, facedown, where it was very dark. I dug five graves and buried my friends. Then I dragged the man's body over to the small burial place."

The first witness stepped down, and the other witness took his place. After being sworn in, he revealed his information. "I'm the one who dug up the deceased for the family and prepared him for a proper burial," he said. "The wound received from Mr. Hayes's rifle was in Clay Prescott's back, high near the right shoulder. It could not have killed him. He had a pistol wound in the chest near his heart. I'm certain this wound is the one that caused his death."

Some of the audience jumped up and caused a disturbance. People moved about while loud murmurs and shouts filled the air. The judge ordered them to be quiet and cleared the courtroom of all onlookers except witnesses, the sheriff, lawyers, and family. Genevieve Markam sat with her mother and dabbed at her eyes with her handkerchief. She looked across the aisle at Peter and whispered, "Thank God!"

Peter clapped his brother on the back. "I knew it would turn out for good, brother. God was on our side!"

The judge cleared his throat and stood up. "Ahem! I haven't made a decision on this case as yet." Everything was quiet as all eyes turned upon the man. Peter held his breath as he focused on the judge.

"I've listened to all the evidence, and it appears to be in order," the judge said. "These two witnesses should have come forward sooner. They withheld important information. I'm convinced they were reluctant due to fear of retribution from the Klan. Do you wish to press charges against them, Mr. Hayes?"

Thomas rose quickly to his feet. "No, Your Honor, I do not. I thank them personally for the strength of character to come forward with the truth at this time. It was a brave thing to do under the circumstances."

"Then I proclaim Thomas Hayes innocent of charges and free to go," the judge stated as he pounded his gavel. "It appears we do not know the identity of the Klansman who murdered Clay Prescott. His murder will remain unsolved unless further evidence is provided."

Those who remained rejoiced as they crowded around Thomas, slapping him on the back and shaking his hand. When Genevieve Markam approached, the others moved away. She walked boldly into his arms. Thomas drew her close and buried his head in her long chestnut tresses. And Peter's heart ached for Louisa.

Chapter 17

You can't leave now, Peter!" Thomas exclaimed. "I need you here for the wedding. You will be my best man!"

The two brothers sat around the breakfast table the following morning and devoured a mound of pancakes. They had returned to the plantation the night before, after a supper meal with Genny and her mother. Anxious to get back to his house after the lengthy time in jail, Thomas borrowed a horse from the Markams' stable. He knew it would be too heavy a load for Powder to carry the two men back to the plantation.

"Anyway," Thomas continued, "I'm just getting used to having a brother. Why not move down here and help me run the place? After your marriage, you and Louisa could live here with Genny and me. This house is too big for us. When I get my cattle delivered, I'll need help. I'll hire some extra hands, but I'd like you to join me. What do you say, brother?"

Peter wiped his mouth with his napkin and stared at his plate. "Thanks for the offer, Thomas, but you and Genny need to be alone after your marriage. Three of us together in this house would be a crowd."

"Three of us!" Thomas exploded. "I mean the two couples—Genny, me, you, Louisa!"

Peter frowned as he faced his brother. "Louisa wrote me some time ago that she was seeing someone else. She could be married by this time."

"But you said nothing! Why didn't you tell me? I'm so sorry. All I've thought about was myself. I never knew you were hurting."

"Thomas, you had enough on your mind. I refused to burden you. Getting your trial over with was important. Now you can get on with your life. You and Genny can be married as planned. I'm happy for you both." Peter's mouth formed a crooked grin. "But I will stay for the wedding. I'd like to share in your happiness. And I needn't hurry back to Waterville. If Louisa is already married, it will be painful for me."

Thomas eyed his brother, brows furrowed. "It's because of me, isn't it? Louisa got tired of waiting for you to come back. That's it, right?"

"Louisa knows nothing about you, Thomas. I left Waterville hurriedly when I got Annabelle's wire. Louisa only knows I had business to attend to and would be back when I completed it. If she really loved me, she should have been willing to wait. It's better this way, I guess. I love her more than I can say. But if she doesn't love me enough—" His voice broke, and he continued huskily, "If she doesn't love me enough, then yes, it's better this way."

That afternoon, Thomas sent Annabelle a wire and asked her to come down for Christmas and the wedding, which would be celebrated two days later, and said he hoped she would stay on with them, at least for a while. The two brothers worked diligently getting the house ready for Thomas's bride and Annabelle's visit. Although they had little time to prepare, Genevieve and her mother took care of the details for the wedding. Genny had purchased her dress several months earlier when she and Thomas had become engaged.

Peter and Thomas checked out the pastures and secured several head of cattle and more horses. They put up a Christmas tree and put forth their best efforts in decorating the tree and house for the holidays. As they stood back to survey their handiwork, they decided it passed inspection.

"Doesn't look too bad for a couple of bachelors," Thomas said as he handed Peter the angel for the top of the tree. "We almost forgot the traditional angel, though, and that's important. It will be wonderful to have a woman's touch on this place. Maybe Annabelle can pretty the house up a bit before the wedding. . .you know. . .feminine touches and such."

"Annabelle will love doing it, Thomas. And her cooking is something else, isn't it? It will be great to taste one of her home-cooked meals again."

Annabelle Hayes arrived two days before Christmas. Her round face and merry smile were a welcome sight. She hugged each of them in turn. "I'm so happy, Thomas," she said. "God answered our prayers and brought you through this terrible situation. And, Peter, I don't know what we'd have done without you."

The two men gave Annabelle a tour of the house, and she oohed and aahed over the large home as she walked through one room after another. Once settled in one of the lovely bedrooms upstairs, she made her way to the kitchen, where she felt most at home. Before long, the brothers sniffed tantalizing odors coming from the cookstove.

Annabelle insisted on preparing Christmas dinner. Mrs. Markam and Genny were invited, and it proved to be a festive occasion. They all talked at great length about the wedding and future plans of the couple. Although Thomas assured Mrs. Markam she was welcome to move in with him and Genny, she said she had made other arrangements. She planned to sell her large home and move in with her widowed sister. "Actually, we'll have a jolly time together, and I'll still be close enough to visit you and Genny."

After a short honeymoon, Thomas and Genny returned to the large plantation and settled in. Genny had ideas and suggestions for some feminine touches in the large house and was anxious to put them into action. "I have so many little things I'd like to add to this lovely home," she said in her sweet Southern drawl. "And Thomas promised me I could let my imagination run wild. . .with certain fabrics and candelabra. It will be delightful fun to make a few changes here and there."

Thomas asked Annabelle to make her home with them. Genevieve agreed with the suggestion and begged her to stay. "Since my mother won't be with us, I'll need some help, Annabelle. I don't think I can run this big house by myself. Thomas has promised me domestic help, but I'd like you here to oversee everything. Please tell me you'll stay. You were Thomas's mother for the first ten years of his life, and he's missed out on so much time with you. It would please us both if you would become a part of our family."

Annabelle flushed, and her round face broke into a wide grin. Her merry little laugh echoed forth as she looked at them with loving eyes. "I appreciate your kind offer, Genny. There's nothing I'd like better than to live here with you and Thomas. There are some things I must take care of back in Boston first. But if you're sure I won't be in the way, I'd love to return and look after the two of you."

"Annabelle," Thomas said with emotion, "we'd like nothing better!"

"What about your little cottage, Annabelle?" Peter asked. "Do you plan to sell it?"

"I don't want to sell it, but I would like to turn it over to the little church. They could keep up the place and use it for visiting pastors or missionaries. Maybe even folk needing a place to stay from time to time. It would give me great pleasure to have it used by the Lord's people. The pastor and church folk have been so good to me over these many years."

"But what about your furniture and things, Annabelle?" Peter asked. "I'll need to help you pack everything and get it to the train."

"Only a few things, Peter. I'll leave the furniture for the new occupants. I have some smaller objects and keepsakes I won't part with. They carry a lot of memories and mean a great deal to me. And I didn't bring all my clothes with me. When we return to Boston, you can crate up my things for me. And we'll visit the cemetery so I can say good-bye to Thomas. Oh, I know he isn't really there. It's just his body in that little plot of ground. His spirit is with the Lord. But I'll miss caring for his grave and tending the flowers. It's such a peaceful spot, and I feel close to him there." Annabelle's eyes misted over, and her lips quivered.

Peter put an arm around her plump body and gave her a gentle hug. "Your husband would want you to be with young Thomas and his bride, Annabelle. That way you won't be alone anymore. It sounds like the perfect situation for you. And when I come back to Tennessee for a visit, I'll be able to see you also."

"Then it's all settled!" Thomas cried as he and Genny hugged Annabelle. "And I liked the way you admitted you would visit us, brother. We'll look forward to many visits from you in the future!"

"Of course I'll be back," Peter said with a mischievous grin. "I plan to leave Thunder with you. He likes it here, and you have plenty of pasture room for him. In town where I live. . .that's no place for a magnificent animal like Thunder. I'll be back to see my horse!"

"Great!" Thomas exclaimed with a chuckle, an arm around his bride. "That piece of horseflesh will be missed more than your own brother! I guess that tells me who is most important around here!"

Peter and Annabelle stayed on with Thomas and Genevieve for another week to help get the plantation restored to its full productive activity. When Peter and Annabelle said their good-byes, it was a touching farewell at the train station in Nashville. They all knew Annabelle would return soon and take up residency with them, but no one knew when Peter would return—not even Peter himself. The two brothers, with moist eyes and a catch in their throats, embraced unashamedly. "Just when I've found you, I'm losing you," Thomas said hoarsely. "We work so well together. I wish you could stay longer and help me run the place. It would be a shared partnership. . .the way I planned to do it with Ben."

"I'll be back, Thomas," Peter muttered as he pulled out his handkerchief and blew his nose. "That's a promise. And it may be sooner than you think."

Peter helped Annabelle onto the train, and they settled themselves toward the back of the coach. Annabelle took her handwork out of her bag and commenced to embroider the fine fabric as the train hastened down the tracks, belching and spitting smoke and steam. Peter leaned back and listened to the *clickety-clack, clickety-clack* of the heavy wheels on the rails. He was bone tired from all the exertion during the past two weeks and longed to sleep. But his mind dwelt on thoughts of Louisa. He visualized her sweet oval face with the softly curved lips, her gray eyes so often wide in wonderment, and her charming innocence as she laid her golden head on his shoulder. How he longed to take her in his arms and never let her go. It pained him deeply to remember she cared about someone else and could be married by now. His face drew into a scowl at the thought. Perhaps she'd had a Christmas wedding, just as Thomas and Genevieve had. She would belong to another then and could never be his. Peter groaned aloud as he tried to put these disturbing thoughts from his mind.

"What's wrong, Peter?" Annabelle asked, turning toward him, uneasy concern lining her face. "Does your body ache from all the hard work you were involved in at the estate? You worked such long hours. Your determination is commendable, but now I expect you are paying for it with sore muscles."

Peter looked into his cousin's eyes and reached to pat her round cheeks. "Annabelle, you seem more like a mother to me than a distant cousin. I appreciate your concern. I had the best laid plans for my life before I got your telegram last September. My lifestyle had changed when I became a Christian. I planned to follow the Lord wherever He led me, marry Louisa, and raise a family. Everything planned out! But I don't ache from the hard work at the plantation. In fact, I relished it. It kept me busy and my mind occupied. Now, when I have time on my hands, I think about Louisa more than ever. The fact that she might be married to someone else pains me. The ache I feel isn't in my muscles. It's in my heart!"

"I understand," Annabelle said softly. "You love Louisa with all your heart. After God, she is the dearest person in your life. I will pray about this situation, Peter."

"Thanks, prayer partner! I feel better knowing you are praying, too."

"Peter," Annabelle said thoughtfully as she stuck her needle into her handwork once again. "I am honored you think of me more as a mother than a distant cousin. It would be a privilege to have a dear son like you. As long as I live, I will pray for you and help you in any way I can."

Jack and Elizabeth Bradford noted a decided change in their daughter. Louisa had matured into a caring, helpful young woman. Her time at the bank proved her ability to buckle down and put her shoulder to the wheel. The days were no longer filled simply with long hours spent doing handwork or joining her mother at teas. It had given her a sense of worth and accomplishment. Her parents delighted in the new Louisa. Her thoughts, once self-centered and childish, were no longer for herself. After a day's work at the bank, she often visited a widow or shut-in from church and took them some broth or small cakes. The ladies welcomed her visits and enjoyed her fellowship. Louisa intended to brighten their lives and encourage their hearts. Often, after her conversations with these dear ones, she came away with the greater blessing.

She still cared about Peter but kept her inner feelings to herself. It had been a mistake—a huge blunder—falling for Roger Evans, who proved to be a no-good renegade. And she had no one to blame but herself. Her parents' warnings had gone unheeded. The letter written to Peter told him of her relationship with Roger. That was the reason he had not written again. Why should he? Her letter, cold and uncaring, left him no alternative. He had resigned himself to the fact she cared for someone else. Louisa shuddered as she considered Peter's reaction to the news. She bit her lip and denounced her cruel actions. Surely Peter could never care for her again!

Christmas came and went quietly at the Bradford home. It was a meaningful time with special church services, concerts, and visits with friends. During this time, Louisa grew in her Christian faith. The birth of the Savior and His eventual death on the cross gave new meaning to her life. Quiet times spent in Bible study and prayer provided her with a peace she had never experienced before. Oh, how much she had missed by living a nominal Christian life instead of feasting on the scriptures and applying them to her life. She sought out passages in the New Testament and Psalms and committed them to memory. They became a great comfort to her.

In mid-January, the full blast of Maine's winter was at its height. Gales from the nor'easters brought in two feet of snow and left the Waterville residents snowbound. All activity came to a standstill. Eventually men with horses and plows managed to pile the huge mounds of white snow along the sides of the main streets. Louisa, anxious to get back to work at the bank after being confined for a few days, bundled herself warmly against the chill. She felt the cold air as it whipped at her cheeks and pulled at her clothing. Snow stuck to her eyelashes as she bent her head low against the wind for protection. Her father had left earlier in the day but insisted she wait and come in later. "There won't be many customers out today after this storm, Louisa," he had said. "Wait until I get the bank warmed up. The temperature in the rooms will be frigid until I heat up the woodstoves."

That afternoon a gentleman from the police investigation committee appeared and asked for Mr. Bradford. The man was plainly clothed in a dark suit rather than a police uniform. His small, beady eyes peered through heavy spectacles as he fumbled with papers he lifted from his briefcase. "I'm J. D. Hackman here to see Mr. Bradford," he said in a hurried tone. "I hope he's in, for I have some news for him regarding the theft here at the bank."

"Yes, Mr. Hackman," Louisa answered. "My father is in, and I'll tell him you are here." Excitement mounted in her chest as she headed toward her father's office. J. D. Hackman followed close behind her and almost bumped into her when she stopped at her father's office door. "I'm sorry, miss. . .but I have urgent news for Mr. Bradford!"

"Well, come right on in, sir," Louisa said as she opened the door. Jack Bradford sat at his desk going over some bank statements and looked up as they entered. "Father, this is Mr. Hackman," Louisa said. "He has important news for you about the bank robbery."

Jack Bradford stood up and extended his hand to the police investigator. "I hope it's good news, Mr. Hackman. We've been waiting for a break in this case for a long time. Please sit down and tell me what has happened so far."

J. D. Hackman settled his large frame into a chair close to Jack Bradford's desk. He leaned forward and spread some papers out in front of him. Tapping his fingers lightly, he pointed to some words written on one of the papers. Louisa held her breath and let it out in a little sigh. She wanted to hear the news herself, but her father nodded his head toward her. It was a clear suggestion for her to leave so the men could discuss the matter. What was the news? she wondered. As an obedient daughter, she closed the door quietly and went back to the front office.

J. D. Hackman did not linger. After a short time, he left her father's office, brushed past Louisa, and hurried out of the bank. She watched him as he walked down Main Street and out of sight. Then she walked briskly to her father's office, where he sat poring over some papers in front of him. "What is it, Father?" she asked breathlessly. "Have the police located Roger? And what about the money?"

The lines on Jack Bradford's furrowed brow relaxed, and he grinned at his daughter. "The news is good, Louisa. The authorities apprehended Roger in

Florida. They believe he planned to hop a ship to South America and stay there until things cooled off up here. He's evidently done that before when he pulled off other jobs. Roger Evans, alias several other names, eluded the police for many years, it seems. But they have him in custody now."

"I don't want to see Roger if he comes back here for his trial. It would remind me of what a foolish person I've been. I've learned a few lessons of late."

"No, he won't be brought back to Waterville. Our bank theft, though serious in our eyes, does not compare to some others he's pulled off. He's been jailed in Boston to await trial. His largest and most serious theft occurred at a large bank in that city."

"Did the police recover the money, Father? I know you've been concerned about the large amount stolen, especially since you had to borrow from Uncle Phillip."

"Roger still had most of the cash at the time of his arrest, but not all of it. Your Uncle Phillip has been patient and never once asked for it. But I want to get this debt paid back. It will lift a heavy load from my shoulders."

"Uncle Phillip has been a dear. He knows you will pay it back as soon as you are able. Did Mr. Hackman give you any idea when the money will be available?"

Jack Bradford removed his glasses and passed a hand over his eyes. A few strands of his neatly slicked brown hair had fallen across his forehead, giving him a little-boy look. "I must travel to Boston in another week for the trial. I'm one of the key witnesses in the investigation. It should be settled quickly due to the evidence and his past record. I will be able to settle my account with Phillip when I get back."

"Boston!" Louisa cried as she smiled broadly and clapped her hands together. Then she whirled and twirled around the room while her full calico skirts billowed out around her. "I want to go with you, Father!"

Jack Bradford turned a perplexed gaze on his daughter. "Why, Louisa? You said you never wanted to see Roger Evans again. What made you change your mind?"

Louisa stopped her whirling and caught her breath. "I don't want to see Roger, Father. Ever again!"

"Then why are you excited about going to Boston, especially when I need you here."

Louisa's face grew serious as she eyed her father. She pushed back locks of gold hair and fastened the tresses with a silver clip. "There is someone I need to see—Annabelle Hayes. She lives in the outskirts of Boston. Peter gave me his cousin's address so I could write to him. I only wrote him one time, and it was an unkind letter. It led him to think I cared about someone else. Maybe Mrs. Hayes can give me some information about Peter."

"Wouldn't that be a little daring and forward, Louisa? It would seem you are pursuing the man. That isn't very ladylike. As I recall, it's the man who is to do the pursuing—not the woman!"

Louisa smiled mischievously at her father, and he noticed the twinkle in her wide, gray eyes. She lifted one graceful hand and patted his cheek. "Fiddlesticks! I don't mind being the pursuer! If our relationship is broken, I'm the one who caused it, and I'm also the one to mend it, if possible. I'll not wait any longer for Peter to return to Waterville. If Annabelle Hayes is the kind of woman I think she is, she'll have some answers for me."

"What if they are not the answers you want, my dear? Have you considered the alternative? Perhaps it will only add to your heartache. You can't toy with a man's affections and expect him to take it in stride. Men have their pride, you know. Peter McClough may have put you completely out of his mind. He may even have a new woman in his life."

Louisa's gray eyes filled with sparks of fire. "I'll fight for him, Father! I will! Peter loved me once! Maybe—" Her voice faltered, and her lips trembled. "Maybe Peter can find it in his heart to love me again."

Chapter 18

When Louisa and her father arrived home that afternoon, they shared Mr. Hackman's news with Elizabeth. She rejoiced with them about the capture of Roger Evans and recovery of most of the funds. Jack Bradford explained it necessitated a trip to Boston for the trial, but he said that with such clear evidence the matter should be settled quickly. Louisa proceeded to tell her mother she planned to accompany her father to Boston and explained her reasons.

"But, Louisa, aren't you being a bit bold?" Elizabeth Bradford asked as she placed their meal on the dinner table. "You don't even know this Annabelle Hayes. She may not want anything to do with you. And I don't want you traveling around Boston alone while your father is at court."

"Mother, I'm not a child anymore. I'll be twenty-one soon—and a spinster at that. I don't need Father with me every moment!"

Jack Bradford coughed as he hid an amused smile and hastened to speak. "I'll go a day early, Elizabeth, and accompany our daughter to Mrs. Hayes's location. One short visit should take care of it. Don't worry, I won't let her traipse around town alone."

Elizabeth sighed with relief. "But, Jack, don't you need Louisa at the bank? Can your two employees carry on the workload without her help?"

"They've been with me a long while, Elizabeth, and proved themselves capable and trustworthy. I'm sure they will do fine. If a problem comes up, they can report to you. Remember, you worked with me some in the early years and have helped out from time to time. I don't see any problem with the arrangement."

"Yes, I have some special memories of those times we shared together. I'll go down to the bank each morning and offer my help. It would be pleasant to work a few days at the bank again. It's a good place to meet people, and I always enjoyed talking to those who came in." Elizabeth fumbled with her apron pocket and pulled out an envelope. "Louisa, I almost forgot about the letter that arrived this afternoon."

A broad smile brightened Louisa's face as she eagerly reached for the envelope. "Is it from Peter, Mother? I've been looking for a letter from him."

"No, dear. It's from Emily out in Pennsylvania. Why don't you read it to us?"

Louisa's brow furrowed. "I hoped Peter would write. Then I could get an idea how he feels about me now. . .and whether there is any hope for us." With a sigh she tore open the envelope. "But I do love to hear from Emily. I miss her so." She smoothed out the pale pink pages on the table before her and sniffed the delicate scent of lavender.

Dear Louisa,

I know I haven't written in a while, but things have been busy at the church. Our Christmas holidays were precious. . .just Robert and me in our own little home. We had some nice activities at the church. . .a special candlelight service on Christmas Eve along with songs by our little choir. I would enjoy singing with the choir, but they need me at the piano. It's fine because I enjoy that almost as well.

Have you heard any further word about Peter? I'm sure he was upset when he learned you were seeing someone else. My brother, Frederic, finally received a note from Tennessee, but Peter didn't go into detail about his situation. He sounded very mysterious and told Fred he wanted to discuss it in person when he got back. However, he gave no indication of when that would be, so it leaves us in the dark.

I do have some exciting news for you. No, I'm not expecting a baby. . .yet. We trust God will bless us with a child sometime soon, but it is all in His hands. My news is about Jim Bishop. He is the difficult man I told you about. It's so wonderful the way God works. This man, so bitter, so spiteful, so intent on causing chaos in the church, has repented of his sinful ways and recommitted his life to the Lord. What a joy it is to see him now! God worked a miracle in his life, and he is not the same man! It was the Christmas program and God's Holy Spirit working together. I told you he had to be disciplined by Robert and the deacons, and he had stopped coming to church. He allowed his children to be in the Christmas program, and his wife helped me with the production. Jim vowed he wouldn't come to see it or darken the church's door again. But he came in quietly at the last minute and took a seat at the back. The Christmas story, with the message of God's love, broke this man's heart. He's a huge hulk of a man, and I wish you could have seen him walk down the aisle and kneel at the front. Tears streamed down his rugged cheeks as he made his peace with God. The rest of us joined him with tears of joy. What a glorious change! It's a complete turnaround. Now he is kind, considerate, and eager to help in any way he can. Robert has channeled Jim's energies in many directions. He's become a dedicated laborer for the Lord, and the Bishops are a happy family unit.

It was dreadful news about Roger Evans and the money your parents lost. We trust the authorities will locate him soon and bring him back to pay his debt to society. It is good you found out about his degenerate nature before you became more interested in this man. I can't imagine my dear friend married to such a person.

THE BEST LAID PLANS

I must close now and start preparation for our evening meal. Please write soon and let me know the latest news.

Love, your friend always,
Emily

"Isn't that good news about Jim Bishop?" Jack Bradford asked. "One man with an embittered spirit can cause so much stress in a local church. I'm thankful to know his attitudes have changed and he is now an asset to the church family. It must be a great time of rejoicing for the Wampum church."

"Yes, Father, Emily and Robert prayed about this concern for a long time." Louisa gathered up some of the dishes and carried them toward the kitchen. She paused at the doorway and turned toward her parents, a smile stretched across her wistful face. "And it's a real comfort to me. It tells me God is still answering the prayers of His people."

The next week Louisa and her father boarded the Kennebec railroad coach headed toward Boston, Massachusetts. Louisa had mixed feelings about her venture, but it was too late to turn back. While her father dozed or read the paper, Louisa considered what Peter's reaction might be if he knew she planned to confront his cousin. And how would Annabelle Hayes respond to her girlish outburst? She had committed to memory her plan of explanation and went over and over the words in her mind. Would Mrs. Hayes consider her fickle and childish? First she cared for Peter, then she didn't. Now she loved him again. It sounded very much like a saga of discontent, and she had been discontented and, yes, childish. But she had changed. The Louisa of yesterday no longer existed. With God's help, she was stable and ready to make a lifelong commitment to Peter. But what about Peter's feelings? Would he believe the change in her was sincere, or would his manly pride stand in the way? Perhaps she had shattered his love to a point of no return. A wistfulness stretched across Louisa's face as she gazed out the window of the coach. The rolling hills and beauty of the countryside could not ease the pain in her heart. Her eyes lingered on the farms with their barns and outbuildings. The snow-covered stone fences stretched across the pastures were especially picturesque. And the little creeks, partly frozen, still bubbled along like a merry melody. She scolded herself and straightened her slumped shoulders. "God's creation is such a delight to behold," she whispered. "I'll feast my eyes upon His magnificent handiwork and allow only good thoughts to permeate my mind. Why despair over something I have no control over? I'll know soon enough where I stand. Peter's cousin may not have all the answers, but she can tell me if there is another woman in Peter's life."

When Jack Bradford awoke from a short nap, he found his daughter in a relaxed and cheerful mood. They talked quietly together, and Louisa pointed out the beauty of the countryside as the train whizzed past towns and rural areas.

Once in Boston, Jack Bradford hired a sleigh to take them to their lodgings. He secured two rooms in town, close to the courthouse.

"Tomorrow is a free day, Louisa," her father said as they ate dinner at a small café that evening. "I'll hire the sleigh again, and we'll ride out to see Annabelle Hayes. I hope the woman will be home, although I really don't understand the reason you wish to see her. She may not have any more information about Peter than you do."

"Oh, she must, Father. She's family. And regardless, I'll feel much better after I talk with her. She can relieve my mind about the seriousness of Peter's business in Tennessee. And," she added thoughtfully, "she may have some insight regarding Peter's love life. . .which I hope includes me!"

Jack Bradford sighed heavily and shook his head. "I'm doing this for you, Louisa, because I love you. Just be prepared for the worst thing that could happen. You told Peter you were seeing someone else, so he might be involved with another woman. Then think about why it wouldn't be so bad after all."

"But it would, Father! It would be very bad, and I would be shattered! Why are you saying these things?"

"Because I love you, as I said, and I don't want to see my daughter hurt any further. Just be prepared, dear. That's all I ask."

Louisa looked down at her plate and toyed with her food. "All right, Father," she said. Her eyes were moist, but she smiled bravely. "I'll be prepared for the worst, but I'll be praying for the best. . .God's best."

Jack Bradford grinned and covered her hand with his. "That's my girl!"

The following morning Jack Bradford rented a team of horses and sleigh from a nearby livery stable. Louisa and her father, bundled warmly against the cold air, headed out of town to find the little cottage of Annabelle Hayes. The keeper at the livery stable was able to clarify Louisa's directions and drew them a small map. "It's a far piece," he said. "But you'll find her place all right."

The ride was invigorating with the chilly temperature and snow in the air. Louisa marveled at the beauty of the countryside with its large farms and outbuildings, stone fences, and small creeks. There were a few animals in the fields, but she envisioned the pastures full of cattle and horses during the warmer weather. For now, she decided, most of the livestock were kept inside the large barns. When they arrived at Annabelle's cottage, Jack Bradford noticed smoke curling upward from the small chimney. "She must be home, Louisa! I'm grateful for that. Hopefully she'll invite us in for a hot cup of tea."

Louisa patted her cold cheeks with her warm gloved hands. "I feel so alive, Father! It must be the cold air. My cheeks feel like two cold apples."

Jack Bradford laughed as he helped his daughter out of the sleigh and tethered the team to the hitching post. In answer to their knock, a short, somewhat rotund woman opened the door. She wiped her hands on her checkered apron and greeted them with a grin that stretched across her round cheeks. "Hello, folks," she said, glancing from one to the other. "What can I do for you?"

"Are you Annabelle Hayes?" Louisa asked rather timidly.

"That I am!" she said heartily with a merry little laugh that echoed on and on.

Jack Bradford extended his hand. "I'm Jack Bradford, and this is my daughter, Louisa. We're from Waterville, Maine."

"Come in! Come in!" Annabelle exclaimed as she reached for each of their hands. "What a lovely surprise! I've heard so much about you from Peter."

Annabelle took their warm wraps and settled them into chairs near the fireplace. "I've got the kettle on for tea," she said jovially, "and we'll soon have you warmed up. It's a long ride from town in the cold."

Louisa glanced around the cozy, homey room and studied pictures on the walls. The cottage was neat and well kept with simple furnishings. Floors of wide-plank pine boards caught her eye, and brightly colored hand-braided rugs were placed in various spots around the room. There were several boxes off to one side filled with miscellaneous memorabilia.

"Don't mind my packed boxes," Annabelle said as she motioned toward the boxes. "I'm planning to move soon." She went to the kitchen and retrieved the kettle boiling on the woodstove. Annabelle bubbled with enthusiasm and kept up a lively chatter as she served steaming cups of tea and small cakes. "What brings you to the Boston area?" she asked, dropping into a chair facing the couple. "Did you hope to find Peter?"

When Louisa hesitated, Jack Bradford spoke up and told Annabelle about his problem. "I need to be in Boston for a court case, Mrs. Hayes. An unfortunate incident happened with one of my employees, and it was necessary for me to make the trip. Louisa decided to come with me."

"I'm sorry about the problem with your employee, Mr. Bradford, but I am glad you and Louisa are able to visit. I'm happy for this opportunity to meet you."

"Mrs. Hayes—" Louisa hesitated, then continued softly, "I've been rather bold coming here like this. I wanted to meet you and ask about Peter's welfare. I understand he is in Tennessee, but perhaps you could assure me that he is all right. He has been so secretive about his travels and when he would return to Waterville. I wondered if he had some serious illness or other cause for alarm."

Annabelle studied the young, uplifted face before answering. "No, Peter is not seriously ill or nigh unto death, Miss Bradford. He has been through a great trauma and difficult time in Tennessee, but it came out well. We are thankful for that. He does suffer pain from another source, however."

Louisa stood up and walked back and forth across the room, twisting her handkerchief in her hands. "I see. Would this other pain have anything to do with me, Mrs. Hayes?"

"Please call me Annabelle, won't you? And I'd like to call you Louisa, if I may."

"Of course, Annabelle. I would like that."

"Peter's pain is indeed because of you, Louisa. When he received your letter saying you were seeing another man and seemed to care about him, he was heartbroken. He kept it to himself for a long while before he finally shared the information. Peter's had a difficult time dealing with your possible marriage to someone else. Has the marriage been consummated yet?"

"Definitely not!" Louisa cried. "I admit I was foolish, Annabelle. . .and fickle. The young man who swept me off my feet is a notorious thief. He was my father's employee who stole a great deal of money from the bank. But I realized our relationship was a mistake before that incident occurred. His character lacked everything I deemed important in a man. At first it was all show and attentiveness. Then he revealed his real personality, which lacked integrity. How foolish I was to let Peter believe I cared for this man."

"Why didn't you write to Peter and tell him it was over, child?" Annabelle asked. "It would have eased the load he carried about his young shoulders."

"I wanted to, but I was afraid. I thought Peter's pride would stand in the way. And I lacked spiritual depth at the time. It was necessary to get my life right with God first, which I did recently. Do you think if I wrote him now, and apologized, he'd forgive me, Annabelle?"

"I think there is nothing that boy would rather hear!" Annabelle smiled broadly as she retrieved their teacups and carried them into the kitchen. "But now I'd like you and your father to do a favor for me. Would you take me over to my church in your sleigh? I have a message for Pastor O'Neil, and he is usually at the church every afternoon. I see the sun has come out, and it has stopped snowing. It's only a short distance from here, and I walk it often. However, a sleigh ride would be nice, and it will give you an opportunity to see more of the countryside. Would that be possible, Mr. Bradford?"

"Of course, Mrs. Hayes," Jack Bradford said as he stood to his feet. "It would be our pleasure. Louisa and I would enjoy seeing your church."

It only took a few minutes for the trio to don their warm wraps and head outside to the sleigh. Annabelle brought along a covered basket with some of her tea cakes for the pastor and his family. "We've been blessed with such a fine minister and his wife for many years," she said, tucking warm blankets around the three of them. "Ours is a small church because we're such a rural area, but the sweet fellowship among the believers has been precious."

With directions from Annabelle, Jack Bradford snapped the reins and headed the team down the road toward their destination. The sunshine glistened like diamonds on the snow-covered fields and caused Louisa to cry out in delight. "I love the way the sun sparkles on the fences and trees, Annabelle! God's beauty and handiwork are all around us!"

"Mrs. Hayes, you mentioned you have plans to move," Jack Bradford said as they made an abrupt turn to the right at the corner. "Aren't you going to miss your church and the people here?"

"Yes, I will, Mr. Bradford. Very much. But it's time to make a change in my life, and I think it will be for the best. I'll tell you more about it later after we get back to my place. The church is just ahead on the right, and you can hitch the team along the front."

Jack Bradford pulled the team to a halt in front of a small, white church complete with steeple and bell. Nestled on a small knoll among a grove of trees, it made a picturesque setting with the countryside as a backdrop. Little puffs of smoke from the church's chimney curled upward toward the heavens. A small cemetery, complete with iron fence and gate, lay off to one side overlooking a valley, with farmhouses and outbuildings beyond. The neat rows of tombstones stood like little sentinels, covered with the pure white snow.

"It's so lovely." Louisa sighed. "It looks like a beautiful painting by a famous artist. I think I shall have to touch it to be sure it's real."

Annabelle's merry little laugh echoed forth and reverberated across the valley. "Louisa, would you mind going into the church and telling Pastor O'Neil I'm here? You are so much spryer than I am."

Louisa threw off her blanket and jumped quickly down from the sleigh. "I'll be able to see if your charming little church is real, Annabelle. I hoped it would be possible to go inside."

Gingerly Louisa approached the heavy wooden door leading into the church. Once inside she blinked her eyes in the darkened building. The sun had been so bright outside it took her a moment to get her bearings. She glanced around the entryway and entered the main sanctuary. There were stained-glass windows along each wall and rows of pews on each side of a center aisle. She could make out a platform at the front and started slowly toward it. Behind the platform a stained-glass window caught her attention. Sun streamed through its multicolored panes in the shape of a cross. The display of various shades bouncing around the room was magnificent. She stared at the array of color and felt a strange sense of peace.

Partway down the aisle Louisa hesitated. She noticed a lone figure sat on the front pew with his head bowed. *What shall I do? I mustn't interrupt Pastor O'Neil when he is praying.* She hesitated and turned to go; but a board creaked noisily, and the man in the pew raised his head.

"Pastor O'Neil," she called. "I'm so sorry to disturb your prayer. Annabelle Hayes is outside, and she has a message for you."

The figure stood up and turned toward her. He pushed back a shock of dark hair that had fallen across his forehead. "Louisa!" he cried, starting toward her. "Louisa, is that you. . .or am I dreaming?"

"Peter!" she shouted, running down the aisle toward him. "Oh, Peter, Annabelle didn't tell me you were here! She let me think you were off somewhere!"

Peter grabbed for her, and Louisa felt the strong arms surround her and draw her close. Her lips trembled as she lifted them to his. "Darling Louisa," he murmured huskily. "I thought—I thought—you had forgotten me."

Louisa's gray eyes searched his dark ones. "I couldn't forget you, Peter. I couldn't forget your boyish grin or the shock of dark hair that falls over your forehead. I couldn't forget how strong and brave you are. I've been a foolish, fickle girl. I was angry with you for going away and not sharing your reason with me or explaining how long you would be gone. In my despair, I drifted away from God and let myself be taken in by an unethical scoundrel. Can you ever forgive me? I've—I've never loved anyone but you."

Tenderly Peter traced the oval of her face with his finger and toyed with the golden ringlets curling along her cheek. Her body trembled at his touch as his dark eyes searched hers. "Those are the most beautiful words I've ever heard, darling," he said, kissing her tenderly on the lips. "Will you marry me soon, Miss Louisa Bradford, and make me the happiest man on God's earth?"

"Yes, Peter McClough. . .oh yes!" Louisa said breathlessly, while tears gathered in the corners of her eyes and trickled down her cheeks.

"What's this? You're crying!"

"Tears of joy, Peter," she said as she smiled up at him. "They are only tears of happiness!" And straightaway he kissed her again.

Epilogue

Roger Evans was brought to justice and jailed for his many crimes. The Bradford family regained most of the stolen money and repaid Jack's brother. By God's grace, Peter's best laid plans finally materialized. The wedding took place the first Saturday in April in their Waterville church, with the present pastor and Rev. Robert Harris from Wampum, Pennsylvania, officiating. Louisa wore her mother's wedding gown and veil, all white satin and lace with fitted bodice and long train. Her hair, pulled back and secured with silver clips, allowed the golden tresses to cascade down her back. Her cousin, Clara, and good friend Emily, dressed in mint green satin with matching headpieces, stood with her.

Peter waited at the front in a black suit, the shock of dark hair slicked back from his forehead. Little muscles in both cheeks twitched from nervousness and excitement. Standing by him for support were his brother, Thomas, and best friend, Frederic Mason. Thomas, Genevieve, and Annabelle had arrived from Tennessee a day earlier to be there for the special occasion. A part of the honeymoon plans included a few days visiting Thomas and Genevieve at their plantation.

Peter felt God leading him to work with young boys. If agreeable with Thomas and Genevieve, Peter and Louisa would spend one or two months each summer at their estate in Tennessee conducting a Bible camp for boys. Along with Bible classes, the boys would learn responsibility. Part of their day would include various chores around the plantation, such as gardening and care of the animals. There would be fun times and an opportunity to learn sportsmanship. Horseback riding, hiking, picnics, and campfires would be included. Louisa shared Peter's enthusiasm and dedication to such a ministry. God had done so much for the two of them, they considered it a privilege to invest time in training young lives for the Lord. The couple's deep love for one another was evident to all their friends and family as they repeated their vows of love and commitment. When the pastor presented them to the congregation as Mr. and Mrs. Peter McClough, Peter pulled Louisa's trembling body close and whispered huskily against her golden hair. "Darling, you are finally mine, and I'll never let you go!" Then he kissed her, long and tenderly, as her eyes once again filled with tears of joy.

A Letter to Our Readers

Dear Readers:

In order that we might better contribute to your reading enjoyment, we would appreciate your taking a few minutes to respond to the following questions. When completed, please return to the following: Fiction Editor, Barbour Publishing, Inc., P.O. Box 719, Uhrichsville, OH 44683.

1. Did you enjoy reading *Maine*?
    ❏ Very much—I would like to see more books like this.
    ❏ Moderately—I would have enjoyed it more if _____
    _____
    _____

2. What influenced your decision to purchase this book?
    (Check those that apply.)
    ❏ Cover   ❏ Back cover copy   ❏ Title   ❏ Price
    ❏ Friends   ❏ Publicity   ❏ Other

3. Which story was your favorite?
    ❏ *A Haven of Peace*   ❏ *The Best Laid Plans*
    ❏ *A Time to Love*

4. Please check your age range:
    ❏ Under 18   ❏ 18–24   ❏ 25–34
    ❏ 35–45   ❏ 46–55   ❏ Over 55

5. How many hours per week do you read? _____

Name _____

Occupation _____

Address _____

City_____ State_____ Zip_____

E-mail_____

If you enjoyed

Maine

then read:

Virginia

Four Inspiring Stories of Valor, Virtue, and Victory

by Cathy Marie Hake

Precious Burdens

Redeemed Hearts

Ramshackle Rose

Restoration

Available wherever books are sold.

Or order from:

Barbour Publishing, Inc.

P.O. Box 721

Uhrichsville, Ohio 44683

http://www.barbourbooks.com

You may order by mail for $6.97 and add $2.00 to your order for shipping.

Prices subject to change without notice.

HEARTSONG
PRESENTS

If you love Christian romance...

$10.⁹⁹

You'll love Heartsong Presents' inspiring and faith-filled romances by today's very best Christian authors...DiAnn Mills, Wanda E. Brunstetter, and Yvonne Lehman, to mention a few!

When you join Heartsong Presents, you'll enjoy four brand-new mass-market, 176-page books—two contemporary and two historical—that will build you up in your faith when you discover God's role in every relationship you read about!

Imagine...four new romances every four weeks—with men and women like you who long to meet the one God has chosen as the love of their lives...all for the low price of $10.99 postpaid.

To join, simply visit www.heartsongpresents.com or complete the coupon below and mail it to the address provided.

✂ -

YES! Sign me up for Heart♥ng!

NEW MEMBERSHIPS WILL BE SHIPPED IMMEDIATELY!

Send no money now. We'll bill you only $10.99 postpaid with your first shipment of four books. Or for faster action, call 1-740-922-7280.

NAME _____

ADDRESS _____

CITY _____ STATE _____ ZIP_____

MAIL TO: HEARTSONG PRESENTS, P.O. Box 721, Uhrichsville, Ohio 44683
or sign up at WWW.HEARTSONGPRESENTS.COM